W9-BXE-571

Venetian Blood

NOV 0 8 2017

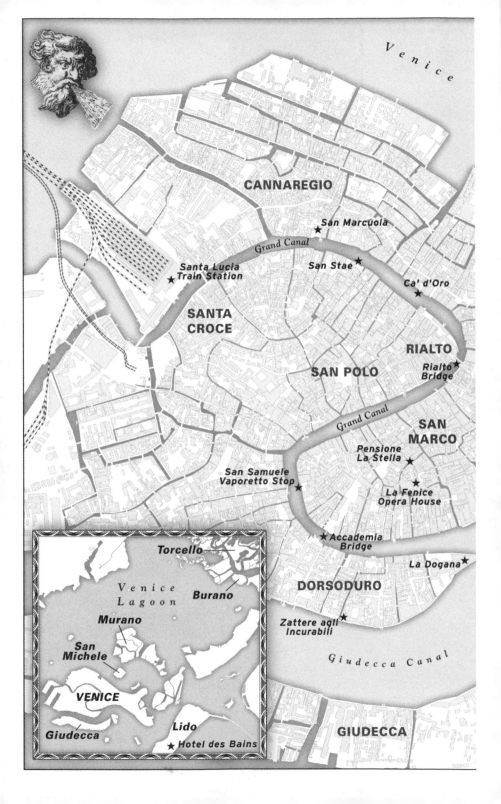

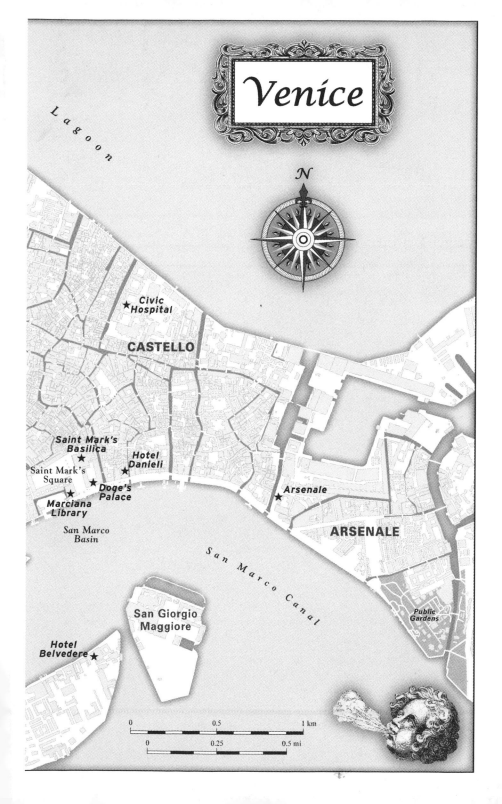

FIC
VOLKER

Venetian Blood

Murder in a
Sensuous City

FAIRHOPE PUBLIC LIBRARY
501 FAIRHOPE AVE.
FAIRHOPE, AL 36532

Christine Evelyn Volker

1391240

She Writes Press, a BookSparks imprint
A Division of SparkPointStudio, LLC.

Copyright © 2017 by Christine Volker

All rights reserved. No part of this publication may be reproduced, distributed, or transmitted in any form or by any means, including photocopying, recording, digital scanning, or other electronic or mechanical methods, without the prior written permission of the publisher, except in the case of brief quotations embodied in critical reviews and certain other noncommercial uses permitted by copyright law. For permission requests, please address She Writes Press.

Published 2017
Printed in the United States of America

Print ISBN: 978-1-63152-310-6
E-ISBN: 978-1-63152-311-3
Library of Congress Control Number: 2017934265

For information, address:
She Writes Press
1563 Solano Ave #546
Berkeley, CA 94707

Cover design © Julie Metz, Ltd./metzdesign.com
Formatting by Katherine Lloyd/theDESKonline.com
Map by Mike Morgenfeld/cartographer

She Writes Press is a division of SparkPoint Studio, LLC.

This is a work of fiction. Names, characters, places, and incidents either are the product of the author's imagination or are used fictitiously. Any resemblance to actual persons, living or dead, is entirely coincidental.

To Stephan,
per sempre e sempre.

For your love, encouragement, and insights
over countless hours. Without you,
my journey would be incomplete.

Contents

The Belvedere Hotel, Venice, Italy 1

1   Santa Lucia Train Station, Venice, Italy 4

2   The Sinuous Voyage 19

3   La Stella 34

4   Beside the Still, Green Canal 37

5   In the Heart of the Faviers 52

6   A Tenuous Connection 63

7   The Murder 68

8   The Money Trail 85

9   The Garden 88

10 The Meeting 99

11 Wanderings 110

12 Of the Incurables 123

13 The Bombshell News 132

14 In the Police Station 141

15 La Biblioteca Marciana 149

16 Caffè Florian 157

17 A Forgotten Place 164

18 St. Mark's 180

19   A Disjointed Message 185

20   Searching 191

21   Dr. Zampone 200

22   The Watch 214

23   Black Hole 221

24   Il Gazzettino 224

25   The Dark Yacana 234

26   Red Dawn 241

27   Napoleon's Gardens 251

28   Leaves of Green 254

29   Dark Star Trails 263

30   La Guardia di Finanza 268

31   L'Ospedale Civile 283

32   In the Shadow of the Doge 288

33   The Lilies of San Stae 297

34   The Golden Lido 303

35   Calle dei Assassini 312

36   The Dream 319

Acknowledgments 329

About the Author 331

The Belvedere Hotel, Venice, Italy

Saturday, September 12, 1992

Count Sergio Corrin gloated. Leaning against a stone pillar, he surveyed the masked revelers. Checkered harlequins tangoed with Columbinas on the veranda, a skull mask floating in their midst. Smiling clown visages and long-beaked Pulcinellas peeked over the feathers of can-can masks. He spotted a joker with flowing red hair, not moving to the orchestra, gazing down from a balcony, still as a mannequin.

The impressive proceeds from this evening's fundraiser would guarantee him yet another year as president of the Preserve Venice Foundation. After the unmasking at midnight, he'd announce, to more thunderous applause, that his valiant efforts had secured an even greater triumph: The twice-stolen Giovanni Bellini painting will regain its rightful spot in the Valier Chapel of Madonna del Orto Church. These feats dwarfed the competition. *They* could only scrape up enough lire to restore a bench outside Santa Maria dei Miracoli. *Madonna and Child* will return, thanks to his magnanimous donation and muscular influence in the art world's darkest corners. The laser-locking system and bullet-proof glass would be the *Pietà*'s equal, protecting Bellini's masterpiece from thieves and the knives of madmen.

He cut through a bobbing sea of painted masks, leaving silk gowns and lilting voices to climb the brick steps to the gardens. Heart-shaped hedges divided the expanse of the lawn, phosphorescent in the floodlights. Gliding past an illuminated sculpture of Venus, he pulled down his Pinocchio mask and inhaled the heady scent of roses. Though hearing light footsteps, he grinned in anticipation of the meeting in two weeks. He picked up a pebble and threw it as far as he could. His spirit soared for having found a talented aide to do his bidding. He would win again.

But his attempts with Anna in the caffè that afternoon had failed so far. Such a memorable body, but an unyielding heart. Firing his arsenal of charm at point-blank range had not swayed her; rather, she had turned heads by trying to snatch the Polaroids he had taken, leaving him no choice. He tapped his pocket. She'd get them under one condition: Grant him the favors he demanded, or her employer would get a nice shock upon opening a plain manila envelope. If she wasn't fired immediately, she'd be forever smeared in disgrace. No matter how hard she scrubbed, traces would linger, like bruises on her delicious derriere. She had shut up after that. Their story hadn't ended. He'd squeeze more, and she'd collapse.

Just a few minutes remained before he would head down and seize the microphone to share the splendid financial results with the upper crust of Venetian society. Enough time to reach his favorite spot, the overlook. As he hurried past a copse of trees, the festive music seemed to die.

He jogged up the stairs and pressed against the railing, like a sailor in a crow's nest high above the roiling sea, savoring the wind. Hugging the distant bank, moored gondolas rocked in unison like dark seahorses nodding. Lamps flickered from the broad promenade. The lighted reflection of the Doge's Palace became a thousand fireflies skimming the water. Plaintive notes from a wooden flute hung in the air as Sergio felt the heart of Venice beating in timeless opulence, showering him with a bouquet of memories. He could live nowhere else.

Waves tapped the metal dock below in a hollow echo, jarring his reverie. Rustling from behind a nearby cypress froze him.

The tree's jagged outline pierced the platinum moon. A long-haired figure bent in the shadows, small golden bells tinkling atop its joker's mask.

"*Signora,*" he said, swaggering over, captivated by her cascading, auburn hair. He spied the glimmer of a coquette's eyes, and full, red lips upturned in a permanent grin.

"*Come si chiama, bella?*" he asked, wanting to know her name.

She tilted her head to one side, then the other. For just an instant, he pictured a cobra, dancing.

The knife held by a gloved hand caught the cold light. In one silent thrust, the masked figure plunged the steel blade deep between his ribs as church bells tolled midnight.

Staggering away in disbelief, he teetered before collapsing onto the Istrian stone, splitting his head open.

1

Santa Lucia Train Station, Venice, Italy

Sunday, September 13, 1992

Anna gulped Venice's brine-filled air as if it could magically erase bad memories. Sergio's last-minute phone call imploring her to come one day early had filled her with the hope that she could get her damn pictures back and never hear from him again. Instead, he had revealed himself to be even more sinister than she had feared. Arguing with him at the caffè, trailing him to the gala, fleeing before speaking to him, her efforts had been a disaster. If she didn't fulfill his demand within five days, a time limit he had termed "generous," she had no doubt that he'd make good on his threat. She needed to figure out how to defuse his time bomb, no matter how much the thought of it made her hands tremble.

Exhausted, she propped herself against a stone wall outside the Santa Lucia train station. The lumpy mattress in the nearby grubby inn last night and the recollection of Sergio flashing a devilish smile while unveiling his ultimatums had sabotaged her sleep. When she'd first met him, he had adopted the guise of a *bella figura*: respectful, courteous, and soft-spoken. Underneath, however, lurked a calculating scoundrel.

Yesterday's clacking train from Zürich had brought her through the blue, towering Alps, past verdant hills studded with sienna villages, until at last descending to the broad coastal plain, with a whiff of salt and a glimpse of the vast Adriatic and its jumble of reedy islands. Seen from the carriage window, Venice's bramble of towers and red roofs had been nearly swallowed by the sea.

Now, in the late afternoon's waning light, she watched somber gondolas slide through a bedlam of water taxis, docking *vaporettos*, and industrial barges as the waters of the Grand Canal washed over the sidewalk just twenty feet away. Ancient stone and brick-clad buildings floated in the distance. Behind her, the sleek mass of the rail terminal rose from demolished crypts and disinterred bones of saints. With *acqua alta*, as her Italian grandfather had called it, the water proclaimed its dominion. Nonno had always feared for her in Venice. You can get confused there, he would say, and step into a puddle only to find that it was really the edge of a canal.

Fidgeting, Anna scanned the crowds. No sign of Margo. Late again, just like all those years ago in college, when Anna would wait for her at Sather Gate after solid geometry class. She stowed her glasses in her purse and rubbed her aching eyes, seeing well enough without her distance lenses.

An aqua speedboat marked *Polizia*—far from the black-and-white squad cars of home, Anna thought—crawled past before docking. Two smartly dressed policemen tied up the boat and alighted. After studying a paper in their hands, they met her staccato glances with penetrating stares as she fingered her chestnut hair.

"*Signora, cosa fa qui?*" the stocky one demanded in a singsong voice, dark brows knit together, wanting to know what she was doing there.

Surprised, Anna labored through her rusty Italian and with an upturned hand told them, "*Aspetto un'amica.*"—"I'm waiting for a girlfriend."

"You tell her thata you be very late," he replied. "Come with us now, please." He grabbed her by the wrist, his calloused hand holding fast as they walked.

His balding partner followed with her bags.

"*Dove andiamo?*" she asked, wagering Italian would help her find out where they were headed. "*Non ho fatto niente. Lasciami stare.*"—"I haven't done anything. Leave me be."

Deaf to pleas in any language, they marched her back toward the train station. People gawked at the lumbering procession while Anna felt her cheeks flush. They crossed the shadows to the door of the police station, set inside the giant maw of the depot. After taking her passport at the front desk, the policemen led her down a dim stairway before nudging her into a cool chamber.

The door thundered shut, the sound magnified by slick floor tiles decayed into a tartared sheen. A wooden table, ringed by mismatched chairs, dominated the space. The pendulum of a wall clock sliced loudly through the dank air as its stark hands pointed to six-thirty. Twin mirrors studded the far wall. Slumped in one of the aged chairs, Anna pictured officers huddling behind the glass, cementing their gaze on her, weighing her every move and expression.

Questions arose like a beggar's chorus. What did I do? What do they want with me? How can I get out of here?

A dripping sound made her pause. How far above sea level is this room, anyway? Feeling queasy, she recalled Nonna's sepia-colored prints of St. Mark's Square submerged beneath wind-whipped waves. She envisioned minnows swimming over the stone pavement and between pedestrians' legs, imagined water oozing through a crack in the corner of the floor, then starting to rise. Calm, stay calm, she told herself. Don't panic. Just think. There must be a mistake, some reason the police had picked her out, one she could deduce by concentrating on it. Nonno had been the first to praise her, saying that her mind was like his. Logical. Analytical.

At home with facts and figures. Her early aptitude in mathematics had foretold her professional success.

Her right leg twitched. She forced herself to determine potential causes for her detention. Sergio had changed his mind. He was making false charges against her, would soon let her know he'd rescue her from jail if she'd help him immediately. Or, the clerk at the Locanda Stazione—the greedy bastard—was accusing her of damaging the room or of stiffing him, to get more money. Maybe he had a relative on the force. She had paid him more than forty thousand lire, roughly forty dollars, for a single, but he hadn't given her a receipt; she had no proof of staying there. Or, worse, what if she resembled the suspect in a crime that the police were hell-bent on solving?

The door burst open and a blond man with a Slavic tilt to his icy, wide-set eyes strode into the room.

"I am Detective Biondi," he announced in a baritone voice.

His well-cut navy suit framed broad shoulders, making him look more refined than she had expected, down to his gleaming wingtips. Biondi pushed his chair close and sat down, scrutinizing her.

"I will like to ask you some questions." He set a small tape recorder on the table, pressed a button, and muttered, "*Niccolò—*"

Just then a female assistant entered the room and placed two glasses of water on the table, earning an annoyed look. Biondi restarted the tape.

"*Niccolò Biondi. Il tredici settembre.*" Having spoken his name and the date into the microphone, he turned to Anna and asked, "Who are you? Why are you in Venice?"

"Anna Lucia Lottol, same as on my passport. I'm on vacation." She struggled to keep her voice steady as she continued, "I've done nothing wrong, so why have you brought me here?"

"I ask the questions."

"I refuse to answer any more. Get me the American Embassy."

"You say you are a diplomat?"

"No. But I know my rights. I work for the US government."

"The FBI told us you work for the Treasury Department."

Anna stifled a gasp, stunned at Biondi's quick contact with US authorities. Maybe he had even talked to her boss.

"We are not so naïve to think that government employees do not commit crimes. We will not treat you any worse than an Italian national under the circumstances."

"What circumstances are those?"

"I can lock you up. It depends."

"Then I want a consular official here."

Biondi glanced at his platinum Reverso watch. Anna recognized it from the Zürich train station displays, its price well above what a detective could afford.

"The nearest consulate is in Milan. They are closed Sundays. Impossible to get here before noon tomorrow, and only if they have nothing better to do than come to your aid. Which I doubt. You may wait here long."

"Why don't you just let me go? You have my passport. I'll come back when they arrive."

"I believe you have a saying, not a snowball's chance in hell? You will enjoy our cozy accommodation, sharing one tiny, dirty cell with the dregs of Venice. Let me see. We hold one aggressive prostitute, another woman scratches herself, thinks she carries bugs. Maybe she is right. Then the drunken woman picking fights with her cellmates—"

Anna sighed. "All right. I'll answer your questions."

"You recognize him?" he asked, sliding a photograph in front of her.

Anna's eyes were drawn to the pool of blood bathing a man's head, tingeing the ends of his white hair a clownish red against the stone pavement. Vacant eyes sunk into folds of skin. Thin lips

8

framing a mouth contorted to one side in a sickening smirk. One pale, veined hand wearing a gold signet ring resting on his crimson-stained tuxedo. A Pinocchio mask crushed under his chin.

"Oh, no!" Anna pushed the picture away, shutting her eyes for a moment, hardly believing what she had seen. Sergio—dead. Vigorous, hateful Sergio. He had been holding his head high, glossy mane moving in concert with his grand gestures as he wove his way through the elegant crowd last night. And now? He looked like a rag doll someone had smashed on the ground.

"You are upset."

Anna took a sip of water, hands unsteady. "Y-you just showed me a photo of a dead man. Of course I'm upset."

"You don't know him?" Biondi asked.

Her forehead throbbed. She thought back through her movements the previous night: crossing the lagoon to the gala Sergio would be attending, entering the hotel from the back, hiding behind a party mask she had found in the ladies room, running up the garden steps to see the dance floor and spy on him, then, losing her nerve to engage him again, dashing down the main stairway, pulling off her mask and jumping into the dark, jam-packed launch back to St. Mark's Square.

"What happened?" she asked, peeking at Biondi, knowing how much pressure he'd feel to quickly resolve the murder of a powerful Venetian count, debating whether she was willing to trust in local justice. "Venetians are as slippery as eels," she recalled Nonno saying.

She took a few coughs. If she said she knew Sergio, Biondi would ask how they met. Once he found that Sergio had been her lover for four whole days back in January, he'd dig until he found more, conclude that she was a jilted inamorata who had traveled to Venice to kill her beloved, and throw her in jail. She blinked, still undecided, before remembering the college acquaintance who

9

had traveled to Asia and spent five years behind bars for a crime he hadn't committed. Lost five years and aged ten.

Last night, near the train station, the somnolent hotel clerk hadn't asked for her passport. She had even scribbled her own name in the guest log to save him the trouble of writing it. That meant there was no central police registry with her name and passport number and a record of where she had stayed. Since she had paid cash, there'd be no credit card trail. And the Italians at the Swiss border hadn't stamped her passport, so who was to say when she had arrived? At least five hundred people must have attended the masked ball, many looking like her—brunettes were scarcely rare here. Scores of people would have known Sergio from business, art, or philanthropic connections. Biondi, she thought, would be very busy sorting them out before finding some illicit deal that would lead him to Sergio's murderer.

Biondi pursed his lips. "I repeat. Did you know him?"

Anna shook her head.

"Subject indicated no," Biondi said into the tape recorder. "I tell you one thing, Signora Lottol. Someone saw a woman running from the hotel last night. Lucky for us he was an artist. Good likeness, no?" He placed a drawing on the table.

Anna examined the rendering of a woman in motion and took a sharp breath. The sketch captured her slender torso, long legs, and broad stride, hinting at her athleticism. The same dark eyes as hers peered from behind wire-rimmed glasses she sometimes wore. But the nose was bulbous instead of straight, the chin weaker. Framed by long, wavy hair, the oval face was unlined, free of incipient crow's feet, making her appear five years younger than her age of forty. A phalanx of cops must have been trawling the train station and airport armed with that sketch. One group or another would have seized her eventually. She felt her skin grow clammy, her eyes drilling into her depiction.

"Well?" Biondi asked.

She felt like retching, but was convinced that recanting her lie would only make things worse. Five years of precious life if she trusted him, she thought, before saying, "There's a resemblance, yes. But, I wasn't in Venice last night."

"You," he stabbed the air with his forefinger, "deny you were at the Belvedere Hotel?"

"The where?" she asked, blanking, her thoughts blurring.

"I already told you—the Belvedere Hotel," he barked. "Where the murder took place."

He's going to end it right here and arrest me now, she thought, hiding her shaking hands in her lap. "Murder . . . God, no. I would never . . . How could I? I was in Zürich—I just arrived here by train this evening. I'm a tourist, like thousands of other people."

"*Porca miseria,*" Biondi mumbled.

Anna understood this to mean "bloody hell." That's where she'd be sent soon, she feared.

"All right, we do this the hard way," he said in a raspy voice. "If you have a train ticket and address book, I would like to see them. Right now."

Pushing away from the table, Anna fumbled in her purse with jerky, abrupt motions, her trembling hand going in circles, her mind struggling to remember his request.

"You need help?" Biondi's voice rose. "Shall *I* do it?"

"No," she managed to say. Her hand brushed against a business card. She tried to control her breathing. In, then out, in, then out, calm, like the cool-down of her aerobics class. She breathed more deeply. Keys, compact, eyeglasses, lipstick, address book, yes. She handed it over.

Biondi shoved the leather book to one side, took her passport out of his pocket, and flipped the pages with manicured hands. "You are married, yet the husband is not with you."

"I'm traveling alone."

"You say you came from Zürich this evening?"

Anna nodded. "I flew to Zürich and took the train here."

"I see the Zürich Flughafen stamp from the airport. You arrived there yesterday morning." He sought her gaze.

She plunged her thumbnail into her forefinger and tried not to flick her eyes away. "That's right. That's what I meant. I . . . I was sightseeing there."

"In Zürich?"

"It's a lovely, historic city," she said. "Venice is not the only beautiful one, you know."

"Gray city. Full of banks and bankers. What did you see?"

"Um . . . watches. I went shopping and saw lots of expensive watches."

"No Künsthaus or Lake Zürich for you?" A scowl washed across his face. "Just watches. You buy any?"

"No." Her right hand jerked, hitting the underbelly of the table. A tangle of gouges, a finger's width apart, had left the wood tortured and raw.

"Missing a stamp here for Italian customs." He flung the passport onto the table.

"You know on the train they generally don't do that," she said, recalling three other times she had entered Italy by rail.

"You think you are an expert? Biondi is a simple man, Signora Lottol. All I know is that we have the dead body of a Venetian count. With a person of interest, looking like you, likely American or British by their accent in Italian. You will need to prove me that you were not here last night. And where is that train ticket?"

"Tossed it out." Anna congratulated herself on having thrown the ticket into a bin by the track as soon as she had arrived.

"Where?"

"I don't remember, maybe outside the station. Do you save

your train tickets?" She smoothed out an imaginary wrinkle in her brown-checkered raincoat.

"Don't get too smug. We speak to conductors and the Ferrovie. Did you ride in first or second class?"

"Second."

"You have receipts from your trip?"

"I got rid of them. I hate clutter." Anna shifted in her chair, struggling to fire up neural connections, despite a sinking feeling that her fabrications were fraying.

"Any people you remember, who might remember you?"

"No."

"Where you stay in Zürich?"

"The Grüner Baum. I do have that receipt." Fishing it out of her saddlebag, victorious, she unfurled it as if it were the captured flag of a vanquished army. "Here."

He took a cursory look.

"This is not proof of your innocence." Biondi planted both hands on the table and brought his face so close to Anna's that she smelled the coffee on his breath. "How do I know you did not arrive in Venice yesterday?"

Well, he was right. The Zürich hotel had charged her in advance, and when she had marched into the lobby, arguing that her plans had changed at the last minute and she wouldn't be staying there, they had refused to refund her money. Tightwads. She'd ended up occupying the room after all, showering and taking a nap before boarding the train to Venice for the meeting with Sergio.

"You come here and kill him at midnight, when the bells ring loud," Biondi continued. "You even could have gone back to Switzerland after that, checked out in late morning, and now you return again with the Zürich train. Perfect alibi. It doesn't matter if you stayed there. The trip is six hours and there are plenty trains."

"Please—"

"You don't look like our typical murderer, but then maybe you are one. After all, women are coming up in the world."

"Not as far as you think. But Detective Biondi, why would I have murdered that man? And if I had, why wouldn't I have left Italy right away?"

"Our killers, not all of them have sense. Some return to the scene. They like very much the thrill. And they want to make Biondi look like a fool."

"This is ridiculous," Anna said, her anger vaporizing her fear. "I'm not a murderer. I can't believe I'm in Italy and not in some dictatorship. Wouldn't the meticulous Swiss have stamped my passport if I had reentered their country by train, like in your hypothesis? You saw they didn't." She studied his stony face. "I have a friend here who's expecting me today. She was supposed to meet my train. Now I've probably missed her."

"Your social life is no concern to me. Except how it intersects the victim's."

Her mouth parched, Anna thrust out her hand for the water glass, bumping the open purse, spilling its contents, and causing thuds and jangles as her heavy wallet and assorted coins hit the floor.

Biondi swung his gaze to the widespread pile. "Let me assist you."

Anna spotted Sergio's thick business card, with its eye-catching, ornate script, lying upside down next to her glasses case. She willed herself not to lunge for it.

"What is this I see?" Biondi asked, reaching down and snatching something.

Anna bit her cheek.

"Do you smoke?"

"No."

"Then why you have matches in your pocketbook?"

"Do I?"

"From Caffè Orientale, quite a walk from here." He waved them at her. "Over by Rio Marin. Impossible to have gone there and back if you just arrived, even if you ran all the way." He looked beneath the table. "In your heels."

She almost didn't recognize the matchbook. She had met Sergio at the caffè yesterday, where they had had a drink and fought.

"Oh those." She forced a chuckle, feeling flushed at the thought that Biondi would now beat a path to its door. "I . . . I bought a Coke at the train station bar and must've grabbed them. Like a memento, I guess."

"I should believe that? Venice has many memorable sites—the Cipriani, the Belvedere, the Gritti Palace, Hotel Danieli, but no, Signora Lottol desires a keepsake from the Santa Lucia train station. How you say—grungy?"

Biondi undoubtedly was congratulating himself on his mastery of American slang, thinking he had caught his mouse. As he made a quick entry in his notebook, Anna unhurriedly leaned down and scooped up Sergio's card, along with her eyeglass case, and secured them in the purse's zippered pouch before allowing herself to steady her hands on the sides of her chair.

Biondi peeked into her wallet before returning it. "I notice this is filled with lire. You know we accept credit cards in Italy, don't you?"

"I want to take advantage of cash discounts," she said, ignoring his taunt, hoping that he wouldn't notice the trickle of perspiration she felt sliding down her forehead.

"Or pay someone off." He pulled a linen handkerchief from his suit pocket. "You look as if you need this."

She laced her fingers together.

"What is your job at the Treasury Department?"

"Financial transaction tracking, modeling, algorithm construction. We help catch bad people like money launderers."

Biondi's eyes widened.

"You have a business card for me?"

Anna looked into her purse and passed him one.

"*Our* bad people spill blood and guts instead of money," he said.

He paged through her address book, seeming to memorize the entries. Thank goodness Sergio had never earned a place in it.

"Tell me, where you stay here?"

"At the home of Count Alessandro Favier, along with my friend."

"Ah, Count Favier—a respected, learned man." Biondi gazed up, as if studying the immobile ceiling fan.

"You know him?" Anna's voice brightened.

"He comes from a very old family," Biondi said in a gentler tone. "Who is this Claudio, Claudio Zampone, living in Dorsoduro? What kind of business does he have?"

"Never met him," Anna murmured. "He's, um, a doctor. A friend of someone back home." Anna was hoping she wouldn't have to consult him, this just-in-case referral from her psychologist in California.

"How long you visit?"

"Ten days."

"Excuse me." Biondi grabbed her passport and business card before leaving in haste.

She sighed and felt the air flow out of her. All she wanted to do at that moment was to crawl away and hide. Her eagerly anticipated, long-overdue vacation hadn't even begun before turning into a nightmare. Given Sergio's outsized charm, glib repartee and command performance at the fundraiser last night, not to mention the ease with which he had issued the venal threats that had turned her life upside down, his death was impossible to believe, despite the photograph. He had seemed too potent and invincible ever to be bashed and bloodied, like a helpless baby harp seal.

Ironically, his murder had not freed her from the danger of his ultimatum but elevated it, as if he were attacking from the grave. Now her pictures were lying somewhere with a destiny of their own. If Biondi had them, he would have brandished them, even crowed about it. Who would find them first? She imagined the police snickering, then arresting her. Even if she could convince them of her innocence, she would still lose her job if Treasury ever learned of her entanglement with a money launderer.

Sergio certainly had been slick. How smooth was Biondi? Given his talent for interrogation, the answer must be plenty. Who was he speaking with now, the FBI? Count Favier? Or checking on her alibi?

She focused on the wall clock. Its ticks sounded ominous, its hands hardly moved. When Biondi returned, she'd surely see the inside of a jail cell. Even if she wasn't arrested for murder, lying to the police would carry some minimum punishment. She tried to estimate how much an Italian lawyer would cost. With some luck, less than the two-hundred-dollar-an-hour legal bills from her divorce attorney. Everything was so complicated in Italy. She frowned at the specter of a capricious, painful process. Do they even have bail here? she wondered. Would she be allowed to make one phone call? To whom? Jack wouldn't care about her wasting away in prison, but his fifty percent of everything they owned would be in jeopardy; if the mortgage payments weren't made, the house would be repossessed. He'd find it in his interest to help her if he were sober enough. Her call would be to Count Favier and Margo. Local connections and someone loyal to her.

When Biondi banged the door open, Anna jumped.

"You are free to go," he grumbled, dropping her passport on the table.

Too relieved to rejoice, Anna hastily stuffed it and the rest of her belongings into her purse while hoping he wouldn't change his mind.

As they walked down the barren hallway, Biondi nodded to the bald officer Anna had met earlier. "*Calvino, vieni qua con le valigie,*" Biondi shouted, looking wan under the bright lights. "He brings your bags."

"Just because I release you now does not mean I believe you," he told her. "If I need to question you more I contact you at Count Favier's *palazzo*. Do not try to leave Venice before checking with me or you find you cannot. We have eyes everywhere. Here, take this." He reached into his jacket and gave Anna his card. "One more thing. No hiding. Remember," he added, tapping the side of his prominent nose with his forefinger, "Biondi will track you down."

"How was he killed?" Anna asked as she claimed her luggage.

"Details are not your business. You must know that specially as a foreigner, we can detain you at any time for questioning." He glowered at her. "For weeks."

"I haven't done anything."

"That is what they all say."

2

The Sinuous Voyage

Sunday, September 13, 1992

Barely believing that she had been freed, Anna staggered outside to the station steps, where she lowered herself into a niche by a planter, not far from the green waters of the Grand Canal. She hugged her knees and closed her eyes as a shiver shot through her.

Sergio murdered? Late last night, dressed in a tuxedo and a Pinocchio mask, he had bounded onto the stage to announce in his gravelly voice that he'd be sharing great news with the crowd at midnight. How much time had elapsed between her rapid exit from the hotel garden and when Sergio, his mask still strapped under his chin, lost his life? Ten minutes and a few hundred yards at most. He had sauntered past without seeing her, heading in the direction of the Casanova grove. His pace had been leisurely, indicating he hadn't been meeting someone there. In fact, the garden had looked curiously devoid of other guests.

She had heard no struggle, no cries, nothing besides the orchestra playing *"Ti voglio tanto bene."* For her own protection, she'd have to be consistent with everyone and never let on that she had known him. And she scarcely had. Those four days in Milan seemed a lifetime ago. Her rash mistake was nobody's business, yet now it was roaring back into her life with its fingers pressing against her throat. Biondi and his officers would be working overtime to uncover everything they could about her. How could she prove she wasn't guilty? She settled her despondent gaze on the canal waters and felt as if she were sinking.

People swarmed down the station steps on all sides, engulfing her in a sea of babble and dim figures: Italians, Americans, Germans, French, Spaniards, and British. Boisterous first-timers snapped pictures of one another by Venice's watery street. Quieter, experienced visitors deftly wove their way to the Grand Canal, gritting their teeth against the entry pandemonium. Oh to be one of those making a grand tour of Italy's art and culture, luxuriating in Venice's dreamlike atmosphere, she thought with a pang. She clutched her purse and stared across the canal at the faded green cupola of San Simeone Piccolo, its pediment depicting the martyrdom of Christ's cousin.

She smelled the moist air and touched the empty space on her ring finger, tempted to cry as the seabirds now did against the darkening sky. She had no one to blame but herself for coming here. The more Nonno had tried to dissuade her, all those years ago, the more she had secretly vowed to see the city for herself one day. Repeating the litany of train stops bringing her to Venice— Zürich, Zug, Thun, Lugano, Milano, Sirmione, Verona, Vicenza, Venezia—led her to wonder whether she should jump onto an outbound train and elude Biondi's travel ban before he made his next move.

As the air grew cool, she felt stranded. The Scalzi Bridge, connecting the train station with the heart of Venice, became a shadowy suggestion. She doubted she could find Count Favier's palazzo, tucked among alleys, away from famous landmarks, on her own. At least she had the phone number. Pulling out her wallet, Anna inspected the coins, growing resentful. Only Swiss francs remained; the five-hundred-lire pieces used in public phones were still on the interrogation room floor. To call the count, she'd have to go someplace and break the tiny thousand-lire notes or buy some slotted *gettoni*, which fit perfectly into the phones.

But if she left the station steps, she might miss Margo altogether. The Zürich train Margo had expected her to be on had pulled in ninety minutes ago. Had Margo come and gone? Hard to say, since Margo Fruhling was rarely punctual. She'd been late more often than not, ever since they had met in English 101 at UC Berkeley twenty years ago. Perhaps it was Margo's small expression of rebellion, or thumbing her nose at the rules, or just her disorganized life. God knows how Margo, a journalist, ever met a deadline.

Anna resolved to return to the station and make a phone call to the count's palazzo. Maybe Margo could direct her to the nearest vaporetto dock and meet her there.

"Anna, is that you?" erupted a familiar voice from the gloom.

"Margo? Really? Of course it's me," Anna said as Margo reached out and embraced her.

Margo was thinner than Anna had remembered; she could feel the delicate bird bones of Margo's back. The savvy dark eyes and the mirth that played around her full, soft lips hadn't changed. Nor had the gleaming jet-black hair, dramatic brows, and fair complexion. Margo's taut skin still could hardly contain her lively spirit and abundant appetites.

"I've been searching for you for more than an hour. I knew it wasn't like you to take a later train without calling. I was so worried I ended up checking with the police. They sat me down with a detective who asked a bunch of questions about you. What the hell happened?"

"They dragged me into the police station, where a Detective Biondi bullied me," Anna said, her voice shaking. "I fit the description of a woman fleeing a murder scene last night."

"How awful! I read the local rag religiously; nothing's been

21

reported. And a murder would make headlines, there's so little crime here. A stolen wallet and the bribes, the *tangenti*, of course." Margo shook her head. "But I don't understand why the police went after you. You just arrived from Switzerland for God's sake. How was it?"

Anna looked away.

"Anna, tell me you weren't here! I swore up and down to that Biondi that you were in Zürich last night. I even threatened to write a piece on Italian police brutality featuring him and his department terrorizing innocent tourists."

Anna groaned. "I arrived yesterday. I needed to take care of something."

"Where did you stay? Why didn't you call me?"

"In some seedy hotel—everything was full. I had to face a . . . situation alone. It was too embarrassing."

"But lying to the police? How long do you think your story will hold before Biondi comes after you like an angry bull? He'll think I was in on it, too."

"I'm so sorry you got pulled into this." Anna pressed Margo's shoulder. "I may have a few days. There was a huge crowd at that masquerade ball."

"What ball?"

When Margo's words were drowned out by a loud throbbing, she arched her neck and scanned. "We'd better run for this boat. There's plenty of room. We might not be so lucky when the next one pulls up." She gave Anna a quick glance. "You look beat."

Margo clicked her tongue a few times before grabbing one of Anna's bags, a sure sign she was nervous. That made two of them, Anna thought.

They ran forward and wedged themselves into the waiting throng, the vaporetto jolting the floating dock as its motor strained into a higher key. The two women clambered aboard and freed themselves from the nucleus of passengers hurtling toward the seats.

"Let's nab a spot outside where we can talk," Margo said. As they crammed onto a bench near the prow, she turned to face her friend. "Tell me everything," she said calmly.

Anna buried her head in her hands. "You can't repeat this, not even to Count Favier."

"I wouldn't before talking to you. But we may need his help."

"I lied to Biondi because I was scared, and I don't trust him."

"But why?"

"Remember early this year when I was so excited about going to Milan to give a talk at that conference?"

"Yep. Boring stuff, nice location."

"I met someone there. Jack and I were talking divorce, so what did I have to hold onto? This Italian was an older man, very bright, charming, accomplished, a count from Venice who owned a bank and invested in art—like a Renaissance man, I thought. We had a fling. I regretted it once I found out more about him." Anna fingered a button on her raincoat. "Someone killed him last night."

"What? Where?"

"At the Belvedere Hotel. Biondi showed me a picture of him lying in his own blood."

Margo gave Anna a soft hug. "That must have been terrifying. A foreign country, the police, and a man you had slept with—murdered. Are you all right?"

"In shock, I think," Anna murmured. "They have an artist's sketch of me. Not perfect, but it's pretty damn good. That's what they used to pick me up. I had stupidly followed Sergio to the ball at the hotel."

As they left Santa Lucia station behind, a cool mist cloaked the resting place of the last doge and lingered beyond the School of the Dead.

"Sergio? Don't tell me. You don't mean Sergio Corrin?"

"You knew him?"

"I met him at the big party he and his wife, Liliana, gave a few years ago, during Carnival. Count Favier invited my cousin Angela and me. How strange."

Was the world really this small, Anna wondered, or was it just Venice?

"Go on."

"Sergio wooed me, showed me around Milan and gave me all his attention—for four days. During that time, I found out later, he took some pictures of me, of us."

"Where?"

Anna's gaze wavered. "In his hotel suite—"

"Like naked in bed?"

"After a lot of Champagne." Anna recalled seeing the two photos of her, of them together, on the caffè table. Along with another surprise—the picture of the confidential file lying on her hotel nightstand, smuggled out of the archives at work, in preparation for her speech. She should never have brought it to the conference.

"When did it end?"

"Before I left Milan. I had even been thinking I could end up leaving California for him. But my flight got canceled, and I returned to the hotel. I was window shopping, strolling along Via Monte Napoleone, and there he was, kissing another woman from the conference. What a fool."

"You should have called me."

"I looked him up in a directory when I got home, a *Who's Who* in Italian finance, which said he was married, with a wife and two kids. Should've mentioned that he was an inveterate skirt chaser."

"I could've found that out for you. What made you want to see him here in Venice instead of just forgetting all about him?"

"I hadn't spoken to him in months. In Milan, when I told him what a sleazebag he was, he just laughed and said he might send something to my boss and get me in trouble. At first I thought he was joking. But then he called me in the spring and told me about the photographs. I asked him to give them back, and he refused, although he didn't say why he wanted them. All these months later, he happened to call me a few days before my flight. Once he heard I was coming to Venice, he pleaded with me to leave Zürich early and meet with him. I figured that if he really had any photos, he'd had a crisis of conscience and I'd get the pictures back. I still thought he was just an awful womanizer."

"What happened?"

"He threatened me. It turned out that he'd been biding his time so that he could use me in an even worse way when he needed to. I'll leave it at that. He wouldn't give me the pictures, and I gave up and left the caffè. Later on, I realized I had to try again. I tracked him to the ball he said he'd be attending, but I chickened out. I didn't even approach him."

"How did he threaten you? What did he want?"

"It's better for you if I don't say."

"I can make an educated guess."

"It'll have to remain just that."

"He could have made copies of the photos and still used them later."

"Maybe he hadn't. Anyway, he's dead now."

"Yes, and you're in a hole with Biondi making book on you."

"Tell me about it." Anna pictured Biondi in a gray office, sifting through a mountain of clues. "How much influence does Count Favier have?"

"Enough to slow Biondi down, not to stop him. Speaking of the count, I couldn't get you in his palazzo. He has too many houseguests: me, my cousin Angela, and more. Once our vacations are over, his home will be empty. But I found you a cute little

25

FAIRHOPE PUBLIC LIBRARY

pensione, only ten minutes away, near La Fenice opera house. I hope you don't mind."

"Staying with all of you would have been great under happier circumstances. I'll need the phone and fax at the pensione to deal with my office."

"Will you be working?"

"Digging. I'd better figure out a way to prove I'm innocent."

"Well, we have a few options, including marching back to Biondi and leveling with him. As bright as you are, you're no match for a detective on his home turf."

"Not a good idea. First, I'd get canned from work once he tells my boss about me and Sergio."

"He was that bad?"

"Worse. Second, how do you know Biondi wouldn't take the easy way out and just pin the murder on me?"

"I don't. But he doesn't have much evidence."

"Who'd care about this American woman he'd say was crazy with jealousy? It'd be a quick solution, and he might get a promotion."

"Nah, you're just one of the leads he's following, Anna. You'd never go to jail, because we'd find you the best attorney in town if need be." Margo squeezed her hand.

A sweater sleeve, sticking out of her suitcase, caught Anna's eye. As she turned to tuck it into the zippered bag, she spotted a trim, middle-aged man in a dark jacket averting his eyes, as if he had been staring at her and wanted to melt back into the crowd. Was this happenstance or had Biondi put a tail on her? She noted the man's features as he intently studied the buildings lining the canal: steel-gray hair, high forehead, protruding ears, sharp nose, small mouth, shorter than the German women chatting next to him in a knot. He was wearing a neutral expression. She'd better keep an eye on him, she thought, not that she could do much about it.

"What's the matter?" Margo asked.

"Those creeps," Anna said. "They must have searched my luggage—totally illegal. Of course they didn't find anything."

"What an ordeal," Margo said, squeezing Anna's hand again.

Anna glanced sideways at the man. He had slid closer but was looking away. She chewed her lip. "Let's take a break, and you can tell me about Venice, as if I'm the tourist I had hoped to be. What's that building?" she asked, pointing to an unfinished-brick church façade, their view quivering under the heavy breath of the vaporetto.

"That's San Marcuola. Behind it lies the old ghetto, probably the first in the world."

"Here in Venice? Never would have guessed."

"People still sail right on by it and never know. In the fifteen hundreds, the local Jews and the banks they owned were forced to move into the old foundry area. The foundry, or ghetto, was horribly cramped, ringed by canals. Jews could come and go during the day, but they had to wear clothing that identified them, and the gates were locked at night. When Napoleon invaded, the gates were torn down.

"I'm doing research on Venice for a series in the *San Francisco Chronicle*. Behind all the gaiety is a lot of tragedy. At the end of the sixteenth century, when almost ten percent of Venetian women were prostitutes, the Council of Ten was at the height of its power, spying, punishing, killing anyone who appeared to be an enemy of the state. Neighbors anonymously ratted on each other, stuffing pieces of paper into the mouths of stone-lion mailboxes."

The bow spray shimmered in the lights as the boat dug into an obstinate wave. Anna pulled her raincoat tight. "Biondi would have had a field day."

"Don't give him more power than he already has," Margo said.

"This unique place and its history are not logical," Anna said.

"Talk about opposites. How can the Venetians have tolerated living in a police state, yet in such a loose society? Were all their escapades a flight from reality?"

"That's what fascinates me about Venice," Margo said. "It's full of contradictions."

The vaporetto made its crooked way down the Grand Canal, the throaty growl of its engines filling the air. Past the angels of San Stae, the boat stopped again, only to groan, tear away from the illuminated buildings, and head into the blackness once more. Each stop was a luminescent island in the dark. The boat was a needle, threading the glowing pearls of an enormous necklace. Did the necklace grace the throat of a vibrant and beautiful woman or that of a trollop, painted and decayed? Venice's enveloping night cloak made it impossible to tell.

Looking at Anna in the light streaming from a nearby palazzo, Margo arched one eyebrow before asking, "Are you feeling better about Jack?"

"I'm not reconciling." Anna recalled their last day together, when winter's overcast skies seemed to never end. No bellowing drunken rants from him, just a stupor, this one courtesy of the whisky bottle hidden in the piano. She had failed to count precisely how many bottles she had discovered over the past six years. It didn't matter, since that was the day she counted the last one. She threw her clothes and some belongings into her car and drove off for the last time, she swore. Never again would his tears and cries persuade her to come back. She had promised herself to sever their insane cycle of breaking up and making up. However much they had tried, they could never get back to their bright beginnings. She had started divorce proceedings after returning from Milan and would be retaking her maiden name by the end of December.

"Is he still calling you?" Margo asked.

"I hang up every time. How could I ever trust him again?"

Anna shook her head, recalling Jack's bleating voice. "He's getting the message."

"Are you sure you don't want to try marriage counseling? Jack seems lost without you."

Anna sighed. "Did he lobby you? Ask you to put in a good word?"

"Don't know if I would phrase it like that," Margo said.

"You remember the old Jack, before he allowed his failures to change him. So do I. He got plenty of second chances. He's out of them now. Frankly, I just think he's feigning caring about me to get a better settlement."

"Sounds harsh."

"I devoted myself to him for fifteen long years. Now I need to think of me. Listen, I can't rehash all of this right now, on top of Sergio and Biondi and everything else, or it'll push me right over the edge. Let's just enjoy the scenery, shall we?"

"We'll pick it up when you're calmer."

Anna rolled her eyes. She's like a pit bull, Anna thought. Jack must have cried on the phone to her and all of a sudden, he's the wronged party. Margo should know better.

"Look to your left," Margo said. "Centuries ago that palazzo was covered in gold."

Gold? Anna could hardly imagine the ostentation and expense as she drank in the delicate columns at the water's edge, the ancient balconies and pointed arched windows, the detailed carvings, like the lions with their flowing manes. The walls' intricate weave of geometric patterns, their textures rising and falling in the wavering light paid everlasting homage to the influence of the East.

"Don't trust the water here," Margo said, her words competing with the thump of the engine. "It can seem serene; Venice is called *La Serenissima*, after all. But the sea can rise quickly, like today, overflowing the sidewalks. And some days are much worse. Maybe we'll take a boat by the Lido. When the tide is right and the sea is calm, you can make out underwater ruins of the old Malamocco. Torn from its roots eight centuries ago, like some little clump of beach grass, and swept out to sea. Gone." Margo snapped her fingers. "Just like that."

Anna squinted at the black waves and shoved her hands in her pockets. Undertows, tidal waves, storm surges, death by drowning—these had always terrorized her. She was not sure if it was an early memory or an old dream, but she clearly recalled the feeling of weightlessness. Of floating face down in dark water, too weak to raise her head. Of holding her breath until her lungs ached. Then being pushed up from below, tumbling into the air.

"Are you cold?" Margo asked, wrapping an arm around her.

"Just thinking." Anna leaned into her friend.

"You know, in a way, all of Venice is a beach," Margo mused. "The city is like a set of sandbars only a foot and a half above the canals. The water floods courtyards and *campi*, the small plazas. It backs up through drains and leaves rusty puddles, or worse. The sea can get anywhere it wants."

"I hope I'm not sleeping on the ground floor. I'd hate to drown in my bed." Anna gave a grim chuckle.

Off to their right, she glimpsed waves strengthened by the boat's wake, invading a marketplace, not pausing at the stone sidewalk barriers but accelerating into the shallower depth, like tiny tsunami landing, careening every which way, into the locked stalls with their canvas awnings, against the ancient columns, the force of each little wave eating imperceptibly into the stone. One day, after the battering of countless waves, the fingerprints, the footprints, and all that man had created here would be wiped clean, crumble away, and be swallowed by the sea, she feared.

They veered under the Rialto Bridge, its grand arch jutting above the water, the shops on its back shuttered for the evening, a huge hanging banner waving in the wind. Pizza parlors and canalside restaurants hugged the bridge's stony flanks. The dampened voices of lone patrons skipped on the water like thin and distant melodies.

Lights illuminated finely detailed buildings with sculpted balconies. Graceful arches framed timbered ceilings. As they floated past Islamic windows, the light from multicolored Murano chandeliers glimmered. Anna caught glimpses of airy blue frescoes, smiling angels, resplendent velvet tapestries. The past persisted.

"Most of the palazzos were born in the fourteenth and fifteenth centuries, when noble families enjoyed a huge influence," Margo said. "Some of them have been beautifully maintained."

"But there are sad ones, too," Anna pointed out, spying a silent abode in the shadows. Alongside the favored palazzos lurked their dark, ignored sisters, the city's abandoned children, tilting into muddy solitude from which they could never be extracted.

"Here's San Samuele, our stop." Margo nodded toward the gleaming Palazzo Grassi.

In a dramatic percussion solo, the vaporetto bumped and scraped the dock until the avalanche of noise came to a whining stop. As they left the boat, Anna peeked at the dark-jacketed man, still aboard and realized it would be child's play to follow them to her pensione. He made no effort to disembark when they alighted, however. The gate clicked shut behind them, the engine revved, and the boat veered back into the mist.

The high water had receded here, leaving scattered puddles. Under the full gaze of the stone Virgin in a narrow niche, past the house of Casanova, they headed down an alleyway, Margo leading them like a seasoned guide in a casbah. They dragged Anna's luggage and trudged by hidden pensioni, wood sculpture, and lace shops.

"You know where you're going?" Anna asked.

"You forget I lived here. It's a bit harder at night, but you remember the way by recalling the stores."

Anna thought of Margo's divorce. "Does it still hurt?"

"I'll be damned if agonizing about him makes me love the city any less."

"Thatta girl."

They zigzagged forward through twisting paths until they turned a corner and faced an empty plaza, nothing but darkened storefronts and bare pavement greeting them.

"Where are all the Venetians?" Anna asked.

Margo paused atop a small bridge. "The city closes early. When there's been flooding, even fewer are out. We're lucky that we can roll your suitcases instead of lifting them above ankle-deep puddles."

A lone gondola glided beneath them like an enormous night insect on dark wings. It unnerved Anna somehow. She had expected a singing gondolier and a crew of raucous passengers. In an instant, the boat rounded a corner and vanished.

In the buildings they passed, human silhouettes played against drawn curtains, like gigantic shadow puppets in a secret ritual. The clicking rhythm of the women's heels on the hard pavement echoed against the stone walls of Campo San Angelo, adding to Anna's unease. Gray, shifting forms drifted in the distant haze before revealing themselves as flesh-and-blood pedestrians. Ah, here are some people after all, Anna thought.

Winding by an old mask shop, Anna glimpsed glittering moons, gleaming suns, porcelain doll faces, and fairy princesses sparkling as if they had been dusted with sugar. A sign on a nearby wall read Calle dei Assassini.

"Street of Assassins, really?" Anna asked.

"Centuries ago," Margo said, as they approached a two-story tan structure on their left. "Here's your hotel, Pensione Stella. The desk clerk's expecting you. You'll join us for lunch at one tomorrow, after you've gotten a good night's sleep. I'll call in the morning with directions."

"Can't wait to fall into bed," Anna replied, managing a hint of a grin. "And tomorrow we have to figure a way out of Biondi's clutches. In the meantime, don't let anyone know about Sergio's murder."

"Right. But remember, no more worrying for tonight." Margo brushed her lips against Anna's cheek, then strode toward a narrow alley, the scent of jasmine lingering in her wake.

Lovers embracing in the shadows of a nearby bridge drew Anna's attention. She shook her head as she opened the pensione's heavy doors.

3

La Stella

Sunday, evening

The desk clerk at Pensione Stella looked up from his book as Anna entered, and flashed a crooked smile. His bushy silver sideburns contrasted with an irregular patch of brown hair, reminding Anna of a bird of paradise she'd seen recently in *National Geographic*. Perched behind an ornate wooden counter, he took hold of a thick, leather-bound log with years of rooms, dates, guest names, and notes written in longhand. After inspecting her passport, he dipped his pen into a crystal inkwell, inscribing her name, room, and passport number with a flourish. Anna felt relieved when he finally handed over her key, an old-fashioned one with the room number notched into a green rubber ball. All the better to float in the canals, Anna thought as she followed him across ceramic floor tiles depicting ancient ships sailing the far blue seas, past a couple of burgundy leather love seats, and up the squeaky stairs to her room.

Had Margo even looked at the Stella's guest rooms? Anna wondered as she opened the door. She surveyed the pale stucco walls, the single bed, the rickety desk, and the nightstand with a lamp so dim, that reading would be impossible. A paisley-upholstered chair and a small sink drooped along the opposite wall. The bath was down the hall. She wouldn't mind staying here, but years ago, traveling with Jack, she would have expected far better.

Resisting the urge to collapse into bed, Anna unpacked and took stock of her garments after the police seizure, noting with satisfaction that no clothes were damaged or missing. Hanging each piece in an artificial-wood armoire, she imposed a semblance of order. When it grew stuffy, she pushed the window and shutters open and stood looking out, breathing in the night air. Across the way, a brick palazzo huddled in the dark, the reflection of the pensione's neon star on one of its windows. An ivory balcony wrapped around the far edge of the building and jutted over the water. The tinkling of piano keys reached her ears, along with the peaceful gurgling of the nearby canal.

The couple on the bridge had moved closer to a filigreed street lantern. The woman sat atop a wide cement railing, at an angle to Anna, her silver dress unbuttoned and pulled up so high, it barely covered the tops of her thighs. Her breasts obscured her lover's face, but Anna caught a glimpse of blond highlights. The woman guided his hands under her panties so as to cup and squeeze her buttocks. Crouching before her, he trailed his lips on her flesh before burying his face between her legs. The woman leaned back and gyrated in pleasure, her dark hair swinging in the weak light.

Dogs in heat, Anna thought. Where were the police? Probably chasing innocent tourists like her. That would keep them busy! A tape of her interrogation played in her mind. It dragged her through loop after loop. She doubted she could sleep without being pursued by visions of Detective Biondi or Sergio.

She slammed the window against the muffled sighs. Despite its glamour, Venice, she realized, consisted of communal living in a maze of little alleys. Whether you liked it or not.

In the depths of the night, Anna awoke, startled by a cry, and threw off her bed covers. The *calle* acted like a funnel, magnifying and mixing sounds in a hallucinating brew. Peering through the window, however, she didn't see a soul on either the bridge or the stone pavement. Then she noticed a faint glow in the brick palazzo. Now that the neon star had been turned off, she could see into the window, where, by the pale light, she made out a teddy bear tossed on a rug. Then she heard the high-pitched sobbing of a child. Somehow, Anna knew that no adult was nearby. She wondered what kind of person could have left such a small child alone. The Italians she knew celebrated and loved children.

In a blur, Anna recalled her own painful quest. She saw herself in a consultation room with oversized photographs of smiling babies looking down from the walls. Needing to believe that a photo of her child would hang there one day, she had concentrated hard, hoping that through the power of positive thinking, she could control the outcome of a science that knew no grays. She had sat there, head down, like a mute soul waiting to learn its destiny. The door had opened and the medical assistant's kind eyes had sought her out. Anna could not remember the face, just the bare legs and clogs on a blustery day. Then the slight Dutch accent, as she leaned close to Anna and said gently, "No. None fertilized. I am so sorry."

Anna had looked out at a passing rain cloud over San Francisco Bay before nodding. That's all right, she had told herself. It was a small chance anyway. We knew this all along. We'll try again. But inside her, a glass had silently shattered.

Sleep finally overcame her when daybreak began painting her room gold. At nine o'clock, the bells began to chime, first one, then more—a never-ending song through the centuries—altos, tenors, baritones, basses. Their individual personalities and locations unknown to her, the bells cried out in a deafening canto. She knew that in bygone days, they had rung to celebrate the survival of the city after the plague, the coronation of a doge, or to warn of a hostile naval force. Now they awakened tourists in their beds.

4

Beside the Still,
Green Canal

Monday, afternoon

A church bell rang out with one deep bong as Anna raced to the count's palazzo. Margo had warned her not to follow the numbers along the streets, since the address of one building bore no relation to the next. Here, addresses were splattered like paint across the district, or *sestiere*. Anna pictured losing herself among randomly numbered buildings in alleyways leading nowhere. Scary, she thought, not being able to trust numbers when she had built her life around them. She had followed a bachelor's degree in mathematics with a master's in physics, gravitating toward astrophysics. All her professors had expressed disappointment when she announced she was not continuing onto the PhD program.

Anna hurried across a stone bridge, her image in a white knit top, navy cotton pants, and red purse blurring against the damask cushions in an antiquarian's window. She passed through a short tunnel, and finally, she glimpsed an imposing ocher palazzo in the distance, alongside a still, green canal.

Just as Margo had described, two sets of pointed arch windows rose above geranium-filled window boxes, and the sculpted head of a bearded god with two faces gazed down from the lintel. One side had been darkened by time and the elements, while the other had remained pure and bright. Searching for a doorbell amid the honeysuckle framing the carved maroon entry, Anna found the outstretched tongue of a tiny brass lion. After a surprised pause, she pressed it.

The door opened with a reluctant buzz into a stone-walled vestibule where the musty cabin, or *felze,* of the family gondola languished in a corner. The place was between worlds, belonging to neither sea nor earth. The wrath of the canal overflowing its banks would be felt here first. Anna imagined waves slowly filling the little room, the felze quivering in the water.

Curious to see where the gondola entered the canal, she drew near the sunlight pouring through a metal gate. Here, a half-dozen steps swept into the canal, each one following its pale stone brother, the lowest hardly visible through the murkiness where shadow and light intermingled with the rhythm of the water. For an instant, Anna glimpsed a woman's grimacing face; then it disintegrated into tiny ripples. Funny what water could do, she thought.

Margo and the others would be waiting for her on a higher floor, the *piano nobile,* not in this desolate spot. A gleaming music box of an elevator answered Anna's call and transported her as she brooded about Sergio's murder and Biondi's interrogation. Margo had given her the right advice on the phone—she needed to put it behind her for a few hours. When the doors squeaked open, Margo was waiting, leaning against a pillar, tapping a sandaled foot.

"You're fifteen minutes late. Where have you been?"

"Sorry about that," Anna said. "This place isn't easy to find. Any news?"

"Nothing about the murder in today's papers. We may not see anything for a while. Everybody I told you about is here. They can't wait to meet you, but let me take a second and introduce you to

Nero, or we'll regret it later when he plunks a giant paw on your lap when you least expect it." Margo turned to a shaggy black dog with warm brown eyes, sitting quietly in a corner, watching them.

Anna calculated his weight at more than a hundred pounds.

"Come here, big boy, and meet Anna. *Vieni qui.*"

The dog bounded ahead, filling Anna with momentary panic, then sniffed her legs while wagging his tail.

"Good thing I passed the smell test." Anna petted him on the head.

Margo ushered Anna into the recesses of the palazzo, over smooth pebbles of Venetian terrazzo and past sumptuously painted mythological scenes. Anna's senses awakened when they entered a drawing room of frescoed parrots and peacocks; on the floor, inlaid mother-of-pearl and lapis lazuli imitated the patterns of a fantastic Persian carpet.

"Those are Alessandro's ancestors," said Margo, tilting her head toward a long hall where busts of the count's forebears overpopulated the top of an ebony credenza set against a red silken wall. A host of lit candles encircled them, as if they were minor saints, Anna thought, smelling the aroma of dusky roses.

After climbing a flight of emerald marble stairs, they emerged onto a grand rooftop terrace. Azaleas and fig trees graced giant terracotta pots, and pomegranates dangled from a small tree. Geraniums and bougainvillea transformed the roof's edges into a miniature jungle. The verdant garden burst with life. Weeds had outnumbered flowers in Anna's backyard. Jack had refused to get his hands dirty, and after a few years, she had given up doing all the work. The view of bare soil from her kitchen window had pained her every time she washed the dishes. An echo, she had thought eventually, of their sterile coupling.

Looking out, Anna caught sight of bell towers rising in every direction and crooked chimney pots angled to the sky. Beyond them lay the glittering swath of Venice's watery arteries and veins narrowing to wispy capillaries, shining in the sun.

Her gaze shifted to the immaculate setting of the rectangular table. Margo had rattled off gossipy snippets about the count and his houseguests: ages, backgrounds, hobbies. As if she had memorized their dossiers. No wonder she was always winning prizes for her reporting. With such talent, she would have been a great spy.

Count Alessandro Favier was seated at the head of the canopy-covered table, smiling at a dark greyhound of a man to his right. That must be the Peruvian consul from Florence, Pablo Morales, Anna thought. Margo's cousin, auburn-haired Angela, sat across from him. She looked as high-spirited as ever, waving her freckled arms as she made an emphatic point. To Angela's left sat Yolanda, Pablo's blonde, olive-skinned wife with tawny, feline eyes. The far end of the table was empty.

"I'm back with my friend, Anna Lucia Lottol." Margo put her arm around Anna's waist as they strode forward. "She's hoping to have a great vacation."

Right, Anna thought. She gave them a wary smile and scanned their pleasant faces, doubting that any of them could have killed Sergio Saturday night.

Gray-haired Count Favier rose and approached the women, stopping them midway to the table. Of moderate height and weight, he carried himself with quiet dignity. His drooping brown eyes gave him an air of sadness. Full lips hinted at a refined sensuousness. Bermuda shorts revealed tanned, well-muscled legs, making him appear more youthful than his mid-sixties.

The count took Anna's hand. "*Un piacere squisito,*" he said, adding in accented English, "Welcome to *Venezia.*" He kissed her on both cheeks and whispered, "And how is the little bird from jail? Do not worry. You will not be hearing from Biondi again."

"Thank you so much for vouching for me, Count Favier,"

said Anna, surprised. "What an awful experience. Did he tell you about the murder?" She wondered if he and Sergio had been good friends.

"Probably a drug dealer or some other criminal. In any case, the relatives must be told first. Family is important here in Italy." He raised his voice. "But you must call me Alessandro." He grinned at Anna and nodded toward Margo and Angela. "They have been hiding you from me."

"Alessandro, she's just arrived," said Margo.

"Besides," Angela said, "she's married, isn't she?"

"Besides," mimicked Alessandro, "she is on vacation with the husband many, many kilometers away. Where did you tell me?" he squinted at Margo. "Berkeley, yes? A lovely city—for him to stay in." He chuckled.

With the mention of Jack, Anna feared she'd be dragged into sharing details of her impending divorce with people she didn't know, who, judging from the half-drained wine glasses studding the table, might ask her embarrassing questions.

"Don't mind him," chided Pablo. "Alessandro calms down once he's been fed."

Anna pivoted toward the count and said, "Your home is so beautiful."

"It was built for my family in the fifteenth century," Alessandro said proudly. With a dramatic sweep of his arm, he added, "I have the original plans and old maps, along with many family documents. Come see my library after *pranzo*."

"Yes," said Margo, "after lunch we can look at the Book of Gold."

Alessandro showed Anna to a seat next to Pablo before easing into his rattan peacock chair. "I offer you a cocktail. Anna, the Bellini is named after one of our famous artists, Giovanni Bellini, living in the fifteenth century. Back then, if you had floated by *palazzi* on the Grand Canal, you would have seen many exteriors adorned with his beautiful frescoes. The drink is made with Prosecco, our bubbling Venetian white wine, combined with juice of peach, thanks to Giuseppe Cipriani."

"*Allora Gaetano, ancora per gli ospiti,*" Alessandro instructed the somber servant lingering at the door, Nero beside him. "I tell him to bring another round of Bellini."

"Anna Lucia, what a beautiful name," Pablo commented.

"Just like Santa Lucia, our saint, buried in San Geremia on the Grand Canal," Alessandro said. "I am happy to have good friends stay here, but it saddens me that I could not fit another lovely guest in my home as we are refinishing the other bedrooms. How are your accommodations at La Stella?" he asked, cocking an eyebrow.

"They're fine. It can be a little noisy, though. I heard a child crying in the middle of the night . . ." She paused, distracted by Gaetano pouring their drinks.

"Where was this comin' from, another hotel room?" Angela asked.

"No, the brick palazzo across the street."

As he was filling her glass, Gaetano knocked against it, barely catching it in time. Moustache twitching, he peeped at Alessandro.

"*Non trascurarti,*" Alessandro said, reminding him not to be careless. Turning to Anna, he corrected her with a toothy smile. "The building you speak of was closed decades ago, when its owners left. It has many, how do you say, *strutturali*, structural, problems, making it unlivable. Like some other palazzi, it is so expensive to fix that no one has touched it. It remains deserted, totally empty, except for a few brave pigeons that have set up housekeeping."

Anna searched his face. "How could that be? Maybe I'm not being clear."

"*Cara Signora* Lottol," Alessandro shook his head, "I am *cento per cento* certain. I have passed there many times. You see, Venice is small, and I have lived here *tutta la mia vita*, my entire life, and invested billions of lire in real estate." He glanced at Pablo. "So I make it a point to know these things. Surely you are exhausted from your voyage, and in the dark, things can get confused. Perhaps you speak of another building.

"Do not forget the cats," he added, shaking his finger at her. "*Piccoli* relatives of the proud lion of St. Mark on our flag. They dominate the city. They sleep by day. They moan in the moonlight, mating. Listening at night, one may think of babies crying. I have thought the same myself."

Anna stifled a sigh. She knew what she had seen and heard. "I can't understand why they haven't torn it down then."

Alessandro erupted into laughter. "Ah, what an American way of thinking! In Venice, our dwellings are very old. Our city was born more than one thousand years before your America was even discovered, by an Italian. What gives a city its character, after all? *Insomma*, its people, yes, but also what they choose to create: art, architecture—things you can see. We restore our buildings. We can make changes on the inside, but their heights, their outward dimensions and details are protected. They are our heritage forever—or at least until the hand of God takes them from us."

"I see," said Anna.

"We wish to keep the harmony we have achieved during many centuries of history. We do not want your McDonald's on the Grand Canal," he snorted.

"To old Venetian buildings," Margo said, proposing a toast. As she raised her glass, the sleeve of her blue linen shirt fell back, revealing a scar the size of two silver dollars. Its swirling patterns resembled a mocha-colored face of the moon.

That was a narrow escape, Anna thought, as everyone joined in. Countless tangy bubbles burst on Anna's tongue and the roof of her mouth, unleashing a stream of pleasure as she closed her eyes, escaping a moment, feeling a warm breeze. Her reverie was broken by flashes of her time in Milan with Sergio, all ending with his red-stained head. She gulped her drink and pushed the vision from her mind.

"Last week, Sergio Corrin asked me to join him in saving Palazzo Tron on the Grand Canal," Alessandro told the group. "We start from the bottom, by replacing thousands of ancient piles sunk in the mud to hold up the ancient walls. Before the cold weather comes, we need to accomplish this foundation work. Then we tackle the floors and the plaster inside. Once we finish, the palazzo will look better than it did originally."

Anna almost choked. Alessandro and Sergio, business partners. She wondered how close they had been and if Sergio had ever said anything about her. Or worse, if he had passed her pictures around in a fit of boasting. Judging from the count's demeanor, that seemed doubtful, unless he was a great actor and had a surprise planned for her in the library. As Margo shot her a knowing look, Anna scrutinized the others. Nobody seemed to have noticed her reaction. Did someone here hate Sergio enough to want him dead? Among the nods at the table, only Pablo was frowning.

"The man does have fine taste in art. I've been buyin' pieces from him for my gallery in Dallas for years," said Angela, pushing her bangs off her forehead. "Isn't that palazzo a few doors up from San Stae? The one sporting a Palladian portal and an extended cornice?"

"Why, yes," Alessandro said.

"You sound like a local professor," Margo said. "How'd you know that?"

"Well, the doctor told me I'd better walk, and I've been exploring four of the six *sestieri*, as they call 'em. I take my map and make notes, remembering my art history courses. Texas isn't filled with hicks, Margo."

"I didn't mean it like that," Margo said, as Gaetano began

serving the colorful antipasti. "Now that our first course is arriving, it's time to talk about food, one of my favorite topics."

"For lack of more interestin' pursuits," her cousin teased.

"Isn't it marvelous how such simple ingredients—tomato, mozzarella cheese, a lovely leaf of basil, and a dab of olive oil—can combine in such a savory way? Italian tomatoes are seized at the moment of perfection, gushing in little explosions when you bite them. American tomatoes taste as if they were ripened on their way to the grocery store."

"You should be food editor at the *Chronicle* instead of girl reporter," Angela said.

"The Italian tomatoes are a lot like their men," Yolanda said. "Many years ago, before my Pablo, an old boyfriend, Gennaro, and I were sunning ourselves in the back of his boat." She took a slow drag from a cigarette and exhaled. "I had brought a dozen cherry tomatoes with me. We had just gone, how you say, swimming with no clothes, yes, skinny-dipping, off L'Isola degli Armeni, where the monastery is. I took one of the tomatoes in my mouth and gently turned Gennaro over. He—"

"*Por favor, mujer. Nunca debes repetir esta historia,*" Pablo snapped, turning his head abruptly, a ray of sun accentuating a jagged scar on his jaw.

"*Jesucristo,* there is such a thing as controlling yourself too much." Yolanda finished the rest of her drink and crossed her arms.

Alessandro cleared his throat and said, "*Basta* with the Bellini. *Più prosecco,* Gaetano."

Limping toward them, Gaetano poured the bubbling prosecco from a carafe of opalescent glass, handmade in Murano, Anna was sure. The diffuse points of sparkling light reminded Anna of distant suns enmeshed in the milky cloud of a nebula, not unlike M8, the Lagoon Nebula in the Constellation Sagittarius—her first. Lying low on the horizon, ten parsecs in diameter, blue stars forming among reddish gases. When she had first glimpsed it through a telescope, she had been awestruck by its beauty. Wondrous new worlds were being born in its midst.

Turning to Anna, Pablo asked, "You have a science background, Margo tells me."

"Math undergrad and master's degree in astrophysics."

"Now working at?" he asked.

She thought about how to describe her current job without getting into sticky details. "I work with financial transactions and modeling."

Her job in the Financial Crimes Enforcement Network, a secretive unit of the US Treasury Department, involved creating algorithms to catch money launderers. The specifics were beyond the ken of most people and her comfort level with this group.

In the rarified world of financial intelligence, a background in math and science was coveted. Mathematical prowess plus scientific precision built models that could capture questionable transactions slithering through the US financial system. Once Anna's division identified a likely launderer, another unit would take over, deepening the investigation, gathering facts, and uncovering the underlying crimes before American agents risked their lives pursuing cartels and kingpins. In her second year at Treasury, Anna had been awarded a certificate of appreciation from the assistant director for preventing the transfer of fifty million dollars to a Grand Cayman account of José Proserpina, a Colombian drug lord and private banking client of Bank Lillobrandt.

"Margo told me you catch drug dealers by following their dirty money," Angela said. "Do you carry a gun?"

Frowning, Anna looked at Margo. Telling Angela anything about her work was a terrible lapse in judgment, particularly when she knew that Sergio had threatened Anna's job. Anna had distinctly sought to avoid what Margo had now stirred up with her irrepressible need to blab. Sergio had partners in crime someplace; she just hoped they weren't sitting around this table.

"Oh, no—far from it," Anna said. "I work in a cubicle with computers all day long. We screen data. I'm sure all of you would find it extremely boring."

"I know I would," Yolanda said. "I need the green places, and I also like to think that life can't be modeled. Who would have predicted that two Peruvians like Pablo and me would be sitting here now?"

Gaetano returned with steaming risotto piled onto porcelain plates edged by crimson crests, a delectable fragrance rising from the saffron cloud.

"Pablo, how did you decide to enter government service?" Anna asked, burying her fork in the creamy rice.

"My medical training in Italy prepared me to deal with the ills of my country," Pablo replied, "but only up to a point. Peru is a poor nation, with mineral wealth, but without great fortunes. My old profession is part art. Often I was frustrated but only able to do so much." He grimly set his jaw.

"I am happier with Consul Pablo than Dr. Pablo," Yolanda said, beaming at her husband. "Maybe next year, Roma. I would like that. Villa Borghese, the Lazio countryside, the Sibillini."

Angela leaned forward and angled her youthful, heart-shaped face toward Pablo. "This is very far from Peru, though. Why did you come here so long ago?"

Pablo fingered his sparse black goatee. "I am a student of history. As a boy, I read that before kidnapping and killing Atahualpa, the Spanish had hoped to seduce him with beautiful gifts and steal his empire in that way. They presented him with a set of Venetian goblets. As a young man, I wanted to visit the place where such marvels were made. I ended up studying at Padua to obtain my medical degree.

"Oddly, the longer I stayed here, the more I recognized connections with my homeland. For me, the Aymara standing while rowing their boats of totora reeds on Lake Titicaca, the birthplace of the Incas, could be the gondoliers of Venice. Coricancha, the Inca palace once covered in gold, the tears of the sun, could be the Ca' d'Oro on the Grand Canal. And our jaguar god could be the Lion of St. Mark. So," he concluded dreamily, "*ya ves*—you see, I had to come here."

Pablo glanced at Angela's polka-dot tent dress. "Is it long before your baby is due?"

"Sixty more days. I wanted to visit now, since it'll be a long time before I come back."

Sixty days, Anna thought. That's how old mine was when it died. Our second try. A tiny sweater still hung in the back of Anna's closet, forgotten by all except her and the moths. Sometimes she pulled it out, inspecting it before burying it again. She took a few more swallows of her drink.

"No one besides Michael back home knows, but I don't mind tellin' y'all." Angela's ivory cheeks blossomed into pink. "It's a girl."

"A baby girl, how wonderful," Alessandro said. "Why not stay? Ask your husband to come over and have the baby born in Venice."

This man lives in a bubble, Anna thought.

"You were here two years ago for Carnival, then early this year for your work when the baby was maybe just a spark in your imagination," he went on. "Too much time has passed since I heard a child's laughter in my home." He reached over and squeezed Pablo's hand. "Pablo will deliver the baby. And Gaetano will make her beautiful wooden toys."

Pablo gagged on his wine. "Alessandro, I *am* a little out of practice."

"Nonsense, it is like bicycle riding, and lovemaking. I am sure—one of those things you do not forget."

Anna certainly could never forget. A child. Or rather, not having a child. How could that void dominate her so? She found herself unwittingly staring at babies, feeling an unwelcome jolt if she passed a store for expectant mothers, condemned always to look in from the outside. Would she never feel the sublime fullness of pregnancy nor the miracle of birth? Try as she might, she could neither expunge nor bury the pain; it was nowhere and everywhere, biding its time, stalking its prey. Just a single brief thought or image would reignite it like an ember hiding under cool ashes, erupting into flame and searing her all over again. The march of time had no balming effect, for time itself was the enemy.

"Pablo is still quite skilled," Yolanda said, flicking her cigarette into an ashtray. "It is no comparison, but recently he set the broken leg of one of our llamas back home. We have a herd of them, more than an hour outside Cusco, not far from the Inca ruins at Ollantaytambo, in the Sacred Valley. Each summer, I host a group of orphans from Cusco at our farm so they can explore nature and understand their heritage. Last year, the boys discovered two llamas had fallen in a ditch. Pablo wrapped one in a blanket and tended to its leg. Its twin was not so lucky. It was a hard lesson for the children. You know, many times he—"

"No. *Cállate*," Pablo said firmly.

"I think Pablo was saying no to your offer, Alessandro," Angela said.

Examining Yolanda's crestfallen face, Anna knew that Pablo was referring to something altogether different.

Angela's green orbs riveted on the horizon, her mobile mouth hinting at a wistful smile. "Alessandro, your offer to stay here is so kind, but it'd be foolish. For one thing, I hardly speak any Italian. I'm fixin' to leave next week."

As they were finishing their risotto, they heard gondolier cries and songs from the water. Craning her neck, Anna glimpsed a flotilla heading up the *rio*. Despite daunting odds, the low-sitting gondolas, overloaded with Nikon-bedecked tourists, were making progress instead of sinking into the murky depths. Above them stood the gondoliers, ribboned hats set at a jaunty angle, pushing their oars against the water, overcoming her resistance.

"Ah, the gondoliers!" Anna cried, happy for a change of subject. "What pleasant songs they sing. I've never been on a gondola. I'm dying to see the city that way. Maybe we can all go together." Looking around the table, she encountered a sea of worried faces. Margo quickly swept her head right, then left, signaling a "no."

More romantic melodies drifted on the air, mocking the brooding tension on the terrace. Alessandro stared at his empty plate, then scowled. With one rapid blow, the exquisite Murano carafe flew onto the brick floor and shattered, the splattered prosecco advancing in a widening circle through the shimmering fragments, like a sinister, exploding star.

Gaetano looked at his master dolefully, lifting his shoulders in a soft shrug.

"What's wrong?" Anna asked.

"O, *Madre di Dio*, I am cursed," Alessandro cried out. "I have been sentenced to hear their maddening voices a dozen times a day and even at night. They know I hate it. They are an eternal brotherhood. They sing louder when they come by. My late, beloved wife kept the windows closed, the curtains drawn, blocking their voices. You, the others will never understand." He looked away, lost in thought, a shroud of melancholy enveloping him.

When a group of gondoliers started a *con brio* chorus, Alessandro rose from the table.

"I must go inside," he said. "*Gaetano, prendiamo la torta e il caffè nella biblioteca.* That is, if it is all right with you, my guests, we have cake and coffee in the library." He surveyed their faces with wild eyes, then threw down his white linen napkin and bolted through the door, Nero right behind him.

Anna sat, shrunken.

One by one, the others slipped from their seats in silence.

In the Heart of the Faviers

Monday, afternoon

What could be better than sitting on your terrace with a million-dollar view of Venice, sipping wine with friends and listening to singing gondoliers?

Anna deeply regretted hurting Count Favier. And yet, she resented feeling guilty. The question of whether rationality applied here gnawed at her. Alessandro's anger about gondoliers made no sense. Her grandfather had warned her about this city's inhabitants, such a temperamental lot, he had said, mercurial as the sea and just as dangerous. While Nonno had lived in New York for decades, he had worked for the Italian consulate and was always coming home with stories of his countrymen.

Anna trailed the others as they descended a staircase curved like a snail, past expanses of Venetian plaster walls and nooks filled with classical sculptures or colorful amphorae. As she came through a burnished gate into the library, Pablo was patting the count's shoulder while he cast a worried glance toward his guests. Nero sat at his master's feet. Anna yearned to rest her eyes on something safe that would not stare back, or look at her with disapproval. Even the dog might be risky.

Light filtering through the leaded-glass windows illuminated floor-to-ceiling mahogany bookcases with carved screens protecting the volumes. Anna assumed the collection extended beyond this cavernous chamber to a far cluster of rooms, rivaling the specialty libraries where she had often retreated on the Berkeley campus. Green mosaic snakes guarding tiny treasure chests of golden tesserae covered the floor. Tallying the repeating pattern to determine the room's dimensions, Anna was halfway through her multiplications when Alessandro called them to enjoy the light cake Gaetano was serving with coffee. He sounded calmer now.

"*Buono*, Alessandro," Angela said with an acute American accent. "This cake's finger-lickin' good." Her plump red lips pressed together.

"*Torta della nonna* is simple to make," Alessandro told her. "A little flour, a lot of ricotta, some lemon. I baked it myself."

"I'm impressed," Yolanda said. "I always tell Pablo he needs to learn. There is nothing like a man who can cook." She licked her fork with the swiftness of a lizard's tongue.

"Well, maybe a man who can work in wood," Alessandro said. "Gaetano's family has served the Faviers for many generations in this way. They are masters. Much of what you see here is made by their hands." He pointed to the gilded ceiling, shaped like an inverted hull, arching above them. In the center hung a gigantic coat of arms: a crimson-and-gold divided sun, raining red drops into a blue sea.

Anna wandered over to a nearby desk where a glass pen rested on some papers: "*L'isolazione l'ha salvata.*" She pondered the written words and translated to herself: "Isolation saved her."

"Alessandro, what are you writing?" Margo asked, peering over Anna's shoulder.

"Merely a history of Venice." Joining them, he gazed at his proud script and repositioned the pen. "From the beginning, the sea protected her from the waves of barbarians invading the Italian peninsula. She existed against all odds. Today is not very different. Our isolation saved us from the tyranny of cars destroying the rest of Italy. Venice is a city where the human voice can still be heard instead of that infernal *macchina* racket."

Alessandro studied everyone gathering round. "Anna, in these bookcases there are many valuable letters and, how do you say, manuscripts, of Venice past." His voice grew vibrant. "I catalog them now, hundreds of years afterward. Even the Cultural Council of Venice has researched here."

"Who are they?" Anna asked.

"An organization working to restore old buildings and churches," Pablo told her. "I was active with them when I was con-sul here in Venice."

Alessandro drew his hands through his hair and proclaimed, "All the birth, marriage, and death certificates of my family are kept in this library. I sit with Nero many times, tracing my past, feeling time flowing in my veins, through the bloodlines of the Faviers."

Steering the group into a broad corridor, Alessandro paused at a marble console covered with sets of smooth plaster hands. "These are a Favier family tradition. This is my friends' favorite section of the library, I think. After they visit, the maid always has to rearrange them. See how refined the women's hands are. Graceful. Well-shaped palms." He halted. "Here is Mamma," he said, caressing an ivory hand with long, tapered fingers. "As a child, I remember her combing my hair, embracing me. She is gone now, of course, with all the others."

Alessandro took Anna's right hand and examined her palm, squeezing the fleshy parts. Relieved that he did not hold her earlier comments against her, she put up with it.

"I remember my grandmother's hands," Anna said, slowly extri-cating hers from Alessandro. "They were always busy, cooking for us, mending, fluttering when she spoke."

"How about your mamma's hands?" Angela asked.

"Both my parents died when I was young."

"I'm so sorry," Angela said.

"That was a long time ago." Anna tried not to dwell on feeling alone in the world. What was it now, five years since she had last seen the glow of twin urns at Woodlawn Cemetery? She had come to the conclusion that even if she spent her whole life trying, she would never unearth any more than she already knew about her parents. The probability of success approached but never touched zero, like in some of her mathematical constructs. She struggled to hold onto that reasoning as she dug her left thumbnail into her forefinger. "Beyond my grandparents, my roots go back to anonymous ancestors."

"America is like that," Margo said, "a break as wide as the ocean from what went before. The place where you go to get another chance."

That only works if you have the strength and perspective to map your future, Anna mused, or else you get stuck in the eddies and just relive the past.

"*Signore*, you are the living bridge between yesterday and tomorrow," Alessandro said. "Nature is stronger than you are. Who knows what is willed to you by the ancestors? You cannot flee and remake yourselves again; no one can run that fast."

"As almost always, we agree, Alessandro," Pablo said, moving closer to him. "Perhaps *el Perú* is a lot like the Old World. It is hard for my people, my country, to change, to escape from the Conquest and tragedy. But when one like me comes to power—"

"Yes, but first, let us enjoy the Favier history." Alessandro smiled. "We start with scenes from Venice of old, then the family portraits."

As he conducted them into a side room with huge seascapes covering the walls, Margo and Anna lagged behind.

"*Ecco*, the battles where my family was distinguished," Alessandro said. "The painting to our left is the Battle of Lepanto, where Sebastiano Venier and Don Juan of Austria fought the Turks. A huge victory." He nodded. "Over there is the Fourth Crusade, led by our blind doge, Enrico Dandolo—a sad time for Constantinople, and in many ways for Venice. In front of us is the Battle of Chioggia, Vettor Pisani's triumph against our enemies, the Genovesi, led by Pietro Doria. Ah, what a great admiral Pisani was."

"This is so boring," Margo whispered to Anna. "Let's go find the Book of Gold, and we can talk." She pulled Anna through a marble-framed doorway and across a green terrazzo floor, past a grand antique mirror, whose nine sections, secured by gold florets, offered divergent, wavering reflections as they walked by.

In the far corner of a paneled room lay an imposing book on a stone pedestal.

"Is this—?"

Margo, already turning the velvet cover, said, "Yes, the marvelous *Libro d'Oro*, a record of Venetian nobility through the centuries. The VIPs. They ended up with all the power. Look how many entries Alessandro's family has." She turned the gilt-edged pages with reverence. "Two doges, a *procuratore* of St. Mark's, a member of the Council of Ten, a senator. You know, both parents had to be noble for their children to be listed. Napoleon burned the book when he conquered Venice, but copies, like this one, survived. Now—"

"Please! We need to get down to business while we can! How can we piece together who might have killed Sergio, and oh, by the way, clear me?" Anna pictured Detective Biondi standing on the station steps in his Armani suit, basking in the adulation of the press as he announced that he had captured the murderess, Anna.

"Right." Margo turned toward the rosewood file cabinets lining an anteroom. "There's a bunch of great material right over here, some of which could involve Sergio. I helped Alessandro catalog hundreds of pages when I was writing a story on Venetian cooking and lived nearby. We'll also need access to any recent news articles, like in a library or a newspaper office."

"Good. How about pretending that you're reporting on Sergio's murder for the *Chronicle*—maybe, I don't know, contrasting it with an American killing? We'd interview people who knew Sergio. Pump them for info. I could tag along as your assistant."

Margo pursed her lips. "Let me think about that."

"Don't take too long."

"Well, to start, his friends will be surprised that a US paper is interested in covering his murder. So we'll have to be convincing."

"Plus, we can't attract the attention of the murderer."

"There are people in town I trust, people I've known for ages," Margo mused. "I guess I can set up a few appointments." She sighed. "Those five tough years with my ex-husband will finally yield something good."

"I'll dig into Sergio's financial transactions through my office back home and see what I can turn up there. I know I'm asking a lot with all of this, but please, stop broadcasting what I do for a living. If people ask, just say I work with numbers for the government."

Margo's shoulders slumped. "Sorry—I only told Angela. She surprised me with her questions."

The sparkle of a gilded picture frame on an adjacent wall drew Anna's gaze to a black-and-white photograph of five adults with San Giorgio Maggiore in the distance. She recognized a youthful Pablo, a brunette Yolanda in a floppy hat and holding a baby, Sergio with an arm around her shoulder. She didn't know the men on the other side of Pablo. The shorter, round-faced one with bowtie and glasses gave a smile so wide it looked as if he were in love with the camera or whoever was holding it. The taller fellow with longish, straight hair and close-set eyes peered ahead sullenly. "I recognize Pablo and Sergio, but who are these other men?" Anna asked.

"The serious-looking one I don't know. The guy with the glasses is Dudley. You'll meet him tomorrow at his garden party."

"And the baby?"

"Must be Pablo and Yolanda's son."

Anna scrutinized the photograph, pondering the relationships and what the intervening years may have brought. "Notice how Sergio is cozying up to Yolanda? How like him." She shook her head. "Well, shall we join the others?"

"Hold on," Margo said, staring at a bit of paper protruding from a carved-wood cabinet. "What's this?" She yanked open the drawer and, by the light of a wall sconce, read in a hushed tone:

Caro Alessandro,

Vedo la tua faccia tra le nuvole e ascolto la tua voce nella canzone suonata dalle campane. Il tocco del vento di scirocco mi eccita. Ci incontriamo questa sera, alla solita ora alla Dogana.

—A.

6 settembre 1954

Margo shook her head. "I can't believe this. It's a love letter."

"I didn't catch part of it."

"I'll translate."

Dear Alessandro,

I see your face in the clouds. I hear your voice in the songs of the church bells. The touch of the Southern wind excites me. Let's meet tonight at the same time at the Customs House.

–A.

September 6, 1954

Just then, voices of the group intruded from a far room. Angela was saying, "It's amazin'. After all this time, I still recognize that room."

"A few of the birds look different in this painting," Pablo commented.

"You have a discerning eye," Alessandro told him. "Those years in the jungle at the Manu clay lick with your macaws and blue-headed parrots made you an expert."

"The red velvet bed with its curved columns and canopy remind me of the altar at St. Peter's," Yolanda said. "Do you really sleep there, Alessandro, with those angels on the ceiling looking down at you?"

"Why, yes. They protect me and make sure that I am very, very good." He chortled.

"I like the wooden cradle," Angela said. "Why is it at the foot of the bed?"

Alessandro didn't respond.

As the group progressed, their voices became garbled, and like the tide, finally receded, leaving Anna and Margo alone in the fresh-washed silence.

"Should we be snooping in here?" Anna asked.

"How else are we going to find anything out? This note's not from Gabriella, Alessandro's wife, that's for sure. Plus, he was married back then."

"Why would he keep a love letter in an unlocked cabinet?"

"He only lets a few people into this part of his home, ones he really trusts. He saves and files everything. This was probably tossed into the middle of God knows what. He's a multimillionaire pack rat who's living in the past but with a history so rich, it could launch a thousand stories. And I could write them."

"You wouldn't do that. Not without his permission, right?"

"I'm awfully tempted." Margo's eyes shone. "What the—" she said with a start, interrupted by heavy panting.

Anna stifled a laugh, glancing at Nero. "We may as well give up now, the dog has found us."

"*Nero, Nero, dove sei?*" Alessandro's voice erupted like a far-away volcano. "Margo, Anna, we miss you. Where are you?"

"Uh oh," Anna muttered.

"He'll be furious if he catches us." Margo clicked her tongue a few times before folding the letter and shoving it into her bra. Stooping, she tried to push the gaping drawer shut, but it refused to budge.

Having witnessed Alessandro's anger once already, Anna feared its gale force. She shook her head. "Forget it. Let's get out of here and go find them, or go to another room."

"It's too freaking late," Margo said as the sound of footsteps grew close. She tried shoving the drawer, then rocking it upward but the age of the wood and Venice's moisture conspired against them.

Anna fidgeted with her bracelet as she knelt beside Margo. She considered diverting Alessandro, using the dog as a decoy. "Maybe—"

All of a sudden, Margo lifted the drawer and finally thrust it into place.

"Aha!" Alessandro said behind them. "Here you are. What are you two doing down there? This is a private area."

"My earring," Margo said, presenting her profile to Alessandro. "I lost it somewhere while we were looking at the Book of Gold."

Alessandro fell to his knees, searching, as Margo deftly pulled the gold loop from her right ear and slipped it into her skirt pocket.

"No. It is not here," Alessandro said. "I send Gaetano or a maid. Do not worry. They will find it. But come now. You are missing the best part."

"That Book of Gold is just fascinating," Margo said, sounding excited as Alessandro whisked the women to a far room where they joined the huddle in front of another interior view of the palazzo.

"I cayn't understand how they look beautiful here and so gaudy in the United States," Angela was saying, admiring the vermilion velvet curtains in the painting. "I sold a portrait with this same old-fashioned color just last month."

"The fabrics, their brilliance, their luxury are bound to our past," Alessandro replied, taking his place in front of the canvas as if picking up his cue. "They speak of Venice's glory, her trade routes to the East. Her empire of spices and silks."

"Ay, *sí*, and lovely to touch," Pablo said. With half-closed eyes, he fondled a velvet wall hanging of deep forest green. "Have any of you ever stroked the pure, fine wool of the *vicuña*, the best wool in the world? It was used for the clothing of royalty in my country."

"We will leave you and your vicuña now and proceed." Alessandro pinched Pablo's arm playfully as he moved into an adjoining room. "Up there is the start of the portrait series," he said, nodding toward a long row of canvases. "Doge Favier is the man with the beard—yes, we had a doge in our family, who ruled in the year twelve hundred. He is followed by Giuglielmo Favier, a procuratore of Saint Marks."

Angela took a tottering step in front of the others. "Alessandro, what is that painting at the far end there, all wrapped up in black?"

After a strained silence, Alessandro replied, "It is mine. My wife. My family." He slowly shook his head. "I cannot bear to see what I lost." He closed his eyes tightly for a moment before turning to her. "The velvet cloth will be removed upon my death, when this palazzo becomes the property of my city. Sometimes I pray that day comes soon." Alessandro's lips drew back to reveal pale gums. "My friends, I am getting old and tired. Why do you not return to the main room for more coffee? I must go now and rest a little."

Watching Alessandro, Anna felt his sorrow. He was the last of the Faviers, she realized. All the pomp and proud history of his family would end in dust. He would never hold the hands of any grandchildren, never witness their growth or their joy. She had taken desperate measures, and so far, she had failed to avoid his fate. The thought haunted her.

After coffee, Anna and Margo took a stroll along the narrow canal. Clouds obscured the sun and a sudden burst of rain pelted down on them. Retreating to the covered entrance of the palazzo, Margo said, "I didn't know he would take us near the family painting. I should've warned Angela. And you, too. I'm sorry. Don't ever mention the gondoliers again."

"But why? And what happened to the rest of his family?"

"I'll explain later. It's incredibly painful for him. I need to get back and see if I can cheer him up. Pablo's prescription drugs don't always do the job."

"When can we tackle the rest of the library?"

"Let's try later tonight. If Alessandro's up to it, he's going to Asolo this evening. In fact, everyone has something planned, even Angela; she's going to visit another art dealer. I'll call you around eight."

Walking back to Pensione Stella, Anna could not shake her sense of impending doom. First learning of Sergio's murder, then of the count's family tragedy, whatever it was. Back home, she had analyzed her share of mysteries, applying logic to deduce their resolutions. She excelled at her job of fishing in an ocean of data for criminals lurking in the depths. But here, she felt logic could only go so far. Now she was enmeshed in the fabric of tragic, interlocking histories of Sergio Corrin and Count Favier. If she pulled on the strands, she was not sure where they would lead.

From the corner of her eye, she saw a gondola sliding past a golden palazzo. The gondolier's song skimmed along the stucco walls lining the canal, his vibrant vocals growing soft, then muddy before fading into nothingness, reminding her of the sounds heard underwater.

6

A Tenuous Connection

Monday, late afternoon

Anna had the pensione clerk dial her office and connect the call to her room. Seeing the hotel's antiquated technology, she shook her head in disbelief before shifting her thoughts to Leslie and what she would say to her boss without lying or making things worse.

When Anna picked up the ringing phone, her assistant, Brian, was on the other end.

"How's *bella Italia?*" he asked. "Didn't think I'd be hearing from you this soon."

"I wish I could say relaxing. Instead, it's confusing. Say, Brian, can you do me a favor?"

"Sure, whaddya need?"

"I've bumped into something questionable here. Look for any accounts belonging to a Sergio or Liliana Corrin, of Venice, Italy. No known aliases. Also, for any accounts that a Banco Saturno has in New York or elsewhere. Run my algorithm on all activity. Find out everything you can about that bank, its ownership, and where it has offices or investments around the world. It's an exclusive, private banking institution, so probe in the locations where money sloshes around and disclosure rules are loose. You know the drill."

"Of course the search won't yield details on his lira accounts back in Italy or other non-US accounts. Should we contact Italian authorities?"

Anna marveled at Brian's usual efficiency. "Not yet. We need to know what we can surmise from our side first."

"Okay. This'll take me awhile."

Examining the results from a broader net could be painstaking. Her brief inquiry before leaving San Francisco had shown that Sergio's bank, Banco Saturno, regularly received funds from nondescript-sounding companies through Granite Bank, its correspondent bank in New York City. The companies were located in San Francisco, Chicago, Los Angeles, Vancouver, and New York. Fedwire transfers were typically split for further credit to one of three different account numbers at Saturno, belonging to investment companies, two with French names, one with a Spanish name.

Within a few days of receipt, those same dollar amounts were sent out by the account holders to a fixed constellation of foreign parties. The sizes were not staggering, generally under five hundred thousand dollars. Anna had expected to see typical investment activity on behalf of wealthy clients involving brokerage firms or real estate companies in the United States. She wondered why the repetitive funds were not making their way to an Italian account holder or an Italian bank. The pattern did not definitely mean that Banco Saturno or its clients were perpetuating a money-laundering scheme, but it had aroused her curiosity. She wondered how Granite Bank, a colossally large correspondent bank, viewed the activity. It hadn't reported anything suspicious to Treasury.

"I have to complete my compliance training due today, or I'll be on the delinquent list and Her Highness will hand me my head," Brian said. "Where and how should I send you the information?"

Anna thought it was just her luck to hit a bureaucratic speed bump when her freedom depended on resolving these questions quickly. Biondi could be preparing an arrest warrant while Brian was taking his damn course.

"Why don't you hold onto it? I'll call you late tomorrow. This is just between us for now, okay? If you're comfortable with that."

"No problem."

"Thanks. I'll bring you back a great bottle of wine. Did the desk clerk give you the phone number of the pensione?"

"Yep."

"Good. Before you go, please transfer me to Leslie's office."

"Okay. *Ciao* for now."

Feeling flushed, Anna sat down on the narrow bed. At least she didn't have to speak to her boss face to face.

After their initial greetings, Leslie said, "I wondered when I was going to hear from you. What have you gotten yourself into?"

Transferred seven months ago from another area within the Treasury Department, Leslie Tanner had specialized in picking Anna's brain, ordering her to produce detailed reports and slides on their program successes and algorithm production, which Leslie presented to higher-ups. With perfectly coiffed light brown hair and wide-set, cornflower-blue eyes, Leslie fit the image of an earnest, trustworthy official, not that of a calculating climber. Anna suspected that instead of keeping her as a valuable asset of the organization, Leslie would eventually find a way to eliminate her as a potential rival. She could almost hear the wheels turning in Leslie's brain when she spoke.

"Did the police call you?" Anna asked.

"Yes, that Italian Detective Biondi. And the FBI to boot."

"There's been some kind of mix-up. They think I look like someone who was running from a murder scene at a fancy hotel."

"Oh, no."

"Didn't they tell you that?"

"Not exactly. Just asked a lot of questions about you."

"Well, I've gotten over my shock about how ridiculous this is, and now I need to find a way to prove my innocence. My word or yours is not going to carry the day." Anna doubted that she could ever count on Leslie's word. On one hand, as ambitious as she was, Leslie didn't seem likely to slander Anna. On the other, she could provide information that would give Biondi a boost in putting the pieces together.

"Do you need legal representation? I could get you some names."

Anna weighed whether lawyers with ties to Treasury or who were friends with Leslie would work to represent her or to protect Treasury's or Leslie's reputation. Better to pass. Count Favier's help would be much better.

"Thanks so much. Not now. I may get recommendations from friends here. But if Detective Biondi contacts you again, please let me know. Brian has my number. Also, I'd appreciate it if you would call the consulate in Milan and vouch for me, in case I need their help later on."

"We'll look into it. Keep me apprised, and tell me if you need any resources going forward. I can't have one of our employees vanish into an Italian prison."

"I hope to avoid that as well."

"I do need to tell you that I've heard a few things from Caroline."

"Caroline—in accounting? What does she have to do with this?"

"She said the report on your Milan trip from early this year looked odd. So few expenses on food, for one thing."

"I got treated."

"Likely beyond the thirty-five-dollar gift ceiling, specified in our policy?"

Anna tried to keep her voice neutral. "It was approved, and I'd be happy to discuss it when I return."

"See you in nine days."

Anna doubted she would make it back to the office by then.

7

L'omicidio, *The Murder*

Monday, evening

The reflections of lamplights on the canal spiraled outward like luminous star trails. As Anna approached the entrance to Palazzo Favier, only the murmur of the canal lapping at the water gate broke the stillness. She pressed the bell and rushed inside once the heavy door buzzed open, revealing the black felze, mildewed and abandoned on the vestibule floor.

Greeting her on the piano nobile, Margo said, "After I called you, I found out that Angela will be here. Her gallery visit was canceled."

"I hope to God she goes to bed early. Or you can convince her to leave us alone. Tell her we need to do some boring, intensive research for your article. I brought a newspaper with me. The murder's just been reported."

"Uh–oh." Margo clicked her tongue.

They entered a spacious living room enlivened with brilliant murals. Angela sat on a velvet couch, surrounded by images of a fanciful jungle. A jaguar crouched low in the grass, mesmerized by a capybara bathing in a swollen river. A flock of green parrots circled the sun. Lavender macaws skirted over broad-canopied trees as an anaconda slithered below.

Angela's green-striped pants transformed her abdomen into a ripe watermelon. Anna asked herself if a baby could have rescued her marriage, already in a ditch when she had gotten desperate, the year Nonno had died. Then came Jack's surprise affair, as he prowled for a big ego boost and to hell with everyone else. Trying to convince herself it meant nothing, Anna had become numb until breaking out of her stupor in Milan.

Angela tapped a button on the portable CD player beside her and started sobbing.

"I told her not to listen to that song," Margo said impatiently. "It makes her cry." Stomping ahead with a "no, no," Margo gently removed Angela's headphones. "You're listening to Eros Ramazzotti sing again."

"So?" Angela looked up at her with reddened eyes.

"I made a promise to Michael that I'd bring you and the baby back safe and sound. I intend to keep it. That means you stay calm." Margo settled in next to her.

"Dad gum it! I can't help being a sap. After years in that itty-bitty tank, those poor dolphins headed for the horizon together, finally free."

Angela must have sat down with a dictionary and the CD notes, Anna thought. She couldn't imagine Margo having the patience to translate lyrics, even for a cousin she tended to baby.

"Don't get excited," Margo said.

"You don't care about Silver and Missie, but I do," Angela said, sounding like a petulant teenager as she pulled her hair back into a pony tail.

"I care more about you," Margo told her. "Here, take some." She poured a glass of water from a crystal pitcher on the marble side table.

"Is everybody else gone?" Anna asked, shedding her backpack and taking a seat.

"Yep. It's just us and the dog—somewhere," Angela said. "Can I see that newspaper stickin' out of your backpack?"

When Anna had bought the evening edition of the *Gazzettino*, broadcasting Sergio's murder on page one, she had been eager to pour over the article with Margo. Alone.

"I didn't think you read Italian," Anna said.

"I'm tryin' to take my mind off a few things," Angela said. "I look at the pictures and guess at the captions."

Anna considered refusing for some reason, but that might raise suspicions when Angela heard about Sergio later. Reading the story together would be hard. Her mind felt scattered. What might be revealed about his life and affairs? Would there be any mention of her? What would she have to ad-lib and lie about?

Handing the paper to Margo as casually as she could, she asked, "Why don't you translate?"

Stalling, Margo flipped through the pages from the back. "Always tangenti," she said. "When will those bribes stop? This is about the *Mani pulite*—you know, that 'Clean Hands' political-corruption investigation."

Angela looked blank and then bored.

"Okay, here's something on the Cultural Council. Gee, they're improving Santa Maria dei Miracoli Church. Meanwhile, the Preserve Venice Foundation is fixing up Madonna del Orto Church. Sounds like dueling organizations. There's an article on acqua alta and MOSE—that's the project planned to stop the flooding."

"Stop the flooding in Venice?" Anna asked. "How? Venice is sinking. It's already lower by ten inches this century. Sea levels are rising around the world, and when they're done, it'll be Atlantis here. Instead of gondola rides, tourists will scuba dive to see how beautiful it was before we ruined everything. A number of scientific journals have shown that if we do nothing, the seacoasts will flood—"

"That's bullshit," Angela said.

"Oh," Margo said, turning to the front page and then blurting, "*Omicidio.*"

"What?" Angela raised her eyebrows.

"Mur-der of Ser-gi-o Cor-rin," Margo translated, pronouncing the words with uncharacteristic slowness, as if she were speaking an unfamiliar language.

Angela plunked her water goblet down. Anna chewed her lip, though in a way she felt relieved. Now Sergio's death would be one less secret to keep.

"We didn't see him on this trip," Margo said, "but his big Carnival *festa* was unforgettable. Remember that incredible art collection, Angela?"

Angela barely nodded, her gaze focused on the doorway.

"We wandered around his home for hours. Sergio had rooms adorned with priceless oil paintings and gardens filled with sculptures. It was like the Getty Museum and made this place look like a dump. And gold, all that gold—plates, tableware. . . unbelievable."

How could he afford it? Anna wondered as she leaned toward Margo, surveying the page. "There are two write-ups?"

"Yeah. The lead story is by Marco Canavotti, the news reporter. This other guy, Filippo Fanfarone, writes the society column. Sergio made a big splash in those circles."

Pointing an unsteady finger at the paper, Angela asked, "What do they say?"

Margo translated smoothly. "Count Sergio Corrin, bank CEO, well-known financier, and patron of the arts, was attending Saturday's masquerade ball and society benefit on Giudecca at the Belvedere Hotel when his life was cruelly cut short by an unknown person as he was savagely murdered on a secluded, winding path. The sixty-seven-year-old count is survived by his wife, Liliana, who hurried back from a Swiss vacation with their two small children, once police located her. Other family includes two adult daughters,

Marinella and Constanza, from his marriage to Arianna Pina Fasolo of Venice, his brother, Giacomo, and a cousin, Silvio Bertone.'

"The Italians are always so melodramatic," she added.

"Sergio was murdered and you criticize the writin'?" Angela screeched. "What's the matter with you?"

"It's terrible, Angela," Margo said. "We all feel bad. But let's finish reading."

"What's next?" Anna asked.

"Lemme see." Margo skipped to the next page. "Okay. It says that Sergio Corrin was born into a wealthy family and fought in the resistance in World War II. Has a law degree and that, after serving as the chairman of CONSOB in Rome for seven years, he worked for the banking giant Mediobanca in Milan before ascending to the vice-chairmanship of Banca Serenissima back here in Venice. He owned a villa in Asolo, a chalet in Cortina, vineyards of enantio grapes near Lake Garda. In 1983 he broke away from his old employer, and four years later, he formed his own successful bank, Banco Saturno, catering to the ultrawealthy."

"Remind me," said Margo, "CONSOB is what?"

"The Italian SEC," Anna said. "They regulate the Italian financial markets."

"Right. Now I'll translate the Fanfarone piece." Turning back to the front page, Margo read, "'This dashing man of exquisite taste opened the borders of Venice by means of his provocative tribal art gallery, welcoming art in all its forms from the four corners of the earth. His genius in selecting, exhibiting, investing, and protecting artistic endeavors is simply irreplaceable. He will be mourned worldwide.'"

"A bit over the top, don't you think?" asked Anna.

Margo shrugged.

"I can still see those lights in the distance from our walk on Saturday night," Angela said. "And the fireworks. A little singin', the sounds of wooden flutes. That fancy hotel, filled with so many people all gussied up. Of all the places to be murdered. Who woulda known it?"

Anna examined Sergio's bright smile in one picture. His shock of hair and limpid eyes were just how she remembered him in life. In a photo that must have been taken the night he was killed, he was holding the Pinocchio mask, its long nose exaggerated. Tapping her thigh, she scanned the news story for a mention of any leads the police were pursuing, like a woman with long hair and glasses, fleeing the scene. What if one of the papers published the sketch of her?

"This article has information on the Corrin family history," Margo said. "They were originally from Spain but bribed their way into Italian nobility centuries ago."

"Diggin' up dirt before he's even buried," Angela complained. "The bunch of 'em genuflecting in front of Sergio, wantin' his money while he was alive."

"The story talks about his international travels and business activities," Margo said. "Back from China, over to Russia, down to South Africa, Brazil, Peru, over to the United States. Sounds like the guy was never home."

Anna wondered what connected it all, then felt a twinge as Margo showed them an image of Sergio embracing twin infants. Having young children certainly hadn't inhibited his extramarital pursuits.

"Rather old to be a father of babies," Margo said.

"You know some men," said Angela. "They figure a young wife'll give 'em the Fountain of Youth. He traded in the wrinkled model for the smooth-skinned one. Why, Liliana's even younger than me. She marries Sergio because of his money and position and gets to ride the gravy train—it's like some goddamn business transaction." She sniffled. "But can we get back to findin' out more about his . . . the murder?"

"There's nothing about how he was killed, just that it was brutal," Margo said.

"Maybe they don't want to broadcast the murderer's m.o.," Anna said.

"You've been watchin' too many *Columbo* reruns," Margo told her. "I'd wager that the cops are keeping the details secret because they don't want some weirdo confessing. That comes from my brief stint as a crime reporter. But murder's so rare here. During the late seventies, maybe you remember, the *Brigate Rosse*, the Red Brigades, killed the Italian prime minister and stuffed his body into the trunk of a car. They were robbing banks and holding tycoons or family members for ransom. Milanese businessmen sent their kids to school here—much less danger of kidnapping in Venice. No cars. Little twisting alleys lined with windows. Harder to escape."

"But why would someone murder Sergio?" Anna asked.

"Could've been anything." Margo tugged at her earring. "Financial underworld stuff—Italian bankers have been killed before—or an unpaid artist, angry investors, hateful neighbors, a mistress, an ex-wife, a jealous wife, the Mafia. Who knows? What's that . . . seven possibilities?"

"Eight," Anna said. "What do you think, Angela?"

Angela was staring at the table. "We did some business together, met his family, but I didn't know him well. Do the news stories mention anything about witnesses? Or people sayin' what they might've seen?"

"Nope," Anna said.

"I was askin' Margo."

Margo shook her head.

"How about Biondi?" asked Anna, hoping he had been taken off the case.

Margo's gaze swept down the page. "Yes, he's still the bigwig in charge. Quotes him as saying that he's going to string up the murderer in the piazza, like in the good old days."

Anna pictured herself hanging between the columns by St. Mark's, looking down at the assembled crowd in her final moments, feet dangling in the air. Biondi's fantasy sounded only too real.

Angela looked surprised. "How do you know the detective's name, Anna?"

"That scary man grilled me about Sergio's murder for more than an hour. Clearly, Biondi even thinks a woman might have done it," Anna said.

"Why're you callin' him Sergio instead of his full name if you never made his acquaintance?"

"I . . . I suppose I just fell into it, hearing you and Margo talk."

"So Biondi suspected you, even before you came to town?" Angela turned to her cousin. "Still the bigwig in charge, huh? Why didn't you tell me? You knew!"

"But not who—he didn't tell Anna Sergio's name. I didn't want to upset you about some unknown man being murdered." Margo shot a sideways glance at Anna. "We should send some flowers to the family, don't you think? Maybe a Mass card. Liliana must be crushed."

"Now that she has all Sergio's money, she's ridin' high," said Angela.

"The article claims Liliana is offering a thirty-million lire reward for a tip leading to the capture of her husband's killer," Margo said.

"You know math's not my strong suit," Angela said. "How much money is that?"

"About twenty-five thousand dollars," Anna told her, almost laughing. The amount was pitifully small compared to the sums in Sergio's bank accounts.

"What a penny pincher," Angela said. "Did she even love him?"

"Who knows," Margo said.

Angela touched her stomach. "I'm not feelin' very well."

"Is it the baby?" Margo turned to look at her.

"I can't believe it. How life can be wiped out so quickly." Angela rose and steadied herself against the couch.

"Do you need help?" Margo asked.

"What I need is to go to bed." Without another word, Angela waddled out of the room and turned down the hall.

"She seems pretty devastated," Anna observed. "What's up with that?"

"Her hormones are raging," Margo said with a drawn face. "You saw her with that song. I worry about her even though she's young and strong."

"Well, we'd better search Alessandro's library while we have the chance," Anna said, snatching up the newspaper.

Sitting on an aquamarine divan, Margo and Anna hunched over the wooden drawer sprawled across their laps. Anna basked in a cocoon of warm lamplight. Around them were musty volumes of Favier family history, lining the far shelves, like a small army ready to do battle, to defend the family honor, even after death. A carved screen gaped open nearby.

"Now that we're here, I'm having second thoughts," Anna said. "We're invading the count's privacy. Do you really think poking around in his private papers is going to get us anywhere?"

Margo jerked her head up. "Not again! Save your moralizing. I'm not the one who decided to lie to the police and got into this mess. I have no idea if we'll succeed, but I do know that you have no chance of finding out much on your own. You'll find financial transactions all right, but with no context for analyzing them. I mean, is the murderer really going to jump out at you from the middle of some money transfers or whatever else you're seeking?

I'm just trying to help you—even if it means lying to my own cousin."

"I hear you. Sorry."

"Any of Sergio's old acquaintances could be linked to his murder," Margo mused. "We might as well start decades ago."

"Someone could have wanted to settle a really old grudge, then."

"Exactly. Or a new one."

"And we're looking for?"

"Hard to say." Margo scratched her forehead. "Something curious. A hint of jealousy, infidelity, betrayal, some kind of cover-up."

"Sounds right up your alley."

"Just as I thought," Margo exulted as she pulled some papers from the drawer, the sleeve of her persimmon-colored blouse quivering. "It's filled with love letters." She extracted a piece of paper as if it were a raffle prize, her eyes gleaming. "Here's a letter from Gabriella, the dead wife, to Alessandro, just after they got married. I think you'll be able to make it out."

10 settembre 1950

Caro Alessandro,

Oggi era un giorno grigio. Non ho potuto scappare dal ritmo costante della pioggia. Esco e mi picchia ripetutamente sulla testa, sulla faccia, in un diluvio di goccie senza pietà. Cerca di farmi diventare un corpo pallido, bagnato, senza nome.

Immagino un letto bianco, con la tua presenza calda, che mi sta aspettando.

Tua moglie, Gabriella

"Did you get it?

"Most of it. Sounds like they were in love."

"Certainly they were in lust. Let me read it."

September 10, 1950

Dear Alessandro,

  Today was a gray day. I could not escape the constant rhythm of the rain. I left and it pelted my head, my face, in a deluge of merciless drops. It tried to turn me into a pallid, wet body without a name. I imagine a white bed, with your warm presence, waiting for me.

  Your wife, Gabriella

"I never receive love letters like this," Margo complained.

"Maybe because you're the first one to leave lately. You don't have relationships that last long enough, or with the right people. So what happened between the time of this love note and the one from that 'A' person?"

"That's the big question."

"Anyway, won't we just see a family tragedy play out in these letters with no clues about Sergio?"

"Can't say."

"Why don't I keep this drawer and you check those others out?" Anna gestured toward the bottom row of the nearest cabinet. "If Alessandro organized the collection chronologically, that area should have things from several years later."

"All right."

Margo sat down in front of a drawer labeled "G" in scrolling handwriting. "I'll see what this yields." Her sturdy fingers flew through the contents as she gathered papers and summarized them aloud. "Repairs on the family gondola at San Trovaso, buying a new felze, receipts for rug cleaning, new dishes, a vase from Venini." She raised her brows. "So far, fascinating. Good thing I'm a speed reader. Here's some more, Murano glass tiles for the bath. A gilded nine-piece mirror specially made at Salviati. One kilo of sardines." She sighed. "This collection goes on forever. I can't believe that Alessandro saved all this crap."

"You're sure it's all his?" Anna asked, pushing a stray wisp of hair from her face.

"It's *his* library. But you know," Margo brought one receipt closer and squinted, "it sure looks like the signature is Gaetano's, and on the others, too. That would make sense given the label on this drawer." She tapped the page down.

"And Gaetano's almost part of the family," Anna said.

"But what could he collect that would interest us?" Margo gazed at the beamed ceiling. "Does he even talk? Since I've been here, maybe he's said ten words to me, all in Italian, most of which have been either *caffè*, or *risotto*."

"Let's settle down and keep looking—for some letters, some notes, some clues, some goddamn something."

"Aye, aye, sir."

Anna drew her hand over the edges of a batch of pages that felt like bristles on a soft brush. Thick cream-colored invitations to balls, holiday-party invites on marbled paper, marriage announcements interspersed with black-framed death notices marked the passage of time as clearly as rings on a tree. She rubbed her finger along an engraved paper with a sketch of the opera house. In gold lettering, it proclaimed that Count Alessandro Favier's wife, Gabriella, was giving a recital on September 20, 1953.

"Was Alessandro's wife a singer?" Anna asked.

"Amateur, I think."

"Apparently good enough to rate a performance at La Fenice."

Margo shuffled through the papers she had randomly pulled from the cabinet drawers before exchanging them for others. "Wait," she said, sounding surprised. "Here's something for you. Looks like a copy of a money transfer." She laughed and passed it to Anna.

Anna held the faint carbon copy up to the light. She could just make out the cable's destination: Dar es Salaam. "This shows that the equivalent of roughly fifty thousand US dollars was sent to Sergio Corrin, and the sender was Alessandro Favier."

"What's the year?"

"1985. What was Sergio doing in Tanzania?"

"You got me," Margo said. "We know he traveled a lot. Charity work . . . then all that art."

"Sergio was rich enough to cover his own expenses. Why was Alessandro paying him? I doubt he ever bought anything from Sergio's gallery. It isn't his taste. You've got to find out from Alessandro if he ever went on a trip with Sergio. Was he investing in something? Was Sergio? We need to know more about this."

"I'll see if I can figure out how to approach him. Check these out, too." Margo placed a set of oversized legal documents on the divan.

Digging into the back of the crammed drawer, Anna pulled out a velvet book adorned with depictions of butterflies. "I found a treasure," she said with excitement, touching the embossed name on the front as she opened it. "Gabriella's diary." Graceful handwriting interspersed with black-and-white drawings of Venetian palazzos filled the pages.

"Well, then," Margo said, rubbing her hands together, "where do we start?"

"Near the end of their marriage, I think. Wouldn't you say that would be around 1954?"

"Yeah, and the beginning of 1955. Do you need my help?"

"It'd be faster."

Margo sat down next to Anna and quietly read an entry.

November 1, 1954

When I am in his arms, I forget that time passes. Piero

showers me with all the warmth, the adoration, that Ales-
sandro, in his aloofness, withholds. Very quickly it seems, it
is time to take up my heavy burden and trudge back to our
cold home.

Monica's little wriggling toes, her smile, remind me that I
am alive. I was starting to think I had fallen asleep.

His mother, his business deals, and even his tennis game
mean more to him than I do. At dinner, once the servants
have returned to the kitchen, he is busy reading La Gazetta,
scowling if his soccer team has lost. He doesn't notice me as
he once did. I have become a couch, a convenient and famil-
iar object he has taken for granted.

For he really is two people. One laughing, a wonderful
host, friend, joking at parties. The other is a bore who would
rather spend time cataloging his family papers. He calls me
"Butterfly," but no longer is it a term of endearment. He
thinks I just flit from party to party, buying jewels and fancy
dresses.

Soon this butterfly will be flying away.

Mamma and Pappa told me Monica and I can live with
them. Pappa never liked Alessandro, thought him a mam-
ma's boy who could not achieve anything on his own.

But leave Venice, leave Piero, my gondolier? I am afraid
I would die.

"Well, this explains Alessandro's reaction today to the gondoliers," Anna said.

"I've been wanting to tell you about that."

"Gabriella sounds as if she lost all hope. But seeking happiness
in the arms of a gondolier when you're a countess?" Anna frowned.

"She paid for it dearly."

"What do you mean?"

"They were all murdered—Gabriella, Piero, and Monica, the little girl. All intentionally drowned."

Anna gasped. "God, no wonder he can't get over it, poor man." She brought her hands to her lips. Alessandro had lost his family in water. She had lost hers in fire. "How did they know it wasn't an accident?"

"There must have been marks or other trauma on the bodies that didn't fit. No one will give me the details. I can't ask Alessandro, of course—he's ready to jump out of the palazzo window if someone even mentions Gabriella's name. And it was so long ago, back in June of 1955, I've never wanted to turn over all the rocks and hurt him to fulfill my curiosity."

"Were the murders solved?" Anna asked.

"No."

"So those murders and Sergio's could be linked."

"After all these years?"

"It's a slim chance, but one we can't ignore. Sergio could have been behind the three murders. The count only found out recently, and he decided to get even."

"Alessandro isn't a killer."

"You saw him explode at lunch. It's like he has a shard of glass sticking out of his chest. He can't hear the gondoliers sing without thinking of her, hating them all for what one did and hating each day he spends without her. If he found the person who took her away forever, I'll bet he could kill him in a minute with his bare hands."

"But why would Sergio murder Gabriella and the others? He was Alessandro's friend. They still were making investments together last week. It doesn't add up."

Anna shook her head.

Margo unfolded a large paper and peered at it. "What did I just say? As these financial documents show."

"Okay, I have another thought," Anna said, "Alessandro murdered Gabriella and Piero, accidentally drowning his daughter, too. Sergio found out, blackmailed Alessandro for years until finally he got tired and stopped paying. Then Sergio threatened to expose him."

"Equally hard to believe."

"In those years, you couldn't get a divorce in Italy. So you murder your cheating wife."

"He still mourns her."

"Maybe he mourns what he had before she started carrying on with Piero."

"Let's see what we can find beyond pure speculation."

"True, but we need to keep our minds open to every possibility until proven impossible."

"Listen, I need to check on Angela. I'll tell you more about Alessandro when we have time. Why don't you take these papers and the diary? There's no way we can read it all here. There must be more than a hundred pages in the diary alone."

"I'm not sure if I should do that, Margo."

"Do you think we can come back any time we want? Alessandro would never allow us to root around. Everyone happened to go out tonight, or go to sleep early; this may be the last access we ever get. And he has so much stuffed away here he won't even notice the diary's missing for several days, maybe longer. If he looks, he'll think he misplaced it. You have a dictionary back at the pensione, right?"

Anna nodded, still unsure.

"I found a ledger for you to look over, too." Margo slid a tiny bound book onto Anna's lap.

"Don't forget, tomorrow we'll attend Dudley and Agatha Filbert's garden party; we can quiz the guests. Oh, and Liliana has agreed to talk to me the day after. Better to keep you out of that conversation. And one more thing." Margo handed Anna a card. "Meet me here tomorrow morning at eleven. Even if you don't want to buy a sumptuous dress for the party, which you should, we can look. This place has beautiful stuff."

"How can you think of clothes when I could be arrested for murder tomorrow?" Anna said, tucking the card, the diary, and other material into her backpack. "I'll return everything as quickly as I can." She couldn't help feeling like a thief, though she told herself she was only borrowing.

8

The Money Trail

Tuesday, early morning

At one a.m., Anna still sat on her bed, puzzling over Gabriella's diary. Tracking her words, immersed in her thoughts, Anna observed the secret world of this woman, almost within touching distance. The emotions that had flowed through Gabriella's hand onto the page had hibernated for decades before seeping into Anna.

She would hardly have noticed one entry, in which Gabriella confided swatting away Dudley to avoid a slurpy kiss, before laughing, had she not been attending his party the next afternoon. Gabriella's remarks about her consuming love for Alessandro, her astonishing singing debut, little Monica's precocious behavior, picayune bickering with Alessandro's mother and her own parents had yielded no clues.

Filled with florid details of the Favier marriage, family, and friendships, the pages had been frustratingly silent about involvements with Sergio save for dreary real-estate investments.

For some reason, Gabriella had disliked and didn't approve of Alessandro's investing or spending time with Sergio. He carried on, and she was powerless to stop it. One year during Carnival, Sergio and his friend Klaus, from Berlin, came dressed as big-game hunters to the Favier ball, and Gabriella had taken pleasure in kicking them out.

Growing desperation engulfed later entries as Gabriella suspected someone of lying to Alessandro, poisoning him against her. Unable to defend herself, she was fighting shadows, she wrote. The villain remained hidden as Alessandro pulled further away, until the marriage unraveled and Gabriella turned to Piero for affection. She wrote her last note in June 1955. On the other side of time's barrier, Anna watched helplessly, knowing, as this woman could not, that she'd be murdered within the month.

As Anna stowed the diary inside her suitcase, she heard singing. "*Poi la nave bianca, entra nel porto,*" the soprano sang. Rather late for an aria, Anna thought, but a welcome respite from the gloom of Gabriella's crumbling life. "*Romba il suo saluto. Vedi?*" soared the voice, nearby. She knew the *Madama Butterfly* lyrics by heart. Anticipating "*è venuto,*" she shoved the creaking green shutters apart. There was no soprano, only silence as she scoured the balcony opposite.

In the morning, Anna fought to forget the phantom singing. Since last night's research brought no new insights about the diary, her disquietude only deepened. Sometimes after concentrating all day on an insoluble work problem, the answer emerged unbidden during the wee hours, if she was alert enough to grasp it. But today, she was seized by despair, unable to escape the mounting fear that a trove of incriminating evidence was being assembled by Biondi, painting an unflattering picture of her as Sergio's spurned lover and handing the detective everything he needed to file charges. She pictured the clock in the interrogation room, with its merciless ticks.

Just as Anna gave up on falling back asleep, a fax appeared under her door. Brian must have finished her project early, carelessly transmitting confidential information to the pensione instead of waiting for her call. Leaping onto the floor, she snatched papers out of her backpack and gathered up the fax. Thank God Brian hadn't printed "Sergio Corrin" on it, though any local might know the connection between Sergio and Banco Saturno, the name printed in bold letters atop each page. Saturno's accounts at the New York clearer, Granite Bank, and a Wall Street investment bank revealed balances bouncing between fifty and one hundred million dollars each month—thousands of transfers at a frenzied pace. Including Liliana's name had yielded benefits. Personal accounts, some exclusively hers, each held between five and ten million dollars.

Saturno's geographic reach crisscrossed time zones and countries, connecting a staggering array of far-flung transactions beyond those she had already noted: Geneva, Frankfurt, Dar es Salaam, London, Palermo, Grand Cayman, Panama City, and even Lima, Peru. What did they have in common? Were Sergio's clients actually his partners in illicit schemes?

Anna brought the faded ledger pages from the Favier library close. She guessed at the faint handwritten notes regarding large sums from the mid-1980s, the wire transfer from Alessandro to Sergio in Dar es Salaam among them. Other entries recorded lira payments to Sergio that continued until 1990. In all, the disbursements totaled three million dollars.

Scrutinizing the legal document Margo had given her, Anna realized it was a copy of a 1987 register of the Societé de Commerce Privée, or SARL, in Luxembourg. Alessandro Favier, Sergio Corrin, and the Fondazione Corrin, a family foundation he must have formed, were listed as shareholders. What to make of it?

She slammed the ledger down in irritation. Watching the tide roll in along San Francisco Bay seemed pretty good right now, but she doubted she'd ever see it again.

9

Il Giardino, *The Garden*

Tuesday, afternoon

"We have to keep our minds sharp during the party, so I hope you're not planning to stew about splurging on your dress," Margo said as they passed an androgynous clothing store in Campo San Stefano in the warm autumn air. "Guilt is a useless emotion. And you should bring home one silken gem from Venice. You look gorgeous, by the way."

Normally, Anna took satisfaction in being thrifty. Her parents had died young; her marriage was over; her Nonno and Nonna were gone—but spending was one thing under her control. As a child, she had earned a nickel for every wine bottle she had washed. Afterward, she had run to her bedroom, deposited the bounty into her Empire State Building piggybank and listened for the reassuring clink. Had Nonno saved the coin bank? Was it among the boxes in the Bronx storage space she could never bring herself to visit?

They climbed the wooden backbone of the Accademia Bridge and soon neared a high brick wall with a sunken bronze plaque proclaiming *Giardino*. Staring at it, Anna doubted how verdant a Venetian garden could be, when stone and water were everywhere, while trees, plants, and earth were scarce. Doubtless a few blades of grass would be all.

When Margo pressed a scarred bell, a clarion sound hung in the air. "Can't wait to introduce you to Dudley and Agatha," she said. "I've known them forever, and they know everybody. Something's bound to slip out on Sergio. Didya find anything last night?"

"Nothing I can decipher. Just lots of transfers to lots of places."

"Maybe our luck will change." Margo jabbed the bell. "What's taking them?"

The weathered copper gate jangled open to reveal a short, plump man with protruding eyes behind thick, horn-rimmed glasses, dressed in a starched white shirt and a red bowtie, neatly pressed gray pants, and shiny charcoal-colored oxfords. He was a senior citizen now, but with the same smile as the man in Alessandro's photograph.

He whispered to Margo, and then kissed her on both cheeks, leaving tiny bubbles of saliva gleaming like sea scum on a smooth beach.

Recoiling, Anna thought fleetingly of Gabriella's encounter and how she had laughed it off.

"Welcome to our garden party," Dudley said in a clipped transatlantic accent after Margo introduced them, staring at Anna's biceps and making her long for the matching shawl she hadn't bought.

"You must go to the gymnasium a lot," he commented, escorting the women toward a lush lawn.

"I run and do aerobics faithfully—high impact," Anna answered uncomfortably. She felt a blush coming on.

"Oh Dudley, please," Margo said with a chuckle. "Stop trying to be such a bad boy, and get us some *vino*. But before you go, have you heard anything at all about Sergio?"

"Leave that tragedy for later," he said. "I want you to enjoy yourselves."

If only that were possible. Anna ached to forget her worries about Sergio's murder, even knowing that the laws of mathematics were against her. Every person she met increased the probability that she'd face someone who would recognize her from Saturday night or had heard about her from Sergio. At least Biondi and his tracker wouldn't be at the party—she hoped.

"Excuse me, *belle signorine*," Dudley said, butchering the Italian pronunciation like a tone-deaf singer destroying a song, before wading to the bar.

Cringing, Anna knew how proud Nonno would have been of her ear for the language, even after all these years. She still remembered the early lessons with him, vowels pronounced with an open mouth, not closed as in English. He made her practice saying their last name: O, Or, Or-si-, Or-si-ni. Just a short trill with the tongue on the roof of the mouth before pronouncing the "s."

"You must know who you are, and how to say our family name in Italian," he had told her. That first time, he had added that there was no use continuing under the old one, for after her parents' death, she was the only Fortunato left.

The women followed Dudley's retreating bulk, past white marble nymphs and satyrs playing in a circle frozen in time among lilac hydrangeas. Climbing roses framed the stately, rust-colored palazzo. Anna felt weighted down as women in designer outfits and men just as expensively dressed, bobbed their heads in her direction, curious about the pedigree of anyone strolling through the gate.

Beyond all of them, the garden bordered the shimmering waters of the Grand Canal where a parade of gondolas, vaporettos, and barges glided by ancient façades of tan and salmon palazzos, more exotic than the canal-side homes on Long Island or the houseboats of Sausalito, perched like seabirds on the water.

"Dudley is a sweetie, once you get to know him," said Margo. "And he adores his wife."

"You told me he's a writer. Of what?"

"Venetian histories—popular ones that make Venice come alive. The wall in his study is plastered with the family trees of all one hundred and eighteen doges of Venice—the guy's an expert in Venetian genealogy. Back in the sixties, he wrote a few historical novels, some in Italian, like *The Doge's Robes*. To this day, the critics are still screaming for more. Maybe you've heard of his last one, *The Gondolier's Prize*, about one of Venice's murdered doges. Even some rulers here met bad ends."

"I'm afraid I'm into science books."

A trim, petite woman in a lustrous fuchsia gown stepped through the arched doorway of the palazzo and headed toward them. Her lively, wide-set eyes and upturned lips gave her an impish look, which a crown of feathery silver hair heightened.

After greetings, Anna remarked, "What a garden! You can't even tell it's here from outside the gate."

Agatha smiled, revealing pearls of teeth. "It's sweeter that way, don't you think? Venice is full of secret gardens like ours. A few are filled with the sound of trickling fountains, so soothing. Others have centuries-old wisteria growing, geraniums tumbling out of pots, honeysuckle climbing the walls, and lots of stone lions, of course. Many are splendid hideaways, to the delight of their owners, like us."

"Have you lived here many years?"

"It's been so long," Agatha replied. "Venice is in our blood, if there can be such a thing. Dudley insisted on getting married here in May, during La Sensa, the annual Sposalizio del Mare festival, when Venice weds the sea. I suppose it's the most romantic thing he's ever done."

"It's the Feast of the Ascension, Venetian style," Margo explained. "Centuries ago, the doge of Venice tossed a gold ring into the water to symbolize Venice's rule over the sea and expansion in the Adriatic. This is reenacted every year. After the ceremony, all the Venetians follow in their boats and go to Mass on the Lido."

What a strange mix of the religious and the profane, Anna thought. So as Christ rises to heaven, the doge is marrying the sea, and the city is celebrating the greatness of its history with Mass thrown in as a bonus.

"I got married in a dress just like yours, Anna," Agatha said. "Simple and elegant. Mine was ivory, of course, but I love the olive color of your Fortuny. Compliments on your good taste."

Anna remembered how the pensione clerk had startled her as she had descended the stairs that afternoon, with appreciative smacking sounds from his wriggling lips, making her hope his reception was not what she'd experience later on. That man, Giuseppe, was an odd duck, arguing with her at breakfast about the early-morning singing, telling her he had heard "*niente*" and nothing like that ever happened in the quiet neighborhood around the pensione.

"Anyway," Agatha continued, "I was a little worried that Dudley would be tempted to fling my ring into the Grand Canal and then have me dive for it." As she laughed, her face breaking into crevices, she splayed the fingers of her left hand, revealing a large heart-shaped diamond set amid swirls of emerald baguettes. "He didn't do it, of course, and I certainly wouldn't have. The jury's still out about who dominates whom, I guess. But there's no question that the sea is his mistress."

"Aren't you jealous?" Margo asked with a wink. "You can tell me. I won't print it in the *Chronicle*."

"I know I have nothing to fear, driven as you are." Agatha patted Margo's hand. "Besides, when we're back in the States we only read the East Coast papers. You know," she sighed, "he does this crazy rowing standing up." Her hands fumbled, tracing circles. "He even rows with other Cultural Council members, sometimes at the crack of dawn."

"Yes," Dudley chimed in as he offered the women drinks on a gold-leaf tray. "I get up at five in the morning and put on my trainers before I'm hardly awake. In summer, the sea and sky are tinged just like the color of this Bellini. I take my trusty steed there." He nodded toward a rowboat bobbing on the canal near a tiny boathouse.

"You go out in that puny thing?" Margo asked.

"Most days, before the water has a ripple in it. I row past the silent palazzi—I call them my painted ladies—showing no sign of life. Then I pick up the tempo and streak past the Arsenale, where you're not supposed to go. Pretty cheeky of me, I know. I row past San Michele and on occasion over to Murano."

His tone grew serious. "I do this for inspiration. You see, my thoughts need room to roam. The horizon is far, and little has changed through time. When I'm out there, who's to say what century it is? Time can stand still or go backwards. Funnily enough, you cannot imagine my progress as I float, cradled by the sea. Sometimes ideas spring from the waves. It's hard to distill the beauty and the evil of the world into a few, almost random drops of ink on paper. I'll always be challenged and plagued by it. 'Tis the writer's curse."

"Right." Agatha's face glowed as she eyed him. "He's hoping since Dante visited the Arsenale then wrote the *Inferno*, that some ancient genius will rub off on him, too."

Margo cackled and grabbed her glass from Dudley. "And he hasn't done too badly, Agatha."

"Doesn't the rowing take a lot of time from your writing?" Anna asked, before sipping her drink and studying him. She could hardly imagine someone looking like an albino turtle fighting the currents and angry waves. Where does he hide his muscles? she wondered.

"Not really. It takes about three hours round trip if I go to Murano, much less if I stay closer or row with other council members. We compete against one another—always training for the next Vogalonga, our little rebellion against the motorboat." He snickered.

"Men will always be boys, but I'm not jealous," said Agatha. "I've grown to treasure the early-morning hours alone. At six, I stretch and get up leisurely, like my cat, Orfeo. I put on my velvet Venetian slippers." She glanced at Anna's feet. "Oh, I see you're wearing a pair. Then in good weather, even if it's a bit chilly, I climb the steps to our *altana*."

"What's that?" Anna asked.

With her ringed forefinger, Agatha pointed to the roof of the palazzo. Balanced on its peak was a little wooden shed-like structure and narrow balcony, the sculpted head of a lion atop each post.

"Instead of bleaching my hair up there like a Venetian courtesan of centuries ago, I sip my tea and gaze out at the city—all the bell towers and alleyways, the palazzos and canals." Her tone became oddly reverent. "I'm like a possessive lover, I guess. Every day I scrutinize Venice for changes, and it never fails to surprise me. A boat's wake, the cry of a seabird, the way the sun's rays strike a window, a flag on a passing ship." Agatha's voice fluttered like the wings of a hummingbird. "I love all of it."

"I can vouch for that—why, I've joined her in the early morning a bunch of times," Margo said. "I swear you have one of the best views in Venice."

Agatha stood straighter.

Anna could not picture night-owl Margo getting up at daybreak to visit a woman with the tongue of a poet, extolling Venice's virtues. Perhaps she stayed over when she got stranded by some man, or was too tipsy to maneuver the bridge steps.

"I imagine this place could spoil you forever, giving you an unreal view of the rest of life," Anna said.

"I wouldn't worry about that, my dear," Agatha said with a

distant look. "I have enough unwelcome memories to last another lifetime."

"Dudley, I'm writing a short piece on Venetian life in the late sixteenth and early seventeenth centuries," Margo said. "Who should I talk to?"

"Ronaldo Gratti," Dudley answered promptly, "who just happens to be here. He's the tall man over there at the bar, an absolute authority and a professor at the University of Venice with impeccable credentials. Headed many art restorations. He'd be happy to put you on the right track."

"Are the best historical sources at the Marciana Library?"

"Now be patient," Dudley said. "Standing next to Gratti is Filippo Fanfarone, an expert on modern as well as old Venetian society. We'll visit with him, too. He's an excellent writer over at the *Gazzettino*, covering culture as well as the society column. Maybe you saw his report on Sergio."

Anna focused on Gratti, wondering if he was the sullen man in Alessandro's old photograph. He looked dark and intense enough. Fanfarone, the columnist, seemed to be of the same vintage. Slim, long-haired, dressed in an elegantly cut pea-green jacket, he was clinking glasses with a woman in a turban, staring at her cleavage. Perhaps she and Margo could turn on the charm and wheedle some information from these men.

"I need to speak to both of them for a second reason," Margo went on. "As Agatha may have told you, I'm writing an article about Sergio for my newspaper back home: I'm calling it 'The Death of a Venetian Count.' It'll be a blockbuster."

"Frankly, you know, Venice has more worthy citizens," Dudley said. "But without a doubt, an article like that would be exciting."

"If people help me with behind-the-scenes information," Margo said.

"By the way, Dudley is too shy to tell you," Agatha said, beaming. "He was just made president of the Cultural Council."

"*Complimenti*, Dudley," Margo toasted.

A sweet duel of cornets and strings drifted from a musical group sitting in a far corner of the garden.

"Ladies, listen to this music," Dudley commanded. "One of the Cultural Council's projects last year involved funding a recording of this coronation piece for Doge Grimani, a popular doge of the fifteen hundreds. Giovanni Gabrielli wrote most of it; he was the organist at the Scuola di San Rocco. Anna, you may know that San Rocco was the patron saint for people suffering from the plague. Treasures restored to their former glory, saving the jewels of Venice, whether music or canvas or stone—our society does it all." His chest expanded in pride. "We get things done. We're not like that other group," he snorted. "They just entertain each other at glitzy snog parties, like the one on Giudecca last weekend."

"They could afford that glitzy party, given all of Sergio's contributions," Agatha said.

"Were they huge?" Anna asked.

"In a word, yes."

"We do more effective outreach," Dudley said. "Harder than writing checks on your own bank account."

Almost against her will, Anna found herself admiring Dudley's fine qualities. His intellect and civic spirit outweighed his pomposity and "bad boy" demeanor. "Margo told me about your books," she said. "I'm impressed with your hard work in bringing ancient Venice alive."

"I'm an old soul, Anna."

"Indeed," Agatha nodded. "Dudley would love to return to the years when Venice was a republic. I can see him addressing the crowds now, wearing a doge's cap." She squeezed his arm fondly.

"I'm afraid not. Unless, of course, I could make you my *doga-ressa*, Muffin." He bowed with a comic flourish.

"Isn't that Alessandro over by the canal?" Anna asked, surprised by the sleek brunette in a leather halter top clutching his arm.

"Looks younger than the last one," Margo said, exchanging a glance with Agatha.

"Where's your pride, man?" Dudley muttered. "What about your name?"

"Could be his granddaughter this time," Margo said.

"He's stuck in a rut," Agatha told Anna, "seeking women around the age Gabriella was when she died. This Flavia is the latest. She does come from an old-line family."

The poor, haunted man, Anna thought. Doesn't he ever look in the mirror and know that he's getting on, notice the curve of his paunch, his silver hair? Just like Jack and his bottles. Sooner or later, life deals everyone a blow. *She* hadn't collapsed. *She* had picked herself up and marched on. One step leads to another on the path to the future, if you can avoid looking back.

"Still searching," Agatha said, her forehead furrowing.

"He'll never find another," Dudley added. "Gabriella was extraordinary. Well, it's up to me to help correct the situation. I'll go and speak with him now that the hussy has left him for the moment." He straightened the gold lion cuff link on his sleeve. "Carry on."

As he took a purposeful step in Alessandro's direction, a black-aproned waiter approached.

"Do try one of these antipasti," Agatha said. "Warm fig, wrapped in prosciutto."

"Leave it to the Italians to dress up their figs, and then crown them with melted gorgonzola cheese," Margo said, putting two on a small plate before offering Anna one.

Anna savored the piquant mix of salty and sweet.

"I was about to say how lucky I was to be a close friend when Gabriella and Alessandro married," Agatha said. "It's not surprising that none of his later attempts at romance worked out. And now . . . a man over sixty, especially a shattered one, and a woman of twenty-five have more to separate them than to bring them together."

She waved to someone across the garden. "I've been neglecting my other guests! I'd better circulate a bit. Why don't you two enjoy the paintings we're showing today? All by local artists. Anna, do come back again, and I'll tell you ways to escape the crowds and uncover the Venice behind the mask," she said in a conspiratorial tone.

10

L'incontro, *The Meeting*

Tuesday, afternoon

"We'll never find out a thing if we're gawking at paintings," Anna muttered.

"Don't be so sure," Margo said. "Sergio was a huge collector, remember. At least some of these artists are bound to have known him." She steered Anna in the direction of a few flamboyantly attired men, one with a long, florid scarf, lounging by the canal. "Oh, there's Andrew McMullan," indicating a thick-necked man in a kilt.

His hairy knees reminded Anna of the furred spider legs dangling from a nest in the corner of her garage. She had hoped to avoid seeing the rest of the creature by asking Jack to get rid of it. That was a waste of breath. "You're a grown woman," he'd said. "Deal with it."

"God, I can't believe what he's wearing!" Margo said. "He lives over on Giudecca, a character, but definitely up-and-coming. Even the national papers, like *Corriere della Sera*, are calling him the next big thing. He has a huge exhibition in Rome next month.

"Nice to see you again, Andrew." Margo's voice rang out like a clean, clear bell.

"And you, too," Andrew said in a burly Scots accent, stopping them at a stone sundial.

As Margo made the introductions, Andrew gave Anna a glance before lingering on Margo. Heavy brows knitting together, he said, "You never showed."

"Sorry. Things got wild at the count's. I couldn't get away."

"What, with that layabout Favier? I dinnae believe it. You have to make it up to me."

"Later," Margo said. "But now, why don't you show Anna and me your new work?"

Linking arms, Margo and Andrew strolled nearer the water as Anna followed toward a long array of easels that looked like the wattle of heron nests. Each displayed a painting. Andrew paused in front of a somber oil. "Yon is a girl from Cannaregio, a bonnie, shy redhead. She was only sixteen, but her eyes are much older, as old as womankind."

Anna studied the gleaming red hair against a dark velvet cloak, the light, beseeching eyes, a gray sea behind her, stretching to the horizon.

"You did a wonderful job," Margo said, pressing his shoulder.

"Aye. Belled the cat on that one," he agreed.

As they rambled along a pebbled walk, Anna studied Andrew's brooding canvases, mainly of people and still lifes in broad brush-strokes and swaths of color. Unlike most artists who had painted in the city, he depicted no Venetian landmarks. The art book on Non-na's cocktail table had featured Francesco Guardi's tempestuous skies, Canaletto's camera-like renderings of the Grand Canal, the watery universe of Turner. Those images captured Venice's ephemeral moods, from the pale light of daybreak to the riotous blues of midday, to otherworldly crimson sunsets to the ghostly mists of night. Andrew, on the other hand, revealed a strongly interior viewpoint. But the melancholy mood, the glistening fabrics, the gilded masks and feathered boas convinced Anna that Venice had seduced him as he projected his shadowy imaginings onto canvas.

He halted before a bold oil titled *Il Redentore*. Anna recalled the church from her guidebook, an ivory beacon, built by Palladio at the end of the plague that claimed almost one-third of Venice's population. Andrew's wrestling reds, umbers, and deep blacks made the church look smeared with mud—earthbound, corrupt, almost unrecognizable.

"Corrin wanted to nick this one," he said.

"Sergio Corrin, the banker?" Margo asked, her pitch jumping an octave.

"Aye, the same sod." Andrew grunted. "He'd lick the butter off my bread. After his lowball offer, I decided not to engage. He thought being rich gave him such great artistic taste, I should be honored by his attention. What an absolute laugh. Over the top with himself and his little hobbies. All he did was lose other people's money making dodgy investments.

"You know," Andrew's voice dipped, "an artist friend of mine was at that party last weekend, goosing buyers for his paintings. Matter of fact, he'll arrive in awee. He told the constables about a woman running from the scene. They kept him back as they were searching the bushes. Seems they found something and put it in a black plastic bag. A waiter, poor chap, looked ill when he told Sean that Corrin had been mutilated. Refused to say one more word."

Anna turned away for a moment. Wasn't killing him enough?

"How awful," Margo said.

"Aye, but that bloke had been out of control." Andrew's face shook like pudding.

"Hardly deserving to be murdered, though," Margo said.

"He could have been gutted like a haddock, and it wouldna matter to me."

"Sounds like you hated him," Anna said.

"Aye, and I'm not alone."

Anna feared Andrew might bite. Best to leave him to Margo. And how much time remained before his friend, Sean, would arrive? She felt like making a mad dash to the gate.

When they reached the last of Andrew's work, abutting the brick wall, Anna paused to admire a delicate painting of porcelain dolls as the artist pulled Margo into an alcove. "I want to paint you," he said, caressing Margo's temple with a ruddy hand. "I can make you look even lovelier with a wee bit of light. You'd be immortal."

Anna imagined those sausage fingers on her skin. How were they capable of such grace and delicacy on canvas?

"Naked. That's it. That's it," he shouted. "You must pose for me in the morning."

"I've never done that," Margo said.

"It would be brilliant. And I should tell you now, I'm sure you would love . . ." Andrew murmured into Margo's ear. She pulled free and blindly rushed past Anna.

This is awkward, Anna thought. "I, uh, understand you live on Giudecca, Andrew. Do you come this way often?"

"Only when the alley cats are making too much noise shagging," he replied. "Are you wantin' one?"

Now Anna hurried away. "Margo," she cried as she caught up with her friend near a whitewashed pergola. "It's a shame that pig has so much talent. He's beyond crude."

Margo gave Anna a beatific smile. "Oh, I don't know."

"Come on, the man is so vulgar. He's trying to bed you, and not doing it tastefully, either. What did he say to you?"

"I really had been thinking of posing for him. I must attract weirdos."

Anna felt the weight of someone's stare and looked up. A compact blond man with intense blue eyes stood on the other side of the pergola. He meandered over and greeted Margo in Italian. His voice was deep and sonorous, like a cello.

"What a surprise," Margo said. "I thought you'd be in Milano by now, working, or cycling up Monte Grappa."

"We Venetians never forget the way home." He kissed Margo lightly on the cheek. "The canals, the sea, they're part of us, so we don't stay away for long." He tilted his head toward Anna. "Who is your friend?"

"Anna. *Ma lei è sposata*," Margo said. "And her husband is a handsome, jealous Neapolitan. Anna, this is Roberto."

Anna could hardly believe that Margo was portraying her as happily married and to a loving Italian, yet, who sounded like he just got off the boat. Ignored and abandoned was more like it. She let it lie; a Latin lover was the last thing she needed right now. Roberto grasped her hand and kissed it. Anna pulled away, fingers brushing against his whiskers. But when she found herself gazing into the cerulean innocence of Roberto's eyes, she stood there, paralyzed, sensing his voice but not hearing his words. Floating in a vast sea, sheltered by an infinite azure sky, she felt herself drift away.

"So, you do not wish to answer; you must be shy," he was saying. "Well, let me introduce myself properly. My name is Roberto Cavallin." He waited, unblinking, concentrating on her.

"I'm . . . I'm Anna Lucia Lottol." Anna collected herself by backing up a comfortable distance. "So tell me, er . . . Roberto, what do you do?"

"That's what I've always wanted to know." Margo laughed.

"Very funny, Margo. You mean, besides go to parties, hide behind statues, and kiss the hands of beautiful women?" He turned back to Anna. "I'm an investment banker. I advise Italian companies on acquisitions, and I invest as a principal. More of this is happening today, before European unification. I work in Milan, but from time to time I come back to Venice to relax. And to enjoy its charms with friends." Roberto opened his arms wide and said, "You both must join me for a ride on my boat."

"Can my cousin Angela come, too?" Margo asked.

"*Certo*, of course. We leave tomorrow around noon-thirty from Florian's. We will go to Torcello for lunch." He took off his jacket.

"Where is that?" Anna asked, distracted by the solid contours of his chest and shoulders.

"An hour to the northeast. The original Venice, the island where it all began. It's a little wild, like me." He gave out a low laugh. "But largely forgotten. It is one of my favorite places. You have not really experienced Venice until you see it from the water, like my ancestors did."

"You'd like it, Anna," Margo said.

"I don't know if I should go," Anna murmured. She spotted Andrew McMullan, his barrel chest bursting through the gate, with a gangly, curly-haired man wearing a cravat, and carrying a big leather portfolio. Quickly, she turned her back to them.

"Why do you say that?" asked Roberto.

"Because I've seen how Italians drive cars. It has to be worse in boats. No rules. Pure anarchy." Anna felt the rush of fear, of accidents on the water. Of sloppy irrationality. Of loss of control. Fear that something might upset the order of her life while underneath it all lurked the fear of getting what she wanted, when her parents had not even gotten to see her grow up.

"Italians! We are Venetians here," Roberto said. "It's true that we like to make our own rules, but we are very careful on the water. There's more courtesy . . . chivalry, you might say. After all, boating is an ancient tradition. Besides," Roberto lightly touched Anna's arm, "I would be very careful with such precious cargo."

"Spare us the crap," Margo said. "The truth is you'd be delighted to be alone with three women."

"Sometimes, Margo," Roberto's eyes danced, "I think you know me too well. Anna, you would regret not going."

Margo lowered her voice. "You heard about Sergio, didn't you?"

"Of course. Sad. Very shocking. But," he glanced over his shoulder, "his life was not without complications. Would anyone like a glass of wine?" he asked. "Valpolicella, Pinot Grigio, Montepulciano?"

"I'll have Sagrantino if they're serving it," Margo said.

"Montepulciano, thanks," Anna said.

"Don't you think he's big-time sexy?" Margo asked as Roberto moved toward the bar.

"Not really," Anna said.

"Oh, come on. Are you blind? You've spent too much time with science textbooks. Just look at the physics of that rear end."

"He's not my type," Anna said. "Much too smooth." In truth, she didn't know what she thought. She'd felt a consuming longing in the early years with Jack. She had no idea if she could or even wanted to feel it again. "Do you think he knows more about Sergio?"

"I'd bet on it. We need to divide and conquer. I'll corner Fanfarone and Gratti. We can try to talk with Agatha together. Why don't you see what you can pry from Roberto? He seems to have taken a shine to you."

"I'll do my best, but I don't trust him. And I may have to leave early. Someone arrived who could identify me—Andrew's friend—the police sketch artist."

"Oh, no," Margo said, clicking her tongue. "Then we'd better start working." She sauntered away, leaving Anna to contemplate her next move.

Several clusters of people reveled together between Anna and the bar. She'd be less conspicuous in their midst, rather than standing in the open with a target on her back, like a mourning dove caught in the gaze of a red-tailed hawk. Starting to seek cover, she heard Andrew booming out in a rich brogue as he said, "Let me introduce you."

She hoped he was referring to an art patron.

Andrew planted himself in front of her, alongside the man with the portfolio.

She turned to leave.

"Stay a moment, Anna," Andrew said. "This is my friend, Sean."

Anna tried to look at ease as she noted Sean's aquiline nose, tiny, alligator-green eyes, and thin lips, his somewhat reptilian look softened by an unruly abundance of sandy-colored hair.

"You look familiar," Sean said with a proper British accent, peering at her.

"Lots of people tell me that. I . . . have one of those faces."

"And American to boot." He cocked his head. "I say, you're the one! You're the woman who ran down the steps from the gardens at the Belvedere Hotel. I sketched you for that detective."

"What!"

"Wearing a raincoat to a formal ball. What were you hiding underneath?"

"Are you accusing me of something?"

"The artist's eye doesn't lie," Andrew said.

"I should call Biondi right now and turn you in." Sean's voice rose with excitement. "There must be a reward in a big case like this. In fact, didn't the widow offer one?"

"I've already spoken to Detective Biondi," Anna said. "Obviously, he let me go."

"He made a mistake. I'll make a positive identification right now—of you in the flesh, not just from a sketch."

"You've got the wrong person."

"Not a chance."

"I was just rushing down to the boat," Anna said.

"You're lying," Sean said calmly.

As heads began turning in their direction, Anna felt someone brush against her shoulder. It was Roberto with her wine. "Here you go," he said, handing it to her with a smile. "You're right," he said to the men. "What did you say your name was?"

"Sean."

"Millbrook?"

"Correct."

"Sean, she *is* lying," Roberto told him.

Anna took a sip of wine, resisting the urge to quaff the entire glass. She couldn't bear the gloating look on Andrew's face.

"She was rushing back to me." Roberto gave Anna a quick kiss on the lips. "Weren't you, dear?"

Anna nodded energetically.

"Why did she have a raincoat on?" Sean demanded.

"We decided last minute to attend the party—how do you say, on a lark, and were in the process of departing," Roberto said. "I told her about the lovely gardens, and she wanted to peek at them before we left."

"Oh," Sean said. Anna couldn't tell if he believed Roberto or not.

"I've heard about your artwork," Roberto said, glancing at the satchel. "Nice to see you've brought some pieces with you. I'd like to take a look at them later. At your work, too, Andrew."

"Come on, Sean, let's put yours up," Andrew said. "Maybe you'll get some offers."

The two artists strolled toward the exhibition space and commenced placing Sean's watercolors on some empty easels. Anna exhaled with a huge sigh. "Are you all right?" Roberto asked.

"Thank you," Anna said fervently. "Even if you did take a liberty."

"I couldn't resist," Roberto said.

"Why did you help me? Couldn't this make trouble with the police for you?"

"You needed it. As you say, the detective released you. You

aren't exactly hiding. I'm sure he could find you if he had more evidence than a drawing. If I am correct, I have embarrassed Sean Millbrook, and he will not broadcast his mistake further. Neither will Andrew McMullan. In any case, I *was* at the ball."

"Really?" Anna asked.

"And so were you. I went because I wanted to contribute money to save Venetian art," Roberto said. "What was your reason?"

Offering a bland smile, Anna tried to concoct an explanation without revealing the tawdry details of why she had gone to the Belvedere. Analyzing numbers was her forte, not fabricating deceptions. Maybe she could just stonewall him.

"My work."

"What kind of work?"

"Treasury work."

"You mean the United States Treasury Department?"

"Yes."

"What is their interest?"

"I can't share that."

"Who are you, the Mata Hari of the Treasury Department? Do you wear a holster on your thigh?" He grinned.

Anna rolled her eyes. "It's not funny. You're a smooth talker. That talent must come in handy."

"As a matter of fact, it does help me close deals. But I'm curious. What is your nationality, I mean, ancestry?"

"Italian. I still go by my married name but not for much longer." Anna had always disliked the truncated Lottol with its dropped vowel, courtesy of Jack's WASP-wannabe father.

"I can't say I'm sorry to hear that. Do you mind me asking your maiden name?"

"Orsini."

"Much better," Roberto said. "Little bears. Cute. More Italian."

Roberto turned as Dudley approached.

"Thank you, sir. Here is my glass." Roberto placed it on the painted tray Dudley held out. "Dudley, you must relax and let the waiters do their job. After all, you are the host."

"Quite right," Dudley said. "I'll go and put my feet up." He retreated to a bench.

"What can you tell me about Sergio Corrin?" Anna asked Roberto.

"What is he to you?"

"I'm helping Margo with an article she's writing, giving her some financial insights. She's on a short deadline."

"So it would seem. That's too bad. Sergio was a complex man."

"Meaning?"

"Many interests."

"Such as?"

"First you attend the ball where he is murdered, now you ask many questions, trying to uncover things. I tell you what. If you come to lunch, I will be happy to share what I know."

"That sounds tempting." At least I'll have chaperones, she thought.

Anna surveyed the crowd. Dudley was in deep conversation with Fanfarone. Margo was sitting, legs crossed, with Gratti. Agatha stood by the entry gate, chatting with a woman in a sombrero. Andrew and Sean were talking with a group of women, pointing to their artwork.

With some luck, she might be able to sneak into Dudley's study.

"Right now, I need to powder my nose," Anna said. "Would you excuse me?" She handed Roberto her wine glass.

"I'll be waiting. Be careful, Anna. Some things are best left alone."

Wanderings

Tuesday, late afternoon

When Anna stepped inside the cavernous palazzo, she wasn't sure where to go. The ground-floor rooms, looming behind etched-glass doors, resembled a warehouse, occasional crates piled high. Did Dudley ship his own books?

She climbed a marble staircase, seeking the piano nobile. Wandering down the hallway on the Grand Canal side of the palazzo, Anna crossed paths with a maid in a trim gray uniform and asked where the bathroom was. "*Il bagno?*"

"*Lì.*" The maid pointed to the end of the corridor and disappeared down a stairway.

Creeping along, Anna peered into the rooms: a music chamber complete with upright piano and gleaming lute; a living room whose walls were garnished with winged lions; a glowing octopus of a Murano chandelier hovering over a baroque dining table, reflecting light onto oyster-colored, silk-clad walls.

Beyond the rear staircase, she spotted a room with a genealogy chart on a Venetian plaster wall. A large breakfront, displaying a collection of oriental fans, hunkered next to it. Pausing, Anna swiveled her neck from side to side, surveying the empty hall before rushing into the room and shutting the carved-wood door.

After nearly tripping on the curved leg of a mammoth couch, she reached a massive desk. A framed photograph claiming one corner showed a youthful Dudley and Agatha embracing aboard a gondola. Papers sat in the middle of the desk, in two neat stacks. Anna took off her glasses, leaning them against the picture frame, hoping that she'd find some clue but steeling herself for failure.

Kneeling on the floor, she tried the drawers on the left side of the desk first. All locked. In the top drawer on the right, she found notes on doges, the Council of Ten, the Gran Consiglio, torture devices in ancient prisons, all written in longhand. Drafts of book chapters, littered with cross-outs and editing, dominated the middle drawer. Crammed into the bottom drawer were a series of personal and professional folders. Anna grabbed one labeled "Investments." Inside, all she found was a 1986 note about a million-dollar investment in a Liechtenstein company in Vaduz, showing the interests of Agatha, Dudley, and Sergio. No indication as to its business.

Then Anna went through the bulky correspondence folder, holding critiques and letters from readers spanning decades. Many praised Dudley's work, while others faulted his portrayal of a piece of Venetian history or a certain doge. A letter sent from Dudley's publisher in 1962 informed the author that he would be receiving a ten-thousand-dollar advance for his next book. How Dudley's fortune had changed over the past thirty years, Anna marveled. Under the letter, she spotted a leaf of cream-colored stationery engraved with animals crossing a stream, jagged mountain peaks in the background. Below that lay a torn black-and-white photo of a woman in profile, an arched window behind her.

Anna hadn't noticed the family cat ensconced in an oversized chair. Now, with a soft meow, the cat sauntered over and jumped on the desk, bumping the framed photograph, which crashed onto the parquet floor.

The sound of footsteps intruded.

Nudging the drawer closed, Anna darted behind the sofa and crouched, barely breathing as the door squeaked open. A male voice shouted, "*Tutto bene? C'è qualcuno là?*" — "Is everything okay? Is someone there?"

As the tabby lounged amid Dudley's toppled papers, Anna spied a decorative mirror in a niche, holding the image of two men in the doorway. One was the big-eared man from the vaporetto, whom she had reckoned was a cop. The other, young and thin-faced, she had never noticed before. She held still, wishing she were lying flat on the floor, knowing if she could see them, they might spot her reflection as well.

"*Vado a vedere da dove viene il rumore,*" said the man from the vaporetto in a deep voice. He took a step closer.

What would he do when he saw her? Arrest her? For what? Invading Dudley's privacy? More likely, he'd get her kicked out of the party after portraying her as a thief, guaranteeing that no one would ever furnish her with information and making her quest perfectly unattainable. He'd report everything to his boss, of course, who already was pulling out all the stops by siccing not one but two undercover detectives on her. Biondi was primed to suspect her of any nefarious scheme, and nabbing her here would only serve to underline her guilt in Sergio's murder. She asked herself if combing through Dudley's study had been worth it. She couldn't assess the value of any one bit of data. Each fragment so far was an unfathomable puzzle piece.

"*Carlo, non essere stupido,*" said the young man. "*È soltanto il gatto.*" — "It's only the cat."

As they left the room, Anna overheard them discussing a woman asking a lot of questions. She wondered what they had heard and if they were talking about Margo, her, or could it be someone else? She hadn't spotted them hovering near her in the garden, but maybe they were skilled at their work.

When the door clicked shut, the green-eyed cat, having finished licking itself, sought refuge in a velvet easy chair. Dashing back to the desk, Anna reopened the correspondence file, anxious to conclude her snooping before the maid or Dudley himself appeared.

The young woman in the torn, yellowed photograph wore her dark hair long. Her forefinger pressed to her lips suggested she had just told a secret. She didn't resemble a young Agatha at all. Could she be an old girlfriend of Dudley's? Or someone's wife? Who was the woman looking at? Her partner, or if not, certainly someone or something that Dudley did not wish to see.

She shoved the folders back into place before glancing at the papers on the desk. Peeking from under the pile of rubble was a thick green book entitled *Intermediate Accounting,* published by John Wiley & Sons in 1960, its author none other than Dudley Filbert. She pondered what had prompted him to write about doges instead of debits.

An array of *murrine* glass paperweights on a copper console table caught her eye, the iridescent glass rods resembling the delicate tentacles of sea anemones. Above the table hung two pictures. The most recent one showed Agatha and Dudley at the Great Wall of China. The older one was of a group: Pablo, with a boy holding his hand, Dudley, and Sergio on a dangling rope bridge. An emerald forest sliced by a wide waterfall lay behind them.

Anna pried open the door and squinted into the hall. When she was sure no one was about, she hurried down the back steps and slipped out through a side exit.

Looking across the garden, she saw Margo, next to a rose bush, waving at her. "Where have you been?" she asked.

"I'll tell you tomorrow. I have to leave."

"What's your hurry? I have a few things to share."

"I'm on the lam from Roberto and the cops."

"Don't be silly."

"Easy for you to say. I'm getting found out around every corner."

"You need to stay. Agatha can talk to us now."

"I didn't want to put a damper on everything, but God, what about Sergio's murder?" Margo shuddered, putting an arm on Agatha's shoulder.

Agatha raised an eyebrow at Anna.

"She's helping me," Margo said.

"Let's go where it's quieter." Agatha led the two women to a stone bench framed by a jasmine-covered bower on the far side of the palazzo. "Others will think we've gone to share some juicy gossip," she said in a hushed tone as they sat down. "Dudley and I have been shaking with the news. Dreadful. New York is one thing, Venice quite another. To have Sergio murdered, just like that," she snapped her fingers. "We're in total shock."

"We were surprised you were still holding the party," Margo said.

"I thought about postponing, but Dudley would not hear of it. Frankly, Sergio had drifted away from us over the years. Became more of an acquaintance. Dudley would see him at an occasional meeting of one charity or another, but I can't remember when we last socialized with him and Liliana."

"Wasn't he running around with someone?" Margo asked.

"Yes. But dears, if that were cause for murder, many men in this city would be dead."

"Not Dudley, though," Margo said.

Agatha's eyes twinkled. "A friend of ours attended that masquerade ball," she told them. "Toward the end, Kitty and her husband took a walk to the gardens. All of a sudden, a waiter rushed out at them, screaming at the top of his lungs about a dead man, a knife, and someone running away. The police descended from everywhere. Our friends were frisked. Later on, one of our artist acquaintances arrived there, too. All were forbidden to say anything until the police announced the murder in the press."

"So he was stabbed," Margo said. "The papers never revealed how he died."

Agatha paused and blinked. "I hope I haven't gotten poor Kitty in trouble."

Margo shook her head.

"The article will take time to write," Anna said. "And Margo may need to talk to Kitty to get the scene straight."

"Ask her in a day or so," Agatha advised. "She was still too unnerved to come today."

"Do you think Sergio was connected to organized crime?" Margo asked.

"Some swear he held hands with the Mafia. They're always trying to figure out a new business, you know, doesn't just have to be burying toxic trash in Naples. In Italy, you're never very far from the Mafia, the Camorra, the 'Ndràngheta. Some shadowy figures visiting his place, who knows? Just like Falcone and Borsellino, those poor Sicilian judges killed a few months back."

"Those were bombs," Margo reminded her.

"For those they can't get close to," Agatha said. "Otherwise, an easily hidden knife will do. With these *tangenti*, I even wonder if Sergio played hardball and threatened to expose a politician."

"Not tough to imagine," Margo said.

"On the first Wednesday of every month, Sergio would hold investment-club gatherings at his palazzo," Agatha said. "He'd give tips. Sometimes they'd meet at the Gritti. Social climbers would be jostling each other to get in."

"Why was that?" asked Anna.

Agatha looked askance at her. "Obviously, to show everyone they have arrived. An invitation from Sergio gave them bragging rights. They could crow about having his phone number here in Venice, at his vineyard, at Asolo, wherever."

Measuring their distance from Sergio as if he were the sun, Anna thought. Empty heads and empty lives.

"You're better than that," Margo said. "Have you heard anything else?"

"One interesting tidbit. Sergio's first wife, Arianna, is working the other side of the aisle from Liliana."

"What do you mean?" asked Margo.

"Liliana offered that pitiful reward for information leading to Sergio's killer," Agatha said. "Meanwhile, the rumor mill has it that Arianna, a hot-tempered bottled blonde with connections, has put out a 'contract' on the murderer himself."

"What? Reaching out to criminals?" Anna asked.

Agatha shrugged. "Who knows if it's true?"

"She'll easily beat the cops," Margo said. "Inspector Clouseau is heading up the police effort here."

"Doesn't *that* make me feel secure," said Agatha. "Margo told me about the police suspecting *you*, Anna, before you even came to town. How incompetent can they be?"

"Yeah, unbelievable," Anna said, trying not to clench her teeth.

"Clearly, they're out of practice."

"How about enemies?" Anna asked her. "Did Sergio have any?"

"He was such a cutthroat in business and in life—always wanting to win, at any cost. Could be it was payback time. Don't know of any specific haters, though."

"Did he invest only here in Italy?" Anna asked.

"No. All over. At least that's what I heard."

"Diversification might be tempting for people, even for you and Dudley," Anna said. "Do you know many others who invested with him? Sergio wasn't killed by accident."

Agatha focused her cool orbs on Anna. "Are you two researching an article, or trying to solve a murder?"

Margo shot a steely glance at Anna. "For a great piece, I need specific details, not just general pabulum."

"We already met someone who disliked him," Anna said. "Andrew McMullan."

"Andrew wouldn't hurt a fly," Agatha said.

Maybe so, but Anna could easily picture Andrew strangling alley cats, if not people.

"He's just sore about the twenty-five-thousand-dollar investment that Sergio lost for him. And then, his artist's pride was probably wounded when Sergio low-balled him for a singular oil painting."

"*Il Redentore?*" Margo asked.

Agatha nodded.

Given Margo's slipups and Agatha's command of gossip, Anna feared it wouldn't take long for Agatha to piece together everything Anna had done in Venice—and when—and broadcast it.

"What kind of investment did Andrew lose money in?" Anna asked.

"Some Sergio import business, I think. You'll have to ask Dudley, he's the reformed accountant, as I like to tease him. I stay as far away from finances as I can."

"What was Sergio doing in all those foreign places?" Margo asked.

"Always on the hunt—for women, most of the time, and art, of course. Beyond that, I don't know. I walked into Sergio's gallery near San Moisè last week to check out his latest exotica from around the world. What a collection. Oh, and on the way back, Margo, whom do you think I saw but your ex, Salvatore, sipping a macchiato at a caffè. He called me over, and we talked for a few minutes. Such a sharp dresser. Still has those big brown eyes, that dark, curly hair pulled into a ponytail. Just the picture of an angel, he is."

"More like *The Picture of Dorian Gray*," Margo said. "What a vile temper."

"I still remember the headlines years ago about his grand-father," Agatha said. "The only one in the family to die without shoes."

"What does that mean?" Anna asked.

"Died in bed of natural causes," Agatha said. "The rest of the men, I suppose, were gunned down or killed elsewhere, given their line of business. Salvatore was the black sheep of a bad family. We warned you not to go near him."

"I have a hard head," Margo sighed. "Those were the worst five years of my life. I still have the scars. All psychological, except this one," she said, touching her forearm. She took a cigarette from her purse, lit it, and took a long drag before exhaling.

"I thought you quit," Anna said.

"I'm having a relapse."

"Kitty said Salvatore attended the party at the Belvedere, too," Agatha said. "I just remembered. She told me the crowd got con-fused when Daniela, Preserve Venice's vice president, made the announcements after midnight, substituting for Sergio at the last minute. No one on their staff knew where he was at that point. It's funny, but Sergio had sent an invitation to Dudley and me, even though we hadn't been friendly for a long time. I really had wanted to go. I have a thing about masquerades. Very intriguing, like a secret affair. Who's behind each mask? What mask do you don, and who are you underneath it? Dudley said no, he had committed to our party today, and one this week was enough.

"Honestly, besides being a tad envious of Sergio, he can be a little hermit. You probably can't tell, but it takes a lot of energy for him to socialize. When his door is closed, I can't get in, even after thirty-nine years of marriage. I don't dare question him, or he clams up even more. Keeps his own counsel. Needs lots of quiet time to research and write, lots of space, lots of rowing, lots of walks. He shares only what he will." Agatha shifted her gaze to the canal.

"On the art front, I've asked Angela to keep an eye out for Paco Rivera's work," Margo said, changing the subject. "He's showing in Lima these days. I know Dudley wants the one with the big splash of yellow."

"He's gone mad for it. Calls it his Rising Sun."

"How much of a premium will you pay Angela?" Margo asked.

"Whatever it takes. He just has to have it. Once Dudley gets something in that head of his, it takes a crowbar to get it out."

After leaving Agatha, Anna and Margo huddled near the Grand Canal.

"Margo, what did you tell Agatha about me?"

"What we told everyone, that you arrived on Sunday."

"Why even mention it? Roberto, Andrew, and his friend, Sean, know that I arrived Saturday. Sean boxed me into a corner."

"How am *I* supposed to know that?"

"And being pulled into the police station?"

"It slipped out."

"Don't say anything more, please. The less anyone knows about me, the better."

"Right."

What was Margo thinking? Anna stared at her watch, its slim hand ticking silently, parsing through five seconds as she tried to keep from exploding. "I have to speak to my office in ninety minutes. Please say goodbye to Roberto and the Filberts for me. A stroll to the Customs House on the way back will help me clear my head." And cool off, she thought.

"Why don't you do it later on?" Margo asked.

"It's already set. They're calling me at the pensione."

Spotting Roberto in the distance, scouring the crowd, Anna hurried to the gate. When she reached it, an accented voice called out to her, and Pablo approached.

"I just love the view from this palazzo," he said, sweeping his arm in the direction of the Grand Canal. "It seems like a fantasy, a watery dream."

Anna smoothed an errant curl, feeling trapped. Not wanting to be rude, she replied, "It can be, I'm sure. But a lot of history took place here."

"Some proud, some sad. Never really a war though, thanks God. Think of the beauty that would have been lost forever. Dudley and I many times have talked about how Napoleon invaded Venice, taking over peacefully from the last doge in 1797. The Venetian nobles were so afraid of anarchy, they surrendered to him and betrayed their country. The French stole the artwork, but didn't destroy the city."

"Yes." Anna had read the John Julius Norwich history of Venice. Gambling had been a national pursuit, the nobles held all the power, debt piled sky high, even caffeine consumption went through the roof. Clearly, it was a society that had lost its way, ready to topple.

Pablo swallowed hard. "How different from ancient Peru where Incan palaces were demolished to build their cathedrals. Art treasures and golden sculptures melted down into gold ingots with one-fifth going to their king. In return, they gave us smallpox, misery, and death."

"How do you mean 'us'? You're part Spanish, aren't you?"

"No. Indian. *Puro.*"

For the first time, Anna noted his regal stance, his skin the color of manzanita, gleaming in the sun.

"I come from those who got away." Pablo's words poured out, like the crimson flow from a wound never staunched. "Atahualpa and his men met the conquistadors, without weapons. Eighty of his most noble warriors, carrying him on a golden litter, refused to let him fall when they were attacked by the Spanish, who cut off their hands. Toledo steel. Toledo swords. Human flesh was no match." Pablo's eyes smoldered. "Their places were taken by others, knowing theirs was the same fate but refusing to let their master go. Despite their sacrifice, Atahualpa became a prisoner. It was then that the other side won. Or thought they did."

Visions of swords piercing flesh, screams, Spaniards slaughtering natives filled Anna's mind. Blood splattering. Hands piling up. Her stomach lurched.

"Yes, Charles the Fifth, *Carlos Quinto*, damn him." Pablo stepped closer. "He had the absurd notion of being the Christian emperor of the world, of bringing Christianity to the heathens, to civilize us, control us. He could not put the two halves together. Had no idea what his conquistadors were destroying: our culture, our wisdom. He did not see the evil in his own men. Endless greed was their true religion. Raping our people, our land. We can never forget."

Anna could hardly recognize the doctor and diplomat she had met at Count Favier's home. She had not realized how ancient sores festered within him. Pablo was revealing himself a revolutionary.

"And the last ruler, Tupac Amaru, 'splendid serpent' in our Quechua language, fled with his wife, about to give birth. She refused to flee in the canoe that would have headed deep into the Amazon and saved their lives. Too scared. Couldn't swim. The Spanish dragged them back." Pablo scowled. "When Tupac was beheaded in the square, their church bells pealed while our people wept. Some of us escaped into the jungle, unconquered, under the waves of green. The rest ended up enslaved."

Anna looked longingly at the exit. Pablo was working himself into a state. "I'm sorry, Pablo. So tragic and ignored to this day."

"It has started once again," Pablo said.

Anna studied him, trying to decipher what he meant and where all this was coming from. Taking a wild guess, hoping to find a nugget about the murder, she asked softly, "Did Sergio do something? What?"

"Corrin!" Pablo glared at the nearest hydrangea.

"*Amorcito*," Yolanda called, coming toward them, holding the hand of an anorexic auburn-haired young woman in a lemon-yellow dress. "I want to introduce you to Constanza." For some reason, the woman stared at Anna.

Strange, Anna thought. "I should be off," she murmured to Pablo, slipping out the gate and vowing to pursue their conversation.

Degli Incurabili,
Of the Incurables

Tuesday, evening

The Filberts' party had become more than Anna could take: suffering Sean's accusations, Andrew's vulgarity, Pablo's alarming rage. With scant progress on solving Sergio's murder, each clue drew her deeper into a thicket.

She took lungfuls of moist air. At San Trovaso, she counted scores of gondolas resting on the sloping ground. Counting was clear and calming, her comfort and her lullaby. She could still recall lying in her bunny pajamas, reciting her numbers in a sleepy voice: "*Uno, due, tre, quattro, cinque, sei.*" The black wooden bellies facing skyward suggested the fertility of an ebony goddess. She had read that the *squero* here was a gondola hospital and birthplace. When the gondola next touched the canal waters, it would be like a baptism.

Her own baptism was lost in the past. Her dress had a long, white satin bow. It was one of the few things to survive the flames. She had spotted it while rummaging in Nonna's dresser drawers, hidden among the handkerchiefs, between drunken sniffs of lavender sachets. The patterns of the lace, delicate as snowflakes, were defined by their empty spaces. She was a big girl of six, she had told herself, and this tiny dress was for a baby. She had tried to refold it as she'd found it, but a picture in the drawer got in the way. She was the infant in the lace dress, clutching a silver rattle. Her mustachioed father was embracing her dark-haired, smiling mother, holding her in her arms. With her pudgy fingers, Anna had touched their faces in the picture, like a blind person struggling to learn Braille, wanting to make them alive again. Years later, the black-and-white photo joined the gallery in their hallway, before it went west with Anna to California.

How tidy and steady her upbringing had been. Nonno and Nonna had loved her with the mellowness of the late-afternoon sun, not its burning brightness at midday. A pat on the hand was good, two pats were better. A peck on the cheek and a soft hug were best. There was harmony and beauty in their love. Like a melodious string quartet by Vivaldi, each instrument enriching and complementing the others. Discordant tones, one member's virtuosity at the expense of the whole, were not part of their world. Anna had sometimes dreamed of what life would have been had her parents survived. How much better, she couldn't say, time having eroded her memories of them into a dusty, evanescent trail. But surely, this gnawing rootlessness would not be a part of her.

Hoping to clear her head, she sought the sharp evening breeze, turning from the small calle to face the broad Giudecca Canal. Fingers of air cooled her forehead, hushing her thoughts. In the distance, the lights of Giudecca twinkled like fallen stars from the far shore of the wind.

Past the Gesuati, she wove along the canal-side row of bustling restaurants where uniformed waiters pirouetted on the sidewalk, racing to serve eager-faced patrons. Pitchers of Prosecco bubbled on the red-and-white-checked tablecloths. Anna could smell the tangy, melted cheese in the *quattro stagioni* and *capricciosa* pizzas.

Shunning such liveliness, she moved on to a dim and deserted stretch of the Zattere promenade, closer to the open water where wind-whipped waves pounded the stone barricades and threatened the sidewalk. Amsterdam had dikes. Venice had only low borders of Istrian stone. How can you keep the waves out? It took discipline and force.

Ruminating on her failed marriage, she knew that Jack and she had loved one another. As the years slid by, she had grown to love him in an orderly way, giving tender, passionless kisses, while embracing a growing stubbornness to endure. She had fallen for an ambitious and confident man who had become as helpless as a baby. Which had come first, the drinking or the failure? Jack had chosen to drown himself under a sea of bottles. One day, his bold canvases had hung in Sutter Street galleries and his calendar had been filled with receptions. On the next, or so it seemed now, he had taken his place among the street vendors and crushed dreams on Telegraph Avenue in the rain. A crisis of confidence, crisis of manhood, and crisis, he had said, in the way she loved, had changed him. She, on the other hand, had not cracked. She had tried not to be bitter as each succeeding year added its weight to the others. Somehow she could never muster the strength or discipline to face the void of life alone.

A plump stone cherub atop a brick wall held out a book, its writings lost to decades of raindrops. Shimmering steps near the Swiss consulate led to a choppy canal. More steps plunged to a submerged stone platform, where the incoming swells gently lifted braids of algae before smacking them down, the next breaker raising them once again. The trembling green filaments resembled the dancing hair of a drowned corpse. Anna imagined descending into the numbing coldness of the water as it darkened the green of her gown before engulfing her face.

Hurrying along to the Zattere degli Incurabili, the section of

Venice that once housed the incurably ill, she witnessed day surrendering to night, as apricot clouds faded into charcoal phantasms flying across the sky. By the time she arrived at the old Customs House, shadows had swallowed its columned porticoes. The triangular mass of stone on which it sat, the angry blackness of the Giudecca Canal on one side and the calmer Grand Canal on the other, cut the water like a silent ship's prow. On the opposite shore, a spectacle of lights illuminated the Doge's Palace and St. Mark's Campanile.

She strode to the edge of the pavement and felt the city's magical rhythm with each beat of the waves. Wind gusting along the water's edge, cold and wet against her skin, drove her back again. A flicker of movement startled her. Peering into the darkness settling on the *fondamenta,* she suddenly felt vulnerable. Coming here, remote from the crowds, had not been a good idea, she realized. You read about these people the next day in the newspapers. Was Sergio's murder really related to some "complication" in his life, as Roberto had claimed, or was a lunatic loose in Venice?

She was turning to flee when a form took shape from the gloom. "Finally, I have caught you," Roberto's voice echoed as he rushed toward her. "Despite those Venetian slippers, you walk fast." His teeth flashed. "It was rude for you to leave me stranded without even saying goodbye. Is that how you treat everyone?"

"I . . . I asked Margo to do it. Sorry, but I became very tired. I suppose I'm not quite over my jet lag." Anna feebly met his eyes and made a half-hearted attempt to laugh.

His gaze flowed down her silhouette, like the caress of the spring rain and a flower bud before ascending again. "You should have taken the fast return to your pensione, not the long and beautiful way back."

"How do you know where I'm staying?" Anna heard her voice rising.

"People talk," Roberto replied matter-of-factly.

"You mean you ask."

He shrugged. "Asking has never been a crime." He tilted his head back and examined the building's blackened dome. "I used to come here, to La Dogana, with girlfriends when I was young. It's very dark, you think?" He turned toward her again.

"What do you want?" She retreated against a wall, the narrow pleats of her dress splaying into an elaborate, quivering fan.

"Nothing, really." He touched her shoulder. "Just to say goodbye . . . properly . . . the Italian way." He came close and whispered, "*Voglio baciarti.*"—"I want to kiss you."

He softly kissed both her cheeks, then paused before sucking his forefinger and tracing the outline of her lips. When he pulled her close, she couldn't help stroking his satiny hair, feeling she could melt into him and perhaps find peace. He was a beguiling undertow. But then, what would become of her, if she lost control?

In that moment, Anna was the observer and the observed. The observer rounded up her fears and summoned the strength to push him away. A distant voice, barely her own, stammered, "I really don't want any of this, Roberto. I just want to be left alone."

"I don't believe you," he said sluggishly, as if emerging from a daze.

"Who are you to say that to me?"

"I don't stay where I'm not wanted. And frankly, Anna, I don't think you know what you want." He tugged at the bottom of his jacket and headed back to the Zattere, disappearing into the curves of the night.

Anna was unsure what she felt. Staring at the white shores of San Giorgio Maggiore, she tried to lose herself in the ballet on the water. The passing ship strewing a frothy organza wake on the obsidian waves. The water taxi buzzing by. The profile of a distant gondola with masked passengers disintegrating into darkness.

Looking up into the arc of heaven, she spotted Deneb, sixty thousand times brighter than the sun, the head of the Northern Cross, and the tail of the swan.

Moving past the wreath of the *Caduti* and the barren steps of Santa Maria della Salute, she zigzagged away from the water, occasionally losing her way. A spooky *sotoportego*, a tunnel under a building, looked like it led nowhere and loomed ahead. A more promising route terminated at the fretted bridge of a single residence. Turning more corners, she strayed into dim culs-de-sac from which she was forced to retrace her steps. Finally, she navigated an improbably narrow passageway that led her through deepening shadows before finally disgorging near the Guggenheim Museum—a solitary star in the darkness.

Maybe I'll avoid wandering all night after all, she laughed to herself, glancing at her watch. It wasn't late, but it might as well have been two in the morning. Not a soul, not even one of the city's ubiquitous cats, was in sight.

Wary of another trap, Anna sought signs to the touristy Accademia Bridge. Then she heard it. Leather on stone, or did she just imagine the sound? Like footsteps hurrying against the light on Market Street in San Francisco. As she passed a cluster of gothic palazzos, she heard the gait persisting. Maybe it was someone like her, heading back to the main part of the island. Could it be Carlo, Biondi's spy from the vaporetto again?

Anna quickened her pace for another fifty feet.

So did her follower.

With the hastening footsteps, droplets of sweat moistened her face and chest. How stupid I was to take such a lonely walk, she thought. First Roberto, and now this. She was tempted to turn and confront her pursuer. That might be a move she'd regret.

The *click, click, click* behind her grew louder. Anna grabbed the flowing skirt of her dress, hiked it up, and broke into a full sprint. Her soft slippers provided no support, and the hard, irregular pavement stones jabbed into the bottom of her feet, like medieval torture devices. Though the pain grew with each step, she accelerated as adrenaline propelled her forward. Back in college, she had run the 100-meter high hurdles at the Edwards Track, winning her competitions more often than not. Thirty-three inches weren't an obstacle to her once she had mastered the technique to soar over them. But that was twenty years ago. Now she had to run as if her life depended on it. And she did.

Looking over her shoulder, she noted the flutter of an occasional shadow as her pursuer raced by a streetlamp. He was closing in, the tapping sounds somehow evoking the tightening circles of the toreador's cape. Soon, he would brandish his sword, and the arena sand would turn red with the tormented bull's blood. Anna pictured herself cornered against a brick wall, fighting a demon.

She managed to stay on the main path, hoping to find a footbridge just high enough for a gondola to glide beneath. She recalled that Venice had four hundred pedestrian bridges, and soon a little one came into view. Summoning her strength and muscle memory, Anna ran as fast as she could, extended her right leg and swooped onto the landing. In another second, she pushed hard off her left leg and descended the bridge in a leap. Her soles cried out in protest as her mind raced. The white letters of a sidewalk mosaic flashed as she flew by. "Save yourself," they seemed to spell out in Italian.

Frantically wondering whether to turn left or right, she could barely read an out-of-focus "Campo San Vio" on one of the buildings she passed. Where had she left her glasses? A blurred sign read "Accademia." Forty feet brought her to another crossing. One, two, three, and she jumped, her body sailing forward, but this time her right foot landed at an angle and she almost stumbled on the top step. She heard her dress rip with a *ssst* as she jerked herself upright before leaping onto the flat path beyond the bridge.

Lights danced on a far alley wall. Anna veered around a corner and almost collided with a couple exiting a building. "*Scusi!*" she cried as she raced past them on the wide, well-illuminated lane. I'll be safe now, she thought. Beyond an antique jewelry store, where tiny golden jaguars stared from the window, she streaked up the wooden steps and reached the safety of the popular bridge. Listening for footfalls, heart racing, she leaned onto her knees, panting hard. When she looked back, the couple was progressing toward her, arm in arm, laughing and sharing confidences. Behind them lay empty pavement. Her pursuer had vanished.

The night clerk was rubbing his eyes when she hobbled into the lobby of the pensione. "*Camera numero sessantasei per piacere,*" she mumbled. He handed her the key, grazing her palm with a long fingernail. Too exhausted to give him a dirty look, Anna limped up the stairs to her room and shut the door.

Somehow she'd have to pull herself together before Brian's call.

In the early morning, Anna dreamed of laughter. Margo, Angela, Sergio, and several people she did not know were at Count Alessandro Favier's palazzo, drinking Prosecco and eating cake on the terrace. One by one, they walked down the emerald marble steps, took the gleaming elevator to the ground floor and gathered by the empty family gondola floating in the water.

When Angela pointed to it, the other guests started to laugh. Anna did not know why, but the count did. Tears were streaming down his face. Sergio Corrin climbed into the gondola and sat rocking back and forth, smirking. Small fish jumped aboard, flailing. A miniature dollhouse, filled with sand and water, doll's feet sticking out a window, lay in the bow of the boat.

Anna had smuggled a cake knife into her purse, and now she brandished it. When she leaned over and stabbed Sergio, he fell sideways and hit his head against the hard wood of the boat. A halo of blood crowned his white hair. The palms of her hands turned red.

Laughter and crying flowed together, reverberating in Anna's ears before becoming a stream of cathedral bells, awakening her once again. Lying in bed with aching feet, hiding her head under her pillow, she told herself it was only a dream. But this was the second time she had had it.

La Notizia Bomba,
The Bombshell News

Wednesday, early morning

Anna strode past a newspaper kiosk, her ankle feeling stronger after a night's rest. With her backup pair of glasses, she noticed a headline, *"Una Notizia Bomba Cade Sulla Società Alta Veneziana — La Domenica,"* promising bombshell revelations about Venetian high society on Sunday. That might shed light on a few things, she thought. In Campo San Fantin, a mélange of centuries-old buildings greeted her: A former guild school, a gothic palazzo, historic caffès and restaurants ringed the cozy square. Standing since the year eleven hundred, the now unused parish church of San Fantin, patron saint of vendors of biscuits and sweets, faced the star of the plaza: Teatro La Fenice, the famed golden phoenix, or *fenice*, stretching its wings over the portal, transfixing Anna. Like the mythical bird, the Fenice Opera House had risen from ashes. In a way, she had as well.

She imagined a dulcet voice breaking into song. *"È bella in ciel sereno, la luna il viso argenteo . . . dolci s'udiro e flebili . . . un trovator cantò."* A maroon tapestry hanging from the balcony heralded the piano recital of Aldo Ciccolini, performing music by

Satie. A passerby murmured in Italian, "Stupendous concert last year. When he caressed those keys, he cast a spell." Eager music lovers were assembling for tickets, their excited voices and laughter filling the square, reminding her of happier times. She felt a spark of hope that her broken marriage would not define her future.

Crossing the plaza, Anna spotted Dudley seated alone at an outdoor caffè, lit by the morning sun and consumed in thought. He happened to glance up, nodded, and pulled out a chair. She sensed his hand brush by her hair as she sat down.

"I'm glad you wandered by," he said with a winning smile. "I'll order a cappuccino at the counter for you. Would you like that?"

"Sure. Thank you."

Dudley stepped inside, affording her a few moments to consider his soured relationship with Sergio. How was it that Dudley, who still had a photograph of Sergio on his wall and had traveled with his buddy decades ago, hosted a party after his murder? Clearly, there was little mourning or caring. Was that everyone's reaction to Sergio's death?

Perhaps Sergio had saved truckloads of Venetian art but not warmed any hearts, even of those attending his monthly soirées.

Anna was scanning the upside-down title of a thin volume with a beige cover when Dudley slipped back into his chair.

She jumped. "You're so quiet. You gave me a start. What is this you're reading?"

Dudley's hazel eyes shone as he patted the book. "It's by Joseph Brodsky, the poet who won the Nobel Prize five years ago. These are his impressions and recollections of Venice. This edition's in Italian: *Fondamenta degli Incurabili*. That's the part of the Zattere bordering the Giudecca Canal, where the old hospital was."

"I went by there last night."

"He paints unforgettable reflections of Venice," Dudley paused, "through the eyes of an exile."

Anna couldn't make up her mind about him. A snob, yet kind and solicitous of her though she was a nobody in his world, a defender of the Venetian upper crust, yet tolerant of roguish artists, and an intellectual writer and art connoisseur who had been the author of an accounting textbook.

"What have you been up to?" he asked.

"Attempting to relax."

"But having a hard time. Agatha and Margo. They talk."

Anna squeezed her thumbnail under the table. Knowing that Margo hadn't drawn any line with Agatha, she'd be foolish to deny what happened. "How can they possibly think I killed him?"

"They're bonkers. I wish I could do something. Truth be told, Alessandro has more pull. To local people, I'm still some foreign writer."

"After all these years?"

"Forty-three to be exact, but they'll never see me as a Venetian, only a quirky American. It's understandable. I'd still rather be here." He took a sip of coffee.

"What made you come originally?"

Dudley rested his gaze on La Fenice, his lips slightly upturned. "Came for a long holiday. Wanted to stay three months, trace the paths of famous writers, see what they saw, hear what they heard, feel what they felt: James, Browning, Dickens, Goethe, Proust, Lord Byron, Mann, Hemingway—actually used to see him a lot at Harry's Bar back in '49. The list is even longer. Then I fell in love. Though Agatha and I split our time, each year we stay here longer."

The waiter set down her cappuccino, and Anna savored the rich aroma. "*Grazie. Due bicchieri d'aqua, per favore,*" she asked. As the waiter turned away, Anna said to Dudley, "Margo showed me an old photo of you in Alessandro's library, with Yolanda, Pablo, their baby, Sergio, and another man."

Dudley nodded.

"How is it you and Sergio grew apart?"

"We met at a Cultural Council meeting back in the fifties. Both of us fretted that Venice, always on the brink of another flood, would lose all the glories of her past one day. After we lived through the flood of '66, we got serious. Sergio could contribute, was born wealthy, and Italy's economic boom only made him richer. But money also filled some hole in his soul; that's if he had one. By the mid-eighties, he had twisted into a monster, always pursuing one ploy or another. And what a bloody ego. Even formed his own art society, and he could never be feted enough. Always wanted more—of everything. Agatha and I began to find him unbearable."

Unfortunate she hadn't known this before she was seduced by him, she thought. "Is that when you pulled away?"

"A hundred kilometers an hour in reverse."

"All that investing . . . what did he invest in, anyway?"

"Once he ceased the financial takeovers, it was real estate, art—tangible things."

"Outside of Europe?"

"I wouldn't know. And he did have his own gallery of African art. Clearly, he must have been paying foreign artists."

Anna mulled over the smattering of information that Brian had dug up and sent her the previous night. Last year, Sergio had transferred twenty million dollars from his New York account to a Klatoki gold mine in Mara, Tanzania. "What about companies or any businesses in heavy industry, like mining, for example?"

Dudley pressed his lips together. "I don't think so. Not glamorous enough. He was above all that."

"Did you lose any money through him?"

"I was too smart. I did have some familiarity with figures."

"Yes, your background must've helped. How'd you ever switch from being an accountant to a writer of history and even some fiction?" Unlike Dudley, she had stayed faithful to numbers. Their perfect, crystalline structure remained unchanged. Now she just applied them differently, in algorithms, instead of in astrophysics. Dudley had deserted them and their logically imposed strictures, balance sheets needing to foot, depreciation needing to tally, accounting rules requiring obeisance. He had chosen a universe in which he made the rules.

He reddened. "Who told you about that?"

"Agatha. In passing."

"Accounting was an early, fruitless part of my life that I'd just as soon forget. And we've talked about Sergio and me too long already. Now it's your turn."

The waiter plunked down their waters.

Anna fell silent, rearranging her napkin.

Dudley leaned his elbows on the table. "You have a degree in physics, of all things, had a flirtation with astronomy or some such, and then you veered into a government job. You're now working at the Treasury Department, combating money laundering, if I'm not mistaken."

"Looks like you do your homework."

"I must admit I check on all the attractive women who come to our parties, heh, heh," he chortled. "Can you blame me?"

Actually I can, she thought.

"Do you do any undercover work?"

"What do you mean?"

"Field work, anything that gets you out of the office and face to face with criminals, maybe even entrapping them. Could be fascinating."

"No way. I'm in the office doing boring calculations. Has Margo been embellishing things, or is your artistic imagination at work here?"

"You've found me out. The latter. Do you have plans today?"

"Meeting up with Margo and Angela at Florian's. Then going with Roberto on his boat over to Torcello."

Dudley peered at her. "Roberto's a charming fellow. Not always sincere. He's a player who chats up ladies. They swoon. He harvests. Like clockwork."

"Thanks for warning me. It won't be a problem. We'll be in a group." Just another reason for being careful with him, she thought.

"Here in Italy, it's different. And he's not married, like you."

"Not for much longer." Her gaze fell on the gray pavement. Three more months, she thought, with little to show for the past fifteen years. Anna took a gulp of coffee. "You and Agatha seem to have found the recipe for a long, healthy marriage."

"Mutual respect—that's what it's all about. Where did you meet your husband?"

"At UC Berkeley."

"Are you from California, then?"

"No. New York."

He stirred more sugar into his coffee, swirling his spoon. "What did your parents think of him?"

"They never met. My parents died when I was young."

"Oh, no. Mine too, when I was a child. Hard to remember them, isn't it? Sometimes an image surfaces, but I'm never sure if it's a memory or a dream. At least you have pictures to remember them by, I would imagine."

She asked herself if he were a kindred spirit beneath all the pomp. "A few. Most burned in the house fire that killed them."

"How terrible. You were lucky to escape."

She tried not to think about the flames. Nonno had pointed to a home in the Bronx a decade later, a new house built where hers had been. "My grandparents were babysitting in their home on Long Island. Maria and Andrea raised me. They came from the old country, from Modena, in fact."

Dudley beamed. "No wonder your Italian pronunciation is impeccable."

"Thanks. Nonno taught me well. He didn't like Jack, my husband, at all. I should've listened."

"Family's important. I know my mother, in particular, would have loved Agatha, if she had only gotten the chance." Dudley wiped one eye with the back of his hand.

She pushed the water glass closer to him.

"It's been years." He took a drink. "Tell me, what does your soon-to-be-ex-husband do?"

"He paints."

"Ah, yes, the creative process. Very demanding, hard on a marriage. And your Nonno?"

"He was involved in diplomacy."

"The world needs more of that."

Anna scratched the corner of her mouth. "You know, getting back to Sergio, I'm helping Margo with her article. What's your take on his murder?"

Dudley drew his brows together. "We've already spent more time on Sergio than I'd like. Margo's the journalist with an intimate knowledge of Venice. Can't she do her own research?"

"She's on deadline and asked me to help."

"I doubt her editors give one whit about Sergio. She's oversold her story. But, all right, one bit then. I don't have any special insight, not having been close to Sergio for almost a decade, but I did hear that he had a special taste for ladies of the night."

Great, Anna thought. Lucky she had taken precautions.

"Anyone could have snuck into the Belvedere garden that night." Dudley fidgeted. "Listen here, Anna, don't let Margo drag you into this, no matter what she says. It's *her* job. After that episode with Biondi, you should be trying to enjoy your vacation. In all honesty, you're getting in over your head."

Anna wasn't sure whether his comments were aimed at throwing her off, warning her, or steering her toward her best interests. She recalled the torn photo in Dudley's desk drawer. Soldiering on, she asked, "How about Arianna, Sergio's ex. Did you know her?"

Dudley swept off a few crumbs from the linen tablecloth. "Sure. She's a pistol. Heartbroken when Sergio left her and the girls. She still loved the louse dearly. After all, she's offering that huge bonanza to the killer of his killer."

"How strange is that? Besides, how would she ever know if someone found the right person and wasn't just wanting to collect the money? Why not leave the police to solve it?"

"They're too slow and inefficient. They'll never catch him—or her. That murderer should be taken down, even if we need the Mafia to do it."

Anna tapped the table a few times with her spoon, reconsidering who her pursuer might have been the previous night. Dudley shot her a quizzical look. "It's not you. I'm a little shaken today."

"Why, if you don't mind my asking?"

"After your party, I took a long walk and someone . . . I think I was followed. Chased, really."

"Where?"

"Past the Guggenheim."

"That's odd. I'd say it never happens, but then I wouldn't have said murder did, either. Did you get a good look at him?"

"Too scared. I almost stumbled at one point."

"Poor dear." He took her hand for a moment. His hand felt cool, dry, and calloused. "Ask Pablo to check your right ankle."

Her muscles contracted. "How'd you know that?"

"It's what we writers do, or try to, and that's to keenly observe. You were favoring one leg ever so slightly when you came toward me today, yet at the party, you walked normally. I was wondering why, but didn't want to pry."

139

Anna sipped her coffee. "I'll be fine."

"If not, you know where to find him. Getting back to the party, I need to tell you something."

She twisted a lock of her hair and prayed for a breakthrough.

"Someone went into my study, rifled through the papers on my desk, smashed a picture of Agatha and me, and left their Italian-made eyeglasses behind." Anna's jaw went slack.

"Can you believe it?" he asked.

"You're kidding. Did he take anything?"

"Not that I can tell. Judging by the type and size of the glasses, I'd wager that he's a she. Not only do we have a murderer of Sergio out there, we have a female intruder. Could it be the same person?"

Anna willed herself to imitate a rock or a tree, overriding her impulse to squirm in her seat. She took a few slow breaths.

"Maybe she was trying to steal my next book," he said. "You can't believe how jealous some authors are. I keep the drafts of the new one secured." Dudley's eyes held a spark of recognition as he nodded curtly to someone.

Anna felt a hand on her shoulder and looked up to see Detective Biondi, scowling. "Anna Lucia Lottol," he said. "You come with me now."

Her stomach fluttered.

"Anna, don't worry," Dudley shouted as Biondi led her away. "I'll call Alessandro and Margo. We'll help you."

14

In the Police Station

Wednesday, midmorning

Anna noticed the curious stares from officers trying to look busy and jostling one another as she passed. Biondi signed her in at the front desk, where she relinquished her passport, then took her into a wood-paneled room with a mirror along one side.

"I have been busy," he announced as they sat down at an oval table.

"Me too—trying to figure out who killed Sergio Corrin." Anna had done her best, but now a sense of resignation overcame her. She felt as if she were standing on a beach, witnessing the enormity of the oncoming swells, incapable of outrunning them but oddly calm in the seconds before they hit shore. Biondi would have at her now.

"Let us strip away your lies and get to the truth." He flipped open a pocket-sized notebook. "You never spent overnight at the Grüner Baum in Zürich. Instead, you leave a few hours after check-in. You board the train for Venice, arrive here on Saturday evening, and pay cash for a room in a fleabite hotel. We have the clerk's statement."

The ceiling lamp seemed to vibrate, its light brightening and dimming like a distant pulsar. Anna felt a little woozy.

"So I ask myself why would she lie to me?" Biondi was droning. "And now I know. In January this year, you flew into Malpensa in Milan and you stay at the Principe di Savoia at the same time—surprise, surprise—as Count Sergio Corrin. Computers, credit cards . . . data lives forever, Signora Lottol. His room-service breakfast was for two persons, and we speak to the server. You made quite an impression. Expensive dinners at Savini and other top Milano restaurants, ditto." He gave her a tight smile.

Anna stared into space and thought about the nights with Sergio that set in motion this disastrous chain of events. "But I had nothing to do with his murder."

"Your denial would carry more weight if you were not a proven liar." Biondi slapped the table. "So you know him. You start an affair, maybe it goes on, maybe not. You fight at Caffè Orientale, hard for staff not to notice. An artist identifies you at the Belvedere gala, running away. He called us again, as a matter of fact, having spotted you, and told us things we already knew. We come to the conclusion that Anna Lucia Lottol had the motive and opportunity to kill Count Sergio Corrin."

Biondi's words were running together, sounding disembodied, like a sentence descending from the sky. Anna's chin trembled slightly. "What . . . what motive would that be?"

"Jealousy. Or to stop him from doing something with these. The likeness is remarkable." The detective pulled two photocopies from a white envelope and passed them to Anna. There she was, smiling, head and arms propped up on a linen pillow, without a stitch of clothing, boldly looking into the camera, like Goya's Maja Desnuda. The next photo showed her and Sergio, naked from the waist up, embracing. How *had* he taken these pictures without her knowing?

Biondi sat back and smirked. "We got the originals from him when we opened the mail today."

Anna shrank in her seat. She was now the laughingstock or the pinup of the Venice police department. She could barely raise her head.

But why would Sergio give up the photographs he was using to threaten her? And where was the third one? Biondi's theory didn't hold water. "Detective Biondi, Sergio did not send these."

"Wrong. He could have mailed them Saturday, before the gala. They are picked up on Monday, the postal worker takes many espresso breaks, and they arrive today."

"Why would he have done that?"

"Leave who and why to us. Maybe he got a death threat from you."

"Him, scared of me? That's absurd."

"Or, these come from an anonymous citizen wanting to help us catch the killer, just like in olden times. We perform a new test on *all* the evidence, called a DNA test. We see if it finds anything."

Anna swallowed. She had touched the Polaroids, along with Sergio's hand. A strand of her hair might have landed on him. What might these tests show?

"I want to speak to the American consulate. They should have been contacted by my office."

"I ask." Biondi used the intercom to relay the request to his staff. "Now, let's get to the murder scene." He unfurled an immense architectural plan and placed it on the table.

"What's this?"

"The plans of the Hotel Belvedere, including all the outdoor, public spaces and the dock. You will show me the location of every single place you walked, circle areas where you stopped, along with what time it was at each spot. If you make a mistake or lie again, I will give no mercy."

Anna struggled to concentrate, banishing any thoughts on the prospect of failure as she studied the rendering. "May I write on it?" Biondi passed her a pencil.

She traced her path carefully from the dock to the back of the hotel, through the hallways, into the ladies room, up the garden steps, and down to the boat again. Shimmering slivers of that night's sights and sounds, as if ruptured by strobe light, accompanied her mental journey. She paused to review her work, mulling it over before deliberating about the times.

"Most of these are estimates," she said as she finished. "It's not like I consulted my watch every time I moved."

Biondi pored over the drawing and then jabbed one spot with his forefinger. "*Ecco.* Here. You stood here, at the beginning of the raised garden, just to the left side of the top of the stairs."

"Yes."

"This is where you ambushed him."

"No. That's where I let him pass, where I lost my nerve instead of trying to speak with him, to beg him for the photos. He didn't see me, because I was next to some bushes."

"How tall were the bushes?"

"Over my head."

Biondi jotted a note on his little pad. "You see him coming, alone, no one else around, you surprise him with a weapon, and force him further into the garden. You kill him there."

"What? Do you think he would just go along with me, like a lamb?"

"You could have tricked him and attack him when he is expecting a kiss from you. Instead, he gets a kiss from death."

"For all I knew, a crowd of people were not far behind him. Why would I take that chance?"

"You seethe with jealousy. You don't think clearly."

"I didn't even have a knife."

Biondi straightened. "We did not disclose that."

"I heard it."

"Where and how?"

144

"From Agatha Filbert, at her party. Someone named Kitty told her."

"Is that her real name or a cat? Kitty who? What is the family name?"

"It's a nickname, I assume. You'd have to ask Agatha."

"*Merda*," Biondi swore. "So why did you run down the steps?"

"To get out of there as quickly as possible. I was embarrassed and didn't want him to spot me. I knew a boat would be leaving any minute."

"You want me to believe that after going to all that trouble—leaving Zürich one day early, meeting him, following him, taking the skiff to the Belvedere, hiding in the garden, desperate to see him again—you change your mind and flee? That does not make sense."

"It's what happened."

"Where do you claim to be at midnight? Still at the hotel?"

"On the boat back to St. Mark's." She pointed to the drawing. "I show my estimate at 11:55 p.m. The campanile was tolling when we were in the middle of the *bacino*. You'd know that already if you interviewed the boatman from the hotel."

"Times of death are not precise, Signora Lottol." A vein on Biondi's right temple began pulsating. "If you are innocent of Sergio Corrin's murder, why did you lie in the first place? You better tell me the truth, if you still remember what that is."

"I was terrified. Totally humiliated about what I fell into with him, afraid you wouldn't believe me if you knew I saw Sergio when I came to Venice, my connection to him, afraid of losing my job. So in a weak moment, I lied. I'm very sorry."

"You made many bad choices. By the way, I did speak at length to your office yesterday, to your boss, a Miss . . ." he looked into his notebook, "Leslie Tanner, who sounded very concerned. Why would you lose your job?"

Leslie would be only too happy to add to his ammunition, Anna suspected. "It's against the department's ethics rules." And common sense, she thought.

"Having affairs? Or 'flings,' you call them?"

"Being associated with money launderers, Detective Biondi."

Biondi let out a whistle. "So now you accuse a dead man of a crime. A man who can no longer defend himself."

"I had begun researching his financial transactions on my own, when he threatened me. In the spring, I asked him to give me back the pictures. After refusing, he called me last week and I told him about coming here on vacation. He asked me to meet him on Saturday. He didn't say why. I hoped for the best, but I had my suspicions, so I analyzed his US bank accounts. I spotted some questionable transfers of funds, not necessarily money laundering, but unlikely to be something else."

Biondi narrowed his eyes. "Your boss said nothing of this."

He would inform Leslie in their next conversation, of course. Anna would be lucky if she had a job as a file clerk when this was over. But what was more important, her job or her freedom?

Anna had run her algorithms against the US dollar accounts of Sergio and his bank, sorting through tens of thousands of transactions. Eventually, she had come to the painful conclusion that nothing with Sergio had been real. He had likely pursued her from the beginning in order to manipulate her. Her bona fides, photograph, and current position at Treasury were well publicized in advance of that seminar for European banking and finance professionals. It had attracted at least one member of the wrong crowd.

"Is he under investigation in the United States then?"

"Not for the moment, as far as I know. But he should be. I work in detection—the nerdy area—not in enforcement."

"Why didn't you tell your boss what you found?"

When Anna had tried to tell Leslie about another potential

money launderer, Leslie had accused her of jumping the gun, of wasting her precious time when it went nowhere. Anna could still hear her condescending tone, making her feel like a schoolgirl getting her knuckles rapped by the headmistress. She had resolved never to go forward again unless she was supremely confident of her data.

"My information was preliminary. I wasn't completely convinced."

"What did he ask of you when you met him here?"

"He wanted me to tip him off and find out what the Italian authorities had on him. He said he'd give me the photos in return—afterward. He'd use them against me if I failed or didn't cooperate."

"Maybe he just cheated on taxes, like many others."

"Oh, no—it was much, much more. That's why he never would have surrendered those photos to you. They were his leverage over me."

"So what were his underlying crimes?"

"I don't know."

"Count Corrin is held in high regard in Venice. You are attacking the man's reputation. He is still presumed innocent. You make claims and give me no proof. So far, all what you have told me has been a lie, maybe this, too. I will see if your new story holds any truth. Even if it does, it would not prove you innocent. Just adds more . . . intrigue."

"You're wrong. During the past few days, I've been in contact with my office in San Francisco about him. If I'm guilty of his murder, why would I be trying to find out more?"

Biondi sneered. "Elementary. To throw us off the scent. By means of this wild tale, you try to broaden the suspect list and take yourself out of the spotlight. Again, your boss did not mention anything. Now we are supposed to look around the world for drug dealers, smugglers, or others engaged in criminal activity with Count Corrin based on *your* word alone?"

Anna sighed. He was single-minded. "I even asked my friend, Margo, to help."

"The one who swore you were in Zürich? You expect me to believe her about anything?"

"She didn't know I had—"

"Now we talk about what to do with you. What to charge you with."

A firm knock came at the door. "*Avanti,*" Biondi said.

When a female assistant came forward, holding out a cell phone, Biondi excused himself. Anna heard him just outside the room, muttering, raising his voice with a "No, no," before growling, "*Fatti i cazzi tuoi!*" She recognized this as a rough, profanity-laced version of "Mind your own damn business."

Anna sensed she was in free fall, not knowing where she would land or how hard the surface would be. When the lives of Count Sergio Corrin and Anna Lucia Lottol were weighed by the system, she knew that the scales of justice in Venice would tip in his direction. Her lying to the police would be an open-and-shut case for Biondi to make. Envisioning a dank, windowless cell with a hole in the floor for a toilet, she imagined more questions from Biondi and others, practiced in the art of breaking people. They'd employ a wide range of tactics: bullying, threats, and worse. They'd figure out where her demons hid and feed them. How long would it take before they'd discover her Achilles' heel, her terror of being immersed in dark water? Her heart palpitated.

The wooden door creaked open, making her jump. "The American consulate tells us they know nothing about you," Biondi announced.

Why am I not surprised, she thought.

"I keep your passport for now. You can leave." He turned abruptly, the door swinging closed behind him.

15

La Biblioteca Marciana

Wednesday, late morning

On the way to meet Margo, Biondi's threats diminished as she surmised that someone was protecting her, presumably Count Alessandro Favier. How long that could last was anyone's guess. As Margo had said, Alessandro could not stop the police, only slow them. If they were lucky, she and Margo might find a clue to the murder in old newspapers stored in the renowned Marciana Library. Housed in a handsome colonnaded building, the library, which required the first copy of every book printed in Venice, was akin to the Library of Congress, only it had opened in 1560.

Anna had always reveled in the smell of old books, the mustier the better. Libraries were like churches to her. At UC Berkeley, she'd wandered the Bancroft Library, its ancient maps, astronomical manuscripts, and rare volumes waiting to be rediscovered. When she closed her eyes and fanned the pages of a faded book, she heard taffeta skimming across a ballroom floor. She pictured the filigreed metal arches and curved ceiling trusses soaring to infinity in Paris's Bibliothèque Nationale. Sometimes she gazed back wistfully, recalling the day she'd forsaken an academic career and all the knowledge she would never gain.

Knowing she was tardy, she resisted the urge to look at paintings by Tintoretto, Titian, Veronese, and other important Venetian artists, and hurried to meet Margo in the cavernous reading room. Watched by a bust of Petrarch, Margo was in a corner, hunched over several thick, spread-eagled volumes. Despite her sometimes scattered ways, Margo had a nimble mind. When she was working on a story, she slept little, speed reading through three or four books at once, working prodigiously, vanquishing deadlines, and turning out enviable pieces.

Tapping her on the shoulder, Anna asked, "Find anything yet?"

"These are for my real article."

Anna glanced at books by Veronica Franco, Coryat, Casanova.

"I've been searching for a story hook." Margo's voice grew animated. "Europeans love the past but Americans won't relate to the life of Venetian courtesans four centuries ago when the events of four years ago have already faded into the mist. How can I make it compelling? Skip the poetry of well-educated prostitutes and add sketches of risqué fashion? That would make eyeballs bulge. Or maybe feature *puttanesca* recipes, prostitute favorites? You know, meals from ingredients gathered between the last customer and the market's close. I could try to write a fictional diary and drag it into a series. Or what about a 'then and now' contrast with a twist: how times have changed the business of prostitution, or have they? Whaddya think?"

"I think we've got to find something about Sergio's murder *pronto* or Biondi is going to lock me up. I'm late because he grabbed me while I was having coffee with Dudley—I ran into him near the pensione—and took me to the police station for more questions. He's put the pieces together; he knows about Sergio and me and when I actually arrived in Venice. He's going to try to pin the murder on me, I just know it." Anna felt a tightening in her chest. "The goddamn Polaroids even showed up in his office. The only good thing is, I don't have to worry about him finding out any more of my lies. There aren't any."

"And he released you?"

"Disappointed?"

"Don't be silly. Why, do you think?"

"He got a phone call from someone who forced his hand. Somebody he could curse at in Italian. Alessandro?"

"Hmm," Margo said, gathering up her things. "Did Dudley have anything useful to say?"

"Not much. He's touchy about being an accountant and not entirely an artiste. And he thinks Sergio might have frequented prostitutes."

"Well, that would fit right into my story idea. Any details?"

"Nope. Sort of heard it on the street. Another thing I need to tell you—I went up to his study during the party and rooted around in his desk."

"You didn't."

"I was desperate. But I came away with nothing. Well, I did see a torn photograph of a woman in profile from years ago. And I managed to forget my glasses on Dudley's desk, which he found, of course. He didn't accuse me of anything, but do you think he's figured out it was me?"

"How'd he act this morning?"

"Matter-of-fact. I was wearing my other pair."

"There were so many party guests I wouldn't worry about it. But he's a sly one." Margo straightened her pile of books. "We do owe him big-time for getting us in here. He even had the head librarian select books in advance for me. I'll plug his latest work to the *Chronicle* book editor when I get home."

"Where do they keep the newspapers?" Anna asked.

"In the microfilm room and only going back to 1960. The space is probably tiny and airless, and we'll slog through everything and come away with squat."

"Can't we wait till we're done to be negative?"

When Margo pushed open the door to the microfilm room, they were overcome by stale air. Her face held the hint of a smile. "See?"

Anna took a second glance at the old microfilm reader, resembling the ones they'd used at college; they'd have to load each reel of film and turn a crank to advance the pages. File drawers held heavy boxes of microfilmed pages of all the local and national newspapers. Margo threaded the reader and started cranking. "I feel as if I'm churning butter back on the farm."

Five reels resulted in blurred nothingness. National politics dominated. For a time, tangenti, Bettino Craxi, and his Socialist Party were all the news. Then Umberto Bossi and the Lega Lombarda anti-political-establishment, anti-immigration separatists, followed by Antonio Di Pietro, the prosecutor for the "Mani Pulite" investigations of political corruption.

"My muscles are aching. How my mother at the age of sixty-two is running the Chicago Marathon in a few weeks is beyond me."

"Save your arms," Anna said. "I'll take over."

In the *Gazzettino*, a picture of a festive Dudley and Agatha during a 1988 Cultural Council celebration at their grand palazzo crawled across the screen. The caption noted that they had just purchased the residence.

In April 1987, a short article lauded Dudley as an expert in international accounting. He'd won some kind of investment-advisor award shaped like the Rialto Bridge. The accompanying photograph showed him accepting the award onstage, with Alessandro in the first row.

"Seems he didn't quit finance as long ago as I'd thought," Anna said, changing reels and speeding through more footage.

"Hold on, I see Sergio's name," Margo said, as a Fanfarone byline from January 1986 came into focus. "Let me translate what he says. 'Exemplary of his art patronage, Count Sergio Corrin is hosting two artists at his sumptuous home for the entire year: Andrew McMullan, from Scotland, along with Azizi Sabodo from Tanzania. Oil painting and wood carving are their respective specialties. An exclusive, joint exhibition at Count Corrin's palazzo is scheduled for October.'"

Anna made a mental note to have Brian add the Tanzanian artist's name to the list she had given him.

"Count Alessandro Favier is back from a South African excursion with Count Sergio Corrin," an early 1985 snippet in the *Gazzettino* reported, showing Alessandro in a safari jacket.

"By the way," Margo added, "Alessandro answered a question about Sergio in Africa."

"And?"

"Last year, Sergio decided to make an investment in a mine," Margo said. "He had problems arranging the funds transfer long distance, which is sort of hilarious, since he owned a bank. Alessandro sent him the money, and Sergio paid him back when he returned to Venice."

Shows how much Dudley knows, Anna thought.

"Alessandro had made lots of investments with him over the years, either in art or in real estate, here and abroad," Margo said. "Sort of like the old trading organizations of ancient Venice."

Changing reels, they spotted a June 22, 1985, article on Sergio's contentious divorce in *La Repubblica*. "Jet-setting Count Corrin, ex-head of CONSOB, dumps wife for nubile student." The *Corriere della Sera* interviewed Arianna along with her two devastated daughters as they were leaving for the mountain air of Cortina. "I hate him," Constanza said. "He deserted us." Arianna added, "I just want to hide." Anna studied her face, trying to imagine it younger and in profile, without success.

"Look at Agatha." Margo had noticed a photograph of an

all-female rowing club in a September 1984, edition of the *Gaz-zettino*. The caption in Italian made them smile: "Ladies practicing for upcoming regatta. Agatha Filbert rowing since 1950."

"She must have been in great shape," Margo said. "Turned the male-dominated sport on its head."

In June 1983, the *Gazzettino* reported that Sergio had resigned from Banca Serenissima to "pursue other interests." Anna knew this was shorthand for anything and everything: being asked to leave, leaving of his own volition, a mutual decision.

The seventies chronicled Sergio's activities heading CONSOB and official actions the regulator took.

"Dullsville," Margo said.

Margo and Anna noticed a positive review in *Corriere della Sera* of a 1969 book written by Sergio: *Transparency and the Italian Stock Market*. Other articles, on Sergio attending society galas, heading up major art restorations, scouring the world for art investments, yielded little.

"Why don't you take the rest out of order?" Margo suggested. "It might spice things up."

When a big portrait of Pablo Morales flew by, Anna flinched. His black eyes had the same intensity she had seen at the party. She reversed the reel, overshooting the page, then undershooting it, before hitting it squarely. "Peruvian Consul in Venice Loses Medical License in Peru," the headline in a 1981 *Gazzettino* screamed.

The story was so long, it was illustrated with two other photographs. One was of Pablo with several native Peruvians in ponchos, the group symbolically pouring *chicha* beer onto the earth for the summer solstice celebration, the snow-capped peak of Salcantay, or "devil's mountain," behind them. Fanfarone's article took pains to point out the translation. The caption read, "Heathens Feeding Pachamama—Mother Earth." The second photo showed Pablo ministering to elderly, comatose patients, all Caucasian, with the caption, "Feeding them drugs."

Margo scanned the article, nibbling on her thumbnail. "Did you get it all?"

"Let's print it out, so I can study it later."

The Italian papers had covered Pablo's disgrace in depth. He had had to return to Peru for a long trial—a huge scandal in a country with an Indian majority and a white upper class in control. "Atahualpa's Revenge: Euthanasia," the *Gazzettino* quoted from *El Sol Cuzqueño*, a Peruvian newspaper.

Switching to other reels of the same vintage, Anna picked up the thread. "Condemnation by the Catholic Church," reported *Avvenire*. "Doctor Death Uses Morphine and Potassium," the *Corriere* proclaimed, along with "Morphine Stock Missing at Hospital in Cusco." One story quoted someone from Clínica San Cristobal: "They only die when he's on duty." Another had Pablo saying, "I was only trying to help." Though he was ultimately found innocent of the second-degree murder charges, he was stripped of his medical license.

"I can't believe it," Margo said.

"Could he have possibly done this? You know him. And how can he still prescribe medicine in Italy?"

"I don't know. I don't know where he got that angry scar on his jaw either. He definitely has a temper. You've heard him yelling at Yolanda in front of everybody. But murdering patients? I can't see it."

"The question for us is did he aim deadly anger at Sergio? Maybe it's just one step from murdering the healthy. I'm sure he can handle a knife well, after practicing for years with a scalpel. But why?"

Looking frantically for a follow-up article, the women finally found a 1985 society column in *La Repubblica*. There was Pablo, resplendent in white tie, toasting government ministers at Lima's Country Club Hotel. After years of self-imposed exile, first in the jungle at Manu, helping indigenous people, then at his llama farm in the Sacred Valley, funding summer camps for orphans, Pablo Morales was back. The article cited the change of government in Lima, Yolanda's family connections, and Pablo reentering favored political circles.

"Who knows if he was unjustly accused," Margo said, turning the page of her notebook. "I've seen plenty of people framed."

Anna mulled over what could have prompted the intense Italian newspaper coverage of one Peruvian man, halfway across the world. She leaned over and glanced at the words written in Margo's notebook. "And men go about to wonder at the heights of the mountains, and the mighty waves of the sea, and the wide sweep of the rivers, and the circuit of the ocean, and the revolution of the stars, but themselves they consider not."

"Oh, that," Margo said. "I read it a long time ago, when I studied here. St. Augustine."

16

Caffè Florian

Wednesday, early afternoon

Anna and Margo luxuriated in the open air. Flanked by columns of polished stone, their comfortable chairs were at the head of a phalanx of little tables leading into the heart of Piazza San Marco. Anna studied the rivers of tourists flowing from all corners of the earth. Swirling together, some tarried by the famed clock tower with its Moorish statues, awaiting the clanging of its bells; others lined up in crowd-control lanes in front of the basilica, while still others formed eddies, snapping photos of humans with pigeon companions. The sun's gentle rays burnished the quartet of bronze horses prancing atop the church's ornate balcony, mouths neighing, plaited manes billowing, hooves lifting. The equine prizes from Constantinople, along with porphyry figures of emperors, and the bones of St. Mark adorned the basilica—treasures of ancient cultures pirated to Venice in carved wooden ships returning from foreign wars and mercantile conquests, now delighting tourists instead of nobles.

Other visitors were wandering at a languid pace, exploring the blown glass and delicate lace stores framing the piazza, or, like Anna and Margo, treating themselves to the pricey but gracious service offered by the two historic caffès on opposite sides of the square. Sun-warmed pigeons patrolled Caffè Florian, hoping for pastry crumbs. A ghostly white pigeon, breaking rank with its brethren, approached Anna, its yellow beak open to reveal a gray, withered tongue. I don't have anything for you, she thought, relieved that the birds, unlike men, were authentic and acted without contrivance.

"Anything new come in from your office?" Margo asked.

"Not as much as I had hoped. I'm having them check on the guests at Dudley's party and everyone staying at the count's palazzo."

"What are you saying? Me and Angela, too?"

"I don't want to be accused of shielding anyone."

"Can't you take us off the list? It's an invasion of privacy."

"Sorry."

"They'll see all my overdrafts."

"Believe me, no one is interested in them. Were you able to speak with Kitty?"

"Yes. She only saw the waiter screaming as he exited the overlook area, but she stayed calm enough to wheedle the story out of him. Sergio's hand had been cut off, and there was a woman running from the body."

Anna tried to avoid picturing it. "Oh, God. Takes a person really hating him to do that. Did the waiter describe the woman?"

"Too dark."

Anna worried about sharp shards of truth and lies crashing together, cutting her.

The noon pealing of bells, with St. Mark's Campanile in the lead, suddenly erupted, drowning the buzz of tourists in the square, the music from church bells big and small enveloping the city.

"My bad hangover headache's coming back with all these bells." Margo rubbed her forehead. "Where the hell's Angela? I told her to come early. God, I need a cigarette; I forgot them at the palazzo. I'm going to order an appetizer for us to share."

Anna wondered where Margo packed the calories. "We're going to eat in an hour with Roberto."

"It'll be longer than that. I'd like to try a red wine from Alto Adige, recommended by a vintner I met at the party. But more to the point, the best hangover cure is more booze." She nodded to a hovering, white-jacketed waiter.

"*Desidera?*" the waiter asked.

"*Prendiamo una bottiglia di San Pellegrino, due bicchieri di vino Lagrein, un piatto di polenta con funghi porcini e formaggio, come lo fanno qui,*" Margo replied.

"And Liliana?"

"It was a short conversation. She slammed the door in my face once she finished calling you a string of nasty names, wrapping it up with *puttana.*"

"The poor woman. She knew my name?"

Margo nodded.

"You think she's broadcasting me as a slut to everyone in town now?"

"Nah. Maybe a few. Otherwise she'd be lowering her own standing."

"How did she find out?"

"I didn't have a chance to ask. One thing I did find out, though. She's keeping Sergio's gallery open. You'd think she'd sell it, or at least close it for a week."

"Guess she can't bear to part with the cash she'd lose by putting up a 'Death in the Family' sign," Anna said.

"Too bad Sergio's funeral won't take place for a while. We could've attended to see who might be acting strange, like in the movies."

Anna doubted that ever worked. "You see Pablo around the palazzo. Can you ask him when we could meet with him?"

"What should I tell him it's about?"

"His fascinating life. Or better, maybe I'm planning a trip to Peru."

"All right. Oh, look, here comes Angela, slow as a tortoise. She has such an orderly existence. Everything in its place."

Anna couldn't imagine that.

"We were starting to worry about you," Margo said to her cousin.

Angela's pale face shone in the sun. Dark circles framed her eyes. "Here you go, Margo." Settling into a yellow woven chair, she pulled a pack of cigarettes from her purse and placed it on the table.

"Well? Were you able to change your flight?" Margo asked.

"Nope." Angela glanced at her with a hint of anguish. "They're completely booked. I'm wore out and stuck here till late next week."

"Angela's homesick," Margo explained. "Don't worry, we'll enjoy the time here together. Anna, we're at the oldest caffè in Europe. This is where Wagner wrote some of his operas."

"He wrote another opera in the humongous Palazzo Rezzonico, where he died, I read," Anna said. "So many famous people have died in Venice."

When the waiter served Margo, Anna couldn't help sampling the delicate polenta, drenched in early-season porcini mushrooms and melted asiago cheese.

"And lived," Margo said. "With fifteen hundred years as a city, Venetians have a lot of history. More than California."

"It depends when you start counting," Anna said, thinking she sounded like Pablo.

"How was your walk back to your hotel last night, Anna?" Margo said after taking a sip of wine. "It must have been beautiful."

"Lovely and a bit windy until I got lost and someone started following me. I ran all the way back to the Accademia Bridge." Her gaze vacillated between the two women.

"Are you sure? Did you see who it was?" Margo sounded concerned.

"Too scared." Anna tasted her wine.

"You still look it," Angela said.

"Someone wanted to catch me, to harm me. I could tell."

"Venice is crammed with people," Margo said as the dulcet concert wound down. "And as I told you, all the dead-end alleys and canals make it so hard to escape, violent crime is rare here."

"Easy to say in the sunlight," Anna replied. "You weren't with me. When it's deserted, the city changes and seems . . . sinister. I don't buy that safe-as-a-church propaganda. The shadows had shadows. What about those murdered doges? And Sergio? Sometimes evil men—I mean, evil things happen here, too."

Margo put her fork down. "All you heard were footsteps," she said, as if she were explaining the law of gravity to Anna. "Those other people had histories here. You don't have any enemies. What would this person have wanted, your purse, your passport? Maybe you just drank too much wine at Dudley's."

Anna felt the sting of betrayal. She wasn't the one with a hangover. "That's a little rich, coming from you just now."

"What I'm dying to know," said Margo in a smoky voice, "is where Roberto dashed off to. He asked questions about you, Anna, and left the party just after you did."

"Maybe Roberto was following you, with lust in his heart, and those were his footsteps," Angela said playfully. "Better 'fess up."

"As a matter of fact, he did track me down—earlier," Anna said. "I ended up pushing him away."

Margo emitted a soft yelp. "I should have known." She lit a cigarette and took a puff.

"He's not my type," Anna said.

"Speakin' about Roberto," Angela said, "he's late."

"I'll call him," Margo said, and disappeared inside the caffè.

"She still throws a hissy fit about her old boyfriends," Angela said.

"Eighteen years later? Really, I have no interest in him. I'm still trying to escape from my husband. I came here to get away from it all, although my plan isn't working."

Angela slid the last bit of polenta into her mouth.

"You have so much to look forward to," Anna said. "You'll be seeing your family and your baby soon." Anna had missed the exquisite rotundity of pregnancy. Just a soft heaviness that ceased too soon and became a stabbing pain.

"Why, thanks. It can't come fast enough."

Margo bounced into her chair. "He'll be here in ten minutes. I caught him working."

"That'll give us time to hear more about Alessandro and his family," Anna said.

Margo looked blank.

"You promised me."

"Oh, all right." Margo shook her finger at them. "This can go no further. As you can imagine, Alessandro became terribly upset when he came back from Milan and found his home empty. So upset that he had a huge fight with Gaetano, who accidentally fell down the stairs."

"What did Gaetano have to do with it?" Anna asked.

"He let Gabriella walk out of the house. The man carried her bags! I can't blame Alessandro for being angry."

"Didn't the police suspect him?" Anna asked.

"Sure. He had a motive: revenge, jealousy. But he also had an alibi and witnesses in Milan, businesspeople who had met with him. Alessandro's not a cruel man. He gave his wife and daughter a huge funeral and buried them in the family crypt over on San Michele. That's how the story of the 'Gondola Murders,' as the police called them, ended."

"And San Michele is exactly where?" asked Anna.

"On the back side of Venice. It's the cemetery island," Angela said.

"For most people, their bones can rest there under a gravestone for a number of years, then have to be dug up and sent to another island," Margo said. "Burial space is impossible here."

"So creepy." Angela's voice squeaked.

"Angela, when you're dead, you're dead. Who cares?" Margo shrugged.

"Betrayal can turn you inside out," Anna said unexpectedly. "It can shatter you and change everything. All of a sudden, you realize that the world that you thought existed was only in your imagination." Her skin felt prickly. She remembered how Jack's model smirked if she happened to drop by his studio unannounced. And Sergio, how he threw back his head laughing with the young woman he had just kissed in Milan. Her voice grew loud. "Part of your goddamn identity, maybe the best, most loving and trusting part of you, just goes up in smoke. Leaving the rage, the hurt."

The women looked at her, wide-eyed.

"Anna's right," Angela said. "It's hard to tell what a person would do in the heat of the moment. Gabriella might have been laughin' at him. His anger could have exploded. And his witnesses—if business people are greedy enough, you can always pay them off."

"I heard Alessandro tried to put a spin on it," Margo said, "that Gabriella had hired the gondolier to take her and her daughter on an outing. I don't think many people bought it. At this point, of course, the tragedy is only a faint memory among a few Venetian aristocrats. Poor Alessandro. The proud Favier line stops with him. The plaster hands are all he has."

"More than anything," Angela said, "what surprises me is Gaetano stayin' with him all these years. Talk about abuse."

"Don't you see?" said Margo. "They are like two trees that have grown together so they don't fall over. Both are maimed."

17

A Forgotten Place

Wednesday, afternoon

"*Ciao, ragazze*," Roberto circled their table with feline grace.

Why didn't I leave before he got here? Anna wondered as Roberto kissed the cheek of each woman in turn. It would be easier not to see him, to be placid and untouched. But surely she could resist his allure by sticking close to Margo and Angela. When he came to Anna, he gazed into her eyes with fresh innocence, lips parted. She offered a frozen smile and pretended nothing had happened. She was good at that.

"*Avete finito?*" he asked them, his eyes lingering on Anna.

"Yes," said Margo, springing up.

"Well then, *andiamo*," Roberto told them. "It takes long to get to Torcello, and the fog might come later."

"I forgot to ask you, Anna, if you got my message about the weather?" Margo said.

"I put my shawl in my tote bag. I could hardly read the writing of that odd desk clerk. You know, the one who wears the crooked wig."

"Giuseppe never fails to make an attractive impression," Roberto said.

"Do you know *everyone* here?" Anna asked him.

"I told you. Venice is a small town." He glanced at their table. "Let me pay. *Ecco Mario, per Lei.*" Roberto's light blue eyes appeared amused as he nodded to the nearby waiter and handed him a hundred-thousand-lire note, with its image of the artist Caravaggio.

"*Molte grazie, Signor Cavallin.*"

"My boat is beyond La Fenice, so follow me." Roberto bounded across the piazza, then past a watery cul-de-sac of bobbing gondolas. A smell of the sea whirled around them, filling their lungs with distilled brine, as heady as the grape residue lining Nonno's wine barrels, Anna thought. As a child, she would descend to the cellar sometimes, just to sniff them.

Roberto veered left near the Alitalia office and led them through a tangled course. Anna rubbed the back of her neck. Twisted lanes, jutting balconies, the outline of Roberto's hips, elevated wooden walkways suspended over wet tumult, the bold blue and white stripes of his shirt, snatches of alleys, arched windows, the memory of kissing his lips, *rioterra* signs for streets reclaimed from the sea. They all became parts of a Byzantine puzzle.

At the end of a dank passageway, he opened an immense cream-colored metal door, revealing the Grand Canal like a monumental magic trick. But the palazzo and the water were real. *La Vittoria* was printed in large gold letters near the prow of a sleek black motorboat tied to one of the gaily painted poles dotting the canal. *Victory*, what a name, she thought, hardly surprising for an investment banker, a species not known for modesty. Anna climbed aboard after the other women, and joined them on the navy canvas bench cushions at the stern.

The motor purred as Roberto coaxed the boat from its slip. The harsh noonday sun exposed the caked and flaking faces of the nearby palazzos. Though their window eyes were blank, many were decorated with colorful, luxuriant drapes, like harlots' false eyelashes, seductively winking at passersby.

The paint had been peeling badly on Anna's home, too, and Jack had steadfastly refused to help repaint it. "You don't understand," he had said. "My hands are my livelihood, like a pianist's. I can't subject them to that kind of abuse. Can't you do it?"

And so she did, pulling the brush across the dry wood year after year, occasional birdsong her only companion. The corner of her yard held a feeder and birdbath. In late winter, the cedar waxwings perched in the juniper, making their high-pitched calls; in the spring, robins and mockingbirds took up the song; in the fall, the migrants, like the chirping white-crowned sparrows, flew in from the far north of Alaska, each just an ounce of feathers on wings, using the stars—Orion and other constellations, rising and setting in a celestial rhythm in the turning sky—for their nighttime migrations. Anna sensed the threads connecting the world.

"I hope no one minds," Roberto shouted to them as they overtook a lumbering vaporetto, "but I thought we would take a *piccolo* detour before we go to Torcello. It might be interesting for Anna Lucia to pass by Saint Geremia, where her namesake, Santa Lucia, is buried."

"Oh, fer Chrissakes," Margo blurted out.

"Please don't do anything on my account," Anna said.

"We just passed the Rialto Bridge," Margo said against the hum of the engine. "Did you know, Anna and Angela, that Michelangelo and Andrea Palladio entered a competition to design it? Instead, a man named Antonio da Ponte won. How could you go wrong with that last name—Bridge? I wonder if he changed it for the competition."

"Now, now, Margo. This is not Hollywood on the Adriatic, after all," Roberto said with a proprietary air. "Do not get cynical."

The Grand Canal was teeming with helter-skelter life. Boat wakes nudged *La Vittoria* as vaporettos, engorged with passengers like orcas with salmon, pulled away from their stops. Brave gondolas, some adorned with oriental carpets, darted in and out of the crushing traffic. "But the wonderful energy Venice had at that time eventually declined," Margo went on, ignoring him. "New ocean trade routes meant less commerce, and by the seventeen hundreds, the wealthy families were borrowing money from the convents."

"I can't imagine nun bankers," Anna said.

"That's the first thing that Napoleon stopped—"

"Do not speak to me about the French!" Roberto snorted, and he jerked the throttle back. The engine hiccupped and died as he glared at Margo. "He did nothing—nothing for Venice. Stole our art treasures, oversaw architectural disasters, wiped out the lion sculptures on our buildings, terrorized the citizens . . . before bankrupting us and selling us to the Austrians."

So much for European unification, Anna thought.

After a quiet minute, Margo said, "We're at the School of the Dead."

How fitting, Anna thought. No one seemed at all concerned that they were stalled and floating like a dead fish in front of the plaque for the Scuola dei Morti, with the sounds of claxons and boat motors besieging them. She imagined the next day's headlines: "Venetian Financier and Three Americans Killed in Fiery Boat Accident." To her astonishment, the other boats simply glided around them, as if following directions from an invisible choreographer.

"How the heck do the dead go to school?" Angela asked.

"This was a school for professional mourners at funerals, like a Greek chorus," Roberto explained. "Venetians believe in doing things correctly." He glanced at his watch. "We do not have time to stop, but you should return here, Anna. Lucia is in a lovely chapel, transported from the church demolished for the train station."

"If we could sneak into Palazzo Labia, nearby, you'd see some real treasures, like the Tiepolo frescoes. I can't believe Sergio inherited it," Margo added.

"Too much for his own good," Roberto said in a firm tone and restarted the engine.

Guiding the boat into a wide U-turn, he headed down the canal. "We will pass through Cannaregio now, near the Madonna dell'Orto Church, where Tintoretto is buried, then out to the lagoon and Torcello."

Margo approached Roberto, putting her hand on his shoulder. "We'd like to go out on the prow, like Angela and I did last time, if it's okay. Just don't go crazy with the speed."

"Not to worry. You know you can trust me." He idled the boat in the middle of Rio di San Marcuola.

"For some things," she winked.

"Remember, I can't swim," said Angela, squeezing Margo's hand as they gingerly made their way forward.

"Pregnant women float better," Margo said. "Anna, why don't you come with us?"

A gold locket dangled from Angela's neck, the filigree catching the sun's rays. *She probably has a picture of her husband in there, and a perfect spot for the baby,* Anna thought, seized by yearning for a home and family. *Would her turn never come?*

"Two forward is the limit," Roberto said. "Do not leave me all alone," he said to Anna as they got under way again. "How about sitting in the first mate's chair? The windshield will protect you from any gusts."

She hesitated before saying, "Oh, all right" and moving up beside him.

Outside the old ghetto, as they headed toward a graceful arched bridge, Margo pointed and raised her voice. "Look. Let's wave."

Dudley and Pablo were strolling near a streetlamp, Dudley looking almost chic in a plaid beret. Margo and Anna waved. Angela held up a limp wrist. Roberto saluted. The duo stopped and waved back before continuing along.

"I know so few people here, it's funny that we bump into two of them," Anna said.

"In Venice, everyone walks, or takes public boats," Roberto said. "They're not hidden in their cars. Our highway is as wide as a hallway. You see every little thing."

"How do you know Dudley?" Anna asked.

"Investments."

"They seem an odd couple, Dudley and Pablo."

"How you say, something about the *uccelli*, the birds? Ah, yes. Birds of a feather."

"I don't understand."

"Right now they are in serious discussions about the shape of the doge's cap, and Pablo is saying how it resembles the Inca emperor's." He laughed. "I am sure they and their culture council would like to bring back the past."

"That sounds pretty extreme."

"But very nice if you can be doge."

As they cut into a rio and Roberto edged the boat past the corners of water-worn palazzos, it seemed impossible to Anna that in such tight quarters he avoided striking the algae-cloaked walls. He steered in small and constant movements, sensing each curve and what lay beyond. This city holds few secrets for him, Anna realized. He could navigate it with his eyes closed.

Stretching out her hand as they were crawling along a tiny canal, Margo grabbed a cherry tomato from a produce boat. She held her bounty in the air, displaying her hunting prowess to Angela's applause, before popping it into her mouth.

"*Non toccare niente*, Margo," Roberto yelled. "You might hurt yourself. And you didn't pay." He reached into his pocket and tossed a five-hundred-lire coin onto the barge deck before continuing through the maze of canals.

"Over there," Roberto indicated a solitary pink house facing the open water, "they used to have great parties. It is a palazzo with a long history and a wonderful, secret garden. D'Annunzio and others visited. They say the Casino degli Spiriti was filled with ghosts."

"You don't believe that, do you, Roberto? I mean you work with math and projections and models. How do you prove a ghost?"

"I did not say that I believed. Yet I do not disbelieve, either. The funeral processions to San Michele sail right by almost every day. Back in the fifties, a prostitute was killed, cut into little pieces, put into a metal box, and sunk in the water near that palazzo. Years later, some boys hauled the box out, covered with crabs. They thought it a treasure chest and eagerly opened it."

The images flooded Anna's brain, and she covered her eyes with her hands.

"I see I upset you by that gruesome tale," Roberto said, touching her arm. "I am sorry."

They emerged into the sudden immensity of the lagoon, where the winds of the Laguna Morta blew in their faces. Stretching to the horizon, the water was olive silk. The reflections on its glimmering surface transformed the channel markers into coiling snakes, their mouths grasping the bottom of the lagoon. Anna pictured the antique Venetian maps she had seen in a store near San Fantin, the drawings in each corner of curly-headed gods with puffed cheeks personifying the four winds. Other ancient maps of varied provenance traced geographies of known worlds beyond Venice, eventually meeting the *terra incognita* of each age, where rationality gave way to imagination and terror.

Roberto shifted and brought the boat to a standstill, its engine barely puttering. He turned to Anna and said, "Come and let us see how you can steer, now that we have reached the other side."

She rose slowly, curious as to how the boat would perform for her.

Roberto peered at her foot. "Are you all right?"

"Only being careful. I almost fell on my walk last night."

"Sitting is best, then."

"I haven't done this since I was a kid, on my grandfather's lap on his sailboat. We're not on the Great South Bay, after all," Anna said, recalling the Long Island shoreline. But it came close, with grassy little islands in the distance, heads barely poking above the level of the tide. What a contrast to the bay near her California home, ringed by hills, wind-whipped, beset by currents, and, even in summer, its bone-chilling water unswimmable. She hadn't dared to sail there.

"If you need help, I'll take over, just like your Nonno would have done."

"You're already using my words against me." Anna gave him a shy smile. "As long as it's daytime, I'm okay. We can go in any direction, hopefully not into a sandbar. The sea, after all, is freedom topped by danger."

"Don't dawdle. We're getting hungry again up here," Margo shouted from the prow.

Anna moved closer, and Roberto placed her hands on the shining mahogany wheel. "Look at that *faro*, that lighthouse ahead, and always aim toward it. Make sure you stay in between the *bricole*, the wooden channel markers."

Anna could feel the warmth of his breath on her hair as he spoke.

"And this is to accelerate." He took her right hand and tapped the throttle. "Make yourself comfortable. I'll stand right behind your chair."

Anna settled into the upholstered seat. "Buckle up," she shouted as she threw the gears forward. The engine rumbled with low-pitched glee, and the boat slapped the frothy waves. Margo and Angela looked at each other, laughing. Wrapped in a cocoon of wind and noise, they clung to the ropes circling the bow.

Anna glanced over her shoulder. Venice was shrinking, as if it had been a mirage.

"Look." Roberto leaned against Anna and pointed to haze shrouding the thin line separating sea from sky. "That horizon reminds me of going fishing as a boy. My mother would pack me a frittata. I would row my boat to one of the *valli*, the fishing grounds, where I would cast my net. The sea was thick with sardines back then. I would put my hand into the water and their shimmering bodies would touch my fingers before gliding past."

He started to trace the widely cut armholes of Anna's sleeveless blouse, making circle after languorous circle until Anna lost count. "When I could wait no longer, I would haul in my net and it would be alive with silver." His hand audaciously wriggled its way inside her blouse. "*Madonna, sei squisita*," he said in an undertone as he explored her hidden cleavage with a delicate touch. "You forgive me for last night?" he asked, and nuzzled her neck.

His sonorous voice, his hands, his warmth, this dream.

Anna murmured, "*Sì.*"

"I would place the sardines in a barrel of water. By the late afternoon, the fog had crept in, isolating me in a white world, like a dream world, really, so confusing. I imagined tall ghost ships, their decks empty, their crews gone forever. Or floating icebergs—at ten, my imagination was very strong. I heard the thundering of ferries and large boats, all magnified in the mist. Were they bearing down on me or sailing by? I could not tell. Sometimes their wakes almost capsized my little boat."

He softly touched her shoulders.

"I never knew if the next moment would bring calamity or calm, danger or beauty. Then the fog would clear, and I would see the rural cabins with their tall fireplaces and thatched roofs, or the colorful island homes that we are passing now. I would always depend on the bricole to keep me from getting lost."

"Do you think you can slow it down?" Margo screamed,

hugging Angela, her hair flying. "We're getting drenched! What are you two doing back there, anyway?"

"Talking about . . . Roberto's . . . fishing exploits," Anna managed to shout over the roar of the engine as she cut back the power. She licked salt spray from the corner of her mouth before turning her head toward the bright buildings, not realizing how close Roberto's face was. Fearful of having no choice but to kiss him if they locked eyes, she averted her gaze and quickly resumed her steering.

"I can still return to those cabins and valli of my youth," Roberto said. "I know all the reeds. The sea breeze that rustles them is mine. But I cannot go back to when I saw everything for the first time."

In the rear-view mirror, she saw his luminous orbs veiled with aching. She didn't know why and didn't feel comfortable asking him. All she knew is that she had fallen for him, even though she had sworn she wouldn't do exactly that. Afraid of where this would end, she realized that she had made it infuriatingly easy for him.

Roberto took the controls. They threaded their way through the sandbar-strewn approach to Torcello, and into an overgrown canal where several swans were paddling. He docked the boat to one side of an arched brick bridge with no railings, and they disembarked onto a walkway.

"Torcello looks so lonely," remarked Anna. She glimpsed pillars collapsed in tall grass, a few buildings dotting the green landscape, a campanile in the distance. "It's nothing like I imagined, and hard to believe that a city was ever here."

"Once Torcello had more than fifty churches," Roberto said. "It was very beautiful. Like the rest of Venice, it rose from the sea, the swamp, and the mud. Those fishermen on the mainland who fled here came because of fear. Fear can make you do desperate things."

Anna considered what she had done, and not done, out of fear. Her successes in scientific, male-dominated fields took talent and gumption. But in the tally of her life, fear had won—the years of childhood worries stoked by Nonno's warnings, the years she'd stayed with Jack because she was too timid to leave—squeezing her into constricting circles, taking shallower breaths, until she was hardly moving at all, like the victim of an anaconda. The four days with Sergio in Milan had helped her break free: to feel again, to start divorce proceedings, to take this trip. She hoped the price would not be too high.

"What were they runnin' from?" Angela asked.

"The killings, the sackings, Attila the Hun, waves of invasions starting back in the five hundreds," Roberto said. "One night the Bishop of Altino saw a low-lying star over Torcello, and thought here they'd be safe from the barbarians, who had no concept of the tides and currents."

"Later on, people left," Margo said. "Torcello was passed by."

"Nature is reclaiming it." Roberto kicked a pebble as they walked along. "Whenever I'm in Venice, I come here to enjoy the silence or climb the bell tower and gaze at the magnificent Alps."

At a pleasant, lemon-colored stucco building with green shutters, Roberto held the door open, and they entered a country inn, with copper pots hanging near the hearth and photographs of luminaries on the walls.

"Locanda Cipriani is a historic place," he said, "but more recent. Your Hemingway stayed here and wrote a book. Churchill came here and painted. *Buongiorno*," he said to the hostess. "*Abbiamo una prenotazione per quattro*."

"*Benvenuti. Che piacere, Signor Cavallin*," she said and led them to an outside table near a grapevine-covered arbor.

Flowers flourished in one section of the garden and herbs in another, a neat geometry that pleased Anna. Two magpies flitted among verdant rows of fruit trees. Nearby, a tall bell tower with ancient arches cast a watchful eye in every direction. Like a silent sentinel, Anna thought.

Once they had ordered and their fragrant Amarone wine had been poured, Margo said, "Roberto, you know everybody. Any leads about Sergio? You've gotta tell us."

Amidst this peaceful scenery, it was hard to believe that Sergio was dead.

Roberto shrugged his shoulders. "Please. I do not work for the police. But, as they say in the mergers-and-acquisitions business, the field of candidates may be crowded."

"How'dya mean?" asked Angela.

"Sergio did not have to work, of course. Born with a platinum spoon in his mouth. Despite the lavish lifestyle, he could have spent centuries just clipping bond coupons. Liliana wanted him working if only to get him out of the palazzo. Always between her legs, she complained. But when he worked for Banca Serenissima as a rainmaker, he got too close to the clients. The bank got bad investments, and Sergio's savings accounts grew fatter."

"Kickbacks?" Anna asked.

"I cannot say for sure. Nine years ago, they parted ways. Then like lightning," Roberto waved his fingers, "he was advising Banca Patriota on a takeover of his old employer."

The name rang a faint bell. Anna would have Brian look it up on the FinCEN list and Banca Serenissima, too, if he hadn't already.

"Silly that they didn't have a non-compete clause," Anna said. "What did the Italian regulators say?"

"His old bank was troubled. They encouraged suitors. Sergio even asked me to write the fairness opinion, but I refused. Banca d'Italia did not approve the purchase anyway. Seems Banca Patriota had questionable people on its board."

"Like who?" Margo asked.

"You don't want to know," Roberto said, lifting his wine glass.

Taking delicate sips of the jammy, ruby-colored wine, Anna marveled at the web of Sergio's financial activity and how smoothly Roberto conveyed the information, all the while pressing his leg against hers.

When a plate of plump, crabmeat-filled mezzelune smothered in light cream sauce, with sun-dried tomatoes and a touch of shrimp, was set down before Anna, she took her time cutting into the pasta and savoring a luscious morsel. She felt like slathering the sauce on her skin. Margo and Angela ate gnocchi in sage butter. Roberto tasted his angel hair pasta in a fragrant fish stew before continuing.

"The latest was that five years ago, Sergio founded his own boutique investment bank, Banco Saturno, investing funds for the rich and famous. He even charged a fee for introducing people. Everyone knew him. On one side would be the entrepreneur needing funds; on the other, the equity investor or venture capitalist. He had the biggest moneyed partners in Venice and beyond—oh, yes, he was expanding, providing private banking services for ultra-wealthy Italians in new markets around the world."

Sounds more like the integration stage of money laundering, Anna thought.

"Sergio has an artist living in his palazzo, brought him over from Tanzania years ago, and gave him an entire wing. There were rumors about the artist and Liliana, but I don't believe them. First the artist painted portraits of Sergio and the family and some seascapes, just masterful. Then, as amusement, Sergio had him paint others on the sly, in scandalous poses. He would have these surprise unveilings at his monthly art society meetings. An adulterer with his mistress. A drunkard with a bottle. A politician being handed bags of lire. Sergio laughed at these paintings and so did everyone else, until it became their turn."

Angela looked dumbstruck. "Why would he go to all that trouble to have people hate him?"

"Why, indeed? The man was an enigma," Roberto shrugged.

There could be dozens of people who wanted Sergio dead, Anna thought glumly. "Are you speaking about Azizi Sabodo? Doesn't he specialize in wood carvings?"

"Where did you hear that?" Roberto asked.

"Read it in a newspaper article."

Roberto had superb connections. Even so, she wondered how he'd come across all these details, no matter how small he claimed Venice was. She could not help speculating about what he might have omitted on purpose.

By the time they finished eating, the fog had come in. They made a brief visit to the Cathedral of Santa Maria Assunta, with its awe-inspiring golden Byzantine mosaic of the Last Judgment, featuring a division of the saved and the damned—those condemned to death by dismemberment, hunger, or water, serpents wriggling through skulls and eye sockets. Anna lagged behind as she studied Fortune's opposite along one wall: the winged wheel of Occasion, the chance that can be seized.

While the others chattered onward to the boat, Anna slipped into the tiny Church of Santa Fosca, with its porch and stilted arches. Inside, the dark stone walls were devoid of decoration. She sat on a bench under the dome, eyes closed, immersed in the cool serenity of the thousand-year-old martyrion, her breathing slowed to a whisper. Exiles had built this place, but they had known where they had come from and where they were destined. She, on the other hand, a refugee from the modern world, possessed little certainty except numbers and the stars. What, she asked herself, could she take hold of?

She caught up with everyone near the bridge. "Roberto was just about to run back and find you," Margo said. "We thought you were lost."

"I was drawn to that little church," Anna said.

"It is lovely," Roberto said as they climbed aboard his boat.

Bound for the Grand Canal, he concentrated on his steering, following the line of bricole, the only solid forms in the shrouds of mist. The crimson orb of the sun wavered behind the haze as speedboats whizzed by like comets, taking shape out of nothingness and disappearing again. In the stern of *La Vittoria*, the three women huddled together, with Anna sharing her shawl.

When Roberto left them at San Silvestro, Anna was the last to depart. He said, "Meet me at nine-thirty at the campanile. Please come."

"I'll think about it." She dashed ahead.

"How about going with us to the caffè, on Giudecca?" Margo asked. "We're joining some friends there in a while."

"I think I'll roam around, maybe eat at Ai Gondolieri, recommended by my guidebook, and study a few things." Like Gabriella's diary, she thought eagerly.

"Come to the count's tomorrow then," Margo said as they parted ways.

Intent on not getting lost, Anna made her way to the Rialto Bridge and strolled through the jungle of T-shirts, sunglasses, and masks covering its haunches. As she reached the far side of the bridge, the warbling notes of a wooden flute accompanied by drum and guitar sailed in the air, reminding Anna of music she'd heard near Maiden Lane in San Francisco. A melodic voice soared like a condor flying in circles against the sky. She pictured the sun on its wings, its eyes surveying life far below, before swooping down for a prize and then returning to its nest, set like an altar in the cliffs.

The musicians' smooth hair glistened like dark, silent waterfalls. Their burnished faces were expressionless, their black, ancient eyes drawing in the light and hiding their dreams. How odd to see these musicians in Venice, so far from the Andes and their own people. For this was the opposite end of the world. Their vibrating tones were magnified by the city's hard stone walls. But then, as Pablo had said, his ancestors had been masters of stone.

Whether they sang of loves and lives lost, of planting crops and changing seasons, of the sun and stars, she did not know. These were songs that Pablo may have heard during childhood, inspiring him, perhaps, with tales of vanquished empires and warriors, or of revolutionaries bent on restoring the harmony of the old ways. She wondered if these musical troupes were a private army or a secret society.

18

St. Mark's

Wednesday, late afternoon

The sun was weakening behind the spire of San Luca Church as Anna joined the throng of tourists exploring the city. Each narrow bridge offered another view. Fading palazzos, with their sagging walls of rose and lime, were knit together in a rickety row. Some were reinforced with iron braces, rusty pins to keep their old bones from disintegrating. Near the waterline, fissured stucco gave way to naked brick, tired and worn, shrouded with snatches of seaweed like funeral wreaths. The oar of a gondola in the distance hit the water in a frenzy, making Anna think of the flapping wings of a drowning seabird, its feet caught in a net.

Pausing in front of a sign indicating Piazza San Marco, Anna chose to walk along Calle XXII Marzo. Sergio's gallery stood close to San Moisè, Agatha had said, Anna guessing that to be the white Baroque church in the distance. She walked slowly, scrutinizing the windows of the storefronts she passed. In one, swirls of colored glass resembled conch shells. Another held a parade of handmade goblets, their shining crystal sister to the sea, born of the same sands. A starry carafe, like the one Alessandro had smashed, stood alone in a spotlight. Anna doubted she could ever afford one.

The neighborhood's walls were plastered with a collage of

colorful announcements: a performance of *Il Bugiardo*, a Goldoni play; an evening of Vivaldi's concertos for viola d'amore; a request from the Cultural Council for funds to restore church doors; President Scalfaro's upcoming visit; Mayor Ugo Bergamo hosting a visiting artist, Fernando Botero.

A cerise sign hung from a striped wooden spear affixed to a nearby lintel announced Galleria Corrin—Arte e Antichità. Anna entered and was immediately greeted by a dark-haired salesman in a black suit. Two gold chains hung from his neck.

"*Buonasera. Voglio soltanto dare un'occhiata,*" she said, telling him she was just looking.

"*Certo,*" he replied.

She sauntered through a cluster of high-ceilinged rooms packed with African tribal art, unsure what she was seeking or what she would find. Stylized masks, pottery with a fusion of animal and human features, a bronze head with bulging eyes, decorated staffs, tapestries in bold colors, woven baskets, mosaics made of butterfly wings. . . . It was all incongruous in Venice, she couldn't help thinking.

Selected totems and sculptures represented religious beliefs, prestige, graduation into male society, or a celebration of female fertility, through depictions of large-breasted women. Anna was taken with a carved staff showing a young girl carried on the back of a woman, initiating her into adulthood. Menacing war masks decorated with animal teeth, a few adorned with cowrie shells, covered an entire wall. Neck bands of dazzling glass beads were displayed in glass cases, along with ornate combs. A sculpture of a woman's head with gold around the orbital bones, her hair a rope headdress, sat on a table. Draped over an arched doorway was a colorful textile of parrots, crabs, lions, elephants, and crocodiles, reflecting the riches of the continent—a veritable Garden of Eden, from which all life had sprung.

Several pieces were centuries old. A petite card accompanied each work, the fine print providing the date, the country or area, and the tribe. Work by the Maasai, the Yao, the Makonde, the Kwere, and the Luguru peoples of Tanzania predominated.

One of the back rooms highlighted an array of spears, gold knives with sheaths, and bold paintings and wooden shields by none other than Azizi Sabodo. In a corner was a small black-and-white photo of Sergio in a pith helmet and carrying an elephant gun, accompanied by a dark-skinned tribesman and a large blond man with a beard. So this is how he'd spent his time after buying tribal art, she thought.

In the farthest chamber reposed a hulking diorama, reminding Anna of those she'd seen on elementary school trips to the American Museum of Natural History. Animals in the foreground, painted landscape and sky behind, the display imitated the three dimensions and fooled the eye. Against the milky blue sky and golden savanna of Africa, a quartet of stuffed, preserved animals was gathered behind the glass: a bushbuck, an impala, a hyena, and a baby elephant. Their fur or skin, their stances, even their marble eyes looked alive. The little elephant's trunk extended out, as if he were trumpeting a warning. What were his last thoughts, his last visions? Anna asked herself. Had his mother been gunned down in front of him before it became the orphan's turn?

Rushing for the door, Anna fled into the fresh air.

Try as she might, she couldn't process it. Was Sergio's fascination with art authentic or was it connected to his money laundering? Given his activities in Venice through the years, it could be the former. She pondered the possibilities as she shuffled along the street, which narrowed before flowing into a large piazza, disorienting her. At the far end, the basilica of St. Mark's sprawled in all of its opulence, as it had for ten centuries. She counted five lead domes piercing the indigo sky.

Weaving past clumps of pigeons and people in the famed square, she entered an enclave of birds. Tourists from every country would feed the feathered creatures, laugh uproariously, and take pictures of others, even toddlers, covered with birds. With a whoosh, the flock of pigeons took flight around Anna, and the sky became a blur of gray feathers. She closed her eyes and caught her breath, waiting to feel a beak scraping her skin or scratching her eyes. This only heightened the sound of their vibrating wings. The air rushed against her face as the birds strained upwards, like souls rising to heaven.

St. Mark's seemed to shift in a searing light. Anna sensed she was floating in the sea, surrounded by votive candles, then flying through a dark galaxy with one pulsating red supernova. The next thing she felt was a soft breeze. When she opened her eyes, she saw a red bridge with blue umbrellas moving across it—a silken fan wielded by a frowning Japanese woman shouting to her family, all circled around Anna, their faces pressing close.

"You okay?" the woman asked, peering down at Anna struggling to a sitting position.

"I . . . I think so." She had managed not to hit her head as she fell. Her pant leg was smudged, but her knee seemed all right.

"Drink water," the woman said, offering a new bottle as the husband helped Anna rise.

"Thank you, I'm fine now."

"Then we go," the woman said, and the family scurried across the piazza, probably to catch up with their tour group.

Anna leaned against a pillar and felt for bruises, then took tentative steps to the cool edge of St. Mark's Basin, sipping the water. Beyond the Doge's Palace, toward Ponte della Paglia, a figure resembling Biondi shook his finger at a man wearing a long jacket. She spun around and strode away as fast as she could, past the gardens, fearing that at any moment she would hear his voice calling after her, "Signora Lottol. Please wait."

She gazed across the peaceful lagoon, drawn, as if by a magnet, in the direction of the Belvedere Hotel. Jutting above the shoreline, its bleached silhouette looked innocent and peaceful. How deceptive, Anna thought. On the far side of the Grand Canal, a statue of Fortune towered over a massive golden globe above the Punta della Dogana. As the wind shifted, Fortune turned her back.

A Disjointed Message

19

Wednesday, night

When she exited Pensione Stella, a figure huddled in the shadows of a clothing store raised a cigarette to an invisible mouth before flicking a fiery ash and starting over. Feeling unseen eyes boring into her, she was relieved to turn the corner. The evening had turned cool, and her light cotton sweater was no match for the chilly temperature. Although she hadn't been able to examine Gabriella's diary with the rigor she would have liked, she was afraid that Alessandro would miss it; in fact, Margo had left a note asking for her to come to the palazzo tonight. At the last minute, she stuck the ledger book in her pocket and brought it with her, just in case.

Hugging the diary, she decided to follow a shorter route to Palazzo Favier, crossing two low-slung bridges before entering a *piazzetta*. Animated voices and announcements on TV game shows from residences overlooking the little square peppered the air. She passed a vacant restaurant with pink tablecloths, closed for the evening.

Anna had been lucky to catch Brian at his desk an hour earlier. She was able to ask him to check the FinCEN and OFAC lists on Sergio's old employers, to run her algorithms on a wider set of accounts, and to perform a few other tests she specified, including one on Azizi Sabodo—all before Leslie found out. After giving him a sense of her desperate situation, Anna insisted that if anyone asked, Brian should say that she told him to perform the work as part of a special project approved by higher-ups. *She* should take the fall for her own mistakes, not him.

A sign for a sotoportego loomed above an arch in the distance. Anna recalled that it led to a walk hugging a narrow canal. When she slipped into the short tunnel, where a few handcarts and boxes were stored, the sound of waves reverberated against the cement walls. The wind was picking up.

Descending the narrow path on the tunnel's far side, she paused at the water's edge and meditated on a slice of the Grand Canal, framed between dazzling palazzos, where boats passed, running lights streaming, motors humming, zooming along mysterious trails in the dark. Advancing to a bulb of pavement jutting into the canal, she looked up and saw Deneb twinkling next to a distant campanile, its light journeying more than a thousand years to reach her. As a little girl, she had gazed at the stars from a hillock by her home, often to a chorus of frogs. She had traced her last name in the big night sky, followed the tail of the Little Bear, the handle of the Little Dipper. Back then, she had thought that one day she might reach out far enough to touch Orion's bejeweled belt and all the stars and nebulae in that constellation. One star was a ruby. Another a diamond. The third a sapphire. Now she saw those distant suns as constants. Constants of normalcy. Of reassuring cool rationality. Symbols of man's triumph in unlocking nature's secrets. Those heavenly bodies obeyed scientific principles that she had studied. Their faithful movements were measured by formulas she had derived, never veering off course. No matter how upset Anna ever became, she could close her eyes and see those stars, etched against the darkness. They were a reminder. And an escape. Parents that had never returned. Grandparents gone. A broken marriage. But the stars, they were always the same.

The clatter of metal wheels shattered her reverie. The sound seemed far away and out of place. At first, she thought she was imagining the high-pitched, grating notes. A tarp-covered pushcart with wooden boxes piled high was bouncing and rolling toward her, just ten feet away now. There wasn't enough room on the pavement for both of them.

She cried out, "*Aspetta, ferma!*"

No response.

Was someone pushing the cart or had it somehow gotten loose from the bunch in the tunnel? At that moment, it didn't matter. She tossed Gabriella's diary against a brick wall and dove into the dark canal, the cart and all of its boxes tumbling in behind her. She sensed a shout from above, a gurgling "Go home," as she sank underwater.

Anna opened her eyes, but even the wavering light from the streetlamps failed to penetrate the blackness. She froze, suspended, forgetting how to swim, the shock immobilizing her, evoking a dim feeling. Her muscles grew slack and retracted from the cold as a jumble of memories crowded her brain: the vibrations of pounding surf at Fire Island, her ear against a striped beach blanket; high school graduation; Nonno walking her down the aisle; her honeymoon at the Grand Canyon; a man yelling, "It's too late now." She was nearly letting go, her brain beginning to slip into a dreamlike state.

Someone she knew was her mother, dancing in a white robe, hair flying, motioned to her as she drifted by.

No. She did not want to join her and the others. Not yet.

Straining to calculate, to jump-start her brain, she estimated how far down she had sunk. Fifteen feet? Assuming she'd surface with a thrust of her legs, Anna forcefully pressed them together and pushed up. Her head plowed into a box, which stunned her, and the waterlogged tarp closed in, one rope like a tentacle tightening around her ankle. She flailed before rising again, but a sharp tug held her back. She realized she was tethered; soon she'd be out of breath and time, drowned like a sea turtle entangled in plastic. This life-giving sea would be her grave.

Ordinarily, the simple act of inhaling never entered her consciousness. Now it was all she could think about. She guessed she'd been underwater for forty seconds. Hoping she had a chance for one last move, she dove deeper and followed the rope along muck-covered rocks, finally reaching the cart, on its back at the bottom of the canal. She pushed and prodded the nylon knot to release the rope's stranglehold on the metal handle, but the cart's runaway journey and crash must have tightened the knot beyond loosening. The end of the handle, however, felt unhindered. She yanked at the knot, trying to slide it off. After a final tug, the rope came free.

With her last ounce of energy, Anna scissor-kicked her way up and popped her head out of the water. She gasped for air, heaving from the effort, her heart pounding. A final surge of strength propelled her to the canal's steep wall, its top looming three feet above her head. Reaching as high as she could, her cold hands barely grasped the pavement's edge. She tried to pull herself onto the walkway, but her feet got no purchase and her arms were too spent. To her left, the canal disappeared around a bend, showing no means of escape.

To her right, a cleft was visible ten yards distant. Worth a try. She crept along until she found a stairway cut into the stone. Hauling herself out of the water, she slumped on the steps, shivering. Slippery tendrils of seaweed clung to her neck. As she bent to unwind the rope on her ankle, she inhaled a pungent odor and realized she was coated with a fishy slime.

As soon as she regained her breath, she tottered back to where she thought she had tossed the diary, searching in the shadows for its soft cover. Sopping wet and cold, she hobbled back and forth around the spot, like a dog circling a buried bone. Finally, sinking to her knees, she crawled on the pavement, feeling around for the precious volume. Damn. Someone had taken it.

Suddenly, she spotted a figure wrapped in a shawl, silently approaching her. Was it someone to fear or someone she could ask for help? Seeing Anna kneeling, a gray-haired woman made the sign of the cross and uttered a quick "*Madonna mia*" before shuffling away.

Anna rose, dejected, and staggered in the opposite direction, her soggy pants chafing her thighs. Once she dragged herself past a clump of moored boats, she recognized a bridge and forced her numb legs forward to the illuminated star of her pensione. The thought of getting warm and dry sustained her.

"*Carina, cosa è successo?*" Giuseppe, the clerk, asked as Anna stood trembling, rubbing her arms, creating a puddle in front of his desk.

She managed to tell him that she had lost her footing and had fallen into a canal.

With mouth agape, he handed her a bath towel and promised to deliver some hot soup to her room. "*Mi sono quasi dimenticato,*" he added. He had almost forgotten, a lady had come in earlier to see her.

Anna just nodded, too shaky to ply him with questions.

The first thing she saw on entering her room was her raincoat, sprawled across the bed. Since she hadn't left it there, who had? But a more immediate question was: Could the pushcart really have jostled free by itself? She was chilled by the thought that while no one in the world loved her anymore, someone hated her enough to attack her.

She limped down the hall for what she hoped would be a hot shower, cursing herself for not having scoured the diary—one of the few things available to her—for clues. Now Gabriella's voice and secrets had vanished, along with another chunk of Alessandro Favier's life—all due to her.

When she heard the campanile tolling midnight, she realized she'd never had a chance to consider meeting Roberto. He must have come to the conclusion that she wasn't interested, which was probably just as well. For some reason, she thought of a poem she loved. Her eyes misting, she recited its verses before drifting to sleep:

My footsteps leave no tracks
My journey leaves no trace
Like a comet without a tail
As my mind plays among the stars
And my body begins to lose its grace

Just another reminder
That the physical passes
But does the spiritual live on?

Or are we trapped forever
Beneath the stony masses
Our consciousness long gone?

20

Searching

Thursday, morning

After breakfast, Anna spoke to Giuseppe, who failed to give a helpful description of the woman who had come in asking for her: English-speaking, reddish-haired, of middle height. That narrowed it down to several thousand women in Venice, Anna thought, sighing. Most of the time, Giuseppe's nose was in a book; yet it was hard to believe his powers of observation or his memory were that faulty.

What about the note? He hadn't seen the person. Had he let anyone in her room, she wanted to know, telling him her raincoat had been moved. Impossible, he replied—well, the new maid, from Tanzania, was still learning the job and might have left the room unlocked. Anna gulped, hoping there was no connection to the artist living in Sergio's palazzo. Then she worried that she was becoming paranoid.

With daylight, there was a small chance she could find Gabriella's diary. She pictured it behind a garbage can or farther down the walkway. Her panicked toss could have been more forceful than she remembered. Wending her way through the warren of alleys, she emerged into the now-lively piazzetta. She scoured the tunnel. Vacant of carts, it seemed much bigger, and she inspected every square inch of pavement.

Along the canal, two men in blue overalls unloaded tomatoes from a barge. "*Basta, Franco,*" the older one said to a younger, dark-bearded man, stacking the last box on a metal cart. Several empty wooden boxes stamped "Ortolano, Bartolomeo e Figli," a local vegetable vendor, lay by the water. Anna looked under each one. She squinted at the barren perimeter of the canal, willing the diary to magically materialize.

The men stopped their work and gawked at her. She asked them if they had found a small diary.

The senior one said no, but they had found their tarp in the water, wrapped around a docking pole. Raising his voice, he accused her of stealing one of their carts to carry her luggage.

Taken aback, Anna replied, "No. *Ma il loro carretto è in fondo al canale,*" telling them their cart was at the bottom of the canal.

"*Disgraziata,*" the older man shouted—"Disgraceful!"

In a wobbly voice, she told them about the cart rolling toward her, ending with her almost drowning in the canal.

"*Poverina,*" said the younger one sympathetically, looking at his colleague. But they always secured their carts with care, he told her, using a sailor's knot to tie the row together. One could never roll away on its own. If someone really had aimed a heavy cart at her, she was lucky to be alive.

Staring blankly at the men, Anna struggled to not give in to fear. She had to forge ahead; otherwise, she'd collapse right on the sidewalk. She looked out at the boat traffic before inquiring if they had seen anyone loitering in the area last night, someone who didn't seem to belong, even a woman.

They only worked mornings, they said.

She asked them to please contact her, Anna, at Pensione Stella, if they heard anything at all about a suspicious person or a diary.

"*Volentieri,*" the young man said—"Willingly."

She thanked them and walked away, chagrined. She alone was

responsible for taking the diary out of the palazzo. Yes, Margo had suggested it, but she was the one to do it, and she had been the one to lose it. It was almost as if Gabriella had been murdered again, gone silent, this time, at Anna's hands.

She'd call Margo later, but for now she wanted to be alone. Her melancholy might ebb in the sunlight, among a tide of unknown faces in a sea of anonymous streets, far from the palazzo or the pensione.

She counted the steps while climbing the Rialto Bridge. *Uno, due, tre.* Turning left at the tiny church of San Giacometto, into which locals had once chased hunchbacks, Anna found herself in a bright, bustling lane. The fragrance of freshly baked bread and sweets evoked her childhood kitchen. Besides making pasta, Nonna had loved to bake. Anna traced the scent to a *panificio* with an array of glistening golden cakes in the window. Entranced, she stood by the door and inhaled. It reminded her of tasting the desserts on Nonna's overflowing table: *crespelli, biscotti, budini, dolci alle pesche.* In later years, as if seeking payment, Nonna would ask, "And when are you getting married?" Once Anna married Jack, it became "When are you having children?"

She saw him then, his back to her, as he made a purchase. She recognized his proud stance and cap of yellow, slicked-back hair, still wet perhaps from a morning shower. She hesitated. He'd spot her in another second. If she stayed, perhaps they'd end up in his boat or his bed, and she'd find some solace.

When Roberto turned, his eyes alighted on her, and he strode over. "Anna. I was standing there at the campanile last night, waiting for you. What happened?"

She started telling him about the cart bearing down on her, about diving into the canal. Stopping partway, she came close to sobbing. He reached out to still her quivering mouth. "Let me make you some caffè, and we talk. My place is near here." He shook the sack he was carrying. "This is my favorite bakery. Funny you found it."

He led her through a lane so narrow, the roofs of opposing buildings almost touched. They passed shop windows with a rainbow-colored stream of merchandise: Turkish lanterns, brass lions, marbled paper, colorful glass beads, painted-velvet pillows, antique jewelry, blue chandeliers, drinking cups supported by bases of red devils with erect penises. It was like being drawn ever deeper into a souk.

Even this could not distract Anna from mulling over her fruitless efforts at finding leads to Sergio's killer. Instead, she had become a target. Perhaps in Roberto's lair, she could forget it all for a while. When she had felt unhappy as a child, she had run outside to her swing and pedaled high up toward the sky, where her cares evaporated into a giddy dizziness. Maybe she could find that bit of peace again. Or maybe this was foolish. She didn't really know him or have any idea what complications he could add to her already disordered life.

By the time they reached a leather store facing a campo, charcoal clouds had suddenly erased the sun. Heavy drops were splattering them, forming rivulets down her curls and tracing hieroglyphics on her lavender silk blouse. "It was sunny five minutes ago only," Roberto said. "This *tempesta* has come from nowhere."

A sudden gust deluged Anna's face. "How much farther do we have to go?"

"Not far." They raced through the alleys, his arm around her. Soon the silk no longer skimmed her flesh but formed a taut and glistening new skin. Only the area underneath Roberto's arm felt dry.

"We're getting soaked!"

"*Mi dispiace, carina.* If I had a jacket, I would wrap you in it. But God does not listen to me—at least not about the weather." He chuckled. When he pulled at the now-transparent white shirt stuck to his chest, Anna glimpsed the tanned skin underneath. "You know what they say about the rain, no?"

Anna squinted at him, anticipating a trick question.

"They say it means . . ." He met her surprised lips with a slow kiss, before whispering, "Fertility."

Anna marveled at that perfectly strange, Old World concept.

They passed through a marble archway, and Roberto opened a metal gate, sculpted with the number eleven, into a verdant garden. The rain released the fragrance of jasmine, its sweet bouquet married to the musky earth. The shrubbery bowed with the wind, quivering like sea kelp. At the end of a curved mosaic path sat a cottage framed by pomegranate trees.

"Is this your home?" Anna admired the pleasant lemon shutters and quaint balcony.

"A little retreat. Sometimes I work here. There is even a canal in back for *La Vittoria*."

His face tensed as he dropped the bakery bag into the arms of a stone nymph and turned toward her. She sensed what was coming. He caressed her hair, and they embraced, his warmth combining with hers in a pagan baptism. When he licked the corners of her lips, it felt as if the world had shrunk and ended just beyond his shoulders.

Pulling away with a sudden movement, he said, "You will get sick out here." He grabbed her hand, and they bolted inside. "I'll make coffee. A robe is behind the bathroom door. You might want to put it on while your clothes dry."

Anna wandered down the olive green hallway, lined with Carnival masks. Passing a library in a nook with two easy chairs, she peeked at the titles. *The Republic*, by Plato. *Physics*, by Aristotle. A collection of classical philosophy next to a textbook, *The Theory of Finance*. Heavy tomes for a retreat, she thought.

She peeled off her sodden clothing in the mosaic-tiled bath and looked at herself in the mirror. Why should she trust this man and not believe the obvious: that he was a brainy lady killer, luring another victim into his love nest, just as Dudley had warned? How much was she willing to risk? She hungered, however, for just one fucking moment of euphoria.

She put on his terrycloth bathrobe, wrapped a towel around her head, turban style, and joined Roberto, who had changed into a dry T-shirt and jeans. In the tiny, aroma-filled kitchen, they sat at a wooden table, drinking espresso from etched-glass cups and devouring ricotta-filled puffs.

"Tell me," his tone grew serious. "Can you talk more about it?"

"About?"

"The attack on you."

She drew a deep breath before describing where she had walked, what she thought she had heard, the runaway cart, and her struggle in the cold, dark canal to save herself. Everything except the diary.

"This is frightening." He reached over and held her hand. "I know exactly where that vegetable barge docks. You reported this to the police, to Detective . . . Biondi, isn't it?"

Anna shook her head. "He'll think I'm lying."

Roberto looked pensive. "What has Margo said about this? Has she not called you when you did not arrive?"

"Not a word," Anna said. "I've been wondering. After we talked at the Dogana Tuesday night, you didn't follow me, did you?"

"I can only take two rejections a day from you. I was already at my limit." He gave her a wry smile.

She melted, almost apologizing before catching herself. "Someone chased me. I was terrified." She put her head in her hands. "I don't understand why this is happening."

"One thing I do know is that you are safe here, with me. What do you go back to?"

"Not much. A job, a divorce."

"No family?"

Anna shook her head. "And you, is there anybody in your life?" She glanced into his eyes before staring at the brick floor, steeling herself for the inevitable news that he was unavailable, untouchable.

"Brothers, sisters, many members in my family, many friends. And a career that I love. You could say it has possessed me."

An Italian workaholic, Anna thought. Approach with caution. "Are you working today?" she said, raising one eyebrow, knowing it was past ten.

He let out a laugh. "I have flexible hours."

She gazed at his biceps, distracted.

"Come, I want to show you something."

When they ventured into the bedroom, a wispy filament of light glowed from a silken floor lamp, while the bed lay in penumbra. A loft arched over the far wall. Anna stared at the huge skylight above it, framing a patch of blue. The sun had come out.

"Sometimes I lie up there on my back and look at the sky," Roberto told her. "The clouds floating, coming together to form fantastic shapes before they pull away from each other, sometimes white, gray, pink, the light always changing. You can feel time passing, the earth spinning, as you watch."

"We forget to lift up our eyes." Anna felt as if they were binary stars orbiting one another, locked in mutual gravitation.

"You may hear stories about me, Anna. Not all of them are true."

"How will I know which ones to believe?"

"When you listen with your heart."

Anna was drawn to a painting of a red-haired young woman staring out to a slate blue sea, her velvet shawl grazing a shy, pink nipple. In the distance, tumultuous waves curled and broke along a curving shore. She wasn't surprised to see Andrew McMullan's signature.

She pivoted away and soon felt Roberto nuzzling her neck and earlobes from behind. When he unwrapped her turban, her hair now falling around her shoulders, she leaned back to kiss him. Then she turned, confronting his bold nakedness. The broadness of his shoulders and chest gave way to a flat, thatched abdomen. Moaning, she clutched him, her robe opening.

He guided her forefinger onto his lips before licking and sucking it. Closing her eyes, she tenderly touched his broad forehead, his brows and cheekbones, his strong chin and neck, his vulnerable Adam's apple. His mouth traveled from her throat, to the concentric circle of her nipple, along the soft slope of her breast to the chalice of her waist.

"*Vuoi stare con me?*" he asked, looking up at her, his eyes glistening.

Yes, I want to be with you, she thought. A hope vibrated within her, about setting sail and never returning. He grabbed her by the arc of her hips, drawing her closer to the bed. She glanced over his shoulder at a bronze duvet with a seashell pattern, and an unwelcome memory arose, of the bed in that Milan hotel, all the lacy pillows. What if another woman lies here tonight?

"I'm sorry, I can't," Anna said, pulling away. "It's too much right now."

The light drained from his face, taking the life with it, making him seem as if he had turned into a frescoed figure blankly staring out from a forgotten wall.

Racing to the bathroom to retrieve her clothes, she yanked open a wooden door in the hallway instead. It was empty except for the video camera perched on a stand, its lens aligned perfectly with a hole in the wood.

"What is this, Roberto?" Her voice shook. "You, too? Is this your own twisted hobby or do you think I'm for sale?" Damn fool that I am, she thought, slamming the door shut.

She threw on her clothes and ran out of the cottage, as a faint voice called, "No, no. Stop. I can explain."

Dashing through the garden, she closed the gate. When she reached the tiny square, she heard the sound of wooden flutes. A breeze tossed the musicians' long black hair. A bright green feather lay on the locks of a flutist. As a conch shell sounded, the plume floated onto the wet ground, to be trampled underfoot.

21

Dr. Zampone

Thursday, noon

Opening her heart, yet again, she had fallen for another Italian user. Was it luck or did she put out some sort of magnetic field that attracted such men?

Trudging through unfamiliar streets, the lyrics of Springsteen's "Human Touch" rumbled through her head as she sought distance from Roberto. She wondered who would betray her next. Who was friend? Who was foe? She had no faith she could distinguish between them anymore. Fearful of what people were hiding behind their smiles, she quickened her pace. Strangers looked placid and unthreatening, she told herself—yeah, like the water's calm surface before a riptide pulls you out and under.

Even if Margo was everything she seemed, Anna's story about Roberto would unleash an eruption. Was there no one trustworthy she could confide in? Angling south, she remembered the address of the psychiatrist her therapist had recommended and searched for Dorsoduro 175 in a tangled nest of numbers. Maybe Dr. Claudio Zampone could help, or at least, listen. Near the Guggenheim, she spotted a tangerine stucco building. Curtains were open, and a curly-haired man sat at a desk, writing.

The doctor greeted her warmly, his navy eyes holding a spark of sincerity. About her age, rangy, with an angular face, he wore a black jacket and gray pleated pants. He had the rest of the afternoon free and was pleased to accommodate her. Dr. Levine, back in the United States, had prepped him in case Anna got in touch.

He led her into an expansive room with floor-to-ceiling bookcases along one long wall and an antique Venetian mirror with tiny black flecks, like age spots, on another. Large windows infused the space with light from the Grand Canal, making Anna, in her damp clothes, eager to soak up the warmth.

"Dr. Levine told me you are working through the pain of your divorce," he said, giving her his card and escorting her to a damask couch. "That is good. You cannot grow if you try to escape by popping happy pills."

He took a seat in a leather chair opposite and peered at her. A writing tablet lay on his lap like a small, obedient dog. "What brought you here today?"

"Frankly, Doctor, I'm at the end of my rope," she said. Her eyes moistened, and she struggled not to grab a tissue peeking from a gilded box. "I can't figure things out anymore." In rapid fire, she told him about an older man she had met in Milan who betrayed and threatened her, along with another here in Venice. She relayed a string of frightening experiences: people denying what she had heard, being chased, almost drowning.

Through it all, Dr. Zampone listened intently, scribbling notes and nodding his head so hard, his dark hair shook.

"Well." He coughed. "You were right to come. You have been through a lot. But please, tell me a little about yourself."

As succinctly as she could, Anna told him about the early deaths of her parents, being raised by her grandparents, the kind of work she did, and her unhappy, barren marriage. "But that's not why I came here."

"I understand. Let us discuss the two men first. Do you think they planned to trap you?"

"Definitely the first one. He had seduced me in order to blackmail me."

"How?"

"I'd rather not say. It was connected to work."

"And the second?"

"With his video camera. Roberto was picking up where the first one left off."

"What do you mean?"

"The older one took embarrassing photos of me. I didn't know it at the time. The second one videotaped me."

"Why do you think they did these things?"

"To force me to cooperate with them, so they could pursue their illegal activities."

"Which are?"

"I don't know all the details, but the first man was a money launderer."

"I see." He made a note. "And do you think this is related to the footsteps you heard following you and later to the rolling cart? Or was that someone else?"

"It doesn't make sense that it'd be them. It was another person. At least one."

"So we have three, maybe four people out to get you. Two for blackmail or coercing you in some way, the rest to scare or . . . eliminate you."

"That's right."

"Did anyone witness the, as you say, attack with the cart?"

"I don't think so. An elderly lady passed me after I climbed out of the canal, but I don't know who she is or what she may have seen. I was in the water for a while."

"So no one was there in the moments when you dove into the canal?"

"No one besides my attacker."

"Who pushed the cart?"

"It couldn't have raced toward me on its own. The carts were tied together. Also, I tossed aside a diary I was carrying, and when I got out of the water, it was gone. Someone took it."

"And did you actually see someone chasing you after the party?"

"I saw shadows on the wall and heard footsteps. They sped up when I did."

He pulled his glasses down and peeked over the rims.

"Have you ever had similar experiences back home?"

"Absolutely not." She looked at him, drawing her brows together. "I'm not making this up."

"I believe you believe it. I keep an open mind." He crossed his legs. "Tell me about what you saw or heard that other people contradicted. If I understand correctly, there was a baby crying and someone singing opera after midnight?"

"Yes."

"How rare do you think this is in the city of Venice?"

"Not very," she said, hunching her shoulders.

"Then why were you disturbed by it?"

"First, because I had seen a light in that palazzo, and a teddy bear, even though Count Favier says no one lives there. When I told the desk clerk about the singing, which I had thought came from the same palazzo, he said I was wrong and that it was a quiet neighborhood."

"So you allow a desk clerk to throw you off balance?"

"He seemed part of a pattern."

"Do not be discouraged. We can work through this."

Anna wondered what he was talking about.

"Are you afraid to leave your hotel room?"

Anna groaned. "Not at all, though I'm no longer going any-where off the beaten tourist track at night. At this point, it would be tempting fate."

"I can understand. But your fate, Signora Lottol, is in great part of your own making."

Ignoring his comment, Anna said, "I haven't told you about something else that scared me." She described her dream of killing Sergio in detail but omitted his name.

Dr. Zampone fingered a button on his canary-yellow shirt. "This dream, where you killed the man you met in Milan, how many times did you have it?"

"Twice." Anna shifted on the couch cushion.

He leaned forward in his chair and spoke in a hushed tone, as if he were giving counsel in a confessional. "*Veda*, dreams, you understand, are expressed in symbols, the language of the uncon-scious. We should not take them literally. They are written in code, like the computer languages you have studied, but they do lend you clues about your existence."

"What do you think this one means?"

"All right. The man is sitting in a gondola, a symbol of romance, of fantasy. He is smirking, not taking it or you seriously. You lost your temper with this man, you are enraged. You wish to sever your sexual relationship with him, but it is very difficult, evidenced by a dull knife. And the cake—you feel you have not been getting your fair share. He is a callous man, a competitive man, making fun of the count . . . the details I do not know. That is my interpretation."

Was this some special talent? Anna wondered. Or some off-the-shelf interpretation—some psychobabble that sounds insightful but means absolutely nothing?

Dr. Zampone focused his eyes on Anna. "Does this man still live?"

"Is everything I tell you held in confidence?"

"Of course, as long as you are not a danger to yourself or others. All my patients need to know they can speak freely."

"He was murdered last weekend."

Dr. Zampone bolted upright in his chair. "I read the papers. So you talk of Count Sergio Corrin."

"Yes."

"Count Corrin, revered here in Venice, using his fortune to help the city?"

"The same one."

"Why did you have relations with him?"

"It's a long story."

"Maybe he was a father figure for a girl who lost hers?"

"Woman. That's disgusting!"

"You had the dream after he was dead, nothing similar before?"

"Yes."

"Why do you think you dreamt it a second time?"

Anna toyed with a lock of her hair. "He's always on my mind. I'm trying to clear my name with the police. Until then, I can't escape thinking about that horrid man."

"One moment, please. What police? You did not speak of them."

"I'm a law-abiding citizen, Dr. Zampone, with a very sensitive job. I made a terrible mistake. I was embarrassed and worried by what had happened with Sergio in Milan. At first, I lied to the detective when he questioned me. Now he views me as a suspect."

"Why did they question you in the first place?"

"I was at the hotel where Sergio was killed, and somebody drew a sketch of me running away."

He rubbed his temple. "How did you weather the interrogation? How did it make you feel?"

"Terrified and angry. They kept me in a dank room and Detective Biondi grilled me, tried to trick me, threatened me, even showed me a picture of Sergio with his head bashed in, blood everywhere." She trembled.

"Do not go there. Do not relive it. But I ask you, are the police out to get you as well?"

She pressed her thumbnail into her forefinger. "Well, later Detective Biondi dragged me to the police department for more questions and was about to charge me with murder, I know."

"But he let you go?"

"For the moment, yes."

"I am sure the police will find the guilty party without your assistance." Dr. Zampone stood up and started pacing on the terrazzo floor. "Let's go back to your dream. I interpret the gondola as a form of transport to a place you were imagining, a place that never existed. The issue, Signora Lottol, may be how you see men: imbued with fantasy, instead of how they really are. I know your life story and now all what you told me about your time in Venice. Perhaps in the dream, Count Corrin was not making fun of Count Favier. Maybe he was pantomiming his escape from you, sliding away in his gondola rocked by the waves. But you stopped him so he could not abandon you, like your father did."

"My father, Antonio, died a terrible death. He didn't abandon me."

"Emotionally, you were left without a father."

"I had my Nonno. And once I found out more about Sergio, I was repulsed."

"Only after a painful lesson, which you nearly repeated, like with that Roberto. In your dream, why did you want to kill Count Corrin?" He stood still, his eyes boring into her. "What were you feeling at the time?"

"Hatred. He was an evil man. And I had to stand up for Count Favier. No one else would."

"Count Favier—a man you just met. Signora Lottol, it appears to me that you have unresolved issues. The fishes in the gondola, they symbolize fertility, life, sexuality, and in the dream, yours are about to die. The dolls, which represent your femininity, are buried in a dollhouse filled with sand and seawater. It has become a death trap."

"I don't understand."

"When we dream about houses of any kind, we are dreaming about ourselves," he said. "Yours is half-buried, littered with what the sea, the great unconscious, the original soup of life, has thrown into it. Your self is not much of your own making. It may be easily overwhelmed. So I am concerned about the strength of your ego, and its boundaries."

There he was, storming ahead, Anna thought, going into the deep end of the pool, yet barely knowing her. She had always prided herself on having a strong will. Could she really have been so weak without ever knowing it?

"It is not easy seeing yourself in a mirror. Most go through life avoiding it. They place one foot after another like sleepwalkers. Sometimes, one day, they awaken, and it is often too late. They cry out, having hoped for a different outcome, now powerless to change it. Brava, Anna, for being courageous. But your instincts get you in trouble. You are caught in a repetition cycle, like a tide that comes in and sweeps you out again. Now you can begin to weaken the pull of others—to work on your relationship with your-self instead of seeking paradise in the arms of men." Before Anna could speak, he added, "Do you feel you made too much sacrifice for your marriage?"

"Yes." She reached for a tissue and wiped her nose. There was no doubt Zampone had hit the mark. He was accurate on the rela-tionship with Jack. How did he glean this from what she had told him and what Dr. Levine had shared? Anna remembered Jack's confident façade cracking in their ninth or tenth year of marriage.

His paintings weren't selling anymore and none of the galleries would show his new works. All depicting local landmarks, they were becoming increasingly surreal and outrageous. The UC Berkeley campanile spearing Oski, the school's bear mascot. Memorial Stadium as a giant fish bowl, with UC Regents and administrators as sharks, the students as bait, Berkeley's mayor resembling a giant blowfish. Coit Tower transformed and renamed "Tower of Babble — City Hall." When the *San Francisco Chronicle*'s art critic had skewered his work, Jack had suspected malevolent political influence. His artistic energies dwindled as his drinking grew. Time limped along. Then came the scandal with his model, her buttocks spread across the canvas, molded onto the face of a local public relations executive.

"Maybe you're the problem," Jack used to say between nirvana-seeking bouts with the bottle. "If you didn't earn a good salary, I'd be more driven. You're too masculine. And you always have to win."

Could it all be her fault? Weighing his claims carefully, like the scientist she was, Anna had sifted among them for a grain of truth. Even if she couldn't find one, what would she do about it, quit her job? She couldn't divorce him, breaking the Roman Catholic hearts of Nonno and Nonna back in New York. They had already sacrificed so much, coping with the fiery deaths of their only daughter and her husband, raising their granddaughter when they should have been enjoying their own retirement. She didn't have the heart to do it. Even after her grandparents died, she couldn't face leaving Jack, telling herself he depended on her. The years deposited their encrustations as she waited for something to change. But nothing ever did, no matter how many pretzel-like contortions she put herself through. Until she went to Milan.

"My dear, what you have told me about the police interrogations would frighten anyone," Dr. Zampone said. "In a few days, the experience will recede. All this stress is feeding on itself, increasing in a geometric progression, making you more anxious, to the point where you believe you have seen or heard something—like the footsteps, the baby crying, or that cart coming after you, always at night."

"What?"

"Add to that the unfamiliar setting, the reflections on the water, the dancing lights, echoes in the shadows. . . . Everything can confuse."

No way, Anna thought. "This all happened to me." How much experience did Zampone have anyway? Maybe he was a brilliant thinker, but a dud as a practitioner.

"Did you report anything to the police when you nearly drowned?"

"They'd never believe me."

"Did you seek medical attention?"

"I didn't need to."

"Why would anyone attack you?"

"I've been asking myself the same question."

He reached over and gave her a reassuring pat on the arm, annoying her.

"Anna, you are at midlife. The psychology of Jung is concentrated in this period. It is where *i sentieri*, the paths of the past and the future, collide. Sometimes the old ways no longer serve. This is where we may have the famous midlife crisis. Integration of the parts, the opposites within us, must take place to feel wholeness. In your case, your keenly analytical mind must merge with your deeply buried feelings."

He scrutinized her. "Have you cried, mourned out loud, shouted to the sky?" he asked gently. "Have you expressed your feelings over the loss of your parents, your grandparents, your marriage, your baby, giving voice to your despair? Or have you silenced and repressed these emotions?"

"I . . . I try not to think about them," Anna admitted. "It hurts me too much. If I start, I'm afraid I'll lose myself."

Dr. Zampone crouched in front of Anna so their faces almost touched.

"Or find yourself," he whispered. "You see, you must free these emotions. Embrace them in a safe place, like here. Better yet, with Dr. Levine, close to home. No more sweeping them under a giant rug. There is no escape from them, you know. I tell you, if your conscious mind ignores those feelings, they only become stronger in the unconscious. Eventually, they crash through. It can be overwhelming."

How could he possibly be right? "What would that be like, Doctor?"

"A vision. A daydream."

"How does it matter?" She wrinkled her nose.

"It hijacks reality. It can turn you against others." He scowled. "It is dangerous for you and for those around you. Do as I say, and things will be fine."

He rose and made a note. "At least you have not lost consciousness."

Anna swallowed. "Just once, yesterday."

"*Accidenti*," Dr. Zampone muttered. "You did not mention this. It is important! Years ago, a patient of mine, not unlike you, woke up one day with his wife's blood on his hands and no idea what had happened. He had killed her." His voice grew clinical and cold. "I think you need to go back to California right away and see Dr. Levine."

Anna felt her chest tightening. "I can't—Biondi is holding my passport. You're scaring me. And when I fainted, it was something different. I was very upset, and I had been drinking wine during the day, with friends, and not much water. As soon as I sipped some water, I was fine."

He cocked his head. "If this ever happens again, call me *subito*, immediately. You have my card with my private number." He made another entry in his notebook.

Anna wondered what damning conclusions he was reaching.

"*Insomma*, my dear, someone following you, pushing the cart, the voices . . . all may be surges from the unconscious mind, trying to bore into reality and dominate. We must remember that for every act, there is a consequence. Not exactly like in physics—Fermi would not have agreed—but not random either. Effects can be delayed, but they will come nonetheless. Sometimes they hide for years, waiting in the shadows, gathering strength, until we deal with them. Or else they deal with us. You need to be on guard against these hallucinations."

She crossed her arms and placed one hand over her mouth. It had been hard for her to sit there and listen to his sometimes degrading, off-the-wall interpretations. Even now, getting up and leaving his office would give her immense satisfaction. But then she'd sacrifice the opportunity that had just occurred to her. It was time to face down her demons.

"Doctor, I need to find something out that has been troubling me for a long time," Anna said. "I have an irrational fear of dark water. Sometimes I shiver just thinking about it. When I jumped into the canal to escape the cart, I froze. It was as if I had never learned to swim."

"Many would find the black water frightening, not knowing what lurks underneath." He tapped his thigh. "Did you almost drown as a child?"

Anna described the December afternoon when she and Nonno were strolling along the boardwalk of Captrec Island. The wind was whipping as she tripped over a pile of rope. Nonno had jumped in and saved her as she had thrashed in the water.

"This incident could be the genesis of your fear."

She scoured her brain. "I feel there's something else, earlier. Another memory, or even a dream, I don't know."

"There is a way to attack that kind of phobia: hypnosis. I am fully licensed to conduct hypnotherapy. I would call such a procedure a tall order for you, though, my dear."

"Why is that?"

"We have not worked together before. There is much unknown. *Una cosa seria,*" he added in a low voice.

Anna doubted that was the entire reason. She worked up a smile. "Dr. Levine told me you were very talented, or she wouldn't have referred me." Anna wondered if she should panic. Was she so desperate she'd put herself in his hands when he probably had just diagnosed her as a paranoid schizophrenic? But if he had, why was he willing to go ahead with hypnosis?

"Actually, she has called me 'gifted.'" Then his voice grew subdued. "We want to make progress, of course. You might fall back, you might crumble. And you're so far from home. Let me concentrate for a moment. *Devo pensare, devo proprio pensare,*" he said to himself. He clicked his pen, eyes fixed in the distance like an athlete on a high diving board, mentally rehearsing before springing into action.

Anna worried that it would be better to wait until she'd see Dr. Levine. She trusted her. With Dr. Zampone, it was trust, once removed. Why was he so reluctant? Was it beyond his abilities? Maybe doing this would be dangerous and she wouldn't wake up. Or she'd lose her mind and become a zombie. But then, how could she stand another odd imagining, another day of uncertainty and fear? She started to silently count to one hundred in Italian.

At *venti*, Dr. Zampone exhaled noisily.

"Very well, I will perform the induction. But I must tell you first some things. This is not science. We are a pair of archaeologists digging through layers of memory, finding only dirt-covered potsherds, puzzle pieces, hypothesizing how the original looked. The truth may be most unwelcome. We may smash forever a cherished memory of yours with our clumsy instruments. The truth may not wish to be found, or we find a false memory instead. We may see just what your unconscious mind has thrown together, like gazing through a broken kaleidoscope and getting lost within it, never reaching the place you want, Anna. But clearly, something is prompting your hunger to know."

Anna hoped Dr. Zampone would stop deliberating and act before she lost her nerve. When he grew silent, she chewed her lip.

"*Allora*, considering what I said, do you still wish to proceed?"

She nodded.

"Then we will see where the journey takes us. If it will make you more comfortable, take your shoes off and stretch out on the couch."

Anna slipped off her pumps and reclined on the couch, her head on a silken pillow, her gaze on the chandelier overhead.

"We will go back to a time when you were a little girl."

22

L'orologio, *The Watch*

Thursday, late afternoon

Dr. Zampone seized a gold pocket watch on a long chain from a velvet box on his desk.

"Look at me and not at the ceiling, Anna." He moved his chair closer to the couch. "I will start by swinging this watch," he said, dangling it in front of her. "When I say 'Sleep,' you will close your eyes and find your way back through time to that place—that other place—where you almost drowned. When I say 'Wake up' and touch you like this," he leaned forward and pressed her right earlobe, "you will come back to the present and open your eyes. You will remember all what you say to me. But before then, if the memory becomes too painful and you want me to stop, you must raise your right hand. Understand?"

"Yes."

"Now, please, eyes on the *orologio da tasca*."

The watch on its gold chain became a blur as Dr. Zampone began swinging it from side to side in a gleaming arc.

"Go ahead and sleep, my dear. Tell me about that day long ago, the day when you were in the water, struggling to breathe. Start at the beginning." The doctor's calm voice faded until it sounded as if it were coming from another room.

Anna closed her eyes.

"Yes, that's right," Dr. Zampone said. "What do you see?"

"Nothing. I don't know. I can't—wait." Anna felt herself drifting through a thick mist. She saw a clearing ahead, and as she got closer, a scene started to unroll, as if in a movie. "I'm in a little boat. The waves are lapping at the sides. It's morning, cool and just starting to get light."

"Are you all alone?"

"Someone is rowing. Everyone is behind me. I hear my mother, Elena, talking."

"What can you see?"

"Boxes are piled high in the boat."

"You say boxes, *scatole?*"

"Yes. Now the boat is turning into a bay. The waves are bigger here."

"Where is this, Anna?"

"I don't know. All the buildings are gray. I hear arguing. My mother is yelling. I look back at her, and her face is scarlet. It frightens me, so I turn and face forward again."

"Why is she angry?"

"I don't know."

"What happens next?"

"She throws one box after another into the water. They splash, and I get wet. The boxes float for a few seconds before they sink. I wonder what's inside. We are getting close to land again, but we're hit."

Anna took a sharp breath.

"By what, by whom?"

"I can't tell. But I fall overboard. I hear splashing, screaming, then grunts and gurgling sounds."

"Are you hurt?"

"No. Bubbles are streaming past me as I start sinking to the bottom of the sea, like the boxes did. Now someone is pushing me up through the water and back into the boat. My eyes are burning from the salt. No, no!" Anna screamed. "I want Mamma! Don't you touch me. Don't touch me." Trembling, Anna tried to raise her right hand, but it barely moved. "Nonno, it's you!"

"Wake up, wake up," Dr. Zampone ordered as he squeezed her earlobe. "Come back. Anna. Anna?"

"No, no!"

"Wake up, wake up, I said."

Anna struggled to open her eyes, dazed, and slowly focused them.

"Are you all right?"

"Doctor?"

"I am Dr. Zampone, here in Venice, Italy. You are safe. You experienced a troubling memory." He grabbed his pen and started to write. "How do you feel?"

"Afraid and confused."

"That is to be expected. This was hard on you. Rest now. Take ten breaths."

Anna followed his instructions, then said, "I need to know what to make of it."

"Come see me tomorrow when you are less upset. Even then, all the terror you feel may not hold the answer you seek."

"I'm getting close, and we need to continue," Anna said stubbornly.

"In my professional opinion, waiting is better."

"I insist."

"As you wish." He made another note. "Why did you try to raise your hand?"

"I was about to see something awful."

"But you don't know what it was, only the panicked feeling?"

"Yes."

"Was your Nonno there all along?"

"I don't think so."

"Was he the one to ram your boat?"

"I can't believe that." Anna started sniffling.

"Too much," Dr. Zampone said, handing her a tissue. "We must continue in another session. What you are experiencing may be too traumatic."

"I have to take the chance. Please, we have to go on." She dabbed her eyes. "I may never gather the courage to try again. Please."

"Let me ask you. Do you have any other recollections? Perhaps where and when this took place?"

"Not more than what I told you. But it must be someplace near New York."

"Think. Think hard."

Anna stared at the floor, meditating on the blue swaths of terrazzo marble chips, rocking back and forth to clear her mind, struggling for any spark of illumination. She took a deep breath. "I can't bring it up," she said, her voice catching.

"I must question whether some things were not true, or you mixed up different times, different memories, maybe taking parts from a dream, and contaminating the original memory," Dr. Zampone said, retreating behind his desk.

"What makes you say that?"

"The tale is too simple. Full of symbols with no details. No complete descriptions—where you were, what the buildings looked like, who was in the boat with you, who brought you up from the water. Your Nonno wasn't there? The whole episode was a floating dream, or nightmare, in this case."

"It felt real."

"I do not doubt you, my dear. And we both know that at some point in your childhood you almost drowned. This could incorporate that. Some of it could be pastiches of what others have told you, like your Nonno and Nonna in bringing you up after your parents' deaths—the kaleidoscope I spoke of earlier. Beyond this I cannot say."

"You've only said what this isn't, not what your opinion is," Anna told him, hearing her voice rise. "Are you refusing to help me?"

"*Basta*, calm down, my dear."

"Stop calling me 'my dear.'"

"I meant nothing by it. What I want to say is that memories are not linear. You expect too much, too quickly. Therapy is not instant gratification, like your American fast food. I cannot say if anyone did anything to you at this point. That is all right. We got a peek at it. We can try again, or you can pursue it with Dr. Levine when you get home. I will write everything up. In any event, you can recover from this early incident even without fully knowing what happened in the distant past. After all, I must tell you, you may never know."

"Never know?" Anna felt her face getting hot. "This is my life we're talking about. I'm not just one of your file folders." Anna squeezed the silk pillow.

"My patients are not file folders to me. They are living, breathing human beings."

Anna just looked at him, challenging him.

Dr. Zampone jutted his chin out, refusing to get angry. "Okay then. I share with you my interpretation, though it is very early. And you will not like it."

"Tell me anyway."

"These thoughts of drowning have come during your stay in this city of too much water, too many reflections. The watery nightmare is your unconscious mind, accusing your mother of squandering the past as she throws the boxes, containing her history and yours, into the water—a past you will never know, since the boxes sink into the sea. Your Nonno tries to rescue you from a rootless past.

And clearly, you feel guilty. Guilty for being alive, guilty, perhaps, over the death of your unborn child. Yet you blame your mother for dying, for leaving you, instead of raising you. But you have twisted it around so that instead she is mad at you. Blaming a poor dead woman is, at some level, overwhelming. So you are drowning in your own guilt. The hand of your own guilt is pushing you deeper in the water as your mother expires. Anna, it is your guilt that is the culprit here! Your guilt is destroying you."

"This doesn't make any sense. You're saying it's all *my* fault?"

"It is not personal."

"The hell it's not. I'm paying you the equivalent of one hundred dollars an hour to be insulted?"

A bronze clock on the desk made a soft chime.

"I will not charge you." Dr. Zampone's voice trembled. "Claudio Zampone will never be accused of cheating a patient. You must remember, this is not a commercial transaction or one of your equations. Today we start to touch something buried, dormant for decades. You think in one session we get to the bottom of the twists and turns of your life for the past forty years? Do things just happen to you or do you make choices? After your childhood, what were your decisions on marriage, children, friends, even coming here to Venice? Was it all drunk Jack's fault, the unraveling of your marriage? It is well past the time of playing the victim. You must start taking the adult role, accepting your past, instead of looking for scapegoats or boogeymen."

"What? Why you are attacking me?"

"Just my point. You will never get to the bottom of your issues this way."

Anna stood up and stalked out, inwardly cursing Dr. Levine along with Dr. Zampone. She had been making progress, adjusting to life after leaving Jack. Today showed her that she should be done with shrinks, too, and save money and frustration while she was at it.

Still steaming when she got back to her pensione room, Anna envisioned relaxing on the count's terrace with Margo later on, relishing the bird's-eye view of the city and sipping an Amarone to dull the ache. She tried to pretend she could leave the past behind like an old, worn-out coat. But she sensed she had failed yet again by blaming Zampone, when it was her own life—her own bad decisions—that had doomed her.

When the phone rang, she shouted into it, "What do you want?"

Leslie's voice answered her.

Black Hole

Thursday, evening

"Anna, I just want to say one thing. You're fired—"

"But, but I was trying to solve—"

"For violating the law, not to mention our policies. Collecting information to help that Italian scumbag? You've been aiding and abetting a money launderer and his gang!"

"That's not—"

"Shut up. You've been trying to clean up after yourself and your tawdry affair. We saw the photograph of the file you took to Milan. His grubby hands on *our* confidential file. You've brought shame on all of us here at FinCEN. You infiltrated the US government and fooled us all. Who are you, anyway, a Mafia princess? Maybe you're related to that Mafia don in prison, Gotti? Nah, you're just a low-level smurf lackey. Your underworld bosses may well snuff you out, now that your cover's blown. We're conducting a top-to-bottom review of your activities and will make a full report to the Justice Department. They'll be looking into charges. At least I didn't hire you. Diane, your first boss—what a sap—is going to be on the hot seat."

"I was not involved with Sergio Corrin."

"From a look at the other photos, I'd say you were closely

involved with him." Leslie snickered. "I've had enough of you and your air of superiority, as if you're the only one with a big brain. Meanwhile, you've brought down a promising employee, playing on his loyalty to you and sabotaging him."

"Brian? What have you done to him?"

"I don't need to tell you."

"No!"

"And whaddya think this does to *my* career? Throws it into the toilet. We'll be sending the dismissal letter to your home. Who knows, maybe you even killed that count."

She heard a thundering crash as Leslie slammed down the phone. Anna pictured her sitting at her abnormally tidy desk, gazing at her perfectly polished fingernails, not a hair on her head out of place. And smirking, having just ripped Anna to shreds.

She curled into a ball on her bed. An image of an astronaut, bobbing in space in a white suit, crossed her mind. Far below him lay the brilliant blue-water planet Earth, this would-be paradise, its sparkling, swirling clouds masking the conflicts and destruction fueled by infinite greed and hatred in a precarious world. Suddenly, an evil alien resembling Leslie flew by and cut the tether to his ship.

Anna recalled all the nights and weekends she had worked late, dueling with shadowy forces behind a money-laundering web until she found the right algorithm, busting the scheme open and spilling its dark secrets. Jack hadn't seen her much then. She had traveled a lot, too. Sacrificing for the future, she had thought; instead it had brought her a kick in the teeth. Even if she ever got out of this mess with Biondi, and another, perhaps, with the Treasury or Justice Department, she could forget about a future government job, because there'd always be a black mark next to her name. The banking industry—like going back to a spot in compliance—out, too. They all knew each other. Maybe she could work for a hedge fund back in New York, building quantitative models, but Anna couldn't get excited about money-making as her purpose in life.

Thanks to the gift package from Biondi, Leslie possessed strong photographic evidence to implicate Anna, but how could she have twisted Anna's research to portray her as Sergio's helper? In any case, Leslie would find a way to prosper from her setback. The firings would make her appear a strong leader, taking resolute action, and with Brian dismissed, there'd be no one to contradict her exaggerations and fabrications. If Anna were allowed to leave Italy, Leslie would make sure federal officers would be there to greet her at San Francisco International Airport, a sick welcome-home party.

Anna closed her eyes, immobilized by an immense force she felt holding her down, sucking in the light and devouring her energy before smashing all her bits of hope. What had she been thinking, running around Venice like an amateur detective, not knowing what the hell she was doing, and with nothing to show for her efforts? In a way, it would be a relief to have Biondi come and lock her up. That would at least end the torture of flailing about. A murder conviction would outrank a money-laundering charge, of course. The Italians could hold onto her for a very long time.

Anna rolled over and dialed the front desk, telling the clerk to hold all calls until the next day, before falling into a fitful slumber.

24

Il Gazzettino

Friday, late morning

When her phone rang, Anna gawked at her clock and realized she had slept for seventeen hours. Gingerly picking up the receiver, she was relieved to hear Margo's cheery hello.

"Gee, you sound groggy," Margo said. "I'm down in your lobby. I was starting to worry about you. Didn't you get my message?"

"Yeah. You mean the note on Wednesday?"

"Huh? No, I called yesterday. Did you forget we have an appointment with Filippo Fanfarone in an hour? And I set you up to talk with Pablo. He'll meet you at five by the bookstore across from the little Bacino Orseolo—you know, where they moor gondolas."

"I'll be right down."

Pulling on a sweater and navy slacks, Anna washed up at the tiny sink, passed a brush through her hair, and rushed downstairs.

"I'm starving," she told Margo, heading into the dining room. "Do you want some breakfast?"

"Sure." She gave Anna a quizzical look. "I phoned you twice yesterday. But you never returned my calls."

"I asked them not to connect any to my room, and I . . ." Anna was concentrating on heaping fruit, prosciutto and cheese, croissants and frittata on her plate, then on finding a quiet table. As soon as the waitress brought steaming coffee and hot milk, she told Margo, "It's time I bring you up to date on a few things."

"Such as?" Margo asked as Anna swallowed a chunk of fontina cheese.

Anna related the attack Wednesday evening after she'd set out for the count's palazzo, as Margo had requested.

Margo seemed to have no trouble believing someone had sent the heavy cart Anna's way. "I never left you a note. If something had happened to you, I could never have forgiven myself." She reached across the table and clasped Anna's hand. "Come stay at the palazzo. Alessandro can put a cot in my room, or we can share the big bed."

"Outside the pensione is where I've had problems. Once we tell him about Gabriella's diary, I won't be very welcome."

"Let me handle that. You're being brave, but very foolish. Think it over." Margo tore apart a croissant. "That note, did it look like my handwriting?"

"At first, I figured you had phoned and a clerk took it down; it was in English. Later that night, he did say a woman had come to see me."

"So someone lured you out of the hotel with a fake message. That's doubly threatening, because whoever it is, knows about me, too, knows we're friends and where I'm staying. Do you still have the note?"

"I can't find it."

"Too bad. But after your scare, why didn't you come straight to the count's the next day? What did you end up doing?"

"I wanted to search for the diary in daylight. I was going to come after that, but I ended up walking around and . . . visiting a shrink," Anna said, leaving out anything about Roberto. The encounter almost seemed as if she had dreamed it.

"You know one here?"

"I'd been given his name as a referral. I really needed to talk to someone."

"You can always confide in me."

"I know. I mean someone with training." Anna sipped the strong coffee. "With everything that's happened since I arrived, I needed to feel calm and centered, pronto, or I'll never be able to think my way out of this."

"Did it help?"

"Not much."

"More than anything, you need to be careful. You shouldn't go out of this pensione alone anymore."

"Please don't make me more scared than I am. You can't always be there. You have your hands full with Angela."

"Tell me about it. She's been crying every night. Guess she's really homesick."

Anna sampled the artichoke frittata. "You know, I visited Sergio's gallery since I saw you last, too. Kind of buried amid all the expensive art and artifacts are carvings and paintings by that artist who's living in Sergio's palazzo. And did you hear that Sergio was a big-game hunter, at least years ago?"

"Nope. Do you think that means anything?"

Anna shrugged.

"What ever came from the searches of everyone's accounts and all the other information you had your assistant track down?"

"He won't be sending anything." Anna's voice dropped.

"Why not?"

"I got canned yesterday. And Brian lost his job, too, thanks to me."

"Oh, no. You always suspected your boss would be up to something, and now this on top of everything else." She put a sympathetic hand on Anna's shoulder.

"Yep. Leslie not only fired me, but she's trying to twist everything

I've researched and done to make it look as if I smuggled information to Sergio and am trying to clean things up. She might even have me arrested in San Francisco, if I ever make it out of Biondi's clutches." She glanced at the floor. "This is becoming hopeless."

"Don't say that. I'm sure we can learn lots more about Sergio from Fanfarone. And if any of this has anything to do with the Gondola Murders, the missing pieces could be right there in the *Gazzettino* offices. After all, you might not have been attacked if you were on the wrong trail."

Anna pondered Margo's words.

They headed out the door toward Calle della Mandorla, a little street pressing in on both sides. As they passed the statue of Daniele Manin, the Venetian patriot, Anna said, "Wait, I need to take a look inside," pointing to an imposing cement-and-metal edifice. The bright letters affixed to the façade spelled out Banco Saturno.

"What are you going to find there? It's a freaking bank, just like any other."

Not entirely, Anna thought. "I'll be quick."

Dashing into the marbled entry, she noted a timbered ceiling soaring above a line of leather-topped desks on oriental carpets. Two classical sculptures of Roman gods stood against the opposite wall: one with a trident, the other with a scythe. Comely tellers sat behind ornate mahogany-and-glass counters, looking bored. Pastries and coffee on silver trays were personally served to waiting customers. Sounds were muted, as well-heeled clients spoke with advisors in hushed tones. One far wall with two rows of plush theater seats in front, was dedicated to TV screens, bringing up-to-the-minute indicators of the Borsa Italiana, the London Stock Exchange, the NYSE, the DAX, and others around the world. Video cameras blinked red from each corner. Decorum reigned.

Returning outside, Anna told Margo, "Let's go," as she mentally scratched any more Banco Saturno branches off her list for clues.

As they approached the newspaper office, Margo said, "The *Gazzettino* stores old issues back to the fifties. Fanfarone will certainly let us into the archives. You can't believe how much I've been buttering him up."

Filippo Fanfarone looked delighted to see Margo and Anna, kissing them each on the cheek, filling Anna with anticipation, a relief after the difficulties gaining building access in the lobby.

"It's such a pleasure to visit you here, at this esteemed newspaper," Margo said as the three went into his office. An antique desk and cushy leather sofa sat atop a thick carpet. A Murano chandelier resembled a giant multicolored crab; a shield carved with a panoply of animals filled one corner. Anna wondered if the *Gazzettino* had spent all the lire on luxury furnishings for his society visitors or if they were Fanfarone's personal contribution. His looks were certainly as dramatic as the décor. A white pageboy framed almond-brown eyes overshadowed by shaggy brows. His hair accentuated pale skin drawn tightly over high cheekbones and a prominent chin.

After serving cappuccinos to his guests, Fanfarone gushed about the upcoming opera season, pulling out swatches of wondrous, silky fabrics that had been commissioned from Rubelli for the costumes. He let them know he had lifelong connections to Venetian socialites, showing off an encyclopedic knowledge of their bloodlines and histories, triumphs and failures.

Anna sipped her coffee quietly, trying to figure out what made him tick. If they approached him properly, she hoped Fanfarone would spill secrets about Sergio and others that would be invaluable.

Turning to Margo, Fanfarone asked politely, "How is your sweet *cugina*, Angela?"

"Enjoying her stay immensely," Margo said.

Fanfarone raised his eyebrows a tad. "Such an art lover, that one. I remember meeting her last year at an event, when a local gallery moved to its new location."

"The Arte e Antichità, the Corrin Gallery?" Anna asked.

"Yes, Sergio's gallery."

"What a shock about his murder," Anna added.

"Venice, I am afraid, will never be the same," Fanfarone said dolefully. "He was so loved."

Margo informed him that she was writing articles on the city for the *Chronicle* back home. She mentioned her visit to the Marciana Library before asking him for help with the *Gazzettino* archives.

"We hope you'll allow us to review the archives for Margo's story, since it goes back in time," Anna said. "I'm working with her on the financial interpretations, drawing on my banking knowledge."

Fanfarone crossed his legs and nodded with a distant look. "I have just one question," he said. "What is the exact subject?"

"Venetian prostitution and Sergio Corrin," Margo said.

Fanfarone's mouth gaped open.

"I mean to say these would be totally separate."

"What! Prostitution? Why do you desire to smear Venice and write about muck worse than what lines our canals? And what does this have to do with Count Corrin?"

"No, no, nothing." Margo blushed. "I told you, I'm writing more than one story. For the prostitution piece, I'm focusing on centuries ago, not the present day—on, you know, courtesans."

"Yes, yes. I am familiar with all the paintings and poems, too. Which of those do you think you will use?"

"I'm not an art critic, but certainly, um, the painting by Carpaccio, um, and—of course poems by Veronica Franco. The second article would be my piece reflecting on the life of Count Corrin, the charity superstar."

"Access to your archives would be critical," Anna said.

Fanfarone squinted at her. "He was a hero, back in the forties, of the Italian Resistance and not even out of his teens. So brave. Did you know that? And later, a supremely successful businessman and investor. He helped enrich many in Venice with his advice. Do you think I could afford to decorate my office on a writer's salary? Such a fine *consigliere*—"

"But some must have lost money with him," Anna said.

"Of course. The market does not rise forever like a helium balloon. The mergers do not always yield as anticipated. But for the majority, his advice worked."

"Then why do you think he was killed?" Anna asked.

"Not because of business. Maybe pleasure? Sergio was catnip to the ladies." Fanfarone leaned down to scratch a bare ankle. "The answer for the archives is no."

Over the years, *Gazzettino* reporters may well have found plenty of dirt on Sergio, and it was not surprising that Fanfarone, as society gatekeeper and publicist, would shield him, dead or alive, from prying eyes. When the low morals of one club member were exposed, it weakened the entire bunch.

"I will take no part in helping people intent on making a sensational splash by sacrificing Venice," he said.

"Nothing could be further from the truth about my story," Margo said. "I lived here for a number of years, you know, and I love the city, too."

Fanfarone leaned forward in his chair. "I have always written about the good that happens here, not the seamy side. Only beautiful people doing beautiful things."

"I knew Count Corrin and his wife, Liliana," Margo said. "Such upstanding citizens. I'm not out to damage their reputations."

Anna couldn't bear to listen to Margo piling it on.

Fanfarone glanced at the glass wall clock. "Beside this, our building is open just half day today. Closes in one hour. I tell you a little about Sergio instead."

230

"Signor Fanfarone, I'm terribly sorry, but I just realized I have an appointment," Anna said. "I'm sure Margo will carry on well without me." He nodded and rose to take her hand as Margo gave Anna an uncomprehending stare.

As soon as she left Fanfarone's office, Anna asked a passing janitor where the archives were, then bolted past the newsroom and up a flight of stairs. She opened the door at the end of the hall and quickly slipped inside, unsure what she could find in one hour. Unless Margo charmed Fanfarone enough for another meeting, to which Anna gave a ten percent probability, this would be her last chance to comb the newspaper's archives.

Massive gray cabinets covered in a film of dust filled the space, their holdings keyed to dates printed on each drawer label. A dehumidifier hummed in the corner. If she recalled correctly, Sergio had been a young, married lawyer in the fifties, not yet a force at CONSOB, or a mover-and-shaker. Anna opted for using Gabriella's death as the central point, calculating that she had at least sixty daily newspapers to review. Diving in, she lugged thirty days' worth of papers, beginning in mid-May, 1955, to a nearby table and plunked them down, scouring the front pages and local sections.

An article from May 27 caught her eye. A group calling itself the Pride Council had sent Alessandro letters threatening both him and his wife. The paper depicted its insignia, which resembled a trident. Anna doubted the menacing notes came from a real organization. Was the story even true? Or had it been concocted by Alessandro before he murdered Gabriella? Anna focused on the trident, hoping the proper application of logic and reason could reveal a solution to the puzzle. Remembering her mythology, Neptune, the god of the sea, carried a trident. Neptune was the son of Saturn. Why had Sergio picked that name, Saturno, for his bank? Then there was the sculpture she had just seen in the bank lobby. Was it a coincidence, or had Sergio just loved the classics? Anna took a piece of paper from her purse and sketched the insignia to compare to the logo of the bank.

She found photographs of Gabriella's funeral, the service at the church of Santa Maria del Giglio, the watery procession out to San Michele. A profusion of white roses, lilies of the valley, and a flower resembling a starfish draped over her casket. Someone had decorated the gondola with angels.

Then she spotted an article dated June 10, written by Fanfarone, with blaring headlines: "Count's Wife Murdered. Autopsy Ordered." Its odd perspective made Gabriella sound like an appendage of Alessandro. But most of the article, all the photographs, and several side pieces had been ripped out—by whom? A few syllables on either side made Anna wish that she had brought her dictionary to unscramble the remnants. The remaining bits mentioned Gabriella's faithful gondolier, Piero Tota, and his twin, Armando, also in the business. Fanfarone must have been attempting to smooth over gossip raging at the time.

When the church bells tolled noon, Anna felt she needed at least another hour of scouring for scraps of information. Surely Dobermans wouldn't be patrolling the *Gazzettino*'s halls. What did they have to protect, yesterday's news?

Her thoughts were scattered by the door banging against the wall.

"*Chiuso*," announced a uniformed janitor, bursting into the archive room followed by a red-faced Fanfarone.

"So this was your appointment?" he asked.

"I know it looks bad, but I'm only trying to—"

"Save your excuses. You took advantage of my good nature. We are closed."

"Please, Signor Fanfarone, I'm not harming anything, just looking at old newspapers. Isn't the *Gazzettino* supposed to inform and serve the public, even a tourist, like me? You have a very important mission, focusing on your city, portraying its culture. So many people are in your debt. The other papers have regional biases and hardly cover anything here except the last flood or scandal."

"*Certo*, we provide an invaluable service to all of Venice. But you should not be here."

"I'm in a terrible spot. I desperately need to find something out. Please help me. I would really appreciate it."

She sensed him wavering.

"*Allora, Silvio, non c'è problema se la signora rimane. Lei può tornare dopo e accompagnarla fuori.*" He told Silvio, the janitor, that it wouldn't be a problem for her to remain and he should accompany her outside when she was done.

"*Va beh*," the janitor said, expressing agreement.

"How much time you need?" Fanfarone asked.

"Only another hour."

He fell silent, weighing her request. "What do you look for?" He stared at the torn-out pages in the open newspaper. In an instant, his languid gaze became furious, smoting her.

"You thief," Fanfarone yelled, pointing to the door. "Out of here!"

25

The Dark Yacana

Friday, early evening

She had taken a chance, hoping that Fanfarone would come to her aid. Now Anna worried he'd report her as a snoop and liar looking into Gabriella's death to God only knew. Maybe to anyone who would listen.

Walking off her frustration and embarrassment despite having proclaimed she was not to blame, Anna meandered to St. Mark's and found herself in front of the Doge's Palace, its filigreed beauty belying the strong-arm secrecy of the old republic. She recalled that in the eyes of John Ruskin, the Victorian art critic, the building, with its delicate pink geometry and airy design, represented the best of what had gone before, a consummation of the three greatest architectural styles: the Classical, the Islamic, and the Gothic. Did every culture's beauty also mask dark secrets? Anna wondered.

She ducked into Calle Fiubera and wandered its byways, the little stores offering glass paperweights, brass ornaments, jeweled trinkets. Ambling toward Bacino Orseolo, she spotted Pablo browsing through an outdoor cart at Passaggio dei Libri, a quaint bookstore, and gave him a peck on the cheek.

"Glad you found me," he said. "Let's get some *cicchetti*. I know just the place, a *bacaro* around the corner."

She welcomed the chance to quiz him at length about Sergio, hoping he wouldn't start recounting the horrors of the Conquest as they dined.

In the dusky bar, a few wide boards were stacked against the stucco wall near the entrance, ready to be set inside the doorjamb as soon as the sirens wailed, with the hope of blocking the gushes of water topping the canal, at least for a while. Anna had seen pictures of hardy Venetians in their high boots during acqua alta, standing at bars, holding their drinks, making wakes in the water covering the tile floors as they moved about their sinking world.

Today, thankfully, the floor was dry.

"Try this," Pablo said, handing Anna an aromatic Sagrantino from Montefalco before bringing several plates of appetizers to their petite window table. She savored the enticing sautéed scallops with grilled radicchio as Pablo deftly cut a morsel of marinated anchovy.

"You know," he said gently, "when we first met, I saw pain in your eyes. Is it more than your husband?"

She wondered what he had heard. "I'm . . . I'm . . . just trying to get over a few things."

"And how is your ankle?"

"Much better, thanks."

"Dudley was concerned. Yolanda and I visit Burano tomorrow with him. Perhaps you like to come along?"

A wave of gratitude washed over her. "Thank you, but no."

"What can be more important than seeing how others live and what they create? The farther we travel, the more we learn about ourselves."

"I have some work to do." The words had slipped out.

"Work? From here? What do you do from here?"

"A few phone calls back to my office today to, uh, complete a project tomorrow." If only that were the case.

"You must visit Burano before you leave. I am intrigued by the lovely lace they make there by hand. How can something so delicate be durable? Yolanda would like a fine lace mantilla. It is much money, but I will buy her one."

Anna knew the cost would be several thousands of dollars. How could he afford the gift on a diplomatic salary? She sipped her wine, then asked him about places to visit in Peru.

He recommended sites along the sea, in the Andes, the Amazon, and the Sacred Valley. When he was done, he gave her a dreamy look. "My people made beautiful fabrics. From the fine wool of the vicuña and, of course, the alpaca. The llama is, how you say, the poor relation—the work horse, the pack animal, the source of the coarser wool for blankets and coats. But so important was the llama that the ancients in Peru observed it in the heavens. They called her the *Yacana*. As a boy in Cusco, I used to gaze at her. She walks along the bright road." He pointed upward with his elbow.

It took a moment for Anna to realize he was referring to the Milky Way.

Pablo grinned. "*Ya ves*, the Yacana's bright eyes are stars. You have heard of one of them, I know. You call it Alpha Centauri."

Anna knew Alpha Centauri almost verbatim from her old textbooks. Twenty-five trillion miles, or 4.3 light years, from Earth; the second closest star, a double star; in the constellation of Centaurus, named after the mythical Chiron, half-man, half-horse, a wise and great teacher. Pointing toward the Southern Cross constellation in the southern hemisphere, Alpha and Beta Centauri help to distinguish it from the false cross.

"She stands next to her dark suckling calf. But the calf, the little *cría*—to see that one is a challenge." He must be speaking about the cloudy nebula nearby, Anna thought. "You need both: the light and the dark. One can't live without the other. Many say—"

"Pablo, all of this is mythology," Anna said, discounting the tale of the two llamas before recognizing her hypocrisy. Why should the Greek and Roman myths of Orion, Perseus, Cassiopeia, and countless others, forever framed as constellations in the "Western" night sky, be superior to the lowly Yacana? The human urge to name and categorize, to make the foreign, faraway stars more familiar—to people the heavens—must be a common way of trying to feel less alone in the infinite universe.

"Mythology and life are bound together." Pablo put his glass down. "Margo tells me you are forty." Anna wondered what else Margo had shared with him. "Forty is the number of wholeness," Pablo went on, sounding like a mystical Dr. Zampone. "There are forty *seques* from the Temple of the Sun in all directions, forty chieftains representing all the people of the Inca Empire, forty dances at the time of Inti Raymi, our June solstice."

"You don't really think—"

"You know," he tapped her arm, "for centuries we honored the sacredness of Pachamama. But now the earth is dying. How will we ride on the broad back of the black dog that will carry us across the river to our forefathers?" He studied her frown. "Sorry. One day Pablo must laugh more and change the world less. That is my challenge, to not live up to my name."

"I don't follow."

"Pachacuti. My nickname. It means 'over-turner' of the earth. Someone who disrupts the old order and starts a new way."

"So you lead revolts?" A smile crept across her face.

"Not enough," he said quietly.

"I understand you have a son," said Anna.

"Stefano," he said, his voice brightening. "He is grown now, with his own family."

"You must be proud. How old is he?"

"Thirty-nine and living in Manu."

"Where's that?"

"In the Amazon, at an outpost. He is a warrior protecting the wild—dangerous work. We couldn't get him back."

"Back?"

"To study medicine in Lima, later to practice in Cusco. That was my dream for him."

Anna asked herself a question she'd never know the answer to: What hopes did my parents have for me?

"But he *is* a doctor in a way," Pablo said. "He tries to heal the forest. The world is spinning like a top, out of balance and getting wobbly. Soon it will crash down on us."

Anna knew he meant what she dreaded: the trickle that would build into a flood, submerging Venice and the low coasts everywhere, turning the wet, oxygen-giving Amazon rainforest into dry savanna. From heaven to hell in one short century. What would life be like then?

"It's too awful to think about; let's change the subject. Pablo, what kind of man was Sergio? I'm helping Margo research her story."

"Why write about him?" Pablo gazed out at the alleyway as people threaded by. "He was evil. He tried to ruin me."

"I saw a picture of you and Yolanda with him in Alessandro's library. Yolanda was carrying a baby."

"That was a long time ago."

"And on my way to the bathroom during Dudley's party," she hesitated, "I got lost, and I . . . spotted a photo of you both in, I think, the rainforest. You were holding your son's hand. You know the one?"

He took a sip of wine. "That, too, was a lifetime ago." Pablo's eyes burned. "He was dead to me long before he was murdered."

"Do you mind my asking what happened?"

"In the seventies, I traveled with Sergio into a corner of the Amazon. I showed him all the sacred, hidden places." Pablo touched his heart. "Where the macaws nest, where the jaguar drinks from the river at dawn, where the harpy eagle flies. The next morning, Sergio woke me, saying, 'Come quickly.' He brought me to the riverbank where the jaguar lay, shot by him—with the gun we had brought for our own protection—for 'sport.' He wanted me to help him cut off the head so he could mount it on his wall back in Venice. Instead of being seized by wonder, he was seized by the need to exterminate. I can see the animal still, the long, white whiskers twitching, the brown-and-tan coat splattered with red, the dying light in his emerald eyes, meeting mine. Some suck the earth dry, not seeing their own future mirrored in the death of what they have destroyed. Sergio boasted about how brave he had been in pulling the trigger. I was so furious, I could have strangled him. Perhaps I should have.

"I left him and made my way to the village of the surrounding tribe; I told them he had killed their jaguar god. Sergio was lucky to escape by boat down the river. I was hoping he'd fall overboard and get eaten by a caiman. But he survived. After that, we had no more contact. Many years later, working in Peru, I made a terrible mistake, yet it was covered by the Italian newspapers as if it was a scandal happening in Rome. I know it was Sergio—Sergio using his influence to turn almost everyone I had known here against me."

If true, yet another reminder of how despicable Sergio could be, Anna thought. The story of a falling out with a dear old friend was sounding familiar. Pablo knew his way around knives and scalpels, and, after years in the rainforest, how to handle a machete. But why would he kill Sergio now if the rupture with him was decades old? There had to be more.

"Did he get along with Yolanda?" Anna asked. "How many years ago did—"

"*No más.* I have said enough."

Deflated, Anna felt like a failed reporter whose life depended on getting answers from people without revealing her desperation. After their goodbyes, she mulled over the message Pablo had for her: the brutality of man, the ruination of the earth, mysterious stories from an ancient, faraway world.

As the sun waned and the darkening world closed in, she wished she had time to explore the Ospedale della Pietà, where Vivaldi, a native red-headed priest who wrote concertos, had taught violin back in the eighteenth century. Nonno had loved his music. But she hurried back to the pensione, anxious to return before sunset.

"*Ecco*," the clerk said when Anna pulled open the lobby door, putting his paperback aside and handing her the room key. Anna recognized the name printed on the yellowing book: *Il Prete Bugiardo*. Dudley, it seems, had also written about lying priests.

In her room, a large glass vase, jammed with red roses, was balanced on the nightstand. Could they be from Roberto? She wasn't sure if she hoped so or not. But, for some reason, Jack had sent them. Wasn't she ever far enough away to be free of him?

26

Red Dawn

Saturday, morning

Anna awoke at six, unable to sleep, worrying about when Biondi would come for her again.

Margo wasn't expecting her at the palazzo for several hours. If I'm going to prison for a crime I didn't commit, she thought, I might as well enjoy my last hours of freedom. Resolving to capture Venice's fragile beauty, to have some record of her time here, no matter how it ended, Anna bolted from bed, washed and dressed, and grabbed her camera. Once she dashed down the stairs, she tossed her heavy room key onto the empty counter before heading for the door.

Jogging past the vegetable barge, she recognized the two workmen she had met while searching for Gabriella's diary. She inquired if they knew an old gondolier by the name of Armando Tota. A good friend, the senior one replied. Soon he would be starting work as usual, at the gondola station opposite the hotel and Harry's Bar.

She crossed the Accademia Bridge to snap the palazzo-lined banks of the Grand Canal before catching the Number One vaporetto as it motored toward the bacino. The cherry orb of the sun shone onto Fortune's globe atop the Dogana when she pressed the shutter. The patterns of the Doge's Palace grew rosy in the gentle light. Anna disembarked and took shots of San Giorgio Maggiore, the basilica, and the campanile. In the deserted piazza, she could hear the shushing sound of a street sweeper's broom, the coos of unseen pigeons, and faint voices rising and falling against the peaceful walls.

After walking along the Riva to the Arsenale, with its proud stone lions, Anna found an outdoor caffè, not far from the Metropole Hotel, where she pondered her next move. She puzzled over what she might gain from Tota about his dead brother. More than a cup of bitterness, she hoped.

Her mind was flooded with warring waves of determination and anxiety as she wondered why she was being followed and attacked. Had she witnessed something at the Belvedere that she did not understand or even recall? Or was it the killer's response to her search for clues?

Servizio Gondole, with its barbershop poles and green fencing, was just a few steps from Hotel Monaco and Grand Canal's picturesque veranda. Blue-covered gondolas rocked in the waves as a young gondolier was tying up his boat. "Where can I find Armando Tota?" she asked in Italian.

"Who wants to know?"

She told him her name, and he disappeared into a shed. A wizened man with tanned, age-spotted skin warily emerged, leaned against the railing, and began speaking in Venetian dialect. When he realized his singsong words were unintelligible to her, he switched to Italian.

Anna said she was helping a friend write about the Gondola Murders for an American newspaper, and they wanted to find out the truth. What did he think was important for her to know?

"American?" His amber eyes lit up. "I have relatives—cousins—in San Francisco."

"That's where I'm from."

"I tell you something then." He clasped his hands together in supplication. "They tried to make him into a monster, and he was not."

"Who?"

"Piero, my twin. We grew up in Burano. He'd look just like me now. Handsome, no?" He passed one calloused hand along the side of his head, ruffling a gray carpet of hair. "They claimed he was being paid off by the count to stay away from her—took lots of lire but didn't leave her alone. Absolutely not. He loved Gabriella. He would have been with her even with no money. They tried to get him kicked out of La Categoria, the gondolier guild. But gondoliers stick together. If the count couldn't have her, he made sure nobody could. So he had her killed."

"I'm sorry, isn't it true that the police didn't solve the murders?"

"Bribed, all bribed. Even the newspapers. They sell their souls for lire. That's if they had any souls to start."

"Who do you think murdered Piero and Gabriella?"

"I just told you, Alessandro Favier—he had his henchman, Sergio Corrin, do it." Armando turned and spit into the water. "I'm glad he met his end. A painful one."

"How do you know it was him?"

"The wealthy think the gondoliers are stupid peasants of the water. We have more than four hundred sets of eyes and ears: a glimpse here, snatches of conversation there. Rich people talking, stumbling, drunk after parties, groping each other. Gondoliers are like a family. We compete, we fight among ourselves, yes. But when one of our own is killed, we find out who did it."

"And take revenge as well?"

"About that, I cannot say. But I did hear he is missing a hand."

When Anna arrived at the piano nobile and entered the living room, Margo was pacing the floor. She jumped when she saw her.

"You scared me! First you give me the slip at the *Gazzettino*, then you slink in here. How'd you get in?"

"The door was open. Who else is at home?"

"Nobody except me and the dog, and he didn't even bark. Some protection."

Anna gave Nero a distracted pat on the head when he came over, wagging his tail.

"Where'd Angela go?"

"Away," Margo said. "She's pissed at me. I was only asking her a few questions last night, following up on things Roberto had told us the other day, and her business with Sergio. She left in a huff around seven this morning. Said she had an appointment."

"That early?"

"You think you know your own relatives!"

"Maybe you were hard on her." Anna knew that Margo would be tone deaf to her own rat-a-tat questioning.

"Nah."

"Maybe she didn't like what you were implying about Sergio."

"From all accounts, he was a bastard except to Fanfarone, who says he was a saint."

"This morning, I spoke to someone who thought he was the devil. Armando Tota, Piero's twin brother. He's still alive."

"How'd you find him? And more important, what did he say about Sergio?"

"The gondoliers pieced it all together, he told me. Sergio killed Piero and Alessandro's family. He was working for Alessandro."

Margo rolled her eyes. "Their hatred and suspicion of Alessandro is to be expected. Class warfare, pure speculation. Nobody actually saw anything. How'd you find out about whatshisname, Tota?"

"Armando was mentioned in a *Gazzettino* article. I snuck into the archives while you were with Fanfarone and was making progress until he barged in and kicked me out. The newspaper I'd been looking at had some pages torn out, and he thought I'd done it."

"Did you?"

"Of course not."

Margo's brow furrowed. "Now we can kiss any other nuggets from him goodbye. Luckily, I found out a few things before I left."

"Such as?"

"More on how Piero and Gabriella died," Margo said.

"He told you?"

"Thanks to my skills as an interviewer. It was awful. She was stabbed, then her hand was hacked off. Bruises around her throat, too."

"Brutal and bloody." Anna jabbed her nails into her palms.

"Why the hand?" Margo asked. "Isn't that a punishment for stealing in some countries?"

"With all of her money?"

"Gimme a break. Rich people steal, too, you know. That's how some of them get rich in the first place."

"Sergio lost his hand, too, if we can believe Armando Tota and Kitty. So we have: one, the same person killing Gabriella and Sergio; two, a copycat; three, a revenge killing if Sergio had murdered Gabriella in the same way; or four, just happenstance. What did Fanfarone say about Piero?"

"Stabbed before drowning." Margo picked up two pieces of paper sitting on an end table. "Look at what I found here, though. Something better than any newspaper article—a confession from Gaetano! If you have trouble with the Italian, call out the word to me. You'd better sit down."

She passed the wrinkled pages to Anna, seated on the edge of the green couch.

She begged me. If I didn't help her to escape her prison, she threatened to kill herself and the bambina. Gabriella was nothing if not headstrong, so I believed her. I could see her

*light fading day by day, until she almost seemed a ghost. I
knew she would leave us one way or the other. Her love was
somewhere else. This made me sad, and I thought that for
all of their money, for all of their high position, I would not
wish to be a Favier.*

*Gabriella warned me that at a quiet time, when we least
expected it, when I was out of the palazzo at the Rialto buying fresh seppie to cook with polenta, or at Jesurum for fluffy
towels embroidered with the Favier crest, she would decide
for both of them.*

*Gabriella was one thing, but how could I bear to see young,
innocent blood forever staining the floors of the palazzo and
my name and that of my father and grandfather, all of us
having served the Faviers faithfully for generations? I had witnessed the wedding, full of promise, then the bambina's birth
at the hands of the Peruvian doctor. Together with my father
(he had such talent) we built the bambina a dollhouse, and
played hide-and-seek with her among the big planters on the
altana. By the Virgin Mary, no, I just could not. I could never
be responsible for her death, for a sin so great.*

*One day, when the count was away on business, Gabri-
ella woke me. It was time, she said. I called the family friend
for counsel, who told me to follow my conscience. I nodded
to Gabriella, who gathered her things. She kissed me, saying
that she would never forget this kindness. I told her this was
not a day to celebrate, but a day to mourn. The door was
so heavy, it did not want to move. Finally, it hissed open.
I lifted little Monica into my arms and gave her a kiss on
the cheek. Once I carried Gabriella's bags to the canal, she
turned to me with thanks in her teary eyes. My heart broke
when I helped them into the gondola. For I did not think
that in this life I would ever see them again.*

I stood there frozen as I watched the retreating boat. Little Monica's dark tresses and Gabriella's head got smaller until they became miniatures, then nothing at all. Afraid of what I had just done, I was afraid to move.

That slick gondolier's accursed face, his monkey arms outstretched with ragged hands. Grasping money (we could never pay him enough to go away), grasping beauty, grasping the life out of this palazzo. How could she love such a creature? Surely he leaves stains on her silk garments. He calls himself a Venetian. Ha! I made inquiries for the count. The Council told me that Tota's grandparents were from Naples.

I entered the quiet palazzo. Then I prepared myself for the storm to come. I finished a few of the Bardolinos and a grappa before the count came home. I dozed in the fading light. Awakening to the sound of his feet on the terrazzo as he hurried from room to room calling for little Monica, I heard her name until I could stand it no more. I slid out from my hiding place and whispered to him that I had something terrible to say. We went up to the altana so that no ears inside could hear us.

My throat closed. I tried to tell him, but how could I explain? I could see his fury rising, his face darkening. I stood awaiting my penance and backed away. Like a roll of thunder, I tumbled down the hard gray marble steps. When I came to, I was in a heap at the bottom of the stairs, ready, perhaps, for the dustbin. I would have welcomed it. Eva, one of the day maids, was screaming. I was bleeding.

The next thing I remember was the count carrying me to the ambulance boat. Rocking with the waves, the starry sky was far away, but it comforted me.

Gaetano Popetta

15 June, year of our Lord 1955

"Heartbreaking," Anna said.

"Gaetano was right," Margo said with a sniffle. "He never did see them again. It's hard for me to think that he had the education to write this flowery language. Someone else, a trusted family friend, like Sergio, must have written it once Gaetano told his story to him."

Anna fingered the pages. "I can't see Pablo harming Gabriella, not after delivering her baby. But whether he murdered Sergio is another question. He told me he had hoped Sergio would die."

"Why?"

"For killing a jaguar and trying to get Pablo involved. Pablo was so enraged, he stirred up the locals against him. Years later, it was payback time. Sergio tried to ruin him after he had made a medical mistake in Peru—the one covered by all the papers here."

"So that's what it was about."

"Maybe. Back to theories about the Gondola Murders. Let's say Alessandro announces well in advance that he's taking a business trip. It's his final test to see if Gabriella will stay—which puts in motion the rest of his plan. He had hired a contract killer to watch the palazzo. That morning, the man follows them and kills Gabriella and Piero, but the daughter accidentally drowns. No wonder Alessandro's a crushed man. Later on, Sergio finds out about Alessandro's role and extorts money from him until Alessandro stops paying. Sergio threatens to expose Alessandro and gets killed before he does. What do you think?"

"Ridiculous. That theory again? Almost forty years later?"

"It's the most logical explanation for all that cash he sent to Sergio. What's yours?" Anna asked.

Margo flinched as a nearby church bell rang. "We should get this back to the library, before Gaetano returns from the fish market."

Just as Margo grabbed the papers, they heard a man's voice

calling, "*Ragazze, dove siete? C'è un'emergenza. Subito. Dobbiamo partire.*"

Margo froze. "How'd Alessandro get back so early from Ravenna?"

"And what emergency?" Anna asked.

Nero barked and Alessandro leaped from the elevator, rushing toward them.

Margo jerked back her hand.

"What are you hiding, Margo?" he bellowed. "Something of mine? Give it to me."

She extended the pages to him with a tremor.

"These do not belong to you!" He tucked them into his pocket.

"I didn't mean any harm," Margo cried.

His eyes darted this way and that. "Both of you, now! Into the elevator!" he said, punching the ground-floor button. "We need to meet Biondi right away."

"What are you talking about?" Margo asked.

Anna squeezed her hand.

"We take the boat immediately," he shouted, sprinting to the palazzo entry, pushing them ahead, then slamming the door so hard that a geranium pot shattered on the pavement. He led them to the canal and jumped aboard his boat. "We have no moment to waste."

On the stern, Anna glimpsed the words *La Farfalla*—The Butterfly.

"Get in," he commanded. "*Subito.*"

Once they boarded, he cranked up the engine and accelerated so hard, the women fell against each other in the aft, like reeds before a fierce wind. As she knocked against a cushioned bench, Anna feared this would be their finale. She imagined a desolate, marshy island on the way to Torcello, where Alessandro would dispose of their bodies. She shouted into Margo's ear, "He's tricked us to get us into his boat. He knows we're onto him. Now he's going to kill us and cut off our hands."

Margo looked as white as the passing stucco walls.

"Biondi called me," Alessandro shouted, the spray punctuating his words, oblivious to their lying sprawled behind him. "They found Angela lying in the Giardini Pubblici. She's been stabbed!"

27

Napoleon's Gardens

Saturday, morning

"Alessandro, talk to me," Margo yelled over the staccato thunder of the wide-open throttle. She pulled herself up from the heaving teak deck, and steadying herself on the gunwale, lurched forward. "It can't be Angela!"

When Alessandro said nothing, Margo pulled on his shoulder. "It's some other American. Angela must be walking around or taking a breather at Florian. She's heading back to the palazzo now, wanting to nap. You know how she likes to sleep." Her voice grew strident. "What does that dumb Biondi know, anyway?"

"Stop it!" Alessandro swatted her hand away. "You must understand. Angela spoke." His voice roared above the blast of the engine as they threaded a gauntlet of low brick bridges. "She said her own name, and mine. Biondi knows more than we do. A lot more." He turned to look at her. "*Insomma*, he is a good detective."

"She's conscious then. Maybe it's not too bad. And the baby . . ."

"No," Alessandro yelled, slamming the throttle. Whining, the boat careened sideways into the quivering expanse of the Grand Canal. He corrected his steering with furious movements.

We may never arrive, Anna thought.

"Biondi told me it is grave," Alessandro said.

"What happened?" Margo asked, slumping into the seat next to him.

"I did not wish to waste time and *chiacchierare* with him on the phone. He would not say—only that if we are too late, we see him at the hospital."

"All of us?" Anna shouted, leaning forward.

Alessandro veered sharply, missing a slow-moving vaporetto before glancing back at her. "Yes, you too. Specially you."

"What about Pablo and Yolanda?" Anna asked, holding onto the side of the boat as it pitched.

"They did not interest him."

Alessandro's hair flew back as the boat picked up speed again and crashed into the waves. The water met the hull with a savage rhythm that reverberated through Anna's body and competed for dominance with her heart. She asked herself what evidence Biondi might have collected since they last spoke. And what slim hope did she have to avoid him when Alessandro will no longer be protecting her, but instead, handing her over like a gift-wrapped present?

Margo's sobs melted into the din of the Grand Canal as Anna took refuge studying the satin marble of Palazzo Dario, the graceful lines of its lunettes, and avoided thinking about herself or Angela. She dug her thumb nail into her forefinger, knowing that soon they'd be out in the open *bacino* and farther from land. No escape.

She fantasized about standing on the edge of the boat, bare toes clasping the wood, before she pushed off and dove into the canal. It would be a perfect dive, like that of a dolphin, taking her deep under the surface. The canal's murkiness would shield her as she swam underwater to reach the floating dock in front of the palazzo. She'd hide beneath it, until everyone was gone, coming up for air only when her lungs were about to burst. They wouldn't search for her long. She could run across the Accademia Bridge, hire a boat to take her to Trieste, and vanish while that arrogant tyrant would still be pacing back and forth at Santa Lucia Station. She'd have to buy a stolen passport and figure out how to doctor it. I should have gone home when I thought about it at the train station, she said to herself.

Margo was crumpled on the forward seat, her head cradled in her hands, immersed in her own private delirium. Anna made her way there to hug her. I may need to be the strong one now, she realized. Turning toward the stern, her gaze lingered on the boat's watery trail as they passed the Dogana, and with it, her faded chance at freedom. She withdrew into a bitter stillness, dreading the sight of Angela suffering.

Past the curve of the hotels along the Riva and the palazzos, the park trees peeked out and bowed, looking sickly and misbegotten. Police boats, tethered to poles on the emerald shore of the Public Gardens, jostled each other in the waves, like a pack of wild dogs. At last, Alessandro slowed down and pulled alongside an ambulance boat. As soon as he docked, the women jumped out, clambering up the jagged steps to a rock path and onto the broad, sweeping entrance to the park. Freed from its bank of clouds, the sun shone brightly. Far to one side and partially hidden behind a shed, police tape marked an area between pockmarked tree trunks. Anna spotted Biondi in the distance.

Margo marched them ahead like the commander of an army, with Alessandro as the rear guard. She tottered a few steps to the barrier and froze. All waited in silence, mustering the strength to go on, as their eyes moved to what lay beyond.

28

Leaves of Green

Saturday, morning

There, in a leafy niche thirty feet away, lay Angela, a jungle-like canopy of trees shielding her from the sun, her sunken eyes set in her ivory face, speckled with dirt. A delicate stream of saliva drizzled from the corner of her mouth. Her chest barely moved in shallow breaths as her left hand dangled from where her sleeve was torn and covered in blood and tissue. Dark stains and bloody puddles encircled her body. The ruby river made Anna retch. How could her baby even be alive with all of that spilled blood? A hot tear slid down Anna's cheek. A maniac had nearly turned vibrant young Angela into a corpse.

Anna recalled the merciless crescendo of her miscarriage: the pressure, the tearing, and just when she could stand it no longer, doubled over in pain, the abhorrent, clotted explosions. She was powerless to stop the endless waves. Her baby's body was somewhere in that discarded tissue. Tiny as a bean. Sixteen thousand dollars in treatments had come to that. She had become as skillful as a junkie, giving herself daily injections, followed by deep, intramuscular ones. Ultrasounds, follicle counts, petri dishes. A roller coaster of hope and despair had propelled her downward as each attempt met a grim fate, ending in unforgettable sorrow.

Angela had felt the joy of her unborn baby's arms moving, feet kicking. Maybe she had even seen a flash of the little girl's face on an ultrasound. It would be doubly cruel to lose a baby after all that. If Angela recovers—and she has to recover; oh, God, please spare her life—she will feel the same hellish void, the same aching emptiness.

Biondi was crouched close to Angela, talking to her and stroking her hair as the paramedics applied pressure to her wounds and readied a stretcher.

Alessandro passed his hand over his face. "*Dio nel cielo*," he cried—"God in heaven." He turned to the solace of the open water, dancing like a mirage between the trees.

"I should have calmed her down!" Margo cried. "Dammit! If she hadn't been so upset, she wouldn't have come here in the first place."

Hearing the commotion, Biondi approached them. Angela's half-closed, haunted eyes followed him as she made a loud, animal-like groan. That was the call to action Margo needed. She ducked under the police tape and darted ahead until a tall policeman Anna recognized blocked her progress. When Margo stepped sideways to move past him, he repeated his maneuver. They were caught in a macabre dance. "*Senta, è mia cugina. Lasciami passare, lasciami passare, per l'amore di Dio*," Margo shouted. "She's my cousin. Let me pass, let me pass, for the love of God!"

"*Signora, mi dispiace, ma questa è una scena del crimine*."

"He is right," Biondi told her. "You cannot get closer. This is a crime scene." He put his arm around Margo's shoulder and brought her back to her friends. "She is barely conscious and cannot be disturbed. She has lost much blood. Whoever did this was interrupted by the noise of the nearby workmen and scared away. They were the ones to rescue her."

"How could someone hurt her?" Margo cried.

"We have a twisted murderer on the loose," Biondi said. His eyes flashed at Anna.

"If she was talking to you earlier, Detective Biondi, could she say who attacked her?" Anna asked.

"She is very weak and could not provide much. She just said, 'Woman.'"

"*Commissario*," one of the policemen called.

"Excuse for a moment," Biondi said. "Wait here."

He joined a group examining an object on the ground near Angela. One of the policemen picked it up with a pair of tweezers and deposited it in a plastic bag. Anna heard Biondi say, "*Buon lavoro*," adding, "*Non dimenticare sotto le unghie*," reminding them not to forget to check under her fingernails.

When Biondi returned, Margo asked, "What about the baby?"

"It does not look good," Biondi said in a distressed voice. "The doctors must diagnose. Our team has done our best to save her life. They will take her to Ospedale Civile. You can visit tomorrow."

"Why not today?"

"Too frail. She needs all her strength to survive."

"But I'm her cousin." By now, Margo was practically nose to nose with Biondi.

"She cannot be excited. Her life depends on it." He motioned to the paramedics with the stretcher. "Besides, *I* make-a the rules here."

"Do what he says," Alessandro ordered.

The paramedics raised Angela onto the stretcher and headed for the ambulance boat.

"Be strong, Angela," Margo yelled. "We love you."

"This has all of you shaken, of course," Biondi said, pointing to the tall policeman. "Giovanni will accompany you to the palazzo, Count Favier. *Guida la sua barca.*"—"He will drive your boat."

"*Grazie.*"

"*Giovanni, vado nella pensione della Signora Lottol, e poi ci riuniamo nel palazzo,*" Biondi said, informing the policeman that he was going to Anna's pensione and would meet later at the palazzo. "Signora Lottol, come with me."

The ambulance siren howled in the distance as Anna gazed at their retreating backs.

"So soon we meet again. We go to my police boat." Biondi's cold eyes appraised her as he led the way. "We find out you don't stay with Count Favier, like you told me. I hope you have more than a flimsy story this time."

"I didn't know he couldn't accommodate me until I spoke to my friend. Detective Biondi, this attack on Angela—only a madman could hurt her."

"Or a madwoman. I rule nothing out, Signora Lottol. A woman who uses her body to manipulate men, twists them around her little finger, clouds their judgment, maybe hires an assassin. What were you doing with Roberto Cavallin?"

"That's none of your business. Did you have me followed?"

"Where were you early this morning?"

"This morning?" Anna hesitated.

"Yes. *Sta mattina,*" he repeated.

"I walked around, took some pictures." She tried to sound casual as they neared the police skiff.

"How many did you take? And where?"

She paused for a moment before regaining her pace. "I can't remember exactly, a number. I went over to Piazza San Marco."

"Miss Arithmetic cannot recall how many? And where else you go?"

"Down to the Arsenale and back."

"Taking you in the direction of the Public Gardens. Where is the film now?"

"In the camera."

He stepped onto the police boat and offered his hand. She declined, and they went forward. Biondi started up the engine. "Did anyone see you leave your pensione? And what time?"

"The clerk wasn't at the desk, so I left my key on the counter. Later, I met Margo in the palazzo, around nine."

Biondi cocked a fair eyebrow, threw the boat in reverse, and they sped off toward the center of Venice. Anna stared at the mahogany stern of Alessandro's boat. "Why don't we catch up to them? My camera's right here in my bag. I can give it to you."

"We need more. Besides, you could have taken those pictures on any morning. And you did not answer me the time you left the pensione." He broke away from *La Farfalla*.

"About six or six-fifteen, I guess. Where are we going?"

"On my special tour," Biondi said, veering into a narrow canal off the Riva. "You will see soon enough. So. You are on vacation, and yet getting up so early in the morning! For what?"

"To take pictures of the sunrise, and the city."

They were passing beneath a dozen clotheslines linking the third floors of several buildings, the drying garments fluttering like flags. Anna looked up at all the colors set against the sky and dreamed of sprouting wings.

"The sun is not up by six."

"Maybe it was later, then. I left right after I woke up."

"I do not suppose," he said, stroking his stubbled chin, "that anyone else out so early, a street sweeper or a bakery worker, could identify you."

"I did have breakfast over at the Riva."

"What time?"

"Maybe eight."

"Before then, you talked to no one, even though you speak Italian."

Anna coughed and tried to control her voice. "The first thing

I did was to return to a canal near my pensione and speak to some men working on a barge. Later, I wasn't paying attention to other people. I was looking for the perfect angle for my photos." He was fishing, testing her reactions like a doctor aiming a rubber mallet at her knees. This time she knew what to expect from his forays, but was uncertain how long her will could hold back her fear.

"Afterward, what did you do, and when?"

"After breakfast, I went over to the gondola station near the Hotel Monaco, to speak to Armando Tota, the brother of Piero, the man who was killed in the old Gondola Murders."

"Do not believe what he says," Biondi said, turning the boat sharply.

They seemed to be going in a circle. The gray, stippled backside of the Palazzo Ducale loomed ahead.

"Even now, you hide something. Here we are. To our left are what we call the *piombi*," said Biondi, like a perverse tour guide. "You have heard of them, I am sure: the 'leads,' the prison—the cramped, dark cells we put criminals in centuries ago. Shame we cannot use them anymore." He peered at her. "You know, they were so frightening, we would get many confessions. We also had torture devices for easing truth from reluctant criminals."

"And lies from the innocent as well, I imagine. Just to stop the pain."

They slid under the Ponte della Paglia and came into the bacino once more, hugging the shore. Biondi pulled back on the throttle and pointed to the twin pillars of the Lion of Saint Mark and San Teodoro.

"Over there, we would hang perpetrators upside down. Very unlucky to walk between the columns. And we would suspend a cage for the criminal against the pink marble of the Palazzo Ducale. Quite cold in wintertime, but such a beautiful view from that height. Have you not been to the top of the campanile?"

"Not yet." Thinking about such a confined space, far above ground, jammed with tourists elbowing one another for the best vantage point, made her queasy.

"Venetians are an imaginative lot." He leaned over until his eyes were level with hers. "Do not force me to get imaginative with you."

"Stop it!" Anna yelled.

"I spoke with Dr. Zampone, Signora Lottol. You know, that 'friend of someone back home' in your address book? You make a habit of lying to me, but I know a little secret now. Even if you do not take the doctor's warning serious, I do. How many bad dreams about killing Sergio Corrin have you had since you come to Venice? How many hallucinations?"

Anna gasped. How could Zampone have betrayed her and the confidentiality he had promised? If Biondi's jilted inamorata theory wouldn't work, he now had a new one: mental illness. She sat fuming at both men.

From the corner of her eye, she glimpsed Biondi half smiling. "Have a glass of water," he said cheerily. "You must be thirsty."

Anna reached over and managed to pour some water from a thermos into a cup without spilling any. The water vibrated with the boat's engine. She sat there meditating on the tiny ripples, hoping an answer would rise from beneath, as if it were a liquid Ouija board. Anna recalled nudges, cuts, and rude comments she had received over the years, including many from Leslie, that she had let pass. However, this was her dignity. Biondi had crossed a line.

At the moment, it didn't matter how much more trouble her actions would bring. She threw the water in Biondi's face and said, "Pumping my . . . therapist is immoral and illegal. You call yourself a police detective, but you're nothing but a lazy bully, trying to pin everything on me."

"I can arrest you for that," Biondi said with clenched teeth, taking out his handkerchief and wiping his face. Anna noted a few stains on his fine charcoal suit, but most of the water had hit its mark. "You are lucky I am interested only in catching *l'assassino*. Some people in your predicament try to bribe me instead of throwing water. But do not think it, because Biondi cannot be bought. I am not a politician."

When they entered the pensione, Anna asked Giuseppe for her key. "*Ma lei ha pagato soltanto per una singola,*" he replied, wagging his finger at Biondi, convinced that Anna was trying to sneak a man upstairs when she had paid for only a single room.

"*Cazzo, questo è un affare della polizia,*" Biondi cursed him, face flushing. "*Sono il Commissario Biondi. La chiave.*"

Cowering, the clerk dangled the room key to Biondi, who snatched it and charged up the squeaking stairs. Anna followed slowly.

"Here is the *mandato di perquisizione*, the search warrant, for your room," Biondi said, unfurling a paper. "My team will be here soon to comb through everything. I start now and give them a little boost." He put on a pair of thin rubber gloves.

Anna sat on her bed, shoulders hunched, surrounded by her belongings, as if on a patchwork quilt sewn by a maniac. She doubted she was capable of much now—like Gaetano at the bottom of the stairs, ready for the dustbin.

She remained still and mute as the police sorted through her purse and every goddamn thing she had brought on her trip—taking items with her fingerprints, pulling hair from her brush, grabbing her raincoat along with a postcard she had started to write. A female officer accompanied her to the bathroom, where she had to strip off her clothing and surrender it. The policewoman examined her for scratches and bruises, inspecting her hands, her fingernails. She took a sample of Anna's saliva for DNA testing.

Back in her room, Biondi counted her money, compared it to

what receipts he could find, and muttered a few expletives when he was unable to reconcile her spending. He stuffed her torn, still-gleaming Fortuny dress, her camera and undeveloped film, and a pair of shoes into a large satchel. He asked her who had sent her flowers.

Biondi frowned when she showed him the water-stained ledger book with its wavy pages. "I was carrying this in my pocket on Wednesday night, when I dove into a canal to save my life. Somebody tried to hurt me in a narrow passage with a pushcart. I got a note asking me to come to Alessandro's palazzo, and I carried, um, a diary I had borrowed from the Favier library. I thought Margo had sent it, but she hadn't. I'm sure the note's someplace in this room."

"We will search for it, and I will have one of our officers take your statement about the dangerous pushcart." As he confiscated the ledger book, he looked as if he wanted to smile. "We do not wish to exclude anything, just in case you tell the truth this time. But maybe you soaked the little book in the sink or the bathtub, to try to make me believe you. And where is the diary you borrowed?"

"I tried to save it by tossing it aside before I went into the canal. But when I looked for it later, it was gone."

"So, in addition to the ledger you took from Count Favier, you stole a diary, which was then taken by another thief?"

"I told you, I was only borrowing them."

"Let me guess. Without permission."

One of the officers reentered the room then and spoke with Biondi. The detective turned to Anna with a smirk and said, "They tell me what the desk clerk recalls. You told him you fell into the canal."

Anna glanced at the bouquet of roses. Petals were falling like tears.

29

Dark Star Trails

Saturday, afternoon

Lying in bed, Anna stared at the ceiling and recalled other trials.

There were no shortcuts to mastering the hurdles. It took two years before she could soar, defying gravity, above them. Sprinting with all her might, driving with one knee, lifting her arms, positioning her trail leg over the side, leaning forward, staying patient, knowing that how she cleared the first hurdle would foretell the other nine. And learning how to not . . . look . . . down.

That had been easy compared with establishing a complex mathematical proof in front of an entirely male audience. Ignoring the roomful of students—squinting at every notation, tittering, ready to pounce—and the skeptical professor, standing in back, she had stayed focused, calmly writing each equation on the blackboard, constructing a thoroughly logical, unassailable edifice when she was done. Undaunted, she had twirled around and beamed in their incredulous faces.

A loud knock at the door brought her back to the present. "*Chi è?*"

"*Sono io.*"

Recognizing Giuseppe's voice, she tugged the door open to

find him holding out several pages from the fax machine. *"Quando è arrivato?"* she asked him.

It had come on Thursday, he confessed with a groan, but had gotten lost under a pile of bills. Anna clapped her hands and kissed him on the cheek. He touched his face and lingered as she retreated into her room and shut the door.

Grabbing a pen, she dashed to the writing desk and slipped into the chair. Despite Anna's complaint, Brian had persisted in sending faxes. They were less noticeable, he had claimed, given Leslie's obsessive scrutiny of phone bills. How wrong that turned out, she thought. When Brian had dispatched this fax to Anna in his final hours at Treasury, he had proved his fidelity. She'd have to find a way to show him hers.

The pages outlined money trails between Sergio and Alessandro, Dudley, Angela, and others. Some may have been just innocent transfers of funds involving investments and purchases of art. Or maybe sinister. Why would Alessandro send fifty thousand dollars to Sergio's personal account in New York, instead of depositing Italian lire locally in Banco Saturno, if not to keep the money transfers from the gaze of Italian regulators and tax authorities? Why had Sergio wired Dudley steady sums, which could represent a handsome rental or annuity stream, at an outsized clip of twenty-five thousand dollars a month?

Sergio's art gallery maintained a separate US dollar account at Granite Bank in New York. This account indicated repetitive transfers, credits of ten to twenty thousand dollars apiece, originating from a Manhattan store called Polo Road, plus funds arriving from Angela, periodic incoming payments from a bank in China, and outlays in Africa.

Nothing linked Sergio to his ex-employers: Banca Serenissima and Mediobanca. A portion of Banco Saturno's account traffic through Granite went to and from US brokerage and investment houses. This made sense given its clientele.

But Saturno's interbranch activity showed high volumes as funds were shifted among locations. Instead of an illuminating trail of stars, the pattern was a dizzying potpourri of transactions from fifteen countries and more than one hundred counterparties. Anna pictured a fun-house pinball machine lighting up as money bounced back and forth, up and down, ultimately finding its way to the bottom, where it fed into Sergio's mouth. Such a maze of twists and turns, with funds skipping through multiple countries, often masked laundering. Criminals know that a given country's regulations and examinations of sources of funds stop at its borders. Money can evade such scrutiny hopping across borders unimpeded, ultimately circling the globe.

If Anna could decipher which origins were legitimate and which illegal, she might get a lead on Sergio's killer. One transfer had caught her eye: On the Monday after Sergio's murder, fifty million dollars from Saturno's sub-account for Le Pont Neuf, a company in Luxembourg, had been sent to a Panamanian construction company, Nuevo Puente de Panamá.

Brian had scribbled the phone number and name of a contact at the local office of the Guardia di Finanza, a specialized Italian police force focusing on financial crimes and smuggling. The Guardia would be very interested in the account of Sergio's US activities that the faxes laid bare. In return, Anna might be able to glean something that could help her solve Sergio's murder.

She phoned the number and was able to make an appointment for five p.m. Either Brian had destroyed this last fax or Leslie hadn't felt she needed to alert the Guardia di Finanza to a potential visit from an ex-employee, whose determination, Anna thought proudly, had been wildly underestimated.

She continued diagramming money flows, noting transaction sizes, dates, senders, recipients, and respective countries where known. The final page of Brian's fax included a handwritten note. "I cross-checked the attendance at the banking conference against all the names of people you provided. Need to review, but I think I found a surprise. Hope to send details tomorrow. Ciao."

Leslie had seen to it that Brian didn't last one more day.

Dressed in her gray pantsuit and low heels, Anna stepped out of the water taxi at the airport and asked for directions to the Guardia di Finanza. The driver pointed to a nondescript white building near the shore.

She cajoled the lobby guard into allowing her to identify herself without a passport, using her California driver's license and Treasury Department picture ID. For a moment, she worried if this was a trap to lure her upstairs and arrest her on behalf of US authorities, before jettisoning the thought. She didn't have to come here to be arrested. That could have happened already.

A smartly attired receptionist ushered her upstairs into an elegant conference room, its picture window framing the steel-gray expanse of the bay, and brought her a cappuccino. On the opposite wall hung a large mural in the bold, bright colors of St. Mark's and the lagoon, the puffy cotton clouds above them evoking a fairy tale. Anna took a seat at a sea-green lacquer table, on which a crystal pitcher, some glasses, and a bowl of fruit were assembled like a still life.

Entering the room, Manfredo Di Tomasso introduced himself and thanked her for coming, saying that they could make use of her information. After a brief discussion, he informed Anna that the agent heading the investigation would take over. She organized Brian's faxes and while she waited, went over her rough analysis of the account relationships. As she spotted more transfers shifting through multiple accounts, she made notes and drew arrows, finalizing the list of countries where funds either originated or were sent. More could be gained through computer analysis, but that would have to wait.

Checking her watch, she noted that twenty minutes had passed. These people were hardly the picture of punctuality, she concluded, suspecting it translated into a low ratio of solved cases.

How rude, Anna was thinking, looking up with a frown as someone cleared his throat.

Roberto stood at the threshold, dressed in a brown suit and tie, holding a thick notebook.

30

La Guardia di Finanza

Saturday, evening

She gawked at him. "What are you doing here? Did they call you in for a tax audit?"

"This is where I happen to work," he said quietly. He shut the door and slipped into a leather chair at the head of the table, gazing at Anna with a cool air. "I've just had to disclose how my video camera was broken. You could have noticed it was aimed at the dining area, not the bedroom. And it wasn't running."

She slumped, recalling the sound of the pantry door slamming.

"I believe you owe me an apology."

"I had no idea. I'm awfully sorry."

When she reached for his hand, he pulled back and crossed his arms. "The camera is a tool to trap tax evaders, smugglers, and money launderers with their own words."

"So you pretend that you'll provide them with financial advice and then record what they say?"

"No different from what your agents do in the United States. You didn't even give me a chance to explain."

"Would you have?"

"I was ready to. You didn't trust me enough to wait."

"I . . . I thought you were an investment banker getting his kicks. And you were once—a banker, I mean."

"Until I found a higher calling."

"But you don't always work undercover?"

"No, I need to stay active in finance, to be credible." He opened a pocket in the table and powered up the computer that popped into view. "Shall we get on, then?"

"One second, please." Anna looked at Roberto and had to ask. "When we were together on Thursday, was it . . . was it for your job?"

He gave her a disappointed look. "Who I get close to is my decision—my life."

"I see," she said, hoping he was telling the truth. "Please let me know if I can reimburse you for the camera—"

"I pay for my own mistake."

Anna sipped her coffee, recalling her early training and the repeated warning not to have intimate relationships with coworkers. This is going to be awkward, she thought.

"Did you hear that Angela was attacked this morning? We saw her before she was rushed to the hospital. There was so much blood. Horrible." She gnawed at her lip to keep from crying.

"I heard. Poor woman. I will call Margo later to see how she is. You know Angela did business with Sergio. We are looking into how much."

"I have data that should shine a light on that and on the rest of Sergio's network."

"Let's make sure we understand each other. *Niente*—nothing—nothing of what we speak can you tell anyone else, even Margo. That includes anything about me."

"I didn't even tell her I was coming here."

"Good." He leaned back in his chair.

"She knows I'm trying to figure out Sergio's crimes on my own, with help from my office, because of Detective Biondi. We're seeking evidence to clear me."

"*Mannaggia!*" He tapped the table after cursing. "Margo talks too much to too many people. We had better get going before someone puts more twos and twos together." He hit a few computer keys. "We've been watching Sergio for a while. Despite owning Banco Saturno and his family wealth and investments, we identified a sizeable gap between his jet-setting lifestyle and his declared income."

"At Torcello, you said he could do very well just clipping bond coupons."

"And I should share what our hard-fought investigations have discovered? No. I only repeated gossip and what is already in the public domain."

"I see."

"Sergio wasn't liquidating assets but adding to them: another yacht in Monaco, his-and-hers 1967 Ferrari Spiders at a second home near Asolo. We suspected him of underreporting the profits from his gallery to evade taxes; the low sales figures did not correspond to the high turnover in artwork. We dug beyond his personal financial statements and the gallery's by studying warehouse receipts and wire transfers. It was very difficult to establish the value of the art pieces. We couldn't back into his stated sales. He continued overspending money, so either he somehow tricked us or he was getting money some other way. And it wasn't from loans."

Roberto looked up as a man opened the door and beckoned.

"Excuse me for a moment." Anna overheard him saying in Italian, "I didn't think he was. On the other hand, go ahead and schedule it."

Italian tax evasion was something Anna couldn't pursue from her end. Roberto and his colleagues had just started to scratch the surface. They were heading in the same direction, but coming from different avenues.

As Roberto took his seat again, he said, "Last week, from our interviews with one of the artists, we found out that Sergio did undervalue much of the artwork."

"Azizi Sabodo?"

He nodded.

"How long have you been investigating Sergio?"

"Ten months."

"And you notified him?" she asked.

"We had to, back in December. Twenty-five percent of the Italian economy is underground, and tax audits do happen here. He fought like the devil. He pulled every string he had, and those went very far and very high. Imagine, he was the chairman of CONSOB two decades ago, now a bank president, an art connoisseur, and a philanthropist, plus a member of the Venetian aristocracy, and we have the audacity or the poor judgment to treat him like any other Italian by trying to inspect his books. It was a very nasty fight."

So Sergio would have been in the midst of this when he sought me out, she thought. Italian companies and nationals were often in the news as they paid back taxes and a fine. But a money-laundering trail, leading to underlying criminal activity, was something else entirely. Sergio was a powerful, connected man with no scruples and his back against the wall. She could easily imagine the damage he could inflict.

"He dragged his feet, but in the end we prevailed, going beyond the financial statements to examine the ledgers for Banco Saturno and his personal bank records in Italy. We interviewed his staff accountant, that type of thing, looking for evidence that he was committing fraud, using the bank itself to fund other enterprises. I went undercover after analyzing his finances, to discover whether his art and extracurricular activities hid something illegal."

"What happened?"

"Last month, we froze the lira account for his gallery. We had seen an abnormally large transfer to a Luxembourg entity, an investment company, a few months before. The gallery account automatically swept funds to two others, one in Frankfurt and the other in Zürich. The Germans won't freeze the Frankfurt account—not enough evidence, according to their judge—and the Swiss . . . well, it's all secret there, that's how they make their money. Sergio was scheduled to come here in two weeks to present my partner with more information on his accounts and businesses."

"And you're thinking others are still running his operation."

"Given the size of it, he couldn't have been acting alone. If there are ill-gotten gains, they sit in someone's account, and we'll bring those people to justice. Maybe he was like the mythical Hydra; you chop off its head, two more spring to life, and the organization continues. We will see."

"I found a recent transfer after his death that'll interest you, a large transfer of funds to an account in Panama. Maybe it was pre-set, but it's something to check."

Roberto looked past Anna at the mural with the church, lagoon, and puffy clouds. When he pushed a button on the console, the cheery image slid behind a wooden panel. In its place was a stark whiteboard map of the world. "This will help."

He pulled an assortment of colored markers from a cardboard container, making Anna think of a giant box of Crayola crayons. She remembered her eagerness as a child contemplating the tantalizing array, deciding exactly which hue to choose. Now she was coloring for her freedom.

"It'll be easier if you view from here," Roberto said. "We'll both use the board."

She came and sat beside him. She caught the spicy fragrance of an aftershave or shampoo and thought about Thursday with a pang.

"What have you brought?" he asked. "Maybe we can piece it all together."

"I'm freelancing, Roberto. I asked a coworker in San Francisco to apply algorithms I had created back home to thousands of funds transfers that he gathered from all of Sergio's US dollar accounts. That included Sergio's and Liliana's personal accounts, the gallery account, and Banco Saturno's. I also focused on the individual accounts of people I've met here. These were distilled to roughly three hundred questionable transactions. My boss isn't even aware of all the implications."

"I see. Why did you take this on yourself? Why should you care?"

Her mind raced. She could invent a story, which might blow up in her face, or she could tell him everything—about her humiliating affair with Sergio, his threats of blackmail, Biondi's suspicions. She couldn't squirm out of this one. Although the Guardia di Finanza was a separate unit, it surely cooperated with local police. Chances are he already knew all about her.

She gazed through the window for a moment and took a deep breath. A pair of spoonbills careened beneath a copper sun.

"I met him at the Italian Banking Association conference in Milan in January."

"I remember the announcement. You were on the program."

"In more ways than one." She felt herself blushing. "He used our liaison to threaten me with some photographs. Before I left for Venice, I checked his US account activities, and they seemed suspicious. We met at a caffè on the day he was killed. He told me he would return the photos if I did him a 'favor.'"

"Which was?"

"He wanted me to use my position to work connections and tell him anything I could find on his financial activities that the Italian authorities were investigating. I refused. Sneaking into the masked ball that night to try to talk with him again and then lying about it to Biondi were huge mistakes. Besides suspecting me of killing Sergio, Biondi has even accused me of trying to kill Angela! He searched my room today. He has a crazy theory that I hallucinate."

"It will not hold up. But you need to stop."

"I don't have a lot of options. Biondi would be happy to arrest me. Both cases could be closed. He can't forgive me for lying to him in the beginning."

"Someone warned you with that cart. If you persist, who knows what will happen? Do you wish to end up like Angela?"

"It's my only chance."

"*Testa dura.*" He took a sip of water. "*Allora*, if we find out something today, will I get you in trouble by contacting your office and officially asking for cooperation if needed?"

"Do what you have to do to get to the truth. I don't know what I'll be going back to—assuming that," her voice cracked, "Biondi will let me leave the country one day."

"He will."

"It won't be to that job in the Treasury Department."

"Why not?"

"My boss fired me. She accused me, if you can believe it, of working with Sergio. I have a history with her, and this provided an opportunity to give me the boot."

"Things will improve. We need to hurry. Let's start."

Anna shared the information she had about Le Pont Neuf, the Luxembourg company, along with what she had found on the involvement of Alessandro, Dudley, and Angela with Sergio. She was pleased that she had asked Brian to look back for a full year. Scrutinizing the list of older transfers, she and Roberto focused on the art gallery and other accounts, tracing each route between countries with a different color. They added codes for size and frequency and made notations on the specific account and any counterparties. Soon a tangle of lines strangled the whiteboard map of the world, connecting Dar es Salaam, San Francisco, New York, Vancouver, Dongguan, in China's Guangdong Province, Shanghai, Grand Cayman, Panama, Lima, Luxembourg, Liechtenstein, and other locations, with Hong Kong sometimes substituting for China. Polo Road had wired US dollars to Sergio's gallery accounts several times a month.

"The size of his dollar-denominated gallery sales surprised me," Anna said. Certainly, foreign purchasers enjoyed more access to and familiarity with the US dollar than the Italian lira, but more likely, this reflected Sergio's desire to spread his transactions through different countries, making him harder to apprehend.

"Suspect, if you ask me," Roberto said.

"Do you think African tribal art sells particularly well in China?"

Roberto got on the phone and muttered something about documentation history. After accessing a file via the computer, he turned the monitor toward her. The image of a letter of credit totaling a hundred thousand dollars, issued by the Banco Saturno branch in Dar es Salaam for ten wooden shields shipped directly to Dongguan, flickered on the screen. Anna noted the Banco Saturno logo, a Roman temple.

A letter of credit, used in large part for trading between exporters and importers, was a conditional guarantee of payment. The bank decided to pay based on the documents submitted and the terms; the merchandise was not inspected. Roberto selected another file that indicated the export of Tanzanian wall hangings bound for Palermo, Sicily. "We assume they were loaded onto trucks and brought here," he said.

"But why have a bank branch in Dar es Salaam in the first place?" Anna asked. "Did Sergio do that much business there?"

"His export company there sent thirty million dollars a year in letter-of-credit volume through that branch."

"That's a lot of artwork."

"Yes. Maybe Sergio was not misappropriating bank funds per se, but was using the bank in a corrupt way," Roberto said. "He had to pay various tribes for the art. A letter of credit made his exports look proper, as if he had nothing to hide."

"Shall we contrast last year's network against the most recent?" A fleeting thought about the dark Yacana crossed Anna's mind. She told herself to concentrate on what was missing, not what was present.

"Of course."

When she posted and summarized the transactions from 1992, the web was smaller. "There's the dividing line," she said, circling the activity in the previous December. China had dropped off the map of gallery transactions. Sergio and Liliana's personal account transfers went from fifteen to five regular counterparties. Banco Saturno's US dollar accounts with brokerages and commodity and foreign-exchange traders remained the same, however, and activity with Angela's gallery in Texas continued.

"*Cazzo.* He switched methods once we started investigating him," Roberto said, nodding. "Before that, everything was visible, very bold. But this year, instead of settling via the New York account in dollars, he used other currencies, or secret accounts in countries like Liechtenstein. We can't get bank information from them, either."

"Did anything revert back to Italian lira accounts, like payments to or from Alessandro or Dudley?"

"Nothing very recent with Alessandro Favier. The Filberts' one account in Italy had no connection with Sergio. They must have stopped making local investments with him."

"But Sergio put twenty-five thousand dollars a month into Dudley's US account until two months ago," Anna said. "And look at this."

She showed Roberto a page of the fax from Brian; after drilling into Polo Road's bank accounts in New York, additional data showed the company had been making payments directly to a Shanghai company. "Polo Road specializes in African tribal art. Let's say Sergio combined his legal gallery business with something illegal to yield more money."

"Right, the old trick of blending the sources of funds. We are to think New York imported African art from China? Ha!" Roberto's eyes flashed. "We have already found a line of artwork leading from Tanzania to Dongguan to Shanghai and New York. It's trafficking in animal contraband, Anna. Ivory, rhino horn, and animal parts are hidden in the art from Africa, and then the art is reshipped with the finished illegal products."

Anna had read about the wildlife-crime epidemic back at Treasury. There had been ten million elephants in Africa in 1930. By 1989, when the uncontrolled ivory trade supposedly came to an end, the elephant population had plunged to six hundred thousand, and the voluntary agreements were failing to stem a rising tide of blood and tusks. After years of trophy hunting, Sergio must have decided to make a second killing. Instead of mowing down an elephant or a rhino in an excruciatingly painful hail of bullets, he was paying others to massacre the animals while orchestrating a global business in their parts.

"Well," Roberto said with a snicker, "we see why Sergio's bank did not provide reports on suspected money launderers. He would have had to turn himself in. We will track down the wire transfers to Africa, additional copies of letters of credit, and receipts from artists. The trail starts with that. We'll also access SWIFT's data on its financial-messaging services. Rebel and terror groups, maybe in the Congo, along with contacts in Mozambique or Zaire, would have been paid for slaughtering the animals. With that money, they buy weapons, the majority made in the United States.

"Poachers cannot resist the money, either. They see the animals as ATM cards, butchered for cash—they get many thousands of dollars for a pair of tusks. Most of the ivory ships out of Mombasa or Dar es Salaam to China, sometimes transiting through Hong Kong, Vietnam, or Thailand. It's processed in Dongguan or elsewhere, carved into artwork, sold in vast numbers to Chinese consumers, and exported to other countries, like yours. Polo Road's true business must be selling illegal ivory. New York is a huge market. San Francisco is a big center. Western Europe isn't innocent, either. And a small amount is sold in the African country of origin, where ignorant or craven foreign tourists end up smuggling it back home."

"What about the rhino horns?" Anna asked.

"Ultimately ground up and used for folk medicine in Asia—more precious than gold on the black market. Not only that, now that the tigers are being killed off, I am afraid that lions and their skeletons are next. We have confiscated shipments here, arrested tourists coming through Italy trying to smuggle animal parts. I—" He stopped, shaking his head.

"This seems personal," Anna said gently.

Roberto stared at his hands. "I've touched the ragged, broken edges of the tusks and horns of those beautiful animals, smeared with their dried blood."

Anna's stomach turned. "Maybe there's a little good news in what we've found. If the funds-flow data is complete, Sergio didn't get too far in Peru." She wondered whether Pablo had had anything to do with that.

"Lucky for the jaguar and the caiman, too. For now."

"These faxes are yours to keep, Roberto. Brian Morrison's name is at the bottom. Please be sure to recognize him in official circles that go higher than Leslie Tanner, my old boss. He went out on a limb to do this for me and was fired as a result. He deserves to be rehired and given a promotion."

"Gladly. I will formally thank you as well. We'll need a few days to analyze everything and pull it together." He looked at his watch. "It's almost eight. I didn't bring my boat today. Shall we take a water taxi back? I can walk you to your pensione, maybe we eat something along the way."

"Are you sure?"

"You've had a rough time. Not to mention, you are not safe here, at least not after dark. Give me a few minutes to advise my partner on our progress." He scooped up all of the material and left the room.

Mulling over the last few hours, Anna felt a flicker of optimism. She wandered over to the window and cast her gaze on the water. The waves were dancing in the reflected lights; some boats were docking, while others headed for the infinite horizon. Her thoughts circled back to Biondi, and the courteous way he had spoken to Count Favier in the Public Gardens, even addressing him formally. Clearly, the count was someone Biondi would never curse. She realized she had been mistaken about the person who had pulled strings to keep her out of jail, although he'd never admit it. He was standing at the door.

"Ready?" Roberto asked. He took her arm, and they headed into the veil of the night.

Once back in the heart of Venice, they chose a canal-side restaurant with brightly colored hanging lanterns that reminded Anna of eating in Japantown. Water taxis and lamplit gondolas floated by as if on a stage, accompanied by the lulling sound of waves lapping against the embankment. But this was real. Anna tried to relax and enjoy the evening. Here was a man with principles, a man who interested her, a bright, worldly man in a fascinating city. Under different circumstances, it would be ideal.

They raised their glasses of fruity Valpolicella to toast elephants, sniffer dogs at airports and seaports, and intrepid park rangers who risked their lives, along with a future where armies fought to protect wild animals instead of making war, and organizations educated local people to change some destructive values of their cultures. With a few more glasses, they had solved the poaching epidemic.

As they savored fragrant chicken spezzatino with peppers and onions, they talked about their childhoods, educations, and lives. He expressed concern about the loss of her parents and showed curiosity about her upbringing. Anna learned about Roberto's father, Edgardo, the moral compass of the family. Under his influence, Roberto had majored in ancient philosophy before pursuing a graduate degree in business at Bocconi University in Milan. This had launched his career, first at Mediobanca, then elsewhere.

This brought them back to the present and Sergio Corrin. Anna confided that she and Margo had been searching Alessandro's library for clues to his murder. She told Roberto about the unsolved Gondola Murders and said there was a possibility they were connected to Sergio's death.

"Chances are there is no connection, Anna. Does Alessandro know what you're doing?"

She shook her head. "There are some similarities, you know, like the murder weapon and especially the mutilation. About Alessandro, what else am I going to do? The way I look at it, the police would need a search warrant. If I find something that helps me, or them, I'll bring it to their attention. Biondi took some of the material from my room." She told him the details of the ledger, as well as of the Liechtenstein document she had seen in Dudley's study.

"Sergio's downfall likely came from the circle of poachers and other criminals he built up around him, not his old friends," Roberto told her. "These will be hardened men. If you crossed any of them, we would be lucky," he said, straightening his napkin, "to find your body."

"I promise I'll be very careful."

Roberto pushed his plate away. "Tell me, what did you ever see in that monster?"

"Nothing of value." Anna shook her head in disgust. "Charm and a fantasy. I was running away from my marriage, in a foreign country, and couldn't think straight. I was an easy mark."

As they shared a caramel and chocolate *budino*, Anna lingered on the first bite. At least I can give in to this tonight, she thought.

After coffee, Roberto grew quiet, meditating on the water. "They mourn their dead, you know."

Anna had been lost in her own thoughts. "Who?"

"I was on a photo safari five years ago, with my ex-fiancée. Our group happened upon an extended family of elephants. The matriarch had been killed—butchered for her tusks, the rest of her bloodied and covered with flies. Her calf, just a few years old, was nuzzling her, wailing."

Anna recalled the baby elephant in Sergio's gallery.

"The elephants made a circle around her body, like they were guarding her," he said. "Some were making low, rumbling cries. Each slowly passed its trunk over her, caressing her, as if they were saying goodbye. Then they threw dirt on her with their trunks. When we passed the spot a day later, they were still standing there, keeping vigil. I tell you, the beauty and richness of these countries are being destroyed for a craving that will never cease until the last animal is dead. That was when I decided."

"What?"

"To, how do you say—chuck—it all?"

Anna nodded.

"To change my life's direction. The funny thing was, then my fiancée changed hers."

"How so?"

"She left me."

"I would think that never happens to you."

He looked at her with the ghost of a smile. "She was in love with Roberto, the investment banker, making tons of lire. She could not love Roberto, working for the Guardia di Finanza. It was a painful, yet excellent lesson."

After dinner, Roberto put his arm on her shoulder as they strolled back to her hotel by way of little alleys with their precious canal views. When they reached Pensione Stella, he gave her a soft kiss. "Let me know when you are leaving. Give me a call. Here," he handed her a card, "it's my undercover one," he whispered, winking before opening the door for her.

She turned around just as he ascended the nearest bridge and disappeared.

31

L'Ospedale Civile

Sunday, early morning

Anna counted the lire bank notes and poured a cascade of silver coins onto the paper pile on her bed. Did she really have the equivalent of just five hundred dollars left? Still in her nightgown, she wandered to the window, opening the shutters onto the tranquil calle. On the balcony opposite, plump cherub faces peeked out from the overgrown ivy.

Dragging herself to her mirror, Anna reached for a comb. Her hair had always disobeyed her. She was tugging at a few rebel curls when she noticed some movement in an upper corner of the mirror. Like a tiny tornado, a clear funnel spun on the surface before clearing. Beyond the sparkling balcony, Anna saw the reflection of an elegantly dressed woman, plaiting a little girl's dark tresses. Transfixed, Anna watched as the mother arranged golden barrettes in her daughter's braids.

Loud knocking interrupted her thoughts. "Anna, it's Margo! We have to go to the hospital now."

"What do you mean?" Anna asked as she opened the door.

"The doctor called me late last night. Things are bad. He's expecting us in an hour. We have to have hope."

Anna looked at Margo in alarm. Is this how it would end? She had needed to believe that Angela wouldn't die, that somehow she would spring back, even if the odds against it seemed great. How could Angela be so vibrant, happy, fecund one day and dying the next? It seemed not only terrifying, but contrary to natural law.

Inwardly, she was fuming. What was the use of hope? The doctors in their white coats would tend to Angela. Amid calculations of probability and statistics, there was no room for hope. Or religion. Hope didn't make the dying live.

"Yes, of course," Anna said. She paused. "I just saw the weirdest thing." Her mind sputtered and leaped to the scene she had witnessed. "A woman was combing a little girl's hair in the palazzo across from here."

"Why was that weird?"

"Let me show you." Anna took Margo's arm and brought her to the window. "There," she pointed.

"I can't see a thing. The shutters are closed."

"They are now."

Margo scrutinized her friend. "Isn't this the building Alessandro said was vacant?"

"He must be hiding something."

"We need to get going," Margo said, her voice tense. "Can't you hurry?"

The Ospedale Civile was buried in the twisted heart of Castello. When Anna crossed its threshold, a familiar smell reclaimed her and spiraled her back in time. She had been aware of death for as long as she could remember. It took the people she loved and left her with nothing.

As they passed the police checkpoint in the hall, the officer barely looked up, his head buried in *La Gazzetta dello Sport*. Entering Angela's room, Anna saw the IV first. One drop of blood slid after another, sealed in the scarlet packet feeding the puncture in Angela's wrist. The deep red liquid did nothing to brighten the ghostly cheeks. An octopus of tubes was feeding and breathing for her. Her heartbeats were oscillating in black on a green screen. Anna felt horrified that they'd been allowed in at all.

In her mind, Angela's room became a medieval painting. At the center was Angela, skin covered in a pearly gleam. Her eyes were closed, one tear poised on her cheek. The tear reflected all the world and His greatness. To her right, a nurse bent over her bed like a lady-in-waiting, holding her hand. To her left, an arched window framed a canal that had felt the ebb and flow of time and eternity. Those waters had carried French kings, Italian popes, Holy Roman Emperors. Hope was a bird on white wings that had no place in Anna's painting.

Because she had been here before, she knew what lay ahead. Back then, she had also dreaded what lay inside the hospital room. Forcing herself to go on without becoming sick or losing control had taken every bit of her courage. The lights of Manhattan had glittered through the window behind him, creating their own meteor trails, constellations, and planets, foreign to Anna's eyes. He didn't know her anymore. He knew no one, lost in the distant solar system of his mind.

Nonno had been just as pale and untouchable as Angela when Anna had visited him for the last time. His body, once so stout and strong, seemed frighteningly dwarfed by the hospital bed. The respirator's measured, mechanical breath forced the air into his unwilling lungs. "Don't leave me," she had begged, digging her nails into her palms. She had wanted him to hear her words of love, feel her kiss on his cold lips. Taking his hand, she had promised him that she would never forget his plea. She thought she had felt a weak squeeze, like that of a tiny baby.

Anna heard Margo's throaty voice—something about Angela staying with her, spoiling the baby together, having fun. "Oh, look, Anna is here to see you," she said, her red-rimmed eyes beseeching. "Come by the bed and spend time with Angela. I need to speak to the doctor."

Angela looked peaceful but lost, without bearings, without wings. Where was Angela: Trapped inside her immobile body, hearing everything and silently screaming for help, ruing her unfulfilled dreams? Or caught in the cold, fatal embrace of nothingness? Anna did not know which hell would be worse.

She pushed herself forward and gently rubbed Angela's yielding upper arm. Once, Anna had been possessed by envy; now, waves of pity tumbled over her as she recited aloud all that Angela had to live for. Everything that had eluded Anna. Looking at young, naïve Angela, she felt she should have warned her to be careful. The money she'd sent from her Dallas gallery was mingling with criminal funds in the witches' brew that Sergio and his accomplices had steeped.

When Margo returned, she took Anna aside. "Her pupils are barely responding," she said in a throbbing voice. "She's deep in the coma. The baby's dead, no heartbeat; operating will yield nothing except weaken Angela more. It's not looking good. Oh, God, what am I saying?" Margo sighed. "They told me she's not going to make it."

"I don't understand," Anna said.

"Blood! She lost too much blood. Her left hand was mutilated. The ring finger's almost gone; they had to amputate it cleanly. Michael, her husband, will arrive in a few hours. I hope he'll be in time to see her alive." Margo was trembling as Anna hugged her.

Margo leaned down to give Angela a kiss before hovering at her bedside, gazing distractedly at the glimmering locket in the hollow of her throat. "I shouldn't leave her jewelry here," she said, bending to open the clasp. The heavy necklace slid into her cupped hand.

"I've always loved this heirloom," she said, holding the locket in the light streaming through the window. "Angela would never show me what's inside," she added, opening it. "Oh, look, a picture of Michael and . . . and . . . a place for one of the baby."

Anna spotted a dark-haired bear of a man.

"It's curling up at the edge here." Margo tried to push Michael's photograph down with a short fingernail, but it kept popping up. "It won't stay down. Something's underneath." Picking at the picture, she peeled it back and slowly revealed a photo of a smiling white-haired man. "Who is—?" Margo gasped. "Sergio!"

How could that be? Anna's mind reeled.

Margo removed Sergio's photograph, bringing it close to her face before examining the back, covered in tiny, bold printing.

"What does it say?"

"To Missie, Love Silver."

"The two dolphins, swimming away together in that Italian song? Did Angela and Sergio plan a getaway, and then he got murdered? Whose ba—?"

"Angela was innocent. How could this have happened right under my nose?"

Anna turned away in distaste. She didn't want to guess how many bodies Sergio's gnarled hands had touched. She doubted he would have run away with any one woman in particular. Their interlude in Milan had probably overlapped with Angela's affair. Maybe they had been seeing each other for years. Anna had hit bottom after Jack and his model. What was Angela's excuse? Happily married to a loving husband and living on her Texas ranch—how had she succumbed to Sergio? What a bastard, she thought, frowning. Surely many women would have wanted him dead.

"Promise me," Margo said. "We can't let Michael know. It'd break his heart. And not Biondi either, that pompous, controlling little man. He'll never find the murderer, anyway, just like the police couldn't find the killer of Alessandro's family in all these years. I don't want Angela's name to be ruined, let alone hurt everyone who loves her."

"Don't worry about me," Anna said. "Biondi and I are hardly on speaking terms."

32

In the Shadow of the Doge

Sunday, late afternoon

When Margo pressed the bell, her hand brushed against a velvety cluster of flowers bursting from a cavity in the bricks. Tiny stars sparkled amid green, leafy tears.

"Did anything ever come from your analysis of account transactions?" Margo asked.

"Nothing to clear me," Anna said. "Only a mess of wire transfers. Or do you mean—"

"Was Angela involved financially with Sergio, beyond the payments for artwork?"

"Unlikely."

"Thank God. Maybe we can still learn something for her sake or yours that's been buried in the past."

"Hope so."

"Stranger things have happened, especially here. I checked the papers before we left—no promised article in the *Gazzettino*. They must have pulled it. Don't forget the Mass for Angela tomorrow morning. Christ, what's taking Agatha so long?" Margo yanked the pale blue head off one of the blossoms. It floated past Anna's outstretched hand as the gate opened and Agatha's face appeared.

"Good to see you," Agatha said, touching her lips to Margo's cheek.

"Where can we go to talk?" Margo asked.

"You don't have to look so worried. We'll go up to my altana. The tea's already steeping there."

Leading them across the lawn, Agatha said, "Dudley, of course, is holed up with his books, laboring over his latest."

"Not surprising," Margo said.

"I swear, he's been working so hard that I worry about his health. He's such a perfectionist, always saying the details need to be impeccable."

"He'd lose credibility pretty quickly if they weren't," said Margo. "What's his new book called?"

"I really shouldn't say. He's superstitious." Agatha lowered her voice as she led them through the tapestry-festooned hallway. "I only know the title because I saw it on a draft. I'll tell you if you promise not to repeat it." She glanced sideways at Margo and Anna. "It's *Keys of Venice.*"

"His secret's safe with us," Margo said.

As they passed the study, Anna spotted Dudley, sitting like a spider at the center of his gossamer web, his shoulders cloaked in velvet, the waves glittering through a window. She was startled to see a silver inkpot near his sleeve.

"Does Dudley always write in longhand and use an old-fashioned pen?" Anna could not imagine the starts, the stops, the pauses as the pen scratched across the page. Dudley's eccentricities made him seem a man from another time.

"Nothing but," Agatha replied. "And only on marbled paper. He says there's something sensual in the pen that sparks his creativity. Imagine his muse contained in a Murano glass pen. Or perhaps she swims in his inkpot." Agatha cackled as they ascended the steps to the altana. "An Italian Tinker Bell."

Anna tried to visualize Dudley's muse. A beautiful sea nymph? A gargoyle, perhaps? In Dudley's books, Margo had said, Venice itself is a character. Once he had seized her on the street and stuttered that he had seen someone who looked like a murdered doge staring at him from across Campo dei Frari. Anna recalled hearing about Dudley imitating a doge on Alessandro's boat years back. Standing on the prow, he had portrayed blind old Enrico Dandalo leading his troops to battle in Constantinople, wildly swinging an imaginary rapier before losing his footing and falling into the bay.

Dudley began each day with a silent communion on Venice's waters. He traced Venice's life through mute backwater rios, then he illuminated the past with his words. Today, for some reason, it was not Dudley's kindness that struck Anna, but his peculiarities, as tangled as a morass of seaweed.

In the altana, Anna craned her neck to see San Vidal and, off to the right, the fanciful domes of La Salute.

"I can never resist this view," Margo said. The serene repetition of red tile roofs seemed to soothe her.

"No need to." Agatha gave Margo's shoulder a tentative pat. "How are you holding up?"

"I'm managing," Margo shrugged. "Angela's the one to worry about."

"Quite," Agatha said, turning to pour steaming tea into porcelain cups before passing them to her guests. The waning sun accentuated the deep worry lines near Agatha's eyes, lending her the countenance of a sad eagle.

"Michael's arranging a special flight if she stabilizes," Margo said. "The doctor called me right before we left with news. They'd said comas can be unpredictable, and Angela really surprised him. This morning, things looked so bleak. Now there's a fair chance she'll come out of it."

"Oh, good, she's improved," said Agatha.

"I hope so," Margo said. "It's all my fault. If I had done something different. . . If I had been able to keep Angela at the palazzo, she'd still be fine, and her baby, too. That's all it would have taken. One little thing could have changed everything."

"Don't think that way," Agatha said. "How could you have expected what happened? She could have been attacked elsewhere. Even if you could have stopped her, that moment is impossible to recapture. I know about these things. You can drive yourself crazy." Stirring her tea, she added softly, "I still can't believe it. First Sergio, then Angela."

Margo asked, "What exactly do you mean?"

"You don't know?"

"Know what?"

"They were . . . an item."

"Why didn't you tell me before now?" Margo said, flushing. "I had to find it out after someone tried to kill her? If I had known earlier, I would have warned her not to see him. Maybe she got mixed up in one of his schemes."

"Both of them were adults." Agatha took a sip of tea. "And you were married to neither. I have a live-and-let-live attitude toward these things. Perhaps I've spent too much time here. Dudley, on the other hand, was revolted. 'Impure,' I think he said. Men—they always see things in black and white. You know, I rather liked Sergio in the old days. I could see some of his ancient Spanish blood in those passionate black eyes, his machismo. I wonder."

"How'd you find out?" asked Anna.

"Was their affair out in the open, then?" Margo asked. "I never realized—"

"Oh, no, no. Dudley saw them early this year on one of his rowing expeditions. Both still dressed in evening clothes. Sergio had her pinned against a wall, their mouths feeding on each other. His hand up her skirt."

"Enough," Margo said, drawing a palm over her eyes. "Maybe I should tell the police . . . but why? I'd end up destroying Angela's family, and for what? How much justice is there, anyway?"

"We each have to decide for ourselves," Agatha said. "I used to argue with Dudley's mother. She treated him so shabbily all his life, always swearing he would never amount to anything. It was terribly cruel and unfair, crippling, really. Then she died, almost out of spite, right before he became successful. Justice, my dears, is in short supply."

"You knew Dudley's mother?" Anna asked, startled.

"Is that strange?" Agatha asked.

"But who'd want to kill Angela?" Margo asked.

"Frankly, I think there's some crazy person doing all this," Agatha said. "Angela was friendly with just a few people around town, mostly gallery owners, a colorful but sane bunch. Fanfarone got a kick out of her. He's harmless, of course."

"Oh, God, I'll have to put all my trust in the police," Margo sighed. "Biondi—what a joke." Her voice hardened. "Agatha, I wanted to ask you about something else. A mystery from long ago. You and Alessandro."

"What's mysterious about being friends?" Agatha shrugged.

"Isn't there something more? Weren't you . . . didn't you have a crush on him?"

"Doesn't everyone?" Agatha's teeth flashed before she looked away. "He can be very charming, as you know."

Margo tossed her head. "Cut it out. I discovered your little secret. It took awhile, but I recognized your handwriting, with a more youthful tilt. It was you . . . the 'A' who wrote the love note about meeting him at the Dogana."

Blanching, Agatha clanged her cup down on the table. "You shouldn't be nosing into other people's lives. Alessandro would be furious if he knew. And in front of Anna, too." She rose and walked to the edge of the altana.

Anna heard the whoosh of the wind and the far-off scream of a gull as Agatha rocked back and forth on her heels, her arms clasping one another. The throaty growl of a vaporetto docking in the canal below hovered in the air. Minutes passed and Agatha continued swaying, as if in a trance.

Shoulders slumped in resignation, she finally turned back to them. "Oh, hell, what's the point? But you can't repeat this, do you understand?" She thrust her pleading face close to Margo's. "Or . . . I . . . will . . . just . . . stop . . . now."

"As long as it's not murder, and it doesn't involve Angela."

"Don't be silly. I'm not proud of it. You have to know that. I'm not the same person now. Swear it. Swear it on Angela."

"I do." Margo nodded.

"Anna should leave."

"She and I have been looking for any scrap of information that can help Angela, even from decades ago. So we're a package."

"As painful as your story is to retell, it might aid us," Anna said. "Please."

Agatha narrowed her eyes. "Maybe it'll make up for a few things," she said, lowering herself into her chair. "But you'll see that there's absolutely no connection."

"Tell us anyway," Margo said.

Agatha sighed. "In many ways, youth is foolish. He didn't really desire me, or ever fully respond. He loved Gabriella. He was toying with me . . . a boost to his ego, a feather in his cap. I tried my best to seduce him. The more he clung to her, the more I wanted him. I even thought that having a part of him was infinitely better than not having him at all. Perhaps it was because I knew I could never have him that I wanted him—the ultimate aphrodisiac for some women, don't you think? Am I making any sense?"

"Yes, but—" Anna said.

"You hope that the years will bring wisdom, but for the life of me, there is still so much I can't explain. Dudley and I were arguing a lot. He had turned inward, leaving me adrift. Alessandro was so . . . so . . . worldly, I thought. What could be more dashing than an Italian count?" Agatha looked up with a smile. "I remember that first night, every minute. I was passing Le Onde, on the Zattere, and from inside the bar, Alessandro called out to me. There he was, drinking Prosecco, eating *sarde in saor,* and generally feeling sorry for himself. At that point, Gabriella was seeing Piero, the gondolier; we all knew. I went in, had a drink with him. We took a walk to the Dogana, where we kissed. I remember his lips and the warmth of his chest pressing against my breasts. He was so masculine, but not rough. We flirted a lot after that. A few weeks later, we made love. On his boat, near Torcello."

"Did Dudley find out?" Margo asked.

"Did Sergio know?" Anna asked.

"No, no. We were careful, and the affair was very brief. Alessandro ended it. He couldn't stop loving Gabriella, despite her infidelity. *'Basta,'* he said. With one word, he crumpled all we had experienced together—the wonderful talks, the touches, laughter, sharing of our souls. All lost, turned to stone. It was as if I didn't exist anymore. I had to accept the sadness of never having him. Not then, not a year from then. Not two. Not three. Not ever. *Never* is a cruel word. To go on, I had to take all those beautiful feelings and crush them. I squeezed them into a secret spot inside, where no sunlight could enter, no food, no water. And so they died. Alone in the dark, they died."

She looked at Margo with watery eyes.

"But in their place came bitterness, jealousy, a feeling of

vengeance. These were stronger, in a perverse way. They made me feel immortal, like some Indian goddess of destruction. I didn't care if I brought about my own. So when Dudley returned with Alessandro's little girl the day Gabriella died, I didn't hesitate to call Gabriella's father, back in the States. Why, after all, should I give Alessandro any joy? I had freely offered my love. He had left me with nothing but heartache."

"I thought his daughter drowned," Margo said, confused.

"Monica is named on the family monument, but her body was never found."

"How were you able to reach her grandfather?"

"Gabriella gave me his number a few months before. She was already thinking about going to live with her parents, and she said she had a bad feeling."

"But what about the little girl?" Anna asked.

"Dudley rescued her. He had been out rowing and came upon her, soaking wet, in Piero's gondola. Gabriella was already dead, on the shore by the entrance to San Michele in Isola. Dudley could do nothing for her. He was terribly shaken. Piero was missing, gone overboard. I convinced Dudley to see it my way. We decided not to tell Alessandro, to lie—to give the girl to the grandfather, as Gabriella would have wanted. After all, Alessandro, I told Dudley, had driven her into the arms of another. He was cruel to her, a weakling who couldn't stop the damage inflicted by his wife. She had died running away with another man. Did he want the little girl to grow up with everyone in Venice knowing all that?"

"Why didn't Dudley go to the police and report what happened?" asked Anna.

"He hadn't seen anything. No other boats, no people were around when he happened to row by. And in hiding the girl, we needed to stay far from the police."

"What became of her?" Margo asked.

"The grandfather booked a flight and got here the next day. He hated Alessandro, of course. He blamed him for abandoning Gabriella, for sending her to Piero in the first place, into the hands of death. I remember that's what he kept saying: '*Le mani della morte, le mani della morte*'—the hands of death. He could never prove it, but he was certain that Alessandro, with all his money and pride, had arranged for both adults to be killed. He got a passport for Monica somehow and whisked her out of the country."

What a perverse start to a life, Anna thought. "Did Sergio find out about this later on?"

"How could he? We certainly didn't mention it. No one else knew."

"Did you see the grandfather again?" Margo asked.

"Only once, when he and his wife came back for the funeral of Gabriella and remembrance for Monica, a month later. They refused to speak to Alessandro. They even paid for a private investigation into the murder."

"I can't believe that all these years you've let Alessandro believe his child is dead," Margo said. "You're supposedly his friend. Don't you think you were heartless? And Dudley, too!"

"We had our reasons," Agatha said. "We played God. Like in one of his books, I suppose. *The Divine Doctor.* We never mention it now."

Agatha paused, gazing into the distance.

"When I awoke from my bitter dream, years later, I couldn't own up to it. How could I tell Alessandro about my betrayal? I took his only child away from him. I let him mourn her for the rest of his life."

33

The Lilies of San Stae

Monday, morning and afternoon

Well past midnight, just as Anna was falling asleep, Margo roused her with a phone call, too excited to wait. Angela was still unconscious but breathing on her own. Now they could give thanks as well as pray for Angela at morning Mass. Maybe Michael's words and embraces had penetrated the iron cloak of her coma, Anna thought, before drifting into uneven slumber.

She glimpsed Angela's pallid face among the spectators at a dance performance. In a Granada cave, a high-heeled gypsy woman in a yellow ruffled dress rhythmically tapped the floor with her heels, awaiting her partner's response. The sound of stomping feet erased the music, then transformed into a loud rattling. With a start, Anna awakened to a racket at her door. Turning on the light, she watched, frozen, as the handle turned in a fury. One, two, ten seconds passed. For the moment, the deadbolt managed to keep the door in place.

"*Chi è?*" she shouted. "Roberto?"

No answer. Just the door handle clicking back and forth. Anna's heart thumped with the knowledge that she could not escape from her room unless she wanted to risk injury by jumping out the window onto the pavement. She grabbed the phone, her mind blanking, unable to recall the police emergency number. As the door heaved and rattled amid loud grunting from the hallway, she dialed the reception desk with a trembling hand. After the fifth ring, she hung up and yelled to Giuseppe as if he were on the line, telling him an intruder was at her door.

When the people in the next room banged on the common wall, the uproar at the door ceased abruptly. Anna waited, but sensed no movement outside her room. Leaving the bed, she scanned the narrow space beneath the door. She saw only light from the hallway lamp.

In bed until daybreak, staring at the doorknob, she focused on one question: Who had tried to break into her room? A thief would have attempted it during the day, while she was out. A drunken, confused hotel guest would have been yelling or swearing in exasperation. That left someone who wanted to harm her while she was sleeping or barely awake and unable to defend herself. Someone who was not very skilled at picking locks.

At ten o'clock, she packed her suitcases before downing a coffee in the dining area and forgoing breakfast. Once again, Giuseppe was not at the desk. She left him a note about the intrusion and demanded he transfer her belongings to another room—one with a strong deadbolt.

At the hotel door, she studied each passerby in the street before summoning the courage to venture outside. She circled the block, wary of any loitering figure, then dove into the sea of humanity flooding the alleyways, hiding in the crowd. Lively travelers were rubbernecking at each small bridge, lining up for endless streams of gondolas and vaporettos, photographing the sights and each other as if nothing were amiss. Umbrellas choked paths broad and narrow as tour leaders marched ahead of their charges, following like ducklings in a row. News of a dead Italian count and an American who'd been attacked hadn't cooled their ardor for all things Venetian.

Traversing the Rialto Bridge, then turning to the north, Anna reached the Baroque white Church of San Stae. Dedicated to Saint Eustache, who converted to Christianity after he beheld a cross between a stag's antlers, it hadn't changed since John Singer Sargent had painted it, early in the century. Angela would like having the Mass said for her here, Anna thought.

Passing into the sanctuary of the majestic building, she was entranced by the dazzling sculpted rays rising above the main altar, which was covered in flowers. Immense displays enveloped the side altars as well, creating a tumultuous fragrance of lilies and incense that soon overwhelmed her. Was it the oppressive scent that weighed on her, or was it familiarity magnified by memory?

Lilies had been Nonna's favorite flower, particularly the pink candy-striped ones, their swollen orange stamens peeking out from their hoods. As a child, Anna had gathered armfuls of Oriental lilies from their garden. She recalled Nonno's crackling voice, telling her that sometimes bees became drunk on nectar fermenting in the blazing sun. When that happened, they would be shut out of the hive by the other workers and die—the cruel discipline of a collective society. Nonna's coffin had been heaped high with her beloved lilies. Nonno's, too. Now Angela's path to recovery was strewn with lilies as well.

The rustling of Pablo's jacket startled Anna as he sat down beside her. "I only come here for Angela, and those that love her. But this," he pointed to the main altar, "I don't believe. Prayer should be high on a mountaintop, a snow-covered *apu*, rising to the open sky. *Rezar libremente*. Far above the jungle, with its infinite shades of green, greener than the jaguar's eye."

A rotund, spectacled priest stretched out his hands to God and began chanting in Latin, commending Angela to a full recovery and a blissful life.

"After this morning, she needs more than prayer," Pablo said.

"What do you mean?"

"You didn't hear? Disconnected from her tubes for many minutes at six a.m., when the policeman outside her door was taking a cigarette break."

"No! How is she now?"

"Stable and assigned added protection. They must get her home. Too dangerous to stay in Venice. She is being hunted."

Anna nodded. A murderer was circling like a shark, and thanks to Detective Biondi, she couldn't go home with Angela but was stuck in the same goddamn fish tank. She was sure the person who had murdered Sergio and Angela's baby, tried to kill Angela, and attacked her was not some random maniac. The hair on her arms rose as a single word came to mind. *Colpevole.* Guilty.

She felt the word like the plucking of a string. It was someone under the dome of this church.

All the people she knew in Venice were in this crowd of solemn faces. Who was the murderer? It would be someone with circles under the eyes, exhausted after the diabolical exertions at the hospital and at her pensione. As her gaze whirled from one visage to another, the features ran together as if the faces were wax masks, melting: Alessandro's hangdog eyes became Dudley's froglike ones; Agatha's aging face transformed into Yolanda's catlike expression, which transmuted to highlight Pablo's black-condor orbs. The art professor's frown became Fanfarone's worried look. Sullen-eyed Andrew McMullan stood in the shadow of a pillar, near an unmoving profile that hinted at Biondi. From the side, she spotted Margo. Only Dr. Zampone was missing. And Roberto.

Her own fawn eyes blinked back at her, caught in a thicket of engraved words on the bronze plaque of the next pew, meaning: "Sea, Venice, Preserve All, donated by the Council."

As the singsong prayers at the altar went on, time seemed to stretch, like the taffy of theoretical physics. Anna was not sure how many minutes had elapsed. Her temple throbbed. She needed air. She made a brief genuflection and swiftly moved up a side aisle before breaking out into the sunlight.

Bathed in astringent brightness, she settled onto a stone bench. Years had passed since she had been to church. First it was every Sunday and Holy Day of Obligation, eventually only Christmas and Easter. Then sometimes. Then never.

Closing her eyes, she contemplated the roulette of fate that separated her from Angela and meditated on the motives of Angela's attacker. To prevent Angela from passing on incriminating information that Sergio had shared? To end the potential scandal of carrying Sergio's baby by finishing her off? Who had Angela planned to meet in the park? Was it the same person who had ambushed Anna, leaving the message to go to the Favier palazzo after dark?

The church doors flew open and people streamed out, their voices rumbling. When Alessandro, Margo, and Michael descended the steps, a crowd quickly gathered around them.

"Anna. We looked over at the end of the service and didn't see you."

Anna squinted in the direction of the voice. Dudley was staring at her, hands on hips.

"I didn't feel very well in there. All those flowers."

"Where did Roberto take you? The boat or the hideaway? Or both?"

"What?"

"Dudley, that has nothing to do with you," Agatha said, pulling on his elbow.

He shook his arm loose and marched closer as Agatha hurried to keep up. "Don't you know that you're just one in a long, long line? That his cleaning lady and his secretary occupy space ahead of you, and behind will be almost every attractive woman in Venice? Roberto needs a revolving door to his bedroom. He was just slumming with you."

Anna cowered briefly, as if hit by a phantom punch. When she struggled to her feet, she sensed her cheeks were wet. Why did he care? Why try to hurt her? There was nothing to say to a man like this. Despite Agatha's presence, she slapped Dudley with all her strength before darting away.

Shouts mingled with the blare of a docking vaporetto before blurring like the alleyways as she ran through them. She wasn't sure if anyone was chasing her, but she was determined to not take chances. Escaping any would-be pursuers, she darted across the Rialto Bridge, zigzagged down the streets leading to St. Mark's, and jogged to San Zaccaria before folding into the mass of people boarding the Line 6 ferry for the Lido. That would be the last place anyone would look.

34

The Golden Lido

Tuesday, morning

Anna calmed herself by meditating on the shoreline of the Lido and recalling details from her guidebook. The Lido's seven miles of barrier sands had long shielded the lagoon and core of Venice from the fury of the sea. As the centuries passed, the Lido had seen its share of glory and tragedy. In the twelve hundreds, the island had sheltered Crusaders bound for Constantinople. In the eighteen hundreds, Byron and Shelley had ridden horses along the Lido shore. Earlier in the month, the Moorish-inspired Excelsior Hotel had glittered with film-festival stars as the Venice Casino's roulette wheels spun, while to the south, the pine-tree sentinels of Alberoni and the ancient ducal seat of Malamocco lay ignored.

After walking half a mile down Viale Santa Maria Elisabetta, Anna had found a row of tiny green-and-white cabanas facing the Adriatic, almost by instinct. Too distrustful to check into a hotel, and having no passport, she climbed into an unlocked cabana at the far end, covered herself with a towel she found, and fell asleep to the sound of the surf.

Awakening near dawn, pacing on the cool sand, she watched the gentle tide rise as plovers peeped and skittered on their orange legs. Feeling safe here, she took her time puzzling over Sergio's killer. Roberto had identified a Sicilian connection to the tribal-art aspect of Sergio's art business. If professionals, Mafiosi or otherwise, were behind the attacks, both Anna and Angela would also be dead. The attempt on her own life had seemed amateurish, hardly the mark of hired killers.

She considered Liliana, offering a pittance as a reward. Perhaps Sergio really had been preparing to leave her for Angela, taking his fortune with him. If she had murdered her husband to inherit his fortune, why not offer a bigger sum to throw off suspicion and stop tongues from wagging? On the other hand, if she didn't care about him, why try to eliminate a rival? That would only make sense if Liliana's real obsession was her own standing in society which gossip about a cheating husband with an out-of-wedlock baby would tarnish. From what Margo had said, Liliana knew about Anna and Sergio; she likely was the person who had mailed the photographs to Biondi. But if Liliana had been Sergio's partner in crime, she would be aware of Anna's profession and might be impelled to stop her.

What about Arianna, Sergio's first wife, or their daughters, already despising him for breaking up their family seven years ago, killing him once they learned that Angela could be carrying a half-sibling to share in the Corrin fortunes? But why attack Anna, an incidental fling?

Pablo, the animal lover and naturalist, might have eliminated Sergio before his forays into Peru swelled the jaguar death toll. What better way to stop this modern-day conquistador than to turn the tables on him and hack off his hand, as his Spanish forebears had done to the Inca warriors? Pablo might have believed that Angela had been helping Sergio somehow. Pablo still bore the scars from the mudslinging of the Italian press, so vengeance could also be a factor. But Pablo's hatred seemed so principled and righteous; Anna couldn't bear to think that he had sunk to Sergio's level. And putting Anna, who labored to catch the Sergios of the world, on his list of victims made no sense.

Fiercely protective of her husband, Yolanda must have suffered during his prosecution in the Peruvian courts and persecution by Italian media. She loved her country's wild as much as Pablo. Perhaps she took action and killed Sergio when Pablo wouldn't? But why harm Angela and Anna—to throw Biondi's bloodhounds off the scent?

The two artists, Andrew McMullan and Azizi Sabodo, weighed in the back of her mind. Sergio might have cheated both of them. But she didn't have enough information to come up with a connection between them, Sergio's murder, and the attacks on Angela and herself. From there, Anna's thoughts alighted on Fanfarone. Clearly obsessed with the cream of society, he felt it was his job to shield them. Since she knew of no motive or financial connections, he was off Anna's list, at least for now, along with Margo, Roberto, and Gaetano.

As rays of sunlight began warming her, Anna scanned the opalescent sea and its rhythmic swells, hinting at creatures swimming below, and thought of Angela, bawling as she listened to the song about the captive dolphins being freed. In the end, Sergio may have decided not to swim toward the horizon with her. Angela could have killed him when she realized that, unlike Silver and Missie, they would never be together. Proving herself a good actress in front of Margo and Anna, she had remained calm but displayed acute interest in the reports of any witnesses to Sergio's murder. After her deed, someone who cared for Sergio could have tried to murder her—perhaps Liliana or even Arianna. Could Arianna still care that much about him? Would jealousy cause either woman to try to harm Anna? And how would they have known Angela was his killer?

Starting to feel hunger pangs, she recalled she hadn't eaten since the day before. While walking beyond Lungo Mare d'Annunzio and over to the Hotel des Bains, she pictured the beach in full summer, with children building sandcastles and playing in the surf. Once she arrived at the hotel's overflowing buffet, the tide was high with well-heeled tourists. Anna filled a plate and sought a table on the cozy veranda, continuing to ponder her list of suspects, fretting that she had forgotten an important detail.

Could Alessandro have killed Sergio for double-crossing him in a business deal? Turning to the darker line of speculation she had discussed with Margo, Anna envisaged Sergio blackmailing Alessandro after somehow discovering that he had murdered Gabriella and Piero. That would explain all those sizable checks to Sergio with no corresponding income. Alessandro had mentioned joint real-estate investments, as if to supply an alibi for the payoffs. Yet seeing him so shaken after the attack on Angela, Anna found it hard to believe that he was a murderer. In any event, he wouldn't have tried to kill Anna unless he was part of Sergio's illegal empire, and the recent funds flows she had discovered did not point his way. She still viewed him as a melancholy soul, wandering in the mausoleum of his life.

As Anna chewed on her vegetable frittata, she recalled her conversation with Armando Tota and wondered about the gondoliers. They were so sure that Sergio had killed Piero and Gabriella, as ordered by Alessandro. But the questions remained: Why now, why not kill Alessandro instead, and why include Angela and Anna?

Margo had helped enormously by recognizing Agatha's handwriting on the old love note to Alessandro. Agatha had unmasked herself as a prisoner of her emotions and desires, which seemed to still be going strong at age sixty-five. Who was to say that she hadn't gotten a late crush on Sergio, even been seduced by him at some point, and become possessed by jealousy? Had Agatha stumbled in telling Margo and Anna that Sergio had been killed with a knife? Supposedly, she had learned about it from her friend Kitty.

Perhaps Agatha had even killed before. After all, she had never even hinted at her talent in rowing to Margo, in all the years of their friendship. Back in 1955, she could have been the family friend whom Gaetano called in desperation that morning. Instead of helping the family, she might have murdered Gabriella. But why choose that particular time, when she'd have to confront Piero as well? She would have had plenty of opportunities to get rid of Gabriella in less risky ways. Better yet, why not let Gabriella flee with Piero and wait for Alessandro to abandon his love for his wife? Agatha had motives, yes. But the timing made no sense. And why include Anna and Angela?

Thinking of Alessandro and Gabriella led Anna to the mysterious group with the trident, the "Pride Council" referenced in Alessandro's complaint to the police before Gabriella died. Anna wondered if this council wrought death on Venetians who brought dishonor to society. She had read about the Signori della Notte, the Lords of the Night, who, starting in the twelfth century, had patrolled Venice each night until dawn, seeking out illicit activity, whether by bigamists, thieves, or assassins. These lords used a "torment" chamber in the ducal palace for their interrogations, questioning the accused while disguising their identities. Anna dismissed the thought of their lurking in the shadows for centuries, not just killing sinning locals but punishing errant tourists like Angela and herself. If that were the case, there would have been an epidemic of murders by now.

That brought Anna to the person she'd had in the back of her mind the entire time. Dudley had already revealed himself as a master of deceit—most recently, yesterday, in front of the church. Anna sipped her coffee and closed her eyes, sifting through Dudley's words and actions. Not only was he a prig, he had lied to her at least twice. He must have told her his own parents had died young in the hope that she'd feel a connection, let down her guard, and he'd discover what she had learned about Sergio. From what Agatha had said, Dudley had never been able to meet his mother's expectations. A man like that could never amass enough wealth or acclaim to feel successful. Was his description of greedy Sergio a self-portrait?

And Dudley had claimed that accounting was far in his past, while he had won an award for his accounting acumen just five years ago. Why would he want to hide this impressive accomplishment, particularly from Anna, working in finance? Dudley certainly could have designed the ridiculously complicated patchwork of Sergio's worldwide accounting. She couldn't imagine Sergio being so patient and meticulous. Thanks to Margo, Dudley had learned Anna's position in the Treasury Department; undoubtedly, he had also heard that she was researching everyone's bank accounts. Knowing that Anna was a money-laundering expert, he'd be doubly sure to hide the skill he had used to help Sergio evade the law.

Dudley's fortunes had jumped in the mid-nineteen-eighties, with a million-dollar investment and the purchase of his Grand Canal palazzo in 1988. The timing coincided with Sergio leaving his old employer and his first wife. But why kill Sergio instead of continuing to rake in the riches? Must have been money. Either Dudley had wanted more and Sergio refused, or they had broken apart, slashing Dudley's financial fortunes. How much Dudley earned from his books was anyone's guess. The twenty-five thousand dollars a month that Sergio had deposited in Dudley's account in the United States had ceased a couple of months ago. Two days after Sergio's death, had Dudley orchestrated the transfer of a fifty-million-dollar nest egg to Panama, a haven beyond the scrutiny of both Italy and the United States? With the money sent from the Luxembourg company, Le Pont Neuf, to the Panamanian construction firm, Nuevo Puente, he'd have a new bridge to retirement. Anna hadn't noticed earlier, but that was the name of each firm in English — New Bridge — a writer's little play on words.

If Dudley had been at the banking conference in Milan — the "surprise" attendee whose name Brian had never had a chance to tell her — he'd have known about her and Sergio, or Sergio could have boasted later about using Anna to win against the authorities. Dudley could have taken the photos from Sergio's body and sent them to Biondi in an effort to frame Anna for the murder. When that didn't work, he tried to scare her away and then eliminate her. While Dudley was a skilled liar, he wasn't a pro at breaking-and-entering.

He had also revealed himself as utterly vindictive, possessed by a strange jealousy of Roberto or, more likely, by a Lord of the Night prudery. What a price Angela had paid for her affair. Did Dudley fear Sergio had confided in her? During their visit to the *Gazzettino*, Fanfarone had discounted Margo's description of Angela's mood, which suggested that he had recent contact with her. Had she told the society writer about Dudley, perhaps a story that Sergio divulged of Dudley stealing from him or being fired? That meant she'd ruin Dudley before all of society before turning him in. Anna remembered the newspapers promising a Sunday bombshell. Perhaps for once wanting to learn the two sides to the story, Fanfarone might have interviewed Dudley first and let him know that he planned to meet Angela in the Public Gardens. Dudley had dismantled the bomb before it exploded. Speaking to Biondi near death, Angela could hardly have discerned whether it was a man, woman, or animal that had attacked her.

Anna still believed in a connection with the Gondola Murders, all those years ago. Let's say when Dudley came to Venice, he fell in love with Gabriella before marrying Agatha. Yearning to enter Venetian society, Dudley could have achieved it by marrying this beautiful woman from a respected family. Instead, his love object married another, whose image Dudley tore from the picture of her he kept hidden in his desk. Dudley was observant, imaginative, and an excellent liar. Cloaking his jealousy and envy in feigned friendship, he eventually poisoned the love Alessandro had for his wife. Gabriella dashed Dudley's hopes by seeking affection from Piero—a gondolier, so far beneath her, beneath them both—instead of him. That would have made him seethe.

On the morning Gabriella fled the palazzo, perhaps Gaetano had called Dudley for advice, giving him the opportunity to unleash a savage revenge. But even Dudley could not bring himself to kill an innocent child. In his crafty way, he might have tricked Agatha into believing it was all her idea to deliver the girl to her grandfather. As a false friend to both Alessandro and Gabriella, he would have known how her father felt about Alessandro. Through the years, while Agatha suffered from her guilt, was Dudley quietly relishing the double dose of pain he'd inflicted on his unwary rival? A vicious, complex story, Anna thought, hard to believe but entirely plausible.

And what about the severed hands of Gabriella and Sergio, and Angela's mutilated ring finger? Could this be Dudley's punishment for rupturing their marriage vows? Anna looked up with a start and realized she was the last person on the veranda. The uniformed staff was standing by the door, too polite to rush her.

Leaving the hotel, she took off her shoes again and walked along the sand, dipping her feet in the frothy water, feeling its energy as the breakers cast their salty white cloaks in the air. Two sets of prints led up from the sea, a human's and a dog's. She saw them in the distance on the shiny shore, the dog with its front paws down, wagging its tail, begging to be thrown a ball. Nearby, flocks of oystercatchers sporting bold black-and-white markings drilled holes in the sand with their flaming red bills, seeking tiny crustaceans.

As sunset approached, the azure sky gave way to streams of

crimson and tangerine. Two passenger ships bound for other ports sailed by, their lights soon twinkling from afar. On the horizon, one passed beyond view as if it had fallen off the edge of the earth.

Near the church of San Nicolò, Anna peeked through the locked gate into the ancient brick-walled Jewish cemetery. Established in the late thirteen hundreds, surviving alternating waves of abandonment and attention, the cemetery and all its dead lay forgotten among the weeds and ivy. The centuries-old gravestones were asunder, some piled in a corner, their carvings of trees of life eroded by salt, sand, and time. How long, indeed, Anna wondered, would anyone be remembered—one, two, three generations? With or without descendants, none of the dead had visitors anymore. Better to spend a God-given span with purpose, truth, and grace, she thought.

Dusk descended as Anna meandered through the streets, bound for the quay. She was reluctant to leave the Lido, the air fresh off the sea, the broad and open streets where nobody knew her.

Drawn to a snug portside restaurant, she ordered the grilled branzino, risotto with radicchio, a glass of Amarone, secretly celebrating her solution to Sergio's murder at her last dinner in Venice. She attempted to turn her back on the misery of her vacation and sensed a light glimmering. After she talked with Biondi, he'd declare her innocent and release her passport. In California, she would gather up the pieces of her life: Roberto would vouch for her, and instead of arranging for her arrest, the Treasury Department would reward her. If Leslie wasn't transferred, Anna would demand to be. In any case, she'd get Brian reinstated. Her divorce would soon be final, and she'd be free to start anew. She relished a tiramisu, and then caught the ferry back to the heart of Venice.

35

Calle dei Assassini

Tuesday, night

Sitting on the ferry's upper deck, Anna took in Venice's gleaming shoreline, from the Public Gardens, where they had found Angela, past the Arsenale, where Dante and Dudley had roamed, centuries apart, and onto the gracious curve of buildings along the Riva. She needed to call Biondi. After they talked, she'd return to the real world and leave this watery illusion behind.

The ferry gently bumped the edge of the dock, and Anna soon disembarked, making her way to the pointed-arch perfection of Hotel Danieli, its fine stone balconies offering a bird's-eye view of the lagoon. Anna sought a phone in the gray-and-white-marble lobby, where filigreed walls towered as staircase arches and balustrades cascaded toward earth in an Arabian dream. When told Biondi would be unavailable for a few hours, she left a message asking him to meet her at La Pensione Stella. Hesitating before dialing Roberto's number, she hung up when she reached his voicemail. A third call let Giuseppe know she was on her way back to the hotel.

The throngs of tourists had vanished by the time she reached the basilica. Finding an open door, she went in, struck by the soft sheen of the floor, the patina of the golden walls, the domes floating high above the Byzantine mosaics. Figures stared down on her from their perches on ceilings, in alcoves, above the grand altar: Saint Mark in a boat, lapped by wavy white lines of water; Noah lounging under a canopy; Adam and Eve in a lush garden. At the center of the main dome was a mosaic of Christ ascending into the blue heavens, gold stars that looked like daisies dotting the sky behind him. If she spun around on her heels, the stars made trails.

Anna thought of her rosary, hanging above her childhood bed. She found a cluster of votive candles and lit seven, for Nonno and Nonna, Pappa Antonio and Mamma Elena, Angela and her baby, and her own unborn child. Reciting snatches of prayers for each, she pondered the fates of the dead and of Angela, still fighting for life. Then she knelt there and cried for them all.

St. Mark's oldest bell, the Marangona, tolled in its ancient voice as Anna left the cathedral. At this hour, the famous piazza was empty; Caffè Quadri and Caffè Florian, on their opposite sides of the square, were silent. Heading toward a far arch, Anna passed the pond of bobbing gondolas and found her way along the Frezzeria. No one knew she'd be coming back to her pensione now, especially after being away last night. But still, returning there might be a mistake. It would be safer to walk to the Favier palazzo and stay overnight. The waning, luminous moon floated above the rooftops, just as it had above the garden at the Belvedere, reminding her to stay alert to every shadow and sound.

As she reached Calle Fuseri, a gang of costumed revelers bore down on her, laughing, singing, beating drums, carrying tridents, and cutting off the path she had intended to take to Margo. Some wore Bauta and Columbina masks; others were hidden behind creepy plague-doctor masks, with the long beak and skull of a ghostly bird. The noisy procession spilled like a torrent into the tiny alley. Anna had to flatten herself against a building and wait for them to pass.

As a red-haired joker with bells went by, he cranked his head in her direction. Then he bumped against her, rubbing up and down before slowly withdrawing. Anna was too shocked to scream, not that anyone would have heard or cared in all the tumult. Shaken and upset with herself for not kneeing the pervert in the crotch, she wanted to crumple up in the nearest doorway. The crowd did not thin and she gave up waiting. She darted across the alley and headed to her pensione, then retreated into a notch between buildings and waited for her emotions to settle.

Just five minutes away from the pensione, she thought—almost there, the nightmare almost over. Making halting progress, she studied the pavement around her. Shrouds of mist covered moored boats and arched doorways as she strained to discern any furtive silhouette. A few musical notes glided overhead. When a shadow darted across her path as she passed a store selling marbled paper and diaries, she almost screamed—a mouse. She tried to laugh at herself as she traversed the deserted campo. At the next corner, the neon star of her pensione came into view. In another hundred feet, she'd be safe. If Giuseppe hadn't moved her to another room, she'd make sure he did so now, and she'd push the armoire against the door for good measure.

Almost tiptoeing alongside dim, narrow Rio Verona, she hesitated by an antique store as she scrutinized her pensione. All looked quiet. As she crossed the bridge over the peaceful canal, the lapping water seemed to say that nothing would harm her here, on her last night in Venice. Basking in slumber, the placid buildings bordering the canal accentuated the mood, as if evil were also sleeping. She decided to walk for just a moment along the fondamenta. Pausing at a lamppost, she looked at her reflection in the shining water and wondered exactly how she'd reassemble the shards of her life. What redress for Leslie's decision would she pursue? How would it feel to be single again?

When an older woman's face appeared in the mirrored surface, Anna let out a small scream and then turned, embarrassed.

"I'm so sorry," the woman said, pushing her thick glasses back. "I didn't mean to frighten you. But I thought you looked familiar. Aren't you Anna Orsini?"

"Not my name now," Anna replied, puzzled.

The woman's lined face contrasted with the lustrous blonde hair tucked under a wide-brimmed hat, and the smiling red lips that revealed yellowed teeth. "My name is Gloria Orseolo. I'm a relation of the first doge of Venice. I saw you at Dudley and Agatha's party."

"Isn't it rather late in the evening?"

"Not for me. I love walking in Venice at night. Keeps me young. I was born in New York, but I live here now, around the corner, actually. A lot of time has passed, I know, but you're related to Andrea Orsini, right?"

"My grandfather. Did you know him?" Anna asked in an uncertain tone.

"We worked together for the Italian government in Manhattan." The woman wore a simple cotton skirt and blouse under an unbuttoned raincoat, and when she took a deep breath, her large breasts pushed against the fabric. "You used to live in the Bronx, then moved out to the Island."

Anna nodded.

"He was such a nice man, and he loved you very much. You're a lovely girl," the woman added, patting her shoulder.

"Thanks. I'm hardly a girl anymore." Anna wondered how much this old woman could tell her.

"Well, you were always your grandfather's little girl. I feel terrible that I lost touch with him. Is he still alive?" She gave Anna a kind look.

"No."

"And your grandmother, your Nonna? Maria, wasn't it?"

"Gone, too."

"Sad to hear." The woman pulled at her scarf with gloved hands. "I remember how upset he was when your parents died. He took a lot of time off from work then. He had the most beautiful picture of you and your mother. You know, you have the same eyes. Do you remember her?"

"Just a little."

"Your grandfather confided a lot in me then." The woman looked as if she had more to say.

Odder things have happened than this midnight encounter, Anna thought, thirsting for information on the missing pieces of her life. Maybe it would give her more to hold onto. And yet, glimpsing a police skiff landing in front of the palazzo on the corner of Rio di San Luca, she began fidgeting.

"I need to go," Anna said, trying to walk around the woman.

"Oh, no, please! Have some consideration for your elders. Young people are in such a hurry these days." The woman paused. "I knew your mother, too."

Anna pivoted. "You did?"

"I can tell you all about her."

Anna's gaze went to the officers scrambling out of the boat.

The woman didn't seem to hear the clamor.

Biondi must have received the DNA and blood results and was coming to arrest her. Dudley had framed her, breaking into her room and contaminating her raincoat. Anna could envision how she'd be treated now—shackled and hung upside down. Her pipe-dream of a happy ending would turn out to be just that.

Anna turned to flee, refusing to be arrested and handcuffed in the middle of the street. But the woman reached out and clasped her arm with a surprisingly fierce grip. "Memories can come back at the strangest times," she said, her voice sounding deeper than before. "When you least expect them."

Anna strained to pull away, but the woman tightened her hold as, with the other hand, she pulled an object from under her rain-coat. When Anna caught a glint of steel, she yanked her arm free but lost her balance, slipped on the slick walk, and fell into the canal. Murky water covered her before she knew it. Then she heard the clang of metal against stone, and a loud splash.

Strong hands were pushing her down, squeezing her throat. She tugged at the woman's fingers, trying to loosen their grip while kicking at someone she couldn't see, but nothing stopped the pressure. Desperate, Anna tugged at the blonde hair, then, unbelieving, watched it float off like a cloud of seaweed. Still kicking, she tried to jab her elbow into the woman's face. She could sense her field of vision darkening, her mind purged of every thought except the need to breathe. Soon she would run out of air.

A dazzling light penetrated the water. Anna sensed a commotion on land, heard a faint voice saying, "*Ferma!* Stop! I order you to stop, or we shoot."

The woman continued to choke her from above. A shot rang out. A crimson trail stained the dark green water, and with it, the pressure on her neck ceased. Giant splashes and bubbles followed. Anna swam to the surface, gasping and coughing, almost sensing hands from below supporting her, a woman's long fingernails digging into her, thrusting her upward as if to say, 'Live,' like the mother whale shoving her newborn calf into the air for its first breath. That is not here, that is not now, that is not real, Anna thought.

"Come, come. Here, take my hands," a man's accented voice shouted. Anna could just make out a blurry figure kneeling at the side of the canal. She flailed at the extended arms before grabbing them and being hoisted onto the pavement. Too weak to stand, Anna shivered and clutched her throat before focusing on the face of her rescuer.

"I am happy to see that we arrive in time," Biondi said. "You are safe. A minute more, and the assassin would have won. We just came from his home. I am very sorry for all this has caused you, Signora Lottol. We get your statement once you are warm and dry and have calmed yourself. A doctor will visit to examine your injury. Officer Palma will accompany you to the pensione. If you excuse me, I must go now with the prisoner."

Anna coughed and nodded. Her voice had deserted her.

Biondi joined the knot of policemen around her attacker, who was facing a stucco wall. A drenched officer was pressing a large white bandage against her assailant's bleeding shoulder. Anna noted disjointed features: a mop of white hair dripping onto a heavily padded bra. Rivulets of water running down hairy calves.

"Dudley Filbert, you are under arrest," Biondi shouted. "You are a disgrace."

"Keep your filthy hands off me," Dudley growled. "You almost killed me."

"It is a flesh wound."

"I was here doing research."

"Liar. *Bestia*! Take him away."

With policemen on either side, Dudley left a wet trail, not unlike the slugs in Anna's garden, as he was marched to the police boat. He boarded without a backward glance.

Officer Palma helped Anna stand up and wrapped her in his dry jacket, then guided her back to La Stella.

36

Il Sogno, *The Dream*

Wednesday, early afternoon

Anna stared ahead, feeling numb in the daylight. She could finally leave Venice and go home. But to what? Charges from the Department of Justice? Seeing the divorce through? Collecting unemployment insurance? She doubted Roberto had ever contacted the Treasury Department. He still wasn't answering his phone or responding to the message she had finally left in her raspy voice. Where the hell was he?

At least she was alive. The horror was behind her. She had signed her legal statement against Dudley and, she hoped, would not have to return for his trial. The doctor had predicted her vocal cords would fully recover in a week. Giuseppe had brought brunch to her room: fresh fruit, a basil and tomato omelet, a croissant, and an exquisite cappuccino capped with foam. It was time for her to relax and heal. With Dudley imprisoned and normalcy reigning once again, she felt sure no more trouble could befall her before she left Venice later that day.

Giuseppe's gaze slipped away from his book as Anna descended the stairs, her suitcases bumping each step. "*Vorrei pagare il mio conto, per favore,*" she said in a hoarse voice, wanting to pay her bill.

He proffered his uneven, toothy grin. "*Sì, carina, lo so.*" He scurried over and helped her with her bags, calling her a dear.

An urgency to leave, to be gone, overwhelmed Anna. To go away—*va via.* Not a minute more, she thought. It was already two o'clock. Once entranced, like many others, by Venice's beauty, she thought now only of murders, rancid canals, crowds of tourists, cat feces, and vanishing lovers.

Dudley had tried to draw her in, so he could kill her more easily. Margo had likely passed on the facts about her grandparents and where she'd grown up. But Anna felt he seemed genuinely afraid of what she might recall, not just what she had recently uncovered. Through his work, had her grandfather been privy to something, or was it possible he had met Dudley and shared . . . something . . . with her, years ago, that might have implicated Dudley in the old murders? She concentrated but bumped into an infuriatingly solid wall. She just couldn't resurrect the memory. When she got home, she'd make a list of Dudley's odd behaviors, assign probabilities to their origins, and solve for the most likely one, similar to her logic at work. On the other hand, she considered whether she should cast off her habitual way of thinking and attack this problem differently.

"*Fra poco, fra poco, carina.*" As she stood there watching him fumble with a calculator, Giuseppe held up his thin, age-speckled hand. "*C'è un piccolo problema,*" he said, telling her there was a problem, and rushed into the back room. Anna heard him on the phone, mentioning that it was "urgent." Just her luck to hit a mechanical breakdown, she thought.

"*Mi dispiace,*" he apologized when he reemerged. He handed over her passport and the sack of personal items that the police had delivered as promised. Just as she finished paying the bill, Margo strode through the door.

"Anna!" she cried, hugging her tightly. "That SOB tried to—"

"Kill me," Anna whispered.

"I'd never have forgiven myself." Margo looked at Anna with moist eyes. "Thank God Biondi got there when he did." Anna nodded as they sat down on the leather loveseat. "But why did Dudley come after you?"

"I figured out he was the killer from the money transfers," Anna said, her voice squeaking.

"You can hardly speak. Did they send a doctor?"

"He said I'll be fine. Somehow Dudley must've known I was going to tell Biondi."

"How many ears did that bastard have around town?"

"You got me. How's Angela? How are you managing?"

"I'm going back with Angela and Michael next week, now that there's no hurry to leave for her safety. She's starting to respond to commands. No one has told her about the baby, yet. Michael and I have been working through how to do it." Margo gnawed at a ragged cuticle. "Unsuccessful, so far."

"Don't blame yourself," Anna said, trying to whisper. "Do you know who she was planning to meet in the Public Gardens?"

"I think she expected to see Fanfarone, although it turned out to be Dudley, of course. Even after Fanfarone heard about the attack on her, it took him until this morning to go to the police with what he knew. Still protecting the leisure class."

"What had Angela told Fanfarone?"

"That Dudley had been stealing from Sergio. She thought it involved artwork sold by the gallery."

"How did you find all this out so quickly?"

"Biondi called Alessandro and filled him in. He also held a press conference this morning. All the papers are on it now—even the national ones have run special editions on the latest 'Death in Venice.' Ha ha. They're calling Dudley 'the snapping tortoise.' The Italians love their nicknames."

"I'll say he snapped."

"Yesterday evening, when the cops finally got a search warrant for his palazzo, they found a stash of wigs. Hairs from one wig were found at both crime scenes. And the knife he used on Sergio was on his library wall in a glass case. I remember seeing it! So evil and creepy. With an ivory handle, yet."

The elephants' revenge on Sergio, Anna thought, with a trickle of satisfaction.

"Murder ran through Dudley's Venetian histories *and* his life," Margo said. "He's already confessed—on one condition."

"Which is?"

"That he's allowed to wear his doge's cap in prison. Biondi and the prosecutor don't care. This'll bring justice more swiftly and save the state money."

"Sounds like he's gone crazy, or crazier. Did they say why he killed Sergio?"

"He cut Dudley off abruptly after he made some kind of mistake. Then the new accountant for Sergio's criminal empire was going over the books and started asking Dudley questions about where millions of missing dollars went."

"And how did Biondi zero in on Dudley?"

"The police were starting to look into money movements. Dudley couldn't show Biondi evidence of investments he had made with Sergio or any legitimate services he had provided in recent years. There was nothing reflected in gallery or bank expenses. So what was he being paid for and why?"

Good questions, Anna thought. She and Roberto should get an award.

"Dudley made up some stories, but they were easy to check. One was that he'd been performing secret audits on Banco Saturno for Sergio, to ensure it was following all the regulations, and that Sergio paid him out of pocket. When the police dug into it, of course, they couldn't find anything to substantiate it,"

Margo said. "I have to hand it to Biondi. When he was certain, he pounced."

"It sure took him long enough."

"I know you felt he was only after you. He was after everyone, though, looking to see what would shake out."

"Come on, Margo. He didn't try to scare the hell out of everyone, interrogate them, or hit them with search warrants."

"Well, you lied to him, and he had the sketch from that artist. And Dudley's disguise threw him off."

"Me, too. But Biondi did end up saving my life."

"Also, when the police searched Dudley's study, they found Gabriella's diary, which you had told Biondi about." Margo's eyes glinted. "Do you want to know the clincher? Biondi reopened the Gondola Murders investigation! Maybe now Alessandro will finally find out what happened and get closure."

Anna shut her eyes for a moment and saw small waves. "Poor man. Have you told him yet?"

"About?"

"His daughter."

"Tonight. It's all happened so fast—too much for him to process. I don't want to give him a heart attack."

"What are you doing this afternoon?"

Margo took a deep breath. "Seeing Angela, of course. And doing a jailhouse interview. Dudley asked for me. What a gift! Maybe he wants to be the dark, misbegotten star of my story. The Italian papers are falling all over themselves to try to get to him, but I'm the only one that'll get the real scoop. The *Chronicle* will love it."

"He would have murdered Angela if those workmen hadn't heard her screams." Anna raised her voice, which broke. "And if your story runs anywhere in the United States, you'll hurt her family! How could you want to spend one minute of your time with him? Don't you think that evil rubs off?"

"Why should I let this plum go to someone else? I'll keep the affair out of it. My questions will be doused with honey, but they'll be daggers, and I'll plunge one into that scumbag for Angela and her baby. Dudley doesn't get to decide how I portray him, just what he says to me. I see him in two hours."

"I still think—"

"Oh, and they nabbed Liliana. The Guardia di Finanza caught her racing to the border in one of her fast cars. Trying to stash money in Switzerland."

Anna pictured Roberto pulling her over. "I'll bet she'll be looking at serious time, given everything else. Have you heard from Roberto?" Anna scoured Margo's face for a sign as Dudley's invective weighed on her. What was the word of a murderer worth?

"No, why would I?" Margo shrugged. "One more thing. The papers reported a big raid on Sergio's warehouse a few nights ago, coordinated with raids in Palermo, Rome, and Milan. Seems that Sergio's warehouse contained illegal animal parts from Africa, like elephant tusks and rhino horns."

"Yes, Sergio made a fortune from massacring them. Dudley must have figured out where to hide the proceeds."

"Disgusting. One paper quoted that Tanzanian artist, Sabodo, who said Sergio used him to steal the wild legacy of his country."

"What an abomination." Anna rubbed her temples. "Instead of highlighting the beauty of Africa for the world to see, a lot of the art Sabodo created was nothing but packaging for animal parts."

"How do you know all this?" Margo asked.

"Part of my job. Listen to me," Anna tapped Margo's arm, "do *not* get into the cell with Dudley. He's stronger than he looks. If he's crazy, he could kill you—with his bare hands, like he tried with me."

"I'm sure we'll be talking through a window. Oh, I forgot one bit," Margo said. "During the raid in Venice, two Guardia di Finanza officers were badly hurt. One might not make it."

Anna felt a sudden tight pressure in her abdomen. "What hospital are they in?"

"I don't know. How about staying in Venice for a few more days to recuperate, instead of rushing back to problems that can wait?"

"I'm not sure." Anna visualized Roberto in a hospital bed, like Angela, connected to tubes. She'd figure out a way to get in touch with him. "I need to get home soon to help someone who helped me."

"And Alessandro wants to see you. He can bring you to the airport, if you insist. But please, don't leave yet."

Anna leaned over and gave Margo a kiss. "I'll think about it. If I go, I'll see you soon anyway, back in California."

Margo waved back at her as she left the pensione.

Finishing her coffee, Anna mulled over her immediate plans. Seized by a desire to view the abandoned palazzo up close, she hurried out to the sidewalk. She arched her neck to admire the balcony, the intricate brickwork; when she blinked, she could imagine when the palazzo had been a home. Hearing faint music, Anna knocked on the door, then turned the handle and wandered in. The terrazzo floor was bare. What had she expected, a room hung with oil paintings and thick, soft drapes to keep out the winter's cold? A woman was singing, operatic notes emanating from a cassette deck on a console table. A bottle of perfume, Fiori di Capri, lay beside it. When she ventured into the next room, the light floral scent followed her and made her think of spring. Strangely, there was a framed photograph on the plaster wall. Anna moved closer, transfixed.

Suddenly, she heard an explosion of barking, followed by frantic scratching noises. Nero trotted into view, followed by Alessandro and Gaetano.

"What are *you* doing here?" Anna croaked.

"I still own this palazzo," Alessandro said. "We were just on our way to see you before you leave, to see how you are."

Gaetano nodded and smiled.

"Were you friends with my parents?" Anna asked.

"Your parents? I never met them," Alessandro said, giving her a blank look.

She turned back to the old black-and-white photograph: her father with his full moustache smiling into the camera, her mother glowing in a white tunic, holding Anna in her lace baptismal dress. Anna could almost feel the warmth of her arms. She had read their names in the cemetery: Elena and Antonio Fortunato. Anna had seen so few pictures of her parents. Her grandparents had talked about her mother with such love; her father, hardly at all.

"Then why do you have this picture of me and my parents on your wall? We had the same one in the house where I was raised. I took it with me to California."

Alessandro gasped before she finished speaking. So did Gaetano.

"Did my Nonno, Andrea Orsini, give it to you?"

Alessandro searched her eyes as Gaetano took his arm. "If I lived to be two hundred years of age, I never thought I would see this day," he said, his voice shaking.

"I'm not sure what you mean," Anna said.

Alessandro drew back to study her. "My family was taken away from me a lifetime ago. Many nights I dreamed of my wife and daughter, and each morning was bitter when I realized they would never return to me. That is how I have existed, if you can call it that. Sometimes I come here late at night, to listen to her singing, and I close my eyes. I pretend they are both here, sleeping upstairs."

He put his hand on her shoulder. "But new life can bloom after tragedy's great fire. You would have gone back to California, and I would have remained here. You would remember meeting an old, very sad Venetian man, and I would remember a bright and charming woman, nothing more. So I would have lost you again. Lost you twice, my daughter."

Anna stood rooted to the floor. Daughter? Father? She looked up at Alessandro and burst into tears. All these years. All that pain.

When he hugged her, Anna felt a spark of recognition fanned by his embrace. Building sandcastles on the sunlit Lido beach, laughing and running among the cabanas; smelling incense in the glowing cathedral; playing hide-and-seek on the altana; splashing about in high boots during acqua alta; listening to music at La Fenice; riding in *La Farfalla*. Holding his big hand. Her mother singing, and reading to her in a melodious voice. The images combined in a rush, like water cascading through a broken dam, the river freed at last, each drop coursing through her carrying the sights, sounds, and scents of the past.

The aching void in her life she had expected to take to her grave was quickly being filled by this man. He seemed like a stranger when she looked at him. But the warmth of his hug, the vibration of his throbbing voice, erased all doubt. So did Gaetano's tears.

"I have grand plans," her father said. "We show you the playroom with the dollhouse Gaetano made for you, the upstairs rooms where we lived, everything. I will tell you all about your life with us, conceived in Capri, where we honeymooned. About your mother and how deeply she loved you. She can rest in peace now."

Anna wanted to see her. She'd bring her lilies.

"We will have your bags brought over to my—that is, the other palazzo." Alessandro raised his hands. "I forget, you are not a little girl anymore. Would you like to stay with us? At least for the next week or so?"

"Of course. We need to get to know each other again. I want to understand what happened to me. Then I can decide what to do. I must take care of a few things back in California."

"Good. We will have a festa here in a few days, to celebrate, before Margo leaves. We pray for Angela and her lost baby. Biondi tells me that your friend Roberto," Anna lowered her eyes, "may be out of the hospital soon."

I will see him before that, Anna thought.

"In time, we renovate this palazzo, to regain the beauty it once had, make it gleam like an old family pearl," Alessandro said.

Anna nodded and reached for his hand.

Acknowledgments

I am grateful to many individuals and organizations that left their mark on this book: Brian Bouldrey, my first writing professor, whose enthusiasm drove me forward; Patrick Zetzman, for reading imperfect drafts with a zeal that never faltered; Laura Accinelli, whose magical introduction to Venice gave rise to my imagination; Pamela Feinsilber, my skillful editor; the Path to Publishing Program of Book Passage, along with two highly talented mentors, Nina Schuyler and David Corbett; all those working to save wildlife and our planet; Phreda Devereaux, for her close review of money-laundering aspects. And to Stephan Volker, my informal editor and co-conspirator.

Thank you, all.

About the Author

photo credit: Ben Krantz

Christine Evelyn Volker became intrigued by foreign cultures at an early age, which motivated her to study Spanish, German, and Italian. After earning an MLS and an MBA, she was drawn to international banking and became a senior vice president at a global financial institution. Her career brought her to Italy, where she immersed herself in the language and made frequent visits to Venice. *Venetian Blood* marks a return to her roots in the humanities. A native New Yorker, she resides with her husband, Stephan, in Northern California, where she leads a local library non-profit organization and writes about environmental sustainability. Exploring both tame and wild places around the world, she is currently at work on her second international mystery, this one set in the rainforest of Peru.